MALCOLM BROOKS

CLOUDMAKER

Grove Press
New York

Excerpt from *Out of Africa* by Isak Dinesen, © 1937 by Random House and © renewed 1965 by Rungstedlundfonden. Used by permission of Random House, an imprint and division of Penguin Random House LLC. All rights reserved; B. H. Pietenpol, excerpts from *Flying and Glider Manual* (*Modern Mechanix and Inventions*, 1932); Amelia Earhart, excerpt from *The Fun of It* (Harcourt, Brace, 1933); Amelia Earhart, excerpt from personal letters (*Letters from Amelia*, Beacon Press, 1982); Aimee Semple McPherson, excerpt from "I Ain't A-Gonna Grieve" (A Negro Spiritual) (Echo Park Evangelistic Association, 1935); Author unknown, excerpt from "Give Me That Old-Time Religion" Public Domain; George Bird Grinnell, excerpt from "Antelope Hunting Thirty Years Ago and To-Day" (*Outing*, vol. 43, 1903); Billy Dixon, excerpt from *The Life and Adventures of Billy Dixon* (Cooperative Publishing Company, 1914); Beryl Markham, excerpt from *West with the Night* (Houghton Mifflin, 1942); Charles Lindbergh, excerpt from We (G. P. Putnam's Sons, 1927); Margaret Culkin Banning, excerpt from "The Case for Chastity" (*Reader's Digest*, August 1937); T. S. Eliot, excerpt from *The Waste Land* (Liveright Publishing Corporation, 1922); Scripture quotations from The Authorized (King James) Version. Rights in the Authorized Version in the United Kingdom are vested in the Crown. Reproduced by permission of the Crown's patentee, Cambridge University Press.

Printed in Canada
Published simultaneously in Canada

First Grove Atlantic hardcover edition: March 2021
First Grove Atlantic paperback edition: March 2022

This book was set in 13.25-pt Perpetua Std by Alpha Design & Composition of Pittsfield, NH.

Library of Congress Cataloging-in-Publication data is available for this title.

ISBN 978-0-8021-5946-5
eISBN 978-0-8021-4633-5

Grove Press
an imprint of Grove Atlantic
154 West 14th Street
New York, NY 10011

Distributed by Publishers Group West

groveatlantic.com

22 23 24 25   10 9 8 7 6 5 4 3 2 1

Also by Malcolm Brooks

Painted Horses

Praise for *Cloudmaker*

"Brooks evokes rural Montana's magnificent beauty in his coming-of-age novel set during the golden age of aviation, an era marked by technical ingenuity and the allure of wide-open skies . . . Brooks has created an entrancing tale about the challenges of pursuing one's dreams and life on American frontiers, old and new." —*Booklist*

"Long and lush, conveyed in masterful prose that captures time, place, and conflicting cultures. Character motivation and backstory are deeply explored. It concentrates on the layers and complexities of people and life, with all their surprises and pain, inching toward goals by way of sidetracks and backslides, with the characters learning hard but profound lessons in the process." —Carolyn Haley, *New York Journal of Books*

"Enthusiastically recommended." —*Library Journal* (starred review)

"Evocative . . . in pitch-perfect dialect that will immerse readers firmly in Brooks's beloved American West, and above it." —*Shelf Awareness*

"Tender friendships and passionate pursuits combine in *Cloudmaker*—a rich, evocative, soaring novel rooted in particulars and populated with characters so nuanced and real you can't help but admire and miss them long after you've turned the last page."
—Erin Lindsay McCabe, author of *I Shall Be Near To You*

"Epic in scope, beautifully crafted in its prose, and always—always—adoring of its cast of unforgettable characters, *Cloudmaker* is a stunner of a novel. A book that absolutely soars."
—Nickolas Butler, author of *Shotgun Lovesongs* and *Little Faith*

Praise for *Painted Horses*

"Brooks's debut captures the grandeur of the American West."
—*Publishers Weekly* (starred review)

"Lush, breathtaking prose that expertly captures the raw essence of an American West known for its wide-open spaces and unbridled spirit . . . Masterful."
—*San Francisco Chronicle*

"Evocative . . . Brooks' prose rings true." —*Seattle Times*

"*Painted Horses* is evidence that the many-peopled, colorific, panoramic, fully-wraparound, pull-you-in-by-the-heels, big-questions, literarily deft 'Great American Novel' still lives." —Carolyn Chute

For Cole and Ethan,
and Samson and Reuben . . .
Fly high, boys.

And for David Comstock, 1914–2005, in memoriam.

In the air you are taken into the full freedom of the three dimensions; after long ages of exile and dreams the homesick heart throws itself into the arms of space . . .

—Isak Dinesen

I'm willing to agree that the editors can make this the best airplane how-to-build that was ever published if I just do the necessary writing. So here goes . . .

—B. H. Pietenpol, 1932 *Flying and Glider Manual*

Prologue

Scorpio slides down and Orion stalks up, and the stars in the October sky otherwise align.

An eight-cylinder Buick roadster with out-of-state plates and nails in two tires had limped in off the highway at dusk. She rests now nine hours later in the wash of light from the open door of the shop, new tubes in place and the convertible top down and the rightful owner in a boardinghouse not two blocks away, unaware of his contribution to any of this.

The kid hits the ignition, and the cold car jolts and roars like a cat. Withered leaves jump in a blast of exhaust, and he works the pedal, feels as much as hears the engine's high-tuned rumble. The leaves skitter again.

He's endured months for hope of this moment exactly, and with the Montana winter lurking just to the north he knows it's either now or hold off until spring. Eternity to a fourteen-year-old. Here is the fastest car to appear in Big Coulee in at least a year. He's actually gone so far as to pray for such, and with the prize dropped right in his lap, he can't help believing he's received not simply an answer but a bona fide green light from God. Even Pop knows the score, put him on the pierced tires with a wink and a nod and made himself conspicuously scarce.

He backs the car around the side of the shop, and Raleigh appears like a red ghost in the taillights, behind him the wide wing of the glider a fainter red blur against the night. Huck walks back and the two of them wordlessly take opposite sides and roll the ship forward, tiny spoked wheels greased and silent, the luminous sailcloth bobbing.

"Looks like a gol dern giant moth," Raleigh mumbles, and he's right, or at least not wrong, or at least not wrong in this diffuse red light. Still, Glider Number One looks to Huck entirely of a piece with the legendary experimental fliers of Orville and Wilbur Wright from four decades past, with its overhead wing and skeletonized rib section connecting the tail and rear flaps to the operator's chair, actually nothing more than a plank atop the axle and a corresponding plank out front for a footrest. Only the cookie-cutter wheels appear truly misfit, repurposed as they are from a baby buggy and looking absurdly out of scale beneath twenty-three feet of wingspan. He wonders if this occurs to Raleigh as well.

They hitch forty feet of hemp line to the bumper and attach the tag to another ten of shock cord with a spliced steel ring at each end, the second of which mates to a release on the ship's footrest. Raleigh straightens up. "All set?"

Huck weaves between cables, ducks beneath the wing. He settles to the narrow plank and reaches for the leather helmet, on self-administered loan from the high school football supply. He screws the helmet down and cinches the strap. He peers up at Raleigh. "How do I look?"

"Like Tom Swift. In his Airship." Raleigh looks over at the bungalow, dark as a morgue. "Reckon your pap's watching?"

Huck tests the scissorlike levers jutting between his thighs, works the pair of them back and forth. He can feel the tips of the wing torque and twist through the tension of the cables. "Pop? Far as I know, Pop's been in bed since nine."

"That is our story. You ready?"

"Born ready. Remember, middle of the street. Get me under the wires at Second and light her up."

"Forty by Fourth."

"Forty by Fourth. Way I've got her figured, I can cut loose by the time you get to the church, and you can hook south and sneak on back. I'll sail out over the ball diamond and set her down."

"Don't crash."

"I might."

"Don't die."

"I won't."

Raleigh crawls out in first gear with the headlamps cut and the parking lamps low. The slack goes out of the rope and the rope comes off the ground and tightens into the shock cord, stretches the elastic out of the cord and yanks the glider forward in a jump. Huck hears the shift into second and steady they roll down the street.

The trees loom on either side, all reaching crooked branches, all dead and dying leaves. With 3:00 a.m. gone they creak past dark cars, past dark porches on darker houses. The wing appears blue-white now against the black of night, bobbing and rocking overhead. Gravel crunches.

By the time Raleigh turns onto Main and the macadam, the left buggy wheel has begun to squeak in its rotation, a whine at regular intervals. The Buick throttles up, and the whine off the wheel hub speeds, too, as the air rushes at his face, rushes around the vibrating wing, and even though they have not yet made the Second Street wires and not nearly achieved their speed ceiling, the ratio of the Buick's whitewalls to the tiny cookie-cutters on the glider nevertheless has the buggy wheels already flat zinging across the pavement. In no time the right wheel wails in answer to the left.

Most of the buildings along Main jut at dark angles, electric bulbs switched off at closing in these struggling times, although the shell-shaped globe atop the gas pump at the filling station beams like a beacon, and low-watt streetlamps glow here and there along the blocks ahead. Raleigh's foot goes deep into the pedal now. Huck watches the black power lines come into view with the moon behind them and seemingly cross the sky above the street like wipers across a giant windshield, an illusion of approach, which then vanishes behind the leading edge of the wing. He realizes he's got about a block and a half to test the warping before the moment of truth.

The buggy wheels fairly shriek, a sound like tangled alley cats. Out ahead the Buick roars. Hot exhaust and chill autumn air. Huck tenuously moves the levers. He feels the tension load in the cables out to the corners of the wings and feels an almost imperceptible shift in the glider's lateral balance.

He goes to try the cables in the other direction and something seizes as the arms scissor past each other, and for a disorienting moment he panics at this unexpected glitch and shoves hard on the right-hand lever, yanks hard on the left.

The pair of them unstick with a nearly violent lunge that sends him deep into the cables, and the torque on the wing in conjunction with the now significant speed of the Buick puts the glider into a hard roll to the right, the left wheel jumping off the ground and the opposite wing veering down. The right wheel speeds on edge along the pavement, throwing a fountain of sparks like a blade to a bench grinder.

He knows full well the technical advance of ailerons over Wilbur Wright's original wing-warping design, and regardless he's built this particular specimen to the earlier patent. Now as he teeters at velocity on one screaming, sparking wheel, it races in his mind that he's an idiot, that he shouldn't have allowed fundamentalism to beat out evolution, shouldn't have been so hell-bent on doing things the old-fashioned way.

He'd wanted to begin at the beginning, is all. The Wrights had the sense to start with actual birds, spending endless hours watching through field glasses the giant gannets and eagles glide and soar with the flex of their wings, and so rule the air. Making sketches and notes and even studying pantomimes with their own arms, until they landed on the first workable method of steering a heavier-than-air ship.

Back in the summer he'd ridden out to a dog town one roaring-hot weekend and shot a hundred or so gophers over the course of an afternoon as they popped and popped out of their dens, cooling his rifle barrel with a wet rag and heating beans in the can for supper and sleeping out overnight with the coyotes and owls.

By midmorning the vultures began to gather, two at first and then six and before he knew it twenty or more, appearing as though thin air and magic were one and the same. He lay in the sagebrush and watched the circling kettle through a telescope he'd built himself the winter before. They congregated impossibly far up and spiraled impossibly down, on the same invisible currents that vectored the slightest carrion whiff to whatever far-flung points they'd originated from. At ground level, even by noon, Huck couldn't smell a thing.

He watched the way the vultures flared their wings while they circled at a single, static elevation. He watched them not merely glide but even climb without flapping so much as a feather, as though air itself were an elevator.

He remembers all this in a cockeyed flash on this crisp October night, careening along on the razor edge of that screaming, sparking wheel, and without really thinking he throws the levers back and reverses the warp.

The glider reverses its roll, slamming back down hard and over-correcting and tipping this time onto the other wheel. The spark shower goes up there as well. He backs off the levers and sets the ship aright.

The sparks don't subside but fly now from both wheels, and both wheels wail like warring banshees, and just about the time he starts to wonder whether the pair of them might fly off or combust or otherwise disintegrate altogether, Raleigh roars across Fifth and the sparking and the shrieking simply stop.

The vibration of the road stops, too. The wheels still whir on either side of him but softly now, silently, spinning by inertia alone. He presses on the elevator pedal.

The macadam drops and in no time he's twenty feet in the air, sailing dead level past the great glowing eye of a streetlamp. Only his stomach plummets.

He hears the rush of air over the curve of the wing. He feels the same rush against his eyes and squints and thinks, *Goggles, I need goggles, like a proper airman.* He squints down and sees Raleigh, glowing green in the dash lights and looking smaller than ever behind the wide wheel of the Buick. He looks up again just in time to realize his right wing is heading straight for a power pole.

He scissors the levers by sheer reaction, and the glider instantly banks away from the pole but sharply enough and steeply enough that he practically slides off the seat. He backs off the levers and levels with his heart in his throat and thinks, *Harness, need to rig a harness.*

He barely has his balance before Raleigh encounters the one wild card on the route, a shallow dogleg where Main Street kinks to follow the natural bend of the coulee. The firehouse sits on the street's inside bend, the New Deal Mercantile directly opposite, and when Raleigh rips with tires squealing through the jog, the glider swings hard sidewise on its tether and the New Deal zooms right at Huck out of the night, twin windows in the second story *right there* like a pair of sinister dark eyes.

Huck braces himself as best he can against the vertical strut and cranks again on the levers and puts the ship into a hard roll as it arcs right up tight to the building. The outer edge of the wing clips the hanging shingle out front with a bang, the hard jolt inextricable from the sickening sounds of indeterminate wreckage, but the tear of fabric definitely in there somewhere. A cascading smash of glass trickles through the dark behind him, finally giving way to the piercing hammer of a tripped alarm.

Raleigh already has the Buick opened up on the straightaway heading out of town. The glider stabilizes with the velocity and climbs a bit higher still. Huck feels the air shift, feels the temperature rise, and is wondering if this warm band in the ether might qualify as an actual thermal when the dead gold leaves of an oak reel by at eye level. The black silhouette of a cross towers into view.

Not a cross. Another power pole, with just enough pale moon behind to show it stark against the sky. He's no sooner eclipsed it when he sees the backlit steeple of the Foursquare church, with its own smaller cross, set just back from the street. This he can't mistake for a single other thing.

The road bends at the ball diamond, and Raleigh's foot comes out of the pedal, he can tell by the drop in the motor. He moves his own foot to the release on the plank and kicks. The tether drops like a gallows rope.

The glider rolls to the left as though to follow the car by default, and he hears again the sound of rending fabric, remembers again the jolt with the sign on the New Deal. He levers the wings and rolls back the other direction and straightens out.

He soars of his own momentum over and past the hard curve in the road, glances to the side, and sees the Buick receding, angling away. Again he sees sparks jump, smaller this time, sporadic, like what fireflies out east must look like. The steel ring on the shock cord bounces and skips along the macadam behind the departing car. Then the glider rolls hard in the other direction as he loses speed, and his field of view rolls with it. The Buick vanishes for good.

He corrects the roll and has to keep back and forth on the levers to hold the ship steady. He's losing altitude, sees the dark mass of the bleachers pass just below. He stays on the levers, works them against the wobble of the damaged wing.

Don't crash.

I might.

Don't die . . .

Even in the dim light of 4:00 a.m. the worn-dirt baseline comes at him like an actual runway.

The crash occurs somehow gently and disastrously at once. The ground lifts up and the wheels touch down and turn against the earth with none of their prior urgency, slow as he's now going, and Huck's just realizing he's all right, just forming the words aloud to himself in utter wonder, when the left cookie-cutter hits some divot in the soil and breaks completely away.

The next thing Huck knows he's airborne again and corkscrewing sidewise, the plank dropping out from under him and then hammering back into his hip, his legs totally akimbo over his head before the whole bucking, twisting contraption slams to a stop.

His head bounces off a wing strut. The sparks this time go up right inside his own brain.

He shuts his eyes, waits for the white lights to dim. When he hazards another look, he thinks he may be seeing actual stars, only in pairs, in twins. He blinks, blinks again, and finally holds just one eye open.

Orion. Betelgeuse. Whatever was out there on the other side.

Back along Main Street the New Deal alarm goes silent but Huck continues to hear the ghost of it ringing in his head, hammering on and on. He opens his other eye and half watches, half forces the merge of the twinned swimming stars. He begins to untangle from the wreck.

He hears the approach of a car, sees the bob and dip of headlights. Probably not Raleigh.

He gets himself loose, limps around on his hip. The ship leans sideways on its left wing, which is clearly broken through the spar. The tip hit the ground when the wheel broke loose, he's sure of it. The right wing juts at a more or less proper cant and appears undamaged.

He's thinking maybe he'll nix the wing warping on Glider Number One and engineer actual ailerons. The left wing needs to be rebuilt anyway, and he's pretty sure he can modify the intact right wing without completely tearing it down. Ailerons would dern sure keep the dern rolling under control.

The headlights are on him now, the car coming up fast and then braking to a hard stop at the edge of the field, and a third beam, like the blaze of the sun itself, hits him square in the eyes. He looks down at his hands, weird and white in the light.

His own name thunders through a loudspeaker as though uttered by God the Father Himself. *"Houston Finn."* Cy Gleason, the town marshal.

He's practically blind, squinting against the light. He shields his eyes with a hand.

Cy booms on. "If I wasn't wearing pajamas, I would tan your cottonpickin' hide. And your old man's, too."

Huck's eyes go back to the ship, flooded with light, and in a flash of clarity he sees that ailerons alone won't do it. The problem is that she's tail-heavy, inherently unstable . . .

"Houston. Can you walk?"

His head throbs inside the leather football helmet. He finds his pipsqueak voice. "I think."

"Then march. You've got a sidewalk full of glass to clean up."

He squints toward the light, unsteady on his feet.

He's not nixing the wing warping—he's nixing Glider Number One altogether. He sees it now, plain as day in the beam of light. He's done with gliders entirely.

"What on God's green earth is that contraption, anyway? Wait, don't answer. I don't want to know."

He takes step after step, the light brighter and brighter, says to himself over and over, *I'm not fixing any dern glider. I'm going to build an honest-to-God airplane . . .*

Annelise

1

Of course, I admit some elders have to be shocked for everybody's good now and then.

——Amelia Earhart, *The Fun of It*

She felt like she hadn't slept in days and in fact had tried to will herself into an outright vigil, tried to summon the same resolve A.E. achieved as a matter of course, up there solo in a ship above the water.

The North Atlantic twice, South Atlantic once. Honolulu to California next. Then nonstop overland, Mexico City to Newark, New Jersey. A woman and her Lockheed like a steady red comet, covering continents in hours instead of months or years or eons. What a time to be alive, whether these nitwits around her realized it or not.

But still. What endless hours they must have become—dark much of the time, cold all of the time. Knocked around by air currents and light in the head from the reek of the gasoline sloshing right there behind her in the extra tanks. Even so, Annelise knew that Amelia used smelling salts to snap herself back when she needed to.

Annelise did not have smelling salts, and she certainly couldn't smell diesel fuel from the sealed canister of a Pullman car, but she went ahead and drank coffee endlessly until her insides felt downright scoured. Her newspaper-shuffling father at first watched and pretended not to, and then tried to ignore her for real and couldn't, and then attempted a conversation that she wouldn't have, and finally resorted to pleading, which she both scorned and enjoyed in a manner exactly parallel to her own equal but opposite monosyllables.

"Are you sure you should be drinking that much coffee?"

"Yes."

"But shouldn't you get some rest?"

"No."

A spell of silence. Then, "This wasn't my idea. You know that, right?"

"Yes."

"Annie, can we stop this? You're making the whole thing worse. Can you just say something real?"

"Would you like a warm-up, miss?" The porter, with a carafe and what could only be described as extraordinary timing.

"Why, yes, sir, I would."

The man had his eyes either averted or steadied on her mug as he poured, but she flashed him her most angelic smile, showed him the little rows of teeth only recently liberated from an expensive set of metal braces and glinting white as a root laid bare. Definitely not coffee teeth. He gave his own small smile and moved along.

Her father tried again. "Hey. Can you just say something to me?"

Again she wouldn't grace this with an actual answer, though she did cast her eyes upon him when she took yet another bitter sip. She'd always been able to punish him, even when she was supposedly the one being punished. She could play this game forever.

Eventually the sun came up over the alkaline flats of the desert. Her father had fallen off hours ago, slumped in his rumpled suit, with his rumpled newspaper, the sleeping berth still folded shut. Her own body had a bone weariness, but her brain rocketed with caffeine, and so she slumped in her seat, too, stretched to a fray by her own warring ends.

She tried to reconcile the two, tried to tell herself this was part of the point. She looked through the crack in the curtain at the dawn.

Then she looked back at her father. His skewed neck would ache for a week. He was getting off easy.

Train travel. What a bore. The Burbank aerodrome and Grand Central in Glendale both routed passenger flights to Salt Lake City these days, although she doubted anyplace in Montana had regular service. She hadn't been there since she was a girl, but she remembered the ranch as a bona fide jerkwater and couldn't imagine much had changed, hence its selection for this whole medieval exercise.

Still. If her parents weren't frozen in Victorian amber, they could at least have cut her father's back-and-forth into something not straight out of the Rutherford B. Hayes era. She'd known better than to suggest air passage herself—Mother had gone so far as to confiscate A.E.'s book, citing it as the root of all the trouble. *The Fun of It*. Ironic, she knew. Practical or not, she'd have crushed the idea on principle.

She held her own against the seduction of sleep right on through to Salt Lake. She watched the pink of the rising sun bathe the toes of the mountains west of the city, watched the same pink wash move up the bare slopes and into the snow at the top. Her father stirred when the train slowed.

They killed a few hours in a diner waiting for her connection north. Annelise freshened up as best she could in the ladies' room. She would be placed in the charge of a conductor who would see her to Butte, Montana, and then east a few hours to Billings. Her father would turn right back around on the next train home.

"You could've flown, you know," she said to him. The first time she'd initiated a conversation in days, and he blinked at her across his hash and eggs as though he were not only hearing but also seeing her for the first time in a year. "We could have flown here even, out of Burbank or Grand Central. We could have saved ourselves a solid day, a day neither of us can ever get back. You know that, right?"

He resumed chewing, and he looked as exhausted to her in the moment as she herself felt. She couldn't recall ever having seen him with stubble on his face before. Now he drained his own coffee and waved for more.

"I mean, isn't that part of it? Not to dillydally your time away? Look alive, because no man knows the day or the hour?"

"Annelise, I own stock in Douglas. My firm negotiated a property dispute for Grand Central. For that matter, I'm the one who backed your flying lessons. I do not by any means regard myself as a Luddite. Remember I told you this was not my idea?"

"Then why do you go along with her? Why don't you put your foot down?"

He shook his head. "Because Mother is not wrong, Annie. And as difficult as this might be for you to see, she has your heart and your soul and your safety and"—he halted, tripped over his own words— "and your *reputation* in mind." He went so far as to point at her across the table. "She is not wrong."

The night's caffeine had run out of her blood like fuel from a tank, even the remnant fumes combusted and gone. She was still in the air but totally without power, and no place in sight to put down. She tried to hold a level gaze across the table and finally went to rubbing her eyes instead. "She called me 'damaged goods,' Daddy. You heard her."

Not only that. They went so far as to haul her to the family doctor to have her put in the stirrups and examined, which she dodged only by finally copping en route to what they already suspected. Her father had practically driven off the road. "Is that what you believe, too?"

He could hardly look at her then, and he could hardly look at her now. "Eighteen is a puzzling age, I'm not going to pretend otherwise. And these are puzzling times we live in, for all of us. Mother included."

"These are wonderful times, if you can see the fun in anything. The opportunity. And if it's occurred to Mother even once that she might not have the answer to every little thing, she's certainly never let on."

He stirred his coffee, stirred and stirred. "You always were head-strong. Even when you were a little thing pulling a red wagon around. Selling books you'd outgrown to the neighbors. You and Mother are too much alike, that's half the problem. Cut right out of the same cloth."

"Too much alike? No, sorry, I live in 1937, not 1837."

"That's not what I'm talking about."

" 'Damaged goods' implies I'd actually stoop to accept a man who wants a piece of property to begin with. Anyone who thinks that doesn't know the first thing about me."

He glanced around, and she realized her voice had risen above the clatter from the kitchen, the clink and clank of plates and knives. A few of the other patrons appeared to notice.

She tried to turn the volume down. "I didn't betray you, you know. It's not even possible."

"I know. I can see why you'd say so."

"I'm not goods, and I am not damaged."

"And I am sorry you had to hear that."

"I mean, is a *widow* damaged? Is Sister Aimee *damaged* after divorce number two?"

"I know—"

"What utter hypocrisy."

"I know. It's just that boys don't . . . always understand that the consequences, for girls, can be disastrous. Socially disastrous. And visible. And permanent. Boys will be boys, but girls . . . the expectations are something different. Because the consequences are different. Fair or not."

Now Annelise did look at him. "*Visible?* Are you hearing yourself?" She felt the slap of her own hands, clapping at her cheeks with minds all their own. "Everyone knows why girls up and vanish midway through a school year, and it's not for a mere . . . indiscretion, or a dalliance, or whatever polite terminology you choose.

"Daddy. People are going to think I'm sent off because I'm *actually in a fix*. Did this not occur to anyone?"

He slid out of the booth and walked toward the counter, and she could tell by his posture and gait how strained he was, by travel in part but mostly by circumstance. She read this like she could read her own name. She wished she could resent whatever pain or exhaustion or judgment he felt, because she was the one with no say in the matter, and no power. But the fire seemed to have gone out of her.

He came back with a fresh newspaper and laid down the front page for her to see: EARHART IS OFF AROUND THE GLOBE.

She looked up at him. "That could be me. Someday."

"I believe you."

"This whole thing is a vast waste of my time. I've already started soloing, and now all this."

He eased into the booth again. "I'm aware."

Something else had occurred to her, too, a subject she hadn't dared broach with her mother around. But she was pretty sure she was right. And as a lawyer *and* a Christian, wasn't he obligated to tell her the truth? "Is this even legal?"

She saw him blink and knew she had him. "That's a bit of a . . . gray area, let's say."

"But if I'd really put my foot down? Refused to go along with this? You'd have done what, kick me out to the street?"

"Lord, of course not."

"But that's the only real recourse you could have had. Am I right?"

He rubbed his bloodshot eyes with fingers and thumb, probably, she imagined, to avoid having to face her. She was yet again in no mood for mercy.

"I became a legal adult clear back in November, didn't I? On my eighteenth birthday. California's one of those states, isn't it?"

"You are . . . not entirely wrong. It's one of those states. One of those *few* states . . . Most are a, ah, sensible twenty-one."

"And now you're sending me to one of them, against my adult will." Her stinger was coming up by the second, her scorpion's defense. "By the standards of the state in which I actually reside. Do I have this right?"

He shook his head at the ceiling, let out a breath. Gotcha.

"Because that's the way it appears. Are you actually breaking the law with this?"

He was still looking at the ceiling. "Not one that any prosecutor would argue before a judge. Or that any judge would enforce, for that matter."

"Why? Because I happen to still be in high school and under your roof?"

"Something like that, yes. Sure. Like I said, gray area."

"And when you wanted to have the doctor examine me against my own free will? Would that have been a *gray area*, too?"

People at other tables were definitely looking now, and he knew it, too, and she didn't give one solitary fig.

"It never got to that point, Annie."

"That's not the question."

"No, you're right. That would have been wrong. Maybe criminal."

"Thank you."

He managed to look at her again without blinking, as though the actual logistics of this punitive circus were finally dawning and he realized he'd better hold her with his eyes while he still had the chance. "Frankly, it probably would've gone better where your mother's concerned if you'd come totally clean and given her a name."

Her one nearly Pyrrhic triumph. Bleary or not, she felt her ire rise even more. "She couldn't beat it out of me. I don't expect you to sympathize."

His own bleary gaze didn't waver. "All right, then. If I can give you one bit of advice beyond that? Going forward, the parole board generally favors model behavior."

"Ha ha."

A little later he kissed her stiff cheek on the platform and put her back on the train. A little after that the train lurched forward, and with the station falling away, she rummaged in her satchel and found the travel kit she'd put together. Toothbrush, toothpaste. Napkins. A perfectly white and perfectly innocent pair of spare underpants, which she unfolded now inside the satchel.

She took out Blix's flight watch, which he'd jokingly let her steal from his wrist that last time. "Careful, now," he'd told her while she undid the buckle. "That's where I get my magic powers."

She let the watch sway in front of him, baited a swipe from his hand, which she neatly dodged. "I'm Delilah," she'd said. She teased and twirled the watch back into his reach, danced a little with her shoulders and neck like a cat about to pounce.

He shook his head, approval in reverse and she knew it. "You're trouble, is what you are."

She held the watch now in her palm, studied again the mysterious dials, the arcane calibrations and elegant blue hands. Blix himself had little practical use for it, outside the few times a year he flew down into Mexico, but he always wore it anyway, as a token. Or a talisman.

She wondered if he regretted letting her take it home on her own wrist that night. Surely he must. She had promised to return it at her next lesson two days later, before fate and her mother elbowed in. Now she tried to tell herself that fate as well had entrusted her to keep it, until finally she could navigate her way back to its rightful place. To her own rightful place.

She thought again of A.E., likely in the air at this very instant and just as likely wearing her own second-setting Longines flight watch. She'd left out of Oakland bound for Honolulu, so hers would be set to the same originating time as the one Anneliese held now. She took some comfort in this even though they were heading in opposite directions. In more ways than one.

She buckled the ticking device in place, the enormous face of the thing feeling more like a clock than a watch against the slim circumference of her wrist. Maybe it could be her talisman, too.

2

He bounced down the washboard above the river and felt the tremor in the motor in the floorboards, distinct somehow from the shake of the road. A prewar Lizzie at least ten years older than Huck himself, all tired springs and tired drive bands and probably tired compression to boot. He hadn't driven far enough to know.

He levered the throttle and felt the wind lift, thumbed the dust off the speedometer. The needle jumped like a live wire between thirty-five and forty. Could that be right? He looked up again and saw the edge of the flat, the road tilting off the plateau and down to the river bottom. He had a moment's distraction at the green blaze along the bank, bright as springtime against winter's remnant brown. He tipped over the lip of the grade and realized he wasn't very dang sure of the brake band, either.

His heart dropped like a hammer with the plunge of the car, a kick to the groin from the inside out. The engine groaned against gravity and wound into a single backfire, then a pause and finally a whole banging barrage, like a pistol shot answered by a fusillade. Now he'd hit forty for sure, the needle when he glanced at it appearing to tremble in place like a setter on point.

He fiddled with the spark and got the backfiring down. The brake appeared near useless, so he pushed on the reverse pedal instead, let off and pushed again and got his speed down and his heart out of his belly and back in his chest where it belonged. He clattered across a rough span of washboard and veered around a buckle of frost heave and bottomed onto level ground.

Two other boys scrambled out of the willows along the river, rods in hand and a mess of fish on a peeled branch. One was a real lunker, Huck could see it even before he'd closed the distance. Raleigh and Shirley, no doubt coming to the racket from the motor. Huck rolled to a stop.

"Dodging the truant officer?" said Shirley. He was nearly eighteen, hadn't made it past the first week of the ninth grade.

Huck twisted in the seat. "Seen one?"

"Ol' Rolly here pulled this dern German brown out. You believe it? This dern far down. Gonna get it to town, sell it to the café. Care to give a lift? We'll let you in on the haul."

"That trout ain't the only thing in this river today," said Raleigh.

Shirley made a show of ignoring him. "Old Man Neuman's rig, ain't it? Been in the weeds two years at least. What'd you do, sweet talk him out of it? Trade a pie or something?"

"A jug, more like it," said Raleigh. He held the dead fish at arm's length to keep the drip off his dungarees. Whitefish and that single, magnificent brown.

Huck grinned. "Gas is down to five cents. Lots of cars coming out of the weeds."

"Running like a real top, from the sound of it." Shirley fancied himself a real wisecracker. "Thought maybe ol' John Dillinger was up here, testing ordnance. Machine Gun Kelly."

"Dillinger's dead," said Raleigh. "All them old boys is. Pushing daisies. Or locked up."

"Yeah, I know that, Rolly."

"I think we ought to get a second opinion."

"Don't need no second opinion. Five cents, you said? This trout'll bring what, twenty? That'd buy some gas. Think this crate can get us to Billings? There's a girl down there who likes me."

Raleigh snorted. "This thing could be a supercharged Duesey and it wouldn't matter a lick. I ain't donating my trout to get you to Billings and back."

"Didn't say nothing about back. All I need is to get there. Worry about back later." Shirley winked at Huck. He tapped the Ford's battered bonnet with his cane pole. "What'd it take to get this trap running in the first place? I know you got a knack, but young Rolly here is right. For once."

"Old Man Neuman tried to run hooch through it a few years back, when gas was pinched. Wrecked the floats in the carb. Ain't done with her yet, but she'll run smooth enough, I think."

"You know what I think." Raleigh studied his dead fish again. The red spots on the trout's long body had already faded and streaks of gray defiled the pale of its belly. "I think we should get a second opinion."

Shirley eyed the narrow tip of his bamboo, made it quiver in the air above his head. "Zane Grey here thinks there's a body down there."

Huck felt the tremor in the motor. "A what down where?"

"A body," said Raleigh. "A dead dern body caught in a snag on the other side of the river. Couldn't get to it with the water this high."

Huck looked at Shirley, and Shirley shook his head. "It ain't no body, it's an inner tube. I promise. A black tire tube with about half the air out."

"Second opinion," said Raleigh.

"How far off we talking?"

Raleigh gestured with his swinging fish. "Two minutes. Right down there."

"Not no two minutes, though. Ten, more like. Look, the blush is already going on this brown," Shirley began, but Huck was already ratcheting the brake with one hand, cutting the magneto with the other. The engine dieseled a bit and shuddered still, and he heard the dull hum of the river all the way up here.

Shirley ran his eyes across the rusted shell of the T. "You sure this heap's liable to start again?"

Huck fell even with Raleigh, flashed a snake-oil grin. "Nope."

"Liar."

"Want a second opinion?"

"Har har. You ladies is going to an awful lot of trouble for a gol dang truck tube."

They went down off the roadway across a swath of cheatgrass greening through the dead stalks of winter, the bitterbrush and sagebrush greening up, too, and the meadowlarks trilling everywhere. The Bull Mountains loomed like a fortress a few miles off, snow glinting yet on the high northern rims. Otherwise the world had warmed.

They dropped into a wash and kicked out a cottontail, which raced ahead and cut and bounced pell-mell like a rubber ball and finally vanished down a hole. The rush of the water rose up louder with the close of distance, not a roar but a hiss, like midnight static after radio sign-off. Raleigh and Shirley walked upriver and cleared a willow brake and threaded their poles through the cottonwoods to get to the gravel along the bank.

The river had already come down from its peak—Huck could see the runoff line a foot or so up the rocks on the far bank—but ripped along anyway brown and fast and high. He saw a butterfly flash in the sun, saw it flit and dip and dart. Mourning cloak, first of the year. That line of azure jewels down each black wing, that yellow edge. Then he saw the body.

Half sunk and bobbing with the racing flow of the Musselshell, in a snarl of dead limbs and flotsam and jumbled planks lodged and upended, akimbo as the wreck of a raft. A torso in a dark suit with one swollen sleeve now visible, now not with the action of the water. A half-submerged cottonwood sweeper nodded and flexed, the root ball still partly attached to the bank.

"Could be a tire tube. A big one, out of a tractor." Had to be. No, a sleeve—there it was again and now gone. Huck squinted and stared and tried to convince himself his first sense had been true. The longer he looked, the less he could swear to.

"Yeah, it could be a tire tube, but it ain't. It's a dern body."

"Tube," said Shirley.

"Corpse. Black suit."

"Okay, look at it. Look. Right . . . *now*," he said, when the convex edge of this conundrum lifted again with the water, breached again in its eddy of foam and debris. "That is an inner tube."

"Huck? What say you?"

The figure again went under. A pair of mergansers rocketed down the corridor, careened and splashed crazily to a landing just down-river. The hen had a topknot like a woodpecker's. "I can't, either way. Could be a tube, yeah. But. It could be a dern body."

"Now hold on already," said Shirley. "This here's enough of a goose chase." He walked to the nearest cottonwood, eyed the crotch ten feet up. He leaned his cane against the trunk. "I'll go up and shimmy out on that limb, get a topside look. Settle this nonsense once for all."

"You're gonna fall right in the dern drink. That'll make two bod-ies in here."

"Not likely. On either count." He studied the crags in the heavy bark, found holds for fingers and toes, and started up. He missed a grip and dropped to the ground once, then tried again and dropped again. "Huck," he said, "you're bigger'n this runt. Why don't you give a hoist."

"Well, you're bigger than the both of us," said Raleigh. "Stouter, at least. Why don't you hoist me?"

"Because it's my idea. Plus I don't trust your judgment."

It was true Huck was big for his age, or tall anyway. Fourteen and he already stood above most men, certainly an inch or more over Shirley. Gangly as a sandhill crane, too—the only pants that fit for length were invariably agape at the waist, cinched into place with a belt that had additional holes in the tongue.

He could see this sparring going round and round, the shadows stretching longer, the day pinched shorter. He stepped over and wove the fingers of his hands into a basket. "You can both climb a tree, for all I care. Let's just get somebody into the air."

"You'd be the man to know, Slim," said Shirley, and he put his foot in the web of Huck's fingers and clambered up at the hoist, and Huck pivoted his shoulders and shifted his hands under Shirley's heft and started to push, and Shirley no sooner got one grip on the crook of the tree than he let out a yowl like he'd been snakebit.

Or bee-stung. A handful of honeybees boiled out of the fork, and Shirley launched flailing and hit the ground scrambling. Huck both glimpsed and felt something thud against the bone near his eye while his breath caught for a jolt that never came, and he found himself pounding gravel right along with the others.

They stopped and caught their breath at the mouth of the wash.

"Left my rod," Shirley croaked. "Jeez, look at my hand. Like a dern catcher's mitt. Bastards got me in the neck, too."

Shirley pulled his hand away and studied it as though the palm might reflect a duplicate of the wound at his nape, what showed to Huck as a rising red boil with an angry white center, the pinprick of the stinger like a bull's-eye. "This ain't good, boys. Last time I got stung I about choked to death. Swelled like that dern truck tube down there. Doc said I dodged a bullet."

Raleigh had relaxed his hold with the fish and now the pale, skewered mess of them bled down the leg of his pants. "So what do we do?"

Shirley looked at him. "Cross our fingers and hope flyboy here can fire that Liz again. And get to it while I can still suck some dern air."

They made their way up the draw. By the time they crossed the cheatgrass the red poison at his nape had worked around to his throat and up into his jowls, a mix of bruise and flush. His lips had ballooned, although his eyes appeared to shrink into slits. He looked like a pumpkin impaled on a barber pole.

Huck felt the anxious smack of his heart, felt a bead of sweat down his ribs. "Almost there," he told Shirley. He pointed at the T, slouched in the lean of the sun. "I'll run ahead, get her going. You want to keep walking?"

Shirley shook his head. He'd begun to wheeze like an engine sucking a vacuum. "Thung thwullen," he said. He pawed at his eyes with his good hand. "Can't thee thit."

Raleigh's peepers, on the other hand, were wide as moons, his mouth taut as a strop. Huck said, "You want to stay with him? Wait, no—come ahead. You're gonna crank."

They started to run, and the sprint went weirdly as if in a dream, seemed to occur in two cosmic places at once. On the one hand, he and Raleigh both ran and ran for what felt like agonizing eternity without ever closing the gap, the Ford always just ahead, just ahead, no closer and no closer and no farther away, either, with every long, desperate stride.

On the other, they seemed to appear at the car in an impossible jolting instant, as though they'd never made the physical dash at all but somehow catapulted not merely over the cheatgrass but also across the very plane of time itself.

Some trick of the mind, some distorted phase of panic. The rush of fear in the blood.

The fish hit the bed with a damp thud, and Raleigh went running for the front. Huck jolted back to himself, scrambled behind the wheel.

Raleigh looked at him across the hood. "Is he gonna die?"

"No." He backed off the spark advance. "Crank it. Keep your thumb clear and get out of the dern way." Raleigh gave him a look, and Huck said, "Wait, hold up. Hold up."

Huck pulled the choke halfway out, experimentally advanced the spark. He and Raleigh watched each other through the cracked glass. The lever hit the top of its arc, and Huck heard the spark pop in the cylinder, saw Raleigh jump as the gas fired and the engine belched and shuddered awake.

"Hot start," he yelled. "Didn't think it would work."

They bounced across the cheat, and Raleigh jumped free before Huck fully managed a stop, helped Shirley fumble into the bed, and then swung back in himself, and Huck stomped her right down into gear again.

Huck ground in low through the trace of his own wheels in the grass and swayed back up onto the roadbed, steered again around the frost buckle and over the corduroy at the base of the grade, and started up. After fifteen feet he thought better of it, let gravity and the brake lever bring them to a stop.

"What are you doing?"

Huck eased back down to level ground. "No way I'm coming down that hill bass-ackwards if the motor cuts on us." He backed around and twisted to see over his shoulder. He glanced at Shirley, prostrate and gurgling in the back, and started up the hill in reverse.

"I thought you put gas in this heap."

"I did. But she ain't near full, and I don't trust the carb yet anyway."

Raleigh snorted. "That's the least of it. Hate to stake my ol' bee-stung hide on a dern jalopy, tell you that much."

Huck gave it more throttle than he needed to and craned his head around to see. The T went up the grade in a steady shot, whining the whole way like the engine might blow a seal. They leveled on the flat up above and he swung around to face forward again and started for town. And a moment along when he stomped her into high, the Ford lunged like a hot-blooded horse and he felt a surge not of speed but of hope. Out of the corner of his eye he caught a flash in the air and he looked and beheld again the mergansers, circling and winging back toward the river, gliding like killer angels—

He caught himself from that same eerie distance, that same angle of refraction. Caught himself thinking, *Please, God, please let there be gas. Please, God, please keep Shirley alive. Please, God, in Jesus's name . . .*

He pried his left hand loose from the wheel. He flexed and unflexed his rigid fingers, his frozen grip. Big Coulee was only two miles off, the tops of the elms showing above the rim at the west edge of town.

"How's he looking back there?" He had to shout above the clatter of the motor, the jostle of loose fenders, and the open rush of air.

Raleigh took in Shirley over the back of the seat. "Not any dern better. Best put the spurs to her."

Huck could still feel the spot on his cheek where the bee struck. A miracle he hadn't been stung smack in the eye. The speedometer bounced and wagged in the general vicinity of forty. "She's full gallop right now."

They hit the macadam outside town, and the rumble of the gravel fell away. For all its roughshod rattles and rust, the T smoothed out across the skim of the pavement, and Huck remembered in a flash that this was how it felt to lift and level and properly soar. Even the raggedy sputter of the motor seemed to settle and glide. He forgot about Shirley, forgot about praying. He just drove and drove and let himself dream.

Huck let the motor wind out again, and the backfiring recommenced, and he backed off the spark, didn't try to brake, just held tight to the wheel with his left hand and throttled up again with his right when they careened around the last bend and leveled onto Main. A dog trotted blithely down the center of the street, and Huck squeezed the bulb of the horn. The dog glanced back at the blare, tucked tail, and cut for the sidewalk like he'd been scorched. Then the siren started.

Raleigh twisted again in his seat. "Guess we had that coming."

Huck took a quick glance himself and caught the grim red mug of the driver barely twenty feet behind, jaw set behind the windshield of the new black-and-white. Not Cy Gleason but his deputy, Junior Joe Candy. Hard to know which was worse.

"Thing's a dern rocket," said Raleigh. The siren wound up to an outright scream behind them, and Raleigh cautioned another look.

The hospital was two blocks down and a block over, and Huck set his jaw and didn't slow a bit, and by the time he reached his turn, people were popping out along the walk like gophers out of their holes, all shop aprons and feather dusters and jaws uniformly agape. He took the turn too wide and skidded sideways, heard Shirley thump around like loose cargo. He fishtailed straight again and in a quick second veered past the line of elms into the circular drive and braked to a hard stop in the covered ambulance bay. The T backfired and stalled.

Out in the street, the cruiser overshot the entry and wailed on down to the exit, squealed in that way and roared on up like the champ to the chump in a Charles Atlas ad, all sinewy lines and gleaming chrome, the V8 badge on the grille like the sneer of a natural-born winner.

Raleigh was already out of the car, already starting for the building. The cruiser braked nose-close, its siren winding down but still unnervingly loud beneath the canopy.

Huck said, "Hey."

Raleigh looked back.

"Best not bring up that inner tube."

Raleigh said, "No shit, Sherlock," and vanished inside the hospital doors.

Huck got out and Junior Candy did, too, ambling around the T's skewed fender. He walked up and stopped just to the inside of what a person with any sense might regard as a polite and sociable sphere, eyes still roving casually around the ceiling or out at the budding trees. He started a slow pink bubble at the precise moment he brought his wandering irises in from the beyond and trained them, like blue gun muzzles, directly on target. The bubble expanded, nearer and nearer. Junior's gaze finally vanished behind the pink balloon.

The bubble popped. Junior worked his tongue and pulled pink spatter back into his maw. Same blue glare. "Houston Finn. We meet again."

Huck could smell the aftershave, smell the hair tonic. His voice had not yet dropped, and to his horror, the first syllable when he found his tongue squeaked out like nails on a blackboard. In that instant, Shirley shot bolt upright in the pickup bed.

He looked like a hydrocephalic farmhouse killer from one of Raleigh's detective magazines. Junior Joe did a double take and heaved out something along the line of "Gid-gadamighty," and the door to the surgery banged open. Doc Lipton and Sonny the ambulance driver and Raleigh charged out with a gurney.

"How long you have this flivv?"

Raleigh spoke above the sputter of the motor, dusk and chill dropping all around. Huck saw a kitchen lamp come on in the house, saw Raleigh's ma peer out the window.

Huck shook his head. "Till she's fixed. Nothing hard and fast."

"She sure ain't that dern Buick we stole."

"Borrowed."

"Right. Borrowed." Raleigh reached into the back and took up his fish again, the bloom indubitably gone even in the lowering light. "Reckon I better get to cleaning these morbid things. Tomorrow, hey?"

Huck cut the motor. "You really think it's a body?"

Raleigh's mother shouted his name from the house.

"I think it's a dern dead body."

Huck chewed his lip.

"You in town or at the ranch tonight?"

"Ain't sure. Pop's been gone all day to Billings, fetching my cousin from the train. That's how come he put me onto this heap."

"Texas kin?"

"California. My ma's kin."

"He older'n us?"

"Yeah, but he ain't a he. He's a she. Twelfth grade, I think."

"Whoa. One in the oven?"

"What all?"

"That's why girls usually get sent off. What they call 'studying abroad.'"

"Huh. You mean a baby."

"Remember Fanny? Rube's sis?"

Raleigh's mother again.

"Hold on, I'm coming," Raleigh hollered. "Gone all last year?"

The door banged at the house.

"Yeah, she had a sick aunt somewhere. What Rube said."

Raleigh snorted. "That's old as the hills, too, Houston. This is your ma's niece, right? Tell me, is your ma sick? I realize that's a touchy subject, but all else being equal."

Huck looked at the moon, full or nearly so, half up now over the far rim of the coulee and blue white and so enormous as to look hardly distant at all. By dawn it would shrink to a speck.

Raleigh squinted at his fish. "Some of us may be studying abroad. Others of us is more like innocents abroad."

Huck continued to look away. "Nobody said nothing about a dang baby."

They were quiet a minute, both of them watching the lavender sky and night coming on, lights at the edge of town winking a mile off, and Sirius, steady as time, in the far beyond. Raleigh changed the subject. "How's the ship?"

Huck nodded. "Starting to look like something. Frame's all gusseted for the fuselage, and I've got about half the wing ribs, too." He thumped the dashboard. "Pop'll let me order the skin once we collect for this crate. Ought to get by to see her."

"I will." His mother shouted again from the house, some threat about dinner. Raleigh started up the walk, then looked back. "Your ma still don't know, hey?"

Huck grinned at the dusk. "Pop says you tell 'em what they want to hear, and you do what you have to do."

"Good man, that pap of yours. Been some kinda day, hey?"

"Shirley's liable to kill us, we head out there and find something without him."

Raleigh turned and walked. "Shirley ain't in a position to kill anybody. Plus he owes us. Don't let on, but that scared the dern daylights out of me."

Raleigh's mother shouted. Raleigh shouted back. Huck set the magneto switch and swung the spark lever. At the top of its arc he heard the snap in the cylinder, felt the engine turn once and wheeze and shudder and still again in the chill blue air. The magnetos whirred like bees swarming from a tree.

Raleigh stopped. "Guess you ain't pulling that stunt twice. Need me to crank?"

3

Much to her shock, her salt-of-the-earth uncle scooped her into a mighty hug on the platform of the Billings depot, squeezing her hard enough to knock the wind out of her.

She barely remembered him from years ago, outside the recollection he'd rigged a little Indian-style headband for her with a couple of turkey feathers and put her in front of him on his saddle horse when he rode out to open an irrigation gate. She'd liked horses ever since, had even owned a little Hanoverian cross in junior high before the local stables suffered some zoning crisis and had to move too far out of San Marino to make regular riding practical.

She supposed on some level she'd assumed Uncle Roy must not be all bad simply because she associated him with her horse, but her parents had said little about him over the years, and with everything else in such a stew, she really hadn't given him a second's consideration.

He let her breathe again, held her at arm's length and took her in. "Well then. Not the little thing I remember."

Crinkly blue eyes and a lopsided smile with one gold-edged tooth. Hat pushed back on his head. She felt her mouth twitch toward a smile for the first time in days, then a pang in her eyes that she fought like a weakness.

The conductor silently handed over a form for Roy to sign, as though he knew exactly why she was here, and his job entailed not only delivery but a suitably solemn one. Damaged goods.

*   *   *

Later in the truck he told her about a shootout a day earlier, outside someplace called Roundup. The very name conjured an image of
horsemen in big hats ambushing each other with six-shooters. Then
he said something about a getaway car and police blockades on the
highways, and it occurred to her that Uncle Roy's hat was a basic fedora, not some ten-gallon Tom Mix, so even a place with a handle like
Roundup, Montana, nevertheless existed in the twentieth century.

"Did they catch them? The robbers?"

"Shot one of 'em. Right off the bridge and into the drink, evidently."

"Wow."

"Never a dull moment," he said. "A few others got plumb away.
They sent a few planes from the airfield here in Billings, to see if they
could spot 'em thataway. Pretty slick idea, really."

This last got her attention. "It is a slick idea. Especially in places
like this, where it's so . . . you know, big, I guess. Empty. I have a
good friend—my flight instructor, actually—who flies for the police
sometimes, too."

She saw his eyes shift at her. "Well, it's a new one in these parts,
far as I know."

They waited through a stoplight, downtown Billings much more
of a bustle than she would have guessed. She looked out the side
window, saw what appeared to be an honest-to-God Indian curled up
in a blanket on the sidewalk. The light went green and they started
forward.

"You said you have a flight instructor?"

She felt herself nod, felt her lips go drum-tight.

"Now that's something. Houston, he'll be green as that traffic
light." He chuckled. "Probably drive you up the wall with questions,
too, so be warned. But he won't mean to be a pest. He's as good a
kid as they come."

If he meant anything with this last, she couldn't detect it. Couldn't imagine it either, on an instant's consideration. "Has he been up?"

"Flown, you mean? Nah. Well—not in an airplane, anyway. There was this glider he built, but that's a long story. You have your license?"

She hooked a curl behind her ear, felt the weight of the watch when she lifted her wrist. "I was getting close. I'd just started soloing when all this . . . you know."

Uncle Roy fished out a pack and shook a Lucky loose and fired it. Smoke rose and swirled, and she realized she'd been smelling it on him all along. Another surprise. He cranked his window down. "Sorry," he told her. "Old habit. Never have much wanted to give it up."

"It's actually a relief. My mother donates to the Anti-Cigarette League, the Anti-Saloon League, the Temperance Union. It's so . . . I don't know, gauche, somehow."

"Not acquainted with that one, miss. Might have to paint me a picture."

"Would you think worse of me if I asked for one?"

"Are you?"

She smirked in spite of herself. "Worse?"

He cracked his own sly grin right around his Lucky. "Asking."

"I guess so."

He handed her the pack, and she drew one out. He handed her his cigarette, and she lit hers from the glowing tip and passed it back. She put her window down. "You didn't answer my question, you know."

He laughed and held up the smoldering V of his fingers. "Obviously I ain't in a position to cast the first stone. Long as it stays between you, me, and the highway."

"Huh. Forgive my sass, but that's a pretty spineless answer."

"I know it. You're preaching straight to the converted." He had his hand on the wheel, and he looked at the burning cigarette. "Used to roll my own, like everybody else in these woolly parts. These tailor-mades are a lot easier to sneak, though." His eyes shifted back to her. "Half of getting by in life is choosing your battles. What your aunt Gloria don't know ain't gonna hurt her."

Annelise held the heat in her lungs, felt the lift in her head. She'd been awake a long time now. "Sometimes I think I was accidentally switched in the hospital. I'm serious. Or adopted." She blew smoke out the window and looked at him. "You can tell me if I was, it won't hurt my feelings. It would explain a lot, really."

"I can't testify to any switch, but you sure weren't adopted. You can bet the ranch on that. Plus, you may not see it, but you look just like her."

"That's what everyone says. And you're right, I can't see it."

The truck went into a climb along the cliff at the edge of the city. The shafts of the sun shot low and yellow through bands of clouds above hazy tables in the distance, mile upon mile of rough, jumbled ground between here and the horizon. She wondered how on earth anyone would make an emergency landing out there.

"She hates my hair, she hates my clothes, she hates my friends. She hates the things that interest me, the books I read. She even hates the *look* on my face."

"Sounds stressful."

She was smoking very quickly, half the cigarette already sucked down. In truth she could count on two hands the number of times she'd smoked in the past, each instance producing exactly the dizzying, borderline nauseating spin she felt now. She tapped the ash on the upper edge of the window.

"My mother called me a whore. She called me a slut. Not my father, my mother. Aren't those ugly words?"

He shifted a little, tilted toward his own window and blew smoke.

"I mean, I assume you know why I'm here."

"Yup. I sure do."

"She grabbed me by the hair, and she literally dragged me to the car so a doctor could examine me."

He looked over, took in her blonde crop. "You've barely got any hair to pull, miss."

"Trust me, there's enough."

A coyote carrying a chicken crossed the road in front of them, out of the bar ditch and then a smooth streak across the gravel to the weeds on the other side, and gone.

"Sneaky bastard," Roy muttered, although he seemed somehow half pleased at the same time, or maybe half amused. He made a quick veer across the center line and back, as though to run down the sneaky coyote's very memory. Annelise swayed with the veer and smirked again in spite of herself.

"Ugly words, sure enough," he told her.

"Right? I don't feel like either of those things. I don't think those things even exist, except in the minds of people who need to believe in . . . believe in . . ."

"Hogwash."

Now her head really did spin. "Right," she said, and reached out her hand and dropped her cigarette to the roadway. "I was going to say *rules*."

"Fair bit of overlap, in my experience."

She tilted her head to the seatback and shut her eyes against the green fog in her mind, and the thought struck her and just popped right off her tongue. "If you're born to fail, how can you be punished for a foregone conclusion?"

He didn't seem to have an answer.

She opened her eyes again, took in the layer of dust on the ceiling. "As if it *is* some huge failure to act like a human. Even with that view of the world, though, where humans are born sinners, doesn't the one thing just cancel the other out?"

He chewed on this, or appeared to. Finally he said something.

"Failure gets to looking downright epidemic, is the trouble. Look at that place, right out across the sage—that's a bust homestead. Door hanging, paper flapping." He shook his head. "I was only born in '86 myself, and nowhere near here, but things have been a last-ditch gamble for most in this country since way back then, at least.

"That's the winter killed all the cows, you know. Or likely you don't, but there's old-timers around can tell you. Dead cattle stacked in the coulees, way the dern slaughtered buffalo must've been five years before. Slaughtered Injuns, for that.

"No end to the troubles ever since, either. Drouth, winds to beat all, Mormon crickets chawing the wheat crop like some Egyptian Bible plague. Damn Spanish flu dropping people from here to Christmas—1918, that one." He was shaking his head now, shaking and driving. "You see enough failure, you start to see it as the way of things. And I guess it does start to look like a dern curse, if you let it. And so I guess you start to tell yourself about heaven, and how on earth you might figure a way to get there."

The road made a bend, and as he steered around to the west, she caught a silver splinter in the last angle of the sun, lost it in a gauze of cloud, and then watched the speck of an airplane emerge. One of the ships looking for the holdup men maybe, but by sheer suggestion, she thought of Amelia's new aluminum Lockheed. That silver-foil flash.

She said, "I don't think humans are born failures. I think we're born animals. The thing that sets us apart is, we can make things that are otherwise necessary into things that are also beautiful. Like . . . I don't know, oysters Rockefeller. Or the Gamble House. It's the opposite of gauche, actually."

He'd kept his eyes on the curve in the road. "I expect you already know this, but you need to brace yourself, miss. You're about to go back in time a bit."

4

When the first edition of the Flying and Glider Manual *was published three years ago, it was inspired by the belief that thousands of young men throughout the country were intensely eager to own and fly their own airplanes.*
    —"Introducing the 1932 *Flying and Glider Manual*"

He came off the highway and took the first left he could to avoid Main, skulking along by the moon's big blare, the idle tuned low as he dared. He turned east again and passed Cy Gleason's side street, cautioned a glance and couldn't make out either the constable's blue Ford or the new county cruiser. He drove to the smithy at the end of the block.

The bulb above the office door put out its usual weak haze, and the porch light on the bungalow next door had been switched on as well, but Pop's REO did not appear to be around. Huck cut the motor and coasted to a stop, nose-in to the sliding shop door. He heard the low babble of the Zenith from inside, which Pop turned on at night for the cat.

He felt like a famine victim out of the Old Testament and knew he should rustle some grub in the house. Instead he let himself into the office. Lindy the cat called to him in the dark, then jumped down from the shelf above the desk and into the wan glow around the radio. *Amos 'n' Andy.* Huck hit the overheads and *tsked* at the cat and went into the shop.

The ship, or what existed of it, rested on sawhorses in the fabrication bay in the back of the smithy. He'd built the frame for each side
flat on the floor over the winter, first chalking out the patterns for
longerons and struts and then driving nails to a half depth around the
scribed lines to function as a jig. The plans called for spruce, which
he and Pop cut in the Bull Mountains in the fall and milled to spec
over at the lumberyard across town. Huck bundled and strapped the
sticks tight and let them cure for a seemingly interminable month
while he read and reread and reread yet again the 1932 *Flying and
Glider Manual*.

He ran the projector and swept stray popcorn in the movie house
when he stayed in town. He socked his pay away in an Arbuckles' can
and stashed the can in the smithy.

Over Christmas holiday he popped the straps on his fir sticks and
bent a lower longeron around the arc of nails in the floor. He laid
the longeron's upper mate into place and fit a row of struts between
the two, then mitered diagonal bracing into each bay. He let the seat
bracing into what would become the cockpit, fore and aft, and cut
gusset plates out of eight-inch plywood. He checked and double-
checked, and when he was sure he had his ducks in a row, he mixed
a batch of casein glue and fused it all together with plates and glue
and brads.

He kept a trapline for muskrat and mink in the slough out on the
ranch.

Over the course of a dead-still and blindingly bright subzero
week in January, he called in and shot six beautifully prime coyotes
and a like pair of red fox using a telescoped .250-3000 Pop had taken
on trade for some machine work.

When trapping season closed, he sent the stretched hides to a fur
buyer in Seattle and cashed a windfall of a check, and this went into
the coffee can as well. He kept on at the movie house, and by March

he had enough to buy a new set of Zenith flight gauges and a war-surplus prop through *Modern Mechanics*.

He built the opposing frame flat again on the floor to mirror the first, and with the casein fully cured a second time, he set the halves topside down on their upper longerons. He pinned them tight at the tail, cut and set the graduated connecting struts on layout, and mitered diagonal bracing into the back three bays. He covered the floor and sides of the cockpit with light plyboard and attached seat-backs and a forward firewall of the same.

The chalk lines from the longerons were scuffed and smudged but still visible on the floor, the arc of nails pulled, but the holes they left like dots properly connected. What he had now resting on the sawhorses and fairly glinting with fresh varnish was the skeleton of an honest-to-God airplane fuselage, sleek and tapered as a rocket. He couldn't stop looking at it.

Lindy had followed him into the shop, and she weaved in and out of his shins. He could smell the high heady sheen off the ribs of the plane, smell also the gasoline and grease on his hands from wrenching on the flivv. His belly growled something fierce, and he knew his head had gone a little light. Hunger and fumes.

A week earlier he'd traced out a jig for the wing ribs. He built two of them the following evening, and by the third night he had a system down and built a half dozen more.

Now he'd been away from the whole project for a few days, and with twenty-two ribs to go, he wanted badly to log some time but knew as well he needed his head on straight. He rocked the fuselage frame a time or two in its berth atop the horses, marveled again at how little this geometric web of sticks actually weighed. Bones of a bird.

He knew by the door lamps and radio that Pop had already been by, that he'd no doubt driven this mystery cousin on to the ranch outside town. Huck had met her once, but too long ago to remember.

Annelise, perpetually the sharp-featured little blonde girl with the Shirley Temple curls in the picture of the family gathering back in '25, hanging on the wall at the farmhouse. She wore a sundress and a thin matching headband, although somebody had stuck a turkey feather straight up behind her head in the fashion of an Indian brave. Huck himself was still in a toddler's smock, looking even then at the sky rather than the camera. He wasn't the shaver in that picture anymore, which meant Annelise was not that little girl, either. But nobody had said a thing about a dang baby.

He reheated a leftover kettle of what Pop called Texas hash on the gas range and forked down about half of it at the table. The first mouthful hit the floor of his belly like a hay bale dead-dropped from a loft.

He still had the jitters. What a day it had been—Doc Lipton had stuck Shirley with two big hypodermics, and sure enough Shirley had quit gurgling and in four or five minutes lost about half the swelling in that balloon of a noggin, and he and Raleigh had started breathing again themselves. Doc Lipton told them they ought to get a medal, and he looked straight at Junior Joe when he said it. Such was the end of the story, other than Junior's unconcealed sour grapes while he filled out his report.

Or so Huck figured. The more he thought about it, Shirley had to be right. Raleigh was known to have a wild imagination, and how in tarnation would a dern body in a black business suit wind up in the river in the first place? Tractor tube, no doubt. What a day, though. His gut churned like a cement mixer. They kept milk in the icebox mainly for the cat, but he went for it now, thinking it might settle the storm.

He spotted the note, there on the sideboard, scrawled on an envelope in Pop's slanting script and with the terse cadence of a telegraph.

Sonny—Took yr. cous. to the ranch, 6:30, back late or in the a.m.? Tx hash in kettle. Big excitement over to Roundup—gang of stickup men busted,

one man shot and washed downriver, others still loose. Lock doors and keep yr.
powder dry. Pops

They made the train trestle with the sun yawning new and long over the coulees and breaks. Huck took his foot out of the pedal and idled down and stopped.

"You have the radio on out of Billings last night?"

"Nuh-uh."

"Hear any news from Roundup?"

Raleigh considered. "Not a thing. What is it?"

He fished the envelope out of his shirt pocket and handed it over. "Not any tire tube, be my guess."

Raleigh took a gander at the note. "Looks like ol' Shirley can pound sand."

Huck turned onto the track and centered the wheels on either side of the left rail. He glanced down once midway across and saw the rip of the water thirty feet below, glimpsed it and glimpsed it again through the metered skip of the ties. He forced his eyes forward. "She cleared any?"

Raleigh had his head craned over the passenger door. "Hard to tell. She's still plenty silty."

He drove out past the plowed and furrowed table and down toward the water as far as the road could take him. He cut the motor and grabbed a rope coil and a shepherd's crook he'd thrown in at the shop.

From a high swell in the shortgrass before the land dropped away to the river bottom, they could look out to the south and see the opposing bench, see the grade Huck had backfired down the day before. Fifteen minutes later they looked downstream at the snag.

The mergansers clattered again off the water, and the both of them jumped like pinched girls. "Glad it ain't just me," Raleigh said.

They walked through a glaze of frost on the green grass by the water where the cold air pooled. They came up onto the snag, and sure enough from a downstream angle they could look back up into the eddy and see the same solid-black bulk when it bobbed up and paused before sinking back again, just shy of the fallen cottonwood.

"We'll have to get out on the sweeper to get a real look," Huck said. "Was hoping we wouldn't."

"You and me both," said Raleigh, but he walked back and climbed up and began to inch his way out against the log's vibrating tremble, and Huck dropped rope and staff in the grass and found his balance and inched out behind him.

Raleigh made the first jutting limb, and with something to hold to, he sidestepped around as quickly as he dared so that Huck could reach for the same limb. They stood then on either side and looked goggle-eyed at each other as the trunk beneath began to lift with the flow like a whale breaching.

They looked down. The river swirled with silt, opaque as fog. The black bulk rolled with the action of the water and lifted and broke through, a human hand protruding and fish-pale by contrast and then the bloated face, assembling through murk and flow and suddenly a half-lidded, blue-tinted ghoul. The dark wreath of hair pulsed around his head like sea wrack.

"Dam-*nation*," Raleigh breathed, and he clutched the limb with both hands and convulsed once or twice and vomited like a firehose, right out across the water.

Huck clutched the limb. The sweeper dipped and his own gorge heaved.

He choked it back. The face and its swimming fronds sank again into the murk. He wobbled for land.

Raleigh finished being sick and followed, stumbled down onto dry ground and walked off by himself, shaking his head and spitting bile. Huck gathered his wits and shouldered the coiled rope. He climbed up on the log and started back.

"Houston. Are you serious?"

Huck kept on. He made the upright limb and put it in the crook of his arm, slid the coil from his shoulder, and tied a running bowline in one end. He could see the black shape through the silt and swirl, was already getting a sense for the timing of the thing. He set a ten-inch loop and let the loop dangle about where the hand would emerge. He looked over at Raleigh. "River's rising again. This body comes loose, no telling where it'll end up."

"Jeepers, who cares? It's a dern dead crook."

"Might be a reward. I need to buy an engine."

Raleigh rubbed his eyes.

The body breached a moment later, the bleached hand with its purpled nails, and Huck dropped the loop and drew the rope taut and tried and failed not to glance again at the face. Eye sockets bruised as plums. The knot in his stomach tightened as well at the solid tug of a waterlogged body, this odd combination of deadweight and buoyancy.

"Now what?" said Raleigh.

Huck steadied himself against the limb when the body again went under. He thought for a moment, tried to work out a plan. He tied the rope to the limb and balanced his way back for the shepherd's crook.

"Water's below the bottom of the trunk in that stretch," said Huck. "Just barely and probably not for long, way she's coming up. I'll send the rope under, snag it, and lead it back here."

"Then what?"

"Then you're going to reel while I crowbar him loose with the staff. Send him under the tree after the rope."

"You're gonna fall in and flipping drown."

"You watch. I think I got it figured."

"Houston. There is a fine line between calculated risk and famous last words."

Huck looked at him. "I don't think he's stuck by much. I think it's mainly water pressure holding him in that pocket. Some weird hydraulic. I got a way to keep from falling, too. You watch."

Huck went back out to the limb with the staff, untied the rope, wound it back to a coil, and dropped it to the water. The body had again gone under. The rope passed beneath the tree on the current, and he turned and grabbed the limb, dipped the shepherd's crook with his free hand, and snagged the rope where it trailed from the dead man's wrist. He hung the crook overhead on a fork of the limb and walked the wet line back to Raleigh. "Anchor it to that bit-off alder. If the current gets him, this might be a real handful."

Raleigh took the rope. "You know this is crazy?"

Huck didn't answer, just headed back out. He made the limb, circled it with his arm, and undid the buckle on his belt. He pulled the long tongue back through three loops on his waistband, ran the leather around the limb, and cinched himself to the tree.

"Houston," Raleigh shouted. "Remember English class? *The Wreck of the Hesperus?*"

"*Christ save us all*," Huck shouted back, and when the body loomed up through the depth, he hooked his foot around the base of the branch and leaned into the bite of the belt. He held the staff in two hands and put the crook down into the water and watched it refract toward the dead man's upper arm.

He tried to hook the arm and felt the crook deflect. He tried again while the dead man bobbed and got the same result, the arm evidently in a rigid lock against the torso. The body rolled a bit against the prod and drag of the staff, and those dead-lidded eyes seemed to divert their attention in a scan of the sky, then bring their fixed stare right back upon him as the body centered again.

He felt the dip of the tree and knew the pull of the water would take its claim again at any second. He thought to try for the dead man's own belt with the crook, and he looked hard through the shimmer and saw only the flapping tail of the black jacket. And when the current began to pull him down, Huck looked full-on again at that ghoul's face with its dancing hair, and he reached down and in one fluid motion set the hook behind the man's neck. He felt the solid tug of contact, the stubborn resistance of a weight that wanted only to sink.

He heaved with both arms and felt something resist and then release below the surface, and the head and chest sat up into the air like a jack-in-the-box, wet wreath suddenly plastered to the skull and a blue bullet hole the size of a dime in the temple. And Huck heard again the words *Christ save us* and realized the wheezing voice that went with them was entirely his own.

He yelled for Raleigh to pull and the body did indeed jump with the current. He heard the rasp of fabric against the bark of the tree as the force of the staff shoved him into his belt, and he let go in reflexive panic and clawed for the limb. Staff and torso both dropped back for the water and slid under the tree, the staff at its skewed angle jutting and knocking against the trunk and torquing down with the heavy pull of the body, scraping under and springing back into the air on the other side.

The corpse floated with the current. Huck's head snapped to Raleigh, struggling to pull against the water, and he forced his fingers from the limb and fumbled with his belt, got himself free, and with one hand clutching his waistband somehow nearly vaulted back to steady ground. He made it to Raleigh in three leaping strides, and the two of them moved downriver, walking and hauling the body toward shore. They reeled him to the shallows, his arm stiff and seized tight yet against his torso, despite the loop at his wrist and the force of the water. The staff jutted.

They steered the body to the gravel and looked at each other. "Houston, your pants are falling down."

"I saw the bullet hole, Rolly. Right in the side of his dern head." Huck hoisted his trousers into place and buckled his belt. "It's blue."

"Aye, yi yi." Raleigh spat a time or two. "My mouth tastes awful."

They moved together toward the body on the bank, its legs trailing into the shallows. One foot was bare beneath the black pant leg, the skin pale as wax and weirdly hairless, the other clad yet in a wingtip shoe.

"He looks like a dern lawyer," said Raleigh.

"Preacher." The word popped out, and Huck immediately regretted it.

Raleigh took a good hard look at the bloated face. Huck could hear him breathing, saw his hands still tight around the rope. He took hold of the staff and twisted the head. "There's where the bullet got him."

"Ho-*ly*." Raleigh looked away, swallowed hard and shook his head and looked back. "Dern thing must still be in his melon, otherwise he'd be missing half his head. That's a .38 at least. Maybe bigger." He seemed to notice his hands and the wet rope for the first time, and he half flung it at the ground, like a thing gone snake-alive in his grip. He looked at Huck. "Now what?"

"Reckon we'd better get to a phone and call Cy. This cuss'll bloat quick out here in the sun."

Raleigh seemed to gather his wits by the second. He looked upriver at the sweeper, then back to the body. "Let's get the rope off him first."

Huck said, "Don't you think we ought to tie him off again? Make sure he don't float away on us?"

"This here is a golden opportunity to get back on Cy's good side after that stunt last fall, is what I think. Walking out on a sweeper and roping a dead guy ain't gonna help your cause."

Huck crouched by the corpse and realized his knees were still shaking. He took the rope close to the stiff white wrist, tried to work the cinched knot with his thumb and index finger only, tried not to make actual contact with cold flesh or sodden cloth.

The body really was stiff as a board. "I don't know if I can get this loose. Dern knot's like a turnbuckle."

He pulled the rope in different directions against what felt for all the world like the permanent grip of death itself, tugged this way and that and round and round, hoping to flex the thing loose from the bite of the knot. The stiff arm jerked, and the wet black cuff of the jacket slouched farther down the wrist. Huck pivoted on his knee to get a better angle and found himself staring at the moving hand of a clock.

Not a clock but a wristwatch, a particularly enormous one, strapped to the inside of the dead man's wrist. Huck watched the metered jump and stall of the second hand, the jump and stall, past the Roman XI and on again toward and then beyond the twelve o'clock apex. He watched the minute hand advance.

"Son of a bitch."

He was not known to swear in the manner of most teenage boys, had in fact a sort of reverse notoriety for exactly the opposite. "Whoa," said Raleigh. "You hurt?"

Huck shook his head. The watch had a gigantic glass face and a steel bezel around the outer rim marked in degrees, one through fifteen, with graduated minutes of angle between each numeral. A prominent onion-shaped winding crown protruded at three o'clock, with a smaller crown positioned at two. LONGINES, in bold if diminutive block lettering beneath high noon. Huck reached over and pincered the two o'clock crown and twisted. An inset dial at the center of the face marked with its own arcane graduations rotated independently of the main Roman dial.

"Son of a bitch."

"What is it?"

Jump. Stall. Huck couldn't peel his eyes away. "It's a Lindbergh flight watch. First one I've ever gotten a real look at."

Raleigh crouched beside him. "Holy—look at the size of it."

"I know it. So a flier can work it with gloves. They also come with a special strap to fit over a flight jacket."

"What all's it do? With the dials and all?"

Jump.

Stall.

"It's for calculating longitude. You set the watch to a radio signal from the prime meridian in England and then figure the hour angle of the sun by the settings on the watch, which gives you your location in the air. I don't exactly know how it works. Colonel Lindbergh came up with it, after the Atlantic crossing. I can't believe I'm actually seeing one."

"So this guy's a flyboy himself, then."

The body. Huck pried himself from the jump and stall and started again at the distorted face of the deceased. He'd become fixated with numerology, with the steady blue momentum of time. He'd forgotten the body altogether.

He looked back to the watch. Worn on the inside of the wrist, like a proper aviator. "Yeah, I guess he must be. Or was." He looked at Raleigh. "I'd give a lot to have enough time with this dern watch to figure out how it works."

"So take it. Start figuring."

Huck shook his head. "More complicated than that. I'd need to study up on the basic science, then figure out the watch after. Plus, I think you're supposed to use it along with a sextant or something. And a radio signal. No way I'm going to make heads or tails before Cy gets here."

"No, Houston, I mean *take* it. As in, take it with you."

"Take it?" Huck watched the needle jump again past twelve, watched the long, pierced point of the minute hand advance. Eight past nine and no doubt dead-on. Sunrise that morning had been shortly before six, and he'd left the shop not long after to meet Raleigh. "You mean steal it?"

"Huck. He's a dern dead crook with a bullet in his head who probably stole the thing himself. Or bought it with stolen loot at least. We hadn't spotted him yesterday, and you hadn't come along with Old Man Neuman's rig when you did, no telling how this would've ended. Eventually he'd have come loose out of that snag and kept right on floating, watch and all. Or the fish would've eaten him. You believe in God, right?"

Huck looked at him.

"You was brought up to believe, right?"

"Was brought up to, yeah."

"Well, maybe God put us in this to get that watch in front of you. Think about it like that. This guy don't need to know the time anymore. Don't need to know his latitude, either."

"Longitude. Latitude's a sight easier."

"Right, longitude. Look, you want to see that watch on Junior Joe's wrist? 'Cause that's exactly where it'll end up."

A streak of a shadow came across the ground at the corner of his eye and passed over the corpse and on and then another in fast tandem, killer angels returning. Huck's eyes flashed up and he beheld again the mergansers, banking and coming back around toward the river, flashing in the morning sun with their plumage and their long fish-killing beaks and that topknot on the hen, like a painted warrior in the Bodmer prints at school. They splashed down against the river.

Huck watched the drake's head go underwater and then his whole body dive. The hen's head swiveled like a ratchet. "I reckon they need to make a living, too," he said, and he reached out and seized the cold dead wrist in his grip and undid the buckle on the watch strap. He handed it to Raleigh and worked the bowline now with his fingers, tried to ignore the bruiselike impression the watch had left behind on the now bare wrist.

He freed the rope and stood. Raleigh handed the Longines back. "Now that's a watch."

"So we just, you know, keep mum about it? Tell 'em what they want to hear?"

"And do what we have to do. Good as any blood oath."

They started back for the T. Raleigh toted the staff and the wet rope. Huck could feel the watch in his pocket, heavy against his thigh.

"How long was the ol' Lone Eagle in the air on that flight? All told?"

"Thirty-three hours," said Huck. "More or less."

Raleigh walked along a minute. "Awake the whole time."

"Reckon he had to be."

"All that dern way, one straight shot, over all that water. Far as the eye can see."

Huck put his hand in his pocket and gripped the watch. "When he could see. A lot of it was in the dern dark."

"Thirty-three hours." They came upon the swell in the shortgrass and angled for the T, setting cockeyed in the sun. "You ever wonder, you know, what if he had to poop? I mean, he's eighteen, twenty hours in, say, and he can't help it, he's just gotta take a crap so bad. What the heck would he do? What the heck *did* he do?"

"You have to wonder. He don't say nothing about it in the book."

"My old man saw him, you know. In Helena. On that big tour he took afterward."

"Yeah. I've met a few people saw him back then. My old man knows a guy who spent a few days with him in that Anaconda country where he holed up for a spell. Guy said he was pretty level, really. Didn't act like a bigshot at all."

"That's what everyone says."

They reached the T and Raleigh went around to crank. He set himself to lean into it but straightened up before he started, looking at Huck through the glass. "Wish we'd been big enough to see him back then."

"I know it. Ten years ago, though. We weren't knee-high to nothing."

Raleigh nodded. "You never did talk to your pap yet, right?"

"No. Not since all this. Why?"

"Just remembered your cousin, is all. Just wondering what's afoot."

"Ain't seen her neither," he said. And nobody had said a thing about a dern baby.

5

She finally let herself cry and finally let herself sleep, in the dark, low-ceilinged bedroom they'd put her in, up in the rafters of the farmhouse. Her cousin Houston's room, ordinarily. Annelise remembered him as a baby years ago, and she could smell him, his basic boyness, in the blankets and pillowcase now.

Not a bad smell—Brylcreem and something like aftershave, although she couldn't imagine he was old enough yet to need it. And although he was her blood cousin and a mere kid, his scent was so reminiscent of Blix's that she found herself sucking massive draughts out of the pillow, clutching the thing almost frantically and burying her face and breathing and breathing, and weeping and weeping at last.

She didn't expect to fall away but evidently she had, because the room was half alight from the narrow window when she opened her eyes.

She could faintly hear voices from down below. Uncle Roy. Aunt Gloria. She couldn't make out what they were saying. She blinked a time or two, studied in the wan light what she hadn't fully processed in the dim glow of the kerosene lamp the night before.

Model airplanes, most of them lined in neat formation on a home-grown table at the far end of the room, and two more suspended from the ceiling overhead. A 1903 Wright Flyer, a Curtiss Jenny. What appeared to be a de Havilland Gipsy. Another that looked like an Avro training plane. A few others of apparently original design and detail, which meant he'd built them from scratch rather than kits. She heard a rooster crow outside.

A voice murmured down below. Annelise pushed the wool blanket back, eased as silently as she could to her feet, and crossed the worn runner in her bare feet down the length of the room.

The models were of a more or less uniform size, with eighteen or twenty inches of wingspan. He'd apparently built each as a true miniature with some sort of fabric, or maybe tissue paper, as a stand-in for muslin, stretched across a fuselage frame and wing ribs, or simply the latter in the case of the Wright plane. Toothpicks for wing struts, strands of thread for cables. Rubber wheels and axles apparently repurposed from toy trucks or other objects. Miniature engines cleverly mocked up out of a variety of things—macaroni noodles, thread spools, tinfoil. Amazing.

She heard a door creak down below. The voice droned on. She realized she was hearing a radio broadcast. She looked back at the Gipsy Moth hanging at a banking angle from the ceiling. Blix had a friend who owned one, a rare plane in the States but famous in Britain and probably more so in Africa. Her cousin had apparently actually laminated thin strips of wood to carve the propeller, and he'd gotten the sinewy, twisting proportioning remarkably right. This kid was either totally obsessive or bored out of his mind, or both, and even in her appreciation for the work itself she realized the latter didn't bode well for her. She wondered how on earth he'd fabricated the cowling behind the prop, bull-nosed manifold cover and all.

The truck door slammed outside and slapped her back. She jumped to the window as the starter on the motor began to cycle, saw Uncle Roy's square-block form behind the shine on the windshield. The starter ground on until finally he quit and popped the door and climbed out.

The day before in Billings he'd had similar trouble and had to get under the hood and fiddle with the choke linkage. "Need to get Houston to fix this for keeps," he'd said, but even so he had the truck started and running in no time, and no doubt would again now. Annelise found her barefoot and pajama-clad self catapulting across the room and taking the narrow staircase two rickety treads at a time. She ran through a wall of pipe organ music from the radio in the kitchen and right past her mother's white-haired sister. The screen slammed behind her.

Uncle Roy was back behind the wheel. The starter whined again, and this time the motor fired to life with a belch of exhaust. He hadn't closed the hood yet. Annelise ignored the gravel beneath her feet and made a beeline.

He reached the front of the truck about the same time she did. He leaned in and adjusted the choke back, then raced the motor a time or two with the throttle arm. The engine settled to a rough idle.

"Cold as a Popsicle," he said to her. He spoke loudly above the shake of the engine, the roar of the fan.

She nearly shouted in response. "Don't leave me out here. Please."

He shifted his eyes to her, blue as ice but kind around the corners. "I wouldn't, if the blood ran the other direction. But it don't, so it's not my play. You've got to get through till Sunday, and then we'll set you up in town for the school week. Right now I've got to get back into town to check on Houston, and we'll likely both be back later today anyway. I don't like the notion of women out here alone when there's a passel of desperadoes on the loose."

Backwoods holdup men frankly seemed the least of her worries.

"I put bathwater on the kitchen stove for you," he told her. "Your aunt will show you the tub."

"I thought she said I had to wait until Saturday."

That gold-edged smile. "I reminded her that cleanliness is next to godliness. That one's hers to begin with."

He looked right at her with those crinkling blue eyes, fedora pushed back on his head, the engine's fan blowing her short curls around. He slammed the hood and the curls settled.

"What if these gangsters show up while I'm in the bath?"

Still with that grin. He gestured with his chin toward the house. "Sic Aunt Gloria on 'em. Tell her they're smokers, drinkers, and gamblers."

"How about whoremongers?"

"That would do it. Look, she can be difficult, but she ain't the Antichrist. You're going to find the rustic accommodations a whole lot more challenging."

"I don't know. From what I can gather, she's even more cuckoo than my mother."

"Crazies are generally pretty harmless. Now go take your bath before the water gets cold."

"Is she going to call me a slut?"

He'd already started for the cab. "Not if you don't behave like one, missy."

She smirked and tried to stick her tongue at him at the same time. She could only get the pink tip out.

"Hold your cards close," he said. "I'll be back."

Annelise watched him drive down the rough lane to the county road. Even from a distance she saw white exhaust on the early air. She hugged her arms, realized she was freezing in her bare feet and pajamas.

The noise of the REO trickled away and she heard something else, some fanlike whirring. Too cold to be the wings of an insect, surely. She cocked her head and tried to locate the source. In another moment she heard a metallic creak at the house, assumed a hinge on the door, and assumed Aunt Gloria had come out on the porch. She felt something lift in pace with the rate of her heart, indignation or petulance, or both.

But when she steeled herself and turned, no one was there. The door on the porch indeed gaped open, and the whine she'd heard came again, not from the door but from what she now identified as the source of the whirring. Some sort of elaborate weather vane mounted to the ridge of the roof. It looked from a distance like one of her cousin's model airplanes, with a propeller spinning out front and a tail fin in back to turn the thing into the prevailing wind. Hence the whine.

She could hear the murmur of the radio from inside. Maybe she'd at least catch an update on Amelia's progress. Undoubtedly she'd left Honolulu by now. Annelise hugged her arms in her thin pajamas. She walked forward.

"She's a powerful, powerful woman. And that scares people, you know. Scares a lot of men, scares them to the soul, even if they're drawn right to that power at the very same time, because it's a force bigger than they are. Ordained to be so, before ever she was born. They have no power in the face of it, and they know it. That's God's honest truth."

Aunt Gloria in her house shift and limp buttoned sweater and tired slippers, creaking around the little kitchen. "They see that sort of passion, that sort of fire, and they envy it and resent it at the same time. They want to possess it and destroy it. Because it's a mirror to their own weakness. That is the plain truth. Fetch me another pail?"

Sister Aimee's voice crackled out of the little Philco on the table beneath the window, half siren's song and half rising tide even through the static, and as familiar to Annelise as the smell of the orange trees outside the windows of another, starkly better and starkly brighter kitchen, two days and half a continent away.

This kitchen smelled of wood smoke. Or coal smoke. The house in San Marino had a gas range and modern plumbing and three or four radio sets, including a glimmering Zenith Stratosphere in the sitting room that made the entire lower floor seem like the nave of Angelus Temple itself, or maybe the orchestra pit of the Vienna Philharmonic.

Annelise stood from the table. Her cropped curls had already dried from the roaring blast of the stove. Sister Aimee had a voice like no other, and she used it now to recall the days of her famous Gospel Car, to illustrate the two-sided sword of progress, with its treacherous roads and broad highways to sin, undercut nonetheless with unswerving opportunities for faith.

"She was the first person to drive from one coast to the other," Aunt Gloria told her. "Not to set a record or to gain for herself, but for the glory of Jesus. Your mother and I, we were touched by that car ourselves when we were girls. Moved by it, you might say, even though we never actually laid eyes on it."

"The first *woman*, you mean. She was the first woman to drive across the country."

To Annelise's bafflement, Aunt Gloria had laid out a pair of her cousin's overalls and a flannel work shirt after her bath, both heavily patched and smelling, like most everything in the house, of stove smoke and lamp oil. She had to roll the legs with cuffs the size of a bucket, and her slim form fairly swam in them otherwise. With her short hair, Annelise knew that from any distance, she must surely look more boy than girl.

"That's right. The first woman." Aunt Gloria held her hands over the hot plate of the stove. The massive Angelus Temple pipe organ had started up behind Sister's voice and, in a moment of simultaneous fadeaway and crescendo, replaced it altogether. "People accuse her of theatrics or sensation. But how do you question the results? She's healed thousands. And saved probably millions."

She rubbed her hands over the heat, and Annelise realized that despite the kitchen's swelter, her mother's sister was actually cold. Something else struck her: Aunt Gloria was not so old as she appeared, although she may well have been exactly as frail. Though her hair had years ago turned snowflake white, she was younger than Annelise's mother, herself just barely forty and though blonde-headed, a ringer for Myrna Loy.

The pipe organ faded out in turn and the Angelus Temple choir started in. Annelise knew the song well—one of Sister's originals called "I Ain't A-Gonna Grieve." Sister sang lead. Annelise gave up hope of hearing any news out of Hawaii. She took the pail and went out to the yard.

She walked off the porch and around the side of the house to the well pump and its concrete pad. She heard that odd weather vane, humming and humming at the ridge of the roof.

She'd already fetched one bucket earlier, to replenish the galvanized water dispenser in a corner of the kitchen. She noticed then that this side of the house, unlike the whitewashed front, was more weather-beaten, with paint peeling like sunburned skin and bare gray siding showing through in patches and streaks. But the pump handle levered and plunged with little more than a squeak, and she could see where grease had been applied to the joints and shaft not long before.

Annelise had always had a vague notion of Gloria's health troubles. Blinding headaches since she was a girl, problems with her back and hips. A near-deadly bout with the Spanish flu at age eighteen that, among other lingering effects, turned her hair permanently the color of raw cotton.

Her sister, Annelise's mother, was by contrast a study in Teutonic vigor, throwing herself tirelessly at luncheons and causes and committees and hardly seeming to sleep. Annelise worked the lever and watched the gush of water splash into the pail and considered with some irritation that under different circumstances, her mother would herself have made quite a distance flier, at least so far as general constitution went.

It was common family knowledge that Aunt Gloria had always been the frail one. The sisters were still close, in a fashion, though they hadn't seen each other in years. They did write back and forth and spoke by telephone every month or so, always on a Sunday afternoon and no doubt, it occurred to Annelise only now, when Aunt Gloria went to Big Coulee for church and thus had available service.

So how on earth could the Philco radio work? Kerosene lamps and a wood-burning stove, although now that she thought about it, a single bare bulb did hang from the kitchen ceiling. Annelise finished filling the pail and left it beneath the pump. She marched in Houston's overalls around the back of the house.

She faintly heard the pulse of the song again from indoors, the lyrics jingling in her head by familiarity more than anything truly audible through the walls.

You can't get to heaven in a rocking chair
The Lord won't have any lazy folks there . . .

The outhouse stood a little way off, amid a cluster of thorn-studded shrubbery. Earlier when she made her first inglorious trip to the thing, an enormous cock pheasant erupted out of the brush like a Chinese rocket, just about the time she mustered the resolve to reach for the door. She'd practically wet herself then, and the memory now made the pressure in her bladder balloon yet again. She ignored it and turned back to the house.

She looked out the lane to the county road. A weathered barn with a tremendous pitch to the roof sat fifty yards or so north and a little east of the house, with two horses in a fenced lot. A squat chicken hutch slouched nearer still, with maybe twenty hens and an enormous copper-colored rooster pecking about in the run. Not a power pole anywhere, and no lines to the house from any direction. An island unto itself. She went back for the pail.

The cold breeze had fallen off completely and the hum of the blades above the ridge of the roof fell, too. The sound of the radio carried on.

Oh some of these mornings bright and fair,
I'll don my wings and fly the air . . .

She stopped so abruptly the pail sloshed. She stood there with water on Houston's overalls, water on his cast-off galoshes—stood there with her eyes clamped shut. She'd forgotten all about that line, and had she still believed in God, she would've taken it as a slap. She held the dripping pail against her leg until the song ended.

She opened her eyes again, stared at the sky, with its powdered late-morning haze. The moon was still up over the long bench east of the farm, small and white and barely a ghost.

The rooster crowed in his run, and she watched him chase down and pin a darting hen. He flapped atop her and went into a sort of brief if somewhat violent electric spasm, then hopped off and puffed up and preened. The hen shook dust in a burst from her plumage and went casually back to pecking. Annelise collected herself and stepped to the porch.

She set the pail by the door and went to free a foot from its rubber boot.

"Keep it on," Gloria told her. She moved away from the stove and took a scarf from a hook by the door. She wrapped her head and ears and eased into a chair. "Hand me those other galoshes. Please."

Annelise looked down and saw what she'd taken earlier for a child's pair of rubber rain boots, mud- and manure-flecked but much smaller than the ones she herself now wore. She stayed on the floor mat and stretched to pass them over.

"Got chickens to feed now. Horses. A few other chores. Lord won't have any lazy folks."

"Like the song says."

"Just like the song says. I'm glad you paid attention."

Annelise looked up at the bulb dangling from its wire in the ceiling and not aglow at the moment. "How exactly does the radio play? A battery or something?"

Aunt Gloria beamed at her spattered galoshes. With her house slippers dropped away, her feet appeared tiny. "That Houston of mine. That's his doing." She slipped a foot into a boot, easy as a silk slipper. "Uncle's too, but Houston—that boy's a wizard. Three years ago, when he was just little."

She tugged on the other boot and creaked around in the chair to look at the squat Philco on the table. Sister's voice had begun to garble, popping and snapping with static and suffering bursts of interference from another broadcast, what sounded like Benny Goodman or the Dorseys, Annelise couldn't quite tell from the snippets. Gloria half stood and gripped the edge of the table with one hand, reached across and moved the tuner.

Benny Goodman, loud and clear. "Moonglow," a song Annelise loved. Gloria moved the dial back, into the stuttering overlap again, then farther yet, into a dead zone on the band. She came up into the clash once more, then once more into "Moonglow" and clarity.

"Does this sometimes," she said. "In the afternoons, usually. Devil's the prince of the powers of the air, you know—says so right in the Word. Sometimes his music runs right over everything else." She killed the radio completely.

"I actually think that's a really pretty song."

"Oh, Satan's not ugly, sweetheart. That's the worst lie of all—horns and a pitchfork. No. He's beautiful. A charmer. Pretty on the surface, just like that song might seem to be. But it's a thin surface, and a dangerous pretty."

Annelise had heard all this before, had run it over and over in her head, and for a couple of years now had kept up her end of an ongoing sparring match with her mother about the same subject exactly. Popular music wasn't totally forbidden in the house, although her mother certainly maintained reservations.

But she looked around this spare kitchen with its one bare bulb and its jumble of milk-carton shelving and mismatched chairs and soot-stained walls, and what mostly rang in her head was Uncle Roy telling her that half of getting by in life was simply choosing your battles.

"Houston," she said. "How exactly did he make the radio work?"

Aunt Gloria straightened up and smiled. "The Lord's got great plans for that one. We didn't have the money for a store-bought wind charger, so he built one. Out of just . . . junk. Used a generator from a wrecked car, I think, and got the propeller from an electric fan, or something—I can't remember. But he did that for me. Before that, Uncle would have to charge a battery at the shop in town, and it wouldn't last the whole week. The Lord's got great, great plans."

"It's on the roof," said Annelise. "Right? Like a cross between a weather vane and an airplane?"

Still with that smile, that terse smile. She nodded. "That's it. That's the power."

"For the light, too, I guess." Annelise shifted her eyes to the ceiling.

"Yes. For the light, too. Enough for the radio and one bulb."

Annelise still stared at the ceiling. "I saw his airplanes upstairs."

Aunt Gloria did not skip a beat. "That's *his* great temptation. His weakness." She shook her head, still with that hint of a smile, and Annelise knew when she looked over that whatever disapproval Aunt Gloria owned, she couldn't avoid the glint of simple pride, either.

"He nearly killed himself sneaking out of the house in the middle of the night with this outlandish glider he tried to fly. Boys, you know. None of us knew a thing about it, that's how sneaky even an honest one can be. I told him you don't have to open your mouth to tell a lie. Speaking, as we are, of lies."

"But he actually flew it? A glider?"

"Evidently. Long enough to crash into the mercantile, anyway. Broke an expensive window in the process, which he had to work to pay off. Learned himself that lesson."

"Those models upstairs are really . . . *intricate*. Somewhat amazing, really—"

"I cannot argue—"

"—so it doesn't seem so surprising that he could build a working glider, but how on earth did he ever launch it?"

"He had an accomplice, obviously. Some partner in crime whom he's taken every bit of the fall for, which should sound very familiar to your own . . . predicament. From what your mother's told me.

"But Houston, now. Apparently he used a car to tow the glider, a powerful car, which obviously didn't drive itself. The sheriff said more than one person heard it that night, on Main Street, just about the time the glass smashed in the mercantile and set off the burglar alarm."

"Could it have been Uncle Roy?" The thought crossed her mind and popped from her mouth in the same instant, and already she'd started flogging herself. *Stupid, stupid.*

"Lord Almighty. What kind of a question is that? Of course not. Not that he was any use nipping it in the bud, God love him. The sheriff's best guess was the car actually came straight from his own shop that night. But your uncle Roy could snore his way through the Rapture itself. One of these days he'll wake up already in glory, never even know how he got there.

"Good Lord chose to preserve him, though. Houston, I mean. Not a scratch on him, broken window and all. Like I said, the Lord has big plans."

This time Annelise actually thought about stopping herself. But her stinger had already risen. "Maybe he'll fly Bibles. To the children, in Africa?"

Aunt Gloria smiled again. "You never do know. God does indeed work in mysterious ways." She looked at Annelise dead-on now, and she held her gaze good and hard. "Part of me thinks that if God wanted us to fly, He'd have given us feathers. But I also know you can't stop progress, and I'm not totally ignorant, regardless of how things around here might seem. Or how you may be inclined to think of me. Heavens, Orville and Wilbur Wright were a minister's sons. Did you know that?"

Annelise admitted she did not.

"But you did know Sister drove an automobile across the entire country when hardly anyone had. So a car can be, well, *stolen* by that boy of mine and used to pull a glider in the middle of the night, or a car can be a vehicle for the work of the Lord. Same with an airplane, I should imagine. Sister's been in one of those, too. Did you know that?"

"The Heavenly Aeroplane," said Annelise.

"The very one. Your mother did her job, I should say. That's a famous sermon, of course."

And an old one, from ten or twelve years back. Annelise had been a little girl the first time she'd heard it. Sister Aimee had chartered a ship to get from one revival to another, and in the usual fashion turned the departure into a publicity spectacle, only to crash and burst into flames on the runway. She got out unscathed and promptly, in the usual fashion, boarded a second plane that flew off without a hitch.

And in the usual fashion, she turned the incident into a sermon the following Sunday. "One plane piloted by the devil," Annelise remembered, "the other piloted by God."

"Gives me hope."

"The Heavenly Aeroplane?"

"No, child. Your mother. She did her job."

Annelise remembered as well an entirely different spectacle, from just about the same time as the famous sermon. Aimee Semple McPherson had vanished while swimming off a Los Angeles beach. Initially feared drowned, she did eventually resurface—but weeks later and a thousand miles away, dragging herself out of the Mexican desert with claims she'd been chloroformed, spirited away, and held for ransom in a Sonoran hovel.

Meanwhile, critics of religion in general, and Sister's many ministerial rivals in particular, mounted a sort of strange-bedfellows' assault on the entire tale. She faced accusations of everything from staging an elaborate publicity stunt to conducting a secret affair with her married radio technician.

To her most ardent followers, the outcry and insinuations were little more than the devil's usual sabotage of an otherwise righteous Christian soldier. Annelise's mother, for example, had never wavered in her allegiance, although Annelise herself had long ago learned to use the whole flap as her own sort of sabotage, the surest bomb to send her mother writhing and clawing for defensive ground.

Because even though Sister not only survived a grand jury inquiry but used it, in the usual fashion, to her advantage, no actual evidence ever surfaced to bolster the kidnapping story. Worse, the rumors of her dalliance with the radio man remained neither proven nor disproven— and as it turned out, he'd gone conspicuously missing himself during the same span of time. Annelise wasn't afraid to wield any of it.

Until now, when she was supposed to be choosing battles. Much as she hated to, she forced herself to avert her eyes from her aunt's, forced herself to look at the dark bulb in the ceiling and the milk crates on the wall and finally down at the ridiculous cuffs in her overalls. Aunt Gloria may as well have read her mind.

"She never was one of the lazy folks. Your mother, I mean. Energy to rival Sister's, if that's possible. That God-given fire, you know. Lord, I wish I had half of it.

"That may be Sister's greatest gift, actually. You can smother a lot, even the plain truth now and again, but a fire like that? That can't be damped down. Not by any slandering panel of men, anyway." Annelise could feel her aunt's eyes upon her. "Although plenty enough have tried."

Annelise finally made eye contact, for the briefest moment only, but long enough to catch a clear challenge in Aunt Gloria's gaze. She shifted her eyes back to the window, watched the daylight sparkle and flash on the bright plumage of another pheasant pecking at the edge of the trees. A handful of much plainer birds pecked in the same fashion, all mottled dun feathering, no white ringneck and no brilliant red comb around the eye. Hens, she realized. She said, "I remember. I live there."

"Oldest trick there is, with men. Especially the sanctimonious ones. Fastest way to kill a woman is by tarnishing her reputation. Throw judgment at her, bring judgment on her. That's a thing you need to remember."

"Well," said Annelise finally, "that's no doubt true. But in my experience, some of the worst judges of women tend to be other women."

Now Aunt Gloria said nothing, and Annelise waited in the rising tick of the stove. She looked back from the window and the pheasants and saw that her aunt no longer glared at her, was not in fact watching her at all.

Aunt Gloria had her head bowed. She pressed hard at her eyes with a finger and thumb.

"We need to get chores done," she said. "I've got a headache coming."

6

"Cy's hard to read, always has been. Cotter pin."

Huck shook the hubcap like a gold pan, watched the nuts and washers roll around and reshuffle until the pin revealed itself. He plucked it out.

Pop leaned in under the hood.

Afternoon was nearly gone, the body hauled in from the river and a Billings newsman already back to the city with his scoop. Huck and Raleigh stood to get their names and pictures in the paper, but the sheriff had seemed downright sour about the whole business.

Pop had returned from the ranch and barely determined that neither Huck nor old Mr. Neuman's rattletrap was anywhere to be found before Cy Gleason roared in waving his arms about a gunshot cadaver, and why in the hell weren't those damn kids in school in the first place, and so on.

"You'll have to log some time in the classroom now, I'll tell you what," Pop told him. He'd pulled the linkage apart, rethreaded a stripped keeper, and about had it all together again.

"We thought we were getting on his good side," said Huck. The REO sat half in and half out of the shop, and it was colder inside at the moment than in the lean yellow sunlight beyond the bay door. He could feel the watch in his pocket, and all he wanted to do was put a fire in the stove and build wing ribs. "Maybe should've just left the thing to wash down the dern river. Saved ourselves the trouble."

"No, you did the right thing, and Cy knows it. He's a classical hard-ass, but put yourself in his position. Charged with the public safety when he's got all you kids running around like wild hellions, not to mention a bunch of guys who spend all day in a coal seam and half the night in the tavern. Not to mention every crackpot farm wife in the Musselshell. At the end of the day he appreciates what you boys done, but that don't mean he's about to gush about it—give you a medal or something. All right, get her fired."

Ten minutes later he had the linkage adjusted and idle mixture tuned and the choke working again. He dropped the hood and disappeared for the washroom. When he returned, Huck had the truck backed into the sunlight.

Pop slid the bay door closed and walked to the driver's door. "Slide over. No sense pushing it with Cyrus."

They drove to the café and sat in a booth by the window. Huck had to recount the tale of the body and its discovery three times in fifteen minutes, once to Hannah, the waitress, and twice again to other diners, and he prayed to God that wherever Raleigh happened to be at the moment, he was sticking to a more or less compatible version of the same abridged sequence. Trouble was, Raleigh had a knack for embellishment even under ordinary circumstances.

"Reckon we'd better get out to the place for the next couple of nights."

He'd seen this coming. "I was sort of hoping to get a little further on the wing."

Pop stirred his coffee, pointlessly because he never put a thing in it. "Yeah, I guessed that. I don't like having women out there alone, though, with that waterlogged rascal's friends still around. No telling where they show up next. Anyways, I got the parts for the tractor and we need to get it back in business, on the off chance we get some water this season. And you ought to see your mother. And meet your cousin."

That other source of dread.

Pop evidently sensed it. "You'll like her, she's a firecracker. And get this, she's had flying lessons. So already you've got something in common."

Now this did beat all. "You didn't tell her about the dern airplane, did you?"

"No, but she'll be starting school next week, which means she'll be living here in town with us some, so she's bound to find out. May as well get that in your head right now."

"She will spill the dern beans."

Pop looked at him. "Did you just hear what I said? Girl's had flying lessons, Houston. That's a big stroke of luck, seems to me."

Huck stared at the bubbles climbing through his Coke bottle. He could feel the watch in his pocket. "You sure they'll even let her into school?"

"Why wouldn't they?"

"Ain't she . . . you know."

Pop looked at him. "Ain't she what?"

He thought of Raleigh, standing in the dusk with his dead fish. "Ain't she 'studying abroad'?"

Pop cracked a grin. He pulled the spoon out of his coffee and set it on the saucer. "No, sonny, she ain't. Although I can see why you'd jump to the conclusion."

"What on earth is she doing here, then? Isn't that why girls get sent off?"

"Yeah, I guess so, most times. But this ain't one of them times."

He took an idle swallow and something else struck him. "I'm on at the Rialto tomorrow night."

Pop looked at him. "Now who's the rascal."

"I just remembered. Honest."

He stirred his coffee again. "Just remembered something myself. Probably is better for one of us to stick it here. I hired a new fella down in Billings the other day, and he's due to show up sometime over the weekend."

"He had flying lessons too?"

"Didn't say. But he's a hell of a smith. Welder and machinist. Young guy, but kind of a character. Name's McKee."

"How young?"

"Well, not real young. Twenty-two? From Utah. Worked at the Browning gun forge down there, actually. Didn't seem Mormon, though."

Huck forked succotash to the side of his plate. "Studying abroad, is he?"

Roy grinned. "You're going to like her, Huck. She's a pistol."

7

Fig. 5-A shows the wing curve I use. I don't know what to call it. I made it up myself after building a lot of wings . . .

When I had found out where the centers of lift were I could place them ahead or behind a little at a time until I had a flyin' sweetheart.

—B. H. Pietenpol, 1932 *Flying and Glider Manual*

Huck fired the stove in the shop and busied himself in the fabrication bay past midnight, building wing ribs in the jig. He finally gave it up when he got out of sequence and tacked two gussets in a row without first applying the glue, and knew he'd gotten too tired and too sloppy to continue.

In the morning he roused himself early, boiled a pot of coffee to cut the fog and took both the coffee and the remains of the Texas hash straight back to the shop. He set another fire and ate the hash cold while the shop warmed, petted Lindy a time or two, and went back to the ribs.

By noon, with the last of them assembled, he stacked them off to the side of the fuselage frame in two columns: fourteen perfectly symmetrical full ribs in one, fourteen truncated aileron ribs in the other, each a single cross-sectional slice of perfect aerodynamic foil. He was close now to needing muslin to sheath the body and wings and in fact already had an order filled out for Sears and Roebuck. Pop would send it off once they collected for Old Man Neuman's T, and Huck went out now and folded the hood open and tinkered a bit underneath. He finally conceded he had the old rattletrap as far along as he could without help.

He went back to the bay and mulled the options. Daylight shot through the clerestory at the top of the wall, weak yellow shafts filtered by a winter layer of coal soot and general grime. He knew he could just drag a ladder around and wash the windows in a legitimate gesture of progress, but one of the yellow beams happened to fall across the fuselage like a spotlight out of heaven itself. Huck found himself unable in the moment to accept a downgrade from airplane builder to gol dang window washer.

What he really wanted to do was lay the ribs out and attach them to the spars, which, along with the fuselage, would represent a nearly complete skeleton of the entire airplane. But the finished wing would span a full thirty feet, and the shop lacked space.

He settled on the flaps instead, to finish off the wing ribs. He went back to the plans pinned to the corkboard on the wall. He'd already partially modified the jig to build the shorter ribs but realized he'd have to fabricate the steel control horns before he could lay in the actual flap frames. He went back to the main part of the shop and rummaged around, found two remnant pieces of twenty-gauge cold sheet and took them back to the bay.

He wondered when this new smith of Pop's would roll in, an intrusion he'd felt in a creeping dread since supper the evening before. McGee, or something. No. McKee, with a *K*. Outside of Huck, Pop hadn't retained a hireling in quite a while and Lord knew he could use one, the way work had been picking up, but still. First this cousin, who in all possibility could at least have been kept out of the shop, and now a guy nobody knew from Adam.

On the other hand, Pop had said this McKee was a heck of a machinist, and welder, too. Huck's own welding skills weren't awful, but they weren't professional, either. Pop was a dern sight better, but also busy. The airplane project had reached a point where a good bead hand might be of real use, provided the guy could otherwise keep mum. Huck prayed to God that this McKee wasn't overly religious, or even particularly talkative.

He worked through the afternoon, laying out and cutting and filing four flat steel halves, two for each horn bracket. He clamped them one by one into the bench vise and hammered the cutaway ear on each to form a mounting strap, hammered a radiused nose on the leading edge where the halves would join.

The shafts from the clerestory climbed the wall behind him as he worked, daylight angling toward evening. He worked right up to requiring weld tacks to fuse the halves into a pair of laminated brackets, what would ultimately serve as the connecting linkage to raise and lower the ailerons, and so steer the ship.

He hauled the big Longines out of his coveralls and checked the time.

The main feature in the movie house turned out to be interesting indeed, given the events of the past few days. A show from six years back called *The Public Enemy*, easily the most violent picture he'd encountered, with machine gun ambushes and back-shootings and gangster hits galore. Women got slapped across the mouth for sass, and a gun moll had a grapefruit shoved in her face at breakfast by the main character, a bootlegger played by James Cagney. Earlier in the film, a mob boss's floozy girlfriend got Cagney drunk and lured him into bed. A horse was tracked down and shot in retaliation for a riding accident. A horse, for crying out loud.

The finale really sunk in. The Cagney character's bullet-riddled corpse was delivered in a standing position on his mother's front stoop, his dead and doughy mug looking for all the world like the one that surfaced through the water the day before.

He could hear already the hue and cry in tomorrow's sermon. Pastor White could get nearly as worked up over movies and dance halls and worldly influence in general as Mother did. While he didn't often refer directly to the Rialto or the downtown saloons from the pulpit, he wasn't above pulling Huck aside from time to time, to suss out what exactly was on import this week from the Hollywood Gomorrah.

"Garbage in, garbage out, Houston," he'd told him not long ago. "Beware of anything that makes bad behavior and corruption appear perfectly normal. Glamorous, even. And let me ask you something serious—is that really where you want to be when Jesus comes back? Is that where you want Him to find you?"

Unfortunately, this James Cagney fellow in particular seemed hell-bent on making the pastor's case for him. A few weeks earlier the Rialto showed another of the star's films, not a gangster tale but a musical spectacle, about a song-and-dance-show producer. *Footlight Parade*.

It was glamorous, all right—Pastor White was right about that. Scores of lissome, underdressed showgirls in all their plucked and silken elegance, long legs scissoring in kaleidoscopic dance numbers. They trickled in a waterfall, folded and opened and reconfigured one to another in unbelievable unison, formed orchestrated geometric patterns that reminded Huck of the magnificent structure of snowflakes.

Nothing cold about any of it, though. Those girls, with their shimmering skin—they looked downright ripe, like exotic fruit. Eve's apple, in a way. Huck sat there in the projection booth not only entranced, but hard as a fence post inside his trousers. Then, midway through a swimming pool number with what must have been a hundred or more glistening beauties all gliding and diving, slipping and sliding, around and over and atop one another, the film snapped in two in the projector.

Huck jolted in his chair, heart clogging his very throat. He lunged for the snapping projector, shamefully, even painfully, aware of the tortured bulge behind his fly.

Catcalls and complaints from the audience down below. He fumbled to find the kill switch and couldn't, bamboozled by the shaft of light blasting out of the projector and by the machine's incessant clacking, the ribbon of celluloid lashing round and round on the reel like a whip. Huck had a panicked vision of the broken film catching on something and unspooling into even greater disaster, and finally he reached around behind the device and found the power cord and yanked it out of the wall.

The stark white shaft of the projection beam vanished. The room went black as ink, although the reel and the lashing celluloid continued to clack in the dark from momentum alone. The sounds of distress in the theater rose in pitch, what sounded to Huck like cries and groans out of the persistent fires of Hades.

He tried to hobble his way for the switch on the wall, keeping his hands on the projector to avoid stumbling into the thing. But even with the present crisis his condition simply would not abate, and halfway around the dark bulk of the machine he had to pause and adjust his own painful angle inside his britches. The whirling celluloid slapped at his head.

To his horror the door to the booth banged open and the overhead light shot on. The manager, Mr. Byers, pushed past and stopped the reel with the heel of his hand. "Quit yer jacking off up here, Houston," he barked, "and grab me that splice kit."

8

"I saw your airplanes. Out there on the farm."

"Ranch. It's more of a ranch."

"Ranch, then," she said. "But your models. They're amazing. How on earth did you know what a Gipsy Moth is?"

They were walking down Main, just about level with the New Deal across the street, which Huck couldn't pass anymore without seeing those upper windows flying toward him out of the dark.

Church had just let out. Pop had sent them home together. Huck was taller and he had no idea what to say to her, but for some reason it rankled that she could so much as name a de Havilland Gipsy.

"Shoot, everyone knows what that is. It's a common ship."

"Have you actually seen one?"

He felt the flush in his face. "Just pictures."

"Well. You did an especially good job, then."

"Thank you."

They trudged a little farther.

He caved. "Have you seen one?"

"I have. A friend of mine owns one. Or a . . . friend of a friend, anyway."

Huck knew people were looking at them as they walked along, from across the street and also from behind them after they'd nodded and helloed in passing, and he knew they weren't looking because of the story in the Billings paper this morning. His cousin had a look to her. In a word, *expensive.*

She said, "I heard about the glider."

That heat around his collar. "What exactly?"

"Oh. Not anything to speak of. I asked your dad if you'd been up, and he said you had. In a glider you'd built yourself."

He'd expected Mother as the source, not Pop. "Yeah, I almost crashed it into the mercantile back there. The New Deal. Actually I sort of did crash it."

"He didn't mention that. Do you still have it? I'd love to see it. Not sure if your dad told you, but I've had some flying lessons myself."

Even after nearly two hours at church and the duration of this walk, he could barely bring himself to look at her. "Actually I burned it."

"I'm sorry?"

"I burned it."

"Oh." She wore a short-waisted baby-blue jacket with two rows of brass buttons above a fairly snug skirt. A darker blue beret cocked at a backward angle on her head, similar to what Shirley Temple sometimes wore. She looked like springtime rising, but nothing at all like Shirley Temple. "Why did you do that?"

He shrugged. "Didn't work right." Out of the corner of his eye he thought he saw her smile.

They turned the corner onto First and walked down the street in the warm air, the maples and elms already out of bud and showing new electric leaves. Early in the year to fill out so fully, though most of the snow had already blown out of the high country with the spring melt. No real rain yet to speak of. A full block from the shop Huck spotted the panel truck, backed up to the open slider door. A Stude, five or six years old. When they drew closer, he made out stenciling on the side, the legend YAKIMA MCKEE BLACKSMITH-MACHINIST-FABRICATOR. Hand-painted, though skillfully done.

The man himself slouched against the workbench inside the shop, perilously close to the fabrication bay. He held a folded newspaper in one hand, a bottle down against his leg in the other. He looked up and took in Annelise. "Hey, cowgirl. Want a beer?"

"McGee, I take it," said Huck.

"I'd love one," said Annelise. She stepped into the shop and crossed the floor toward the bench.

He reached behind for a fresh bottle. "McKee, with a *K*," he said to Huck. "Highland clan. McGees are Lowland." He set the paper down, grabbed a cold chisel off the bench and popped the cap. He handed the beer to Annelise, but he looked now at Huck. He tapped the newspaper. "Reckon you'd be the local hero. Heck of a write-up this morning."

It was true. Pastor White had preached half a sermon on the events of the previous days, with a copy of the same morning paper for effect. He called Huck and Raleigh heroes, pointed to their God-given industriousness and tenacity and plain Christian courage to do right. Huck had sat there feeling like an idiot in a spotlight the entire time, the Lindbergh watch fairly burning in his pocket.

Annelise pulled on her beer. "I think he autographed twenty papers after church."

He'd managed to scan a good bit of the article in the process. He and Raleigh came off like characters in a boys' adventure novel, under the banner YOUNG SLEUTHS STAGE DARING RECOVERY OF GUN-SHOT BADDIE!

Although the both of them had glossed right over the most dangerous parts of the escapade, the newspaper managed to make the whole thing sound pretty sensational anyway. Raleigh, as usual, had the take-home quotes, one of which appeared in italics beneath the main headline: *"The problem with putting two and two together is sometimes you get four, and sometimes you get twenty-two."*

"They call you Huck, eh?" said McKee.

"Yeah, some people. Rolly does, that's why it's in the paper. He's the one who started it, actually. On account of my last name."

"He must be a real piece of work," said Annelise. "That quote under the headline? It's from a detective novel."

"That would figure."

He noticed something else. McKee had toted Pop's ancient single-shot out from the office, had it lying now on the bench beside the beer. Usually the rifle hung high up on the wall in a blanket of dust, a token of what Pop called "them wild old days." Nobody had fired it in years, or even taken it down in as long as he could recall. Now McKee had evidently cleaned and oiled it.

He'd looked back to Annelise. "So what do they call you, cowgirl?"

"I am not a cowgirl. I'm an . . . aviatrix."

"Oh *ho*." He hooked a thumb toward the fabrication bay. "So that's your build back there, I take it?"

Not good.

Annelise frowned. "Build? Why on earth would I have to build anything?"

"Strictly the flier, then. Reckon that leaves Junior here to be the shipwright." He winked at Huck. "Already had that last part figured out, by the way."

"I'm the builder *and* the dern dang flier." The words just popped out and now he realized he needed a change of subject, pronto. He said, "That's Pop's rifle."

This worked better than expected. McKee visibly lit up, in fact seemed to forget all mention of anything else. He pivoted and set his beer down and hoisted that beast of a gun from the bench. He cranked the breech open, looked down the bore like he was looking through a railway tunnel.

"Two-and-a-half-inch Sharps, Big Fifty. Not one you run across every day. Good solid bore, too, hard living or no." He levered the breech block again, a sound like the clank of a vault. "See how the wood's dished out in the fore-end? That's from riding across a saddle." He glanced up at Huck. "A *lot*. How long's he had this baby?"

Annelise cut in before Huck could answer. "Speaking of a good solid bore, let's stop living in the past, shall we? The future awaits." She stepped straight for the fabrication bay.

Huck found his tongue. "Wait. You can't go in there."

She did pause, however briefly. "The cat's out of the bag, Houston. Or it's about to be, if I'm guessing right. I'm on your side, believe me." She pushed through the door.

McKee shifted the rifle to one hand and retrieved his beer bottle with the other. "So. Pancho Barnes in there ain't your sister, I take it."

He knew he should follow her, but for some reason he thought to stave off the whole business, folly though it no doubt was. He looked at McKee. "Cousin. From California. I barely know her."

McKee nodded. "Cousin. Well." He winked and sauntered after her, rifle in hand.

"It's a start, at least." She was on the other side of the fuselage frame, eyeing the passenger compartment.

"Yeah, she's getting there," Huck mumbled.

"I take it your mother doesn't know."

"No, and she ain't gonna find out, either."

Annelise fixed her own gun-barrel eyes on McKee. "Not from me she's not, that's for sure."

McKee threw up his arm as though shielding a blow. "Mum's the word, sister. I can be as tight-lipped as the next guy."

"Hmm. Somehow you strike me as not quite able to help yourself. This is important, Mr. McKee." She turned her stare to Huck. "Judging by your models, I have no doubt what you're doing here is, well, extraordinary."

"You actually flown anything before?" said McKee.

The sun angled again through the clerestory and struck the opposite wall lower down, struck in trapezoids and skewed quadrilaterals, and struck Huck in the moment square in the face. He was faintly aware of the radio, murmuring away in the office.

"He has, actually," said Annelise. "He's already built his own glider."

She looked into her bottle a moment, swirled the contents as though to divine something in the deep brown glass. Highlander, Huck noticed, a Missoula brew from the west side of the state. Scotch plaid on the label. McKee not McGee, and no Lowlander with his beer choice, either. Annelise looked back up. "So what was wrong with the glider exactly?"

"Tail-heavy. I built it with old-fashioned wing warping, like the Wrights used, and at first I thought that was the problem. It wasn't, though—ailerons wouldn't have fixed it."

"But you're pretty sure about this?" She rocked the frame on the horses. "Pretty sure it's right? I know what you can do. It just looks like an awful lot of work."

He nodded. Mother and Pop would show up at any minute, he could practically smell it. He pointed at the plans on the corkboard, then turned for the office. "Come with me. And for the love of Mike, close the dern door."

He wove through the machinery in the shop and went into the office, rummaged around on the desk and found the *Flying and Glider Manual*. The radio murmured with an ag broadcast, a forecast with no rain and the usual dire predictions of drought.

Lindy jumped onto the desktop. Huck picked her up and dropped her to the floor. Annelise moved beside him, and he flipped the manual open at the dog-ear, to a chapter titled "THE PIETENPOL 'AIR-CAMPER' . . . a Ford Powered 2-Seater Monoplane."

"It's this. Built around a Model A engine. But it's a real airplane, homemade or not." He swiveled his head toward her. "The glider was my own ideas, mostly. But this is proven to work. I ordered the plans directly from the designer, in Minnesota. Mr. Pietenpol."

McKee had moved in and even he seemed to take some interest. "Model A's a heavy damn engine." He set his bottle down and started flipping pages. "Gravity-fed, too. I don't know much about airplanes, I admit. But whoever figured this out, well. I doff my hat." He stopped at the motor-conversion diagrams, pored over them for a moment. "If it actually works, I mean."

"It does. There's a bunch of them flying already. Two in Montana, that I know of."

"Well, I—"

"Shush," said Annelise sharply.

They both looked at her, but she'd turned to the radio.

"... and in Honolulu, Miss Earhart's silver Lockheed has crashed upon takeoff on the second leg of her attempt to circle the globe at the equator. Neither Lady Lindy nor her crew have been injured, but damage to the airplane will mean at least a month's delay. In other news, tensions continue to rise in the northern regions in Spain, where . . ."

"Goddamn it," said Annelise.

Huck and McKee both looked at her. Huck's ears actually seemed to ignite, as though those words out of those lips held the very breath of the devil.

"What?" she said. Then, "First one of you makes a crack about women pilots, I swear I'll come at you with this bottle."

"So you do fly planes, then? That's for real?"

She looked McKee smack in the eye like a mongoose at a cobra. Or a queen to a drone. "I'm working toward my license. Yes, I've flown. Quite a lot."

He looked at Huck. "And you built all that back in there yourself, right? Plus your own glider?"

Huck nodded.

"You want help?"

He gave a start. "What all?"

McKee waved a hand at the manual on the desk. "You're some hand, that much I can see, but this looks to be a whale of a lot of work. Now I got no earthly doubt you can manage it, but the three of us, together? We'd get this sucker off the ground in no time."

"I'm in," said Annelise. She turned to Huck. "If you want the help, I mean."

Huck didn't quite know what to think. The thing had been a sworn secret for months, and other than Pop and Raleigh, nobody had sussed out a thing. Now in the turn of an hour it was all this.

Pop's REO rumbled up outside. "Better stash those bottles," he said.

Annelise downed hers in a gulp and glanced around and finally just lowered the brown glass to the floor and rolled it under the desk with her foot. McKee for his part took another slow swig and went back to studying the engine schematics. Huck heard the doors clank on the truck, one then two, heard feet on the gravel.

He looked at Annelise. "What if she smells it on your breath?"

She gestured with her chin toward McKee. "I'll tell her the new fabricator here kissed me full on the mouth."

"Guilty as charged," said McKee. "Even if I don't know your name."

"Annelise," she said. "Or Miss Clutterbuck, to you."

McKee tilted his bottle at her. "Annelise it is." He shifted back to Huck. "You have the motor yet?"

Huck's nerves were already up and whatever was happening between these other two wasn't helping. "Nope."

The door swung open and hit the transom bell, and Pop held the door for Mother. Her eyes went first to Huck, then to McKee's beer, then to the rifle positioned with its muzzle on the toe of his boot, and finally back to Huck.

Pop mainly appeared amused. He said, "Working hard, or hardly working?"

"We're working hard *at* hardly working," said McKee. "This being the Lord's day and all." He looked at Mother. "Howdy-do, ma'am. Beer?"

"This is my new man," Pop told her. "Mother, Enos McKee."

"Call me Yakima," he said.

"*Enos?*" said Annelise. "Really?"

"Sort of," said McKee. He looked a little sheepish.

"I don't imbibe," said Mother.

"Enos," Annelise repeated, as though the very combination of letters and syllables were some exotic if dubious flavor in her mouth. "Is that a, um, family name?"

"Annelise. Don't tease the man. Besides, Enos is a good Christian name in the Word. A direct ancestor of Jesus, in fact."

"Just call me Yakima," McKee said. He glanced at Annelise. "My friends all do."

"Well, what sort of a name is *that?*"

"It's a place," said Pop. "Out on the Palouse. By all means, call the man what he wants to be called. And keep your nose in your own business."

She grinned at him. "Mea culpa. That's a legal term."

"That sounds about right," Pop told her, with an unusual twinkle of his own, and Huck realized with an odd flash of chagrin that his cousin already had his old man wrapped right around her finger.

Mother seemed not to notice. She'd moved up beside him and taken his arm, and he felt himself tense the way he always did these days. What she said next made him feel some chagrin about that, too.

"I'm going to fix you a hero's supper, Houston. Pastor was very proud of you. Why don't you and Annelise bring the groceries from the truck for me? Let Papa and Mr. McKee have some grown-up time."

Huck glanced at Annelise. Her blue-gray eyes looked like shards of ice above the sky-colored wool of her jacket, and when they made contact now with his own she widened and then narrowed them again in a way that made him think of signal lights, surging and dimming through a fog. He wondered if she was sending a message.

She winked and removed all doubt. Otherwise her face was a stone.

"Mr. McKee, will you be joining us?"

"Well, ma'am, I'm not one to impose. Or to insult a lady's invitation, either."

"How gallant of you," said Annelise.

Everyone looked at her. She looked back at each in turn and finally blinked, and Huck realized that despite the steady coolness in her eyes, she really didn't know quite what to do in the moment, either. She pushed her sleeve back to check the time, a gesture he took more as a cover for nerves than anything else.

He saw the watch on her wrist.

"Son of a—" he blurted, and caught himself in the nick of time. "—gun." His hand shot in the same instant to his pocket, and Mother's grip tightened on his arm. Reflex unto reflex. "That is one . . . big ol' watch."

"Speaking of guns," said Roy mildly, "I see you've given ol' Juno the once-over."

McKee seemed to have momentarily forgotten the fourteen-pound howitzer balanced on the toe of his boot. He regarded it with fresh eyes. "Why, yes. I think I may be in love, in fact. Never have actually seen one before."

"You can dance with her," Pop said, "but she's true to me."

"You're a lucky man. Get her off some old buffalo rounder or something?"

Mother still had Huck's arm like a clamp. His hand still gripped the watch through the cloth of his trousers. Jump.

Stall. His eye caught the open manual on the desk. He needed to get her out of the shop altogether. Annelise stepped for the door as though she could read his mind.

"Son, that big Sharps belonged to my daddy, and I reckon he did some damage with it the way all them old boys done. I rode with it across my saddle clear from Texas when I was ten years old. Been in Montana ever since. Me and Miss Juno both."

"Clear from Texas," said McKee. He ran his hand over the concave dish in the fore-end, worn into the wood by the sway of a horse, mile after mile, state after state. "Now that is sure enough something. Reckon I'd like to hear that story one of these days."

Roy winked at Annelise, still with her hand at the door. The big Longines had once again vanished into her sleeve. "Set a plate for him, Mother," he said. "Reckon I might as well tell it."

Roy

*In 1873 I hunted in eastern Nebraska, on the Cedar, a tributary of
the Loup River, not more than 130 miles west of the city of Omaha,
and saw numerous bands of elk. A little further to the west and south,
buffalo were plenty.*

—George Bird Grinnell, 1903

*There was never a more splendidly barbaric sight. In after years I
was glad that I had seen it. Hundreds of warriors, the flower of the
fighting men of the southwestern Plains tribes, mounted upon their
finest horses, armed with guns and lances, and carrying heavy shields
of thick buffalo hide, were coming like the wind.*

—Billy Dixon, 1914

In the last hours of life Roy's pa saw again the constellations of fire,
flickering pinpricks like he'd watched in the picket camps across the
Susquehanna in a war thirty years gone, or later in the lodge fires
of the fighting tribes in Nebraska and Texas. Rifle fire and mortar
bursts, lapping and lapping out of the darkness of his own delirium.
Coal fires and streaking cinder in the Glasgow smelters he'd witnessed still earlier in his youth.

Only nine years old himself, Gilroy had been raised from birth by
his father alone, and he'd heard most of the stories already. But what
he did not apprehend until the last was the haunting beneath the
surface of the tales, as though the wandering souls of the annihilated
plodded quietly, grazing sorrowfully along, never ceasing and never
arriving, in the canyons and plains of memory itself.

*　*　*

His father had come into the world a ghillie's son, on a grandly faltering estate outside Aberdeenshire, and been christened Lachlan Graham Finn after Old Norse ancestry on his father's side and the staunchly native clan on his mother's. He took to the land and its creatures from the time he could toddle, turned loose like a hound sprung from the master's kennel to roam and rout whatever might jump and run, and the chase got fully into his blood.

By six he was already an asset with hawk and fox control. At fifty paces he could hit the eye of a rook or a rabbit with a pea rifle. His father kept him in powder and lead as a matter of professional interest, and while he might not as a rule slay the lord's proper game, he was encouraged and even rewarded for exterminating anything that might compete with or raid the lie of or otherwise itself slay the lord's game.

He excelled at this assignment right up until the estate fell bankrupt and into receivership in 1862, his fourteenth year. His father stayed on with the new laird, and the youngest of Lach's siblings of course remained as well, but Lachlan and his older sister were bound for teeming Glasgow, where aunts and uncles caught up and displaced by either the famine or the Clearances, or both, had already migrated. The two arrived to a cramped and stinking tenement and relatives they didn't know, breathing coal dust and rat pestilence and squalor, and the first bloom of trouble opened in his lungs.

Though he'd hoped to apprentice to a gun maker the real boom was occurring in the Glasgow shipyards, on account of the war between the American states. Glaswegian boatbuilders came to specialize overnight in blockade runners for the Confederacy, with daredevil Scotch sailing men running the ships first to the Bahamas, then into Charleston or Savannah with munitions, then back to British ports with bales of cotton.

Starting with a menial job in a shipyard, Lachlan within six months had signed as crew to a steam-powered side-wheeler, a low and lean vessel with both extensive armor and an almost unfathomable capability for speed.

Roy knew there were gaps in his knowledge of the paternal history. He knew that the steamer berthed without incident in North Carolina and that his father did not make the return voyage, would not in fact ever return to his homeland again. He knew as well that the lung trouble originating in the industrial tenements would be with him for life, flaring and then subsiding for months at a time and then flaring and easing again, before finally pulling him full under into that last, fast decline.

And though his father came into America under the pretext of the Southern cause, Roy knew he somehow wound up not merely in the North, but also killing for it. As a sharpshooter.

"Dinnae aisk a man in these western lanes his name, his religion, his politicks. Any one a' them ca' buy ya' trouble, and in big letters. Ne'er stray from that, laddie."

He himself appeared almost wholly without either religion or politics, so Roy could never rightly say what compelled him to the Northern ranks. He never doubted, however, that philosophy or any sort of burning conviction had anywhere near as much sway as the simple chance to acquire one of those long-range Sharps breechloaders and put it to use.

"Made me way to the nearest Yank garrison, an' fibbed me way into a Berdan trial. Told 'em I's a member of the Ninety-Fifth Rifles, and a real long-range hand." Roy remembers the gleam in his father's eye, the wink. "Nae quite a galvanized Yank, I'll say . . . but a long-ranger, well. Turns oat I was."

His father never much mentioned the total number of graybacks killed or wounded, and likely did not rightly know himself. The war is not what he talked about anyway, for the most part, because whatever he participated in during that time, conducted at distance and hence remove, paled in comparison with what came after, when he

mustered out of service with his Sharps and his sniper's pay, then
made his way west by rail and paddleboat to Council Bluffs, Iowa.

He hired on with the Union Pacific Railroad as a meat hunter. If his
bullets-to-mark tally remained uncertain from his days hunting men,
his record of ungulate kills for the railroad was precise as an abacus.
In two years, with the steady progress of the railbed unfurling across
the plains of Nebraska and much of Wyoming, he shot 4,552 buffalo, all with the breech-loading Sharps. Sometimes he roamed out
overland with a wagon and team and a contingent of meat cutters,
sometimes he rode the supply locomotives and utilized the roof of a
train car as a shooting platform.

A few times he and others engaged Cheyenne or Arapaho raiding
parties, and he killed a few there as well, although the formidable
range of the rifles generally made for short-lived rebuff.

"Ye'd knack one or two dane," he regaled the boy, "or flaiten th'
pony beneath th' raider, and they'd lose the taste quick enough."

He followed this work long after the last golden spike put the trans-
continental road into business, supplying meat for various spur crews
through the late sixties and finally striking out as a straight-up hide
hunter in the seventies. Roy would eventually understand that these
latter were the slaughters that truly ghosted the old man, the ones that
woke him in the shape of nightmares two and three decades hence.

In Omaha he acquired a Sharps New Model .50-70 cartridge
gun, chambered in the standard U.S. arsenal round and a definite
improvement over the earlier paper-case rifle. He teamed with a pair
of skinners, put cash down for a wagon and rolled out with an entire
procession of like entrepreneurs on the vast level reaches across
Kansas and Colorado.

At first they encountered the big shaggies in pockets and bands
and they killed as they went, peeling the hides and taking the tongue
for trade and what choice cuts they needed for camp meat and otherwise leaving waste in their wake, the dead beasts opium-eyed like

naked overgrown larvae, marbled pink and white and laced with veins, and ghoulishly comic with their furred heads and horns still attached.

Farther along an actual river of bison, thousands upon thousands the way he first saw them on the rail line to the north, stretched across the muted yellow plain like the stark black aftermath of a brush fire. He and his crew pitched camp a few miles out from the next wagon. They set up shop and got down to business.

He killed more than one hundred the first day. His skinners did their work through the second day, while he primed and repacked cartridges for the Sharps at the wagon. The herd continued to drift but never disappeared. The boom of heavy rifle fire rolled over the plains from different directions until nightfall, sporadic but steady.

Buzzards, blowflies, and, by the scorching middle of the third day, stench. The dead bison began to bloat, badly, their legs stiff with rigor but elevating awkwardly anyway into the air as the gas in their guts inflated them like dirigibles. Some of the bodies burst, either spontaneously or from the peck of birds or the orgiastic swarms of snapping coyotes and snarling wolves. A few of these Lachlan rolled to kingdom come on general principle, five hundred grains of accelerated lead the practical equivalent of a Jovian thunderbolt.

The skinners peeled those hides, too. They finally headed for the nearest rail depot with scant breeze and the temperature certainly north of ninety. The wagon fairly groaned beneath a mountain of green stinking hides, Lachlan's lungs fairly scorching with sputum and blood, as though the air itself contained a writhe of some insidious pox.

So it went for three seasons in the Ogallala country and then west along the Saline River around Fort Hays, until the herds there had so diminished by 1873 that the trains began to run more or less on schedule.

The following season Roy's father and several hundred others cast their eyes south, toward the Staked Plains. The herds there had rebounded after good years of rain, and besides that, the dry hot air might ease his crippled lights.

He knew as all of them did that this was hostile country, still con-trolled by the last holdout bands of Comanches and Kiowas, a bloody and no-nonsense bunch indeed. So the outfit fairly bristled with guns and ammunition, not only the cannonlike tools of the buffalo-killing trade but also a pair of repeating Winchesters per man, and a like quantity of Colt's revolvers modified to take the same cartridge. Enough ammo to mount an insurrection.

He'd also upgraded the Sharps yet again, acquired in Dodge what would turn out to be the last and most mythic incarnation in the design's evolution—the rifle that Roy would eventually lug around the West like somebody else's cross to bear. A Model 1874 two-and-a-half-inch .50, capable of propelling a titanic 600-grain slug. A rifle engineered for one thing and one thing alone: to drop a one-ton buf-falo dead in its tracks, even at extreme range. OLD RELIABLE, read the legend on the barrel. Big Fifty, in the parlance of the trade. Lachlan dubbed her Juno.

By now he'd again lost count of his actual take, the numbers noth-ing short of astronomical and the hides sold not by the unit but by the ton. Wherever they rode they encountered the scatter of bones and middens of carcasses, even the scavengers unable to deal with them all. After a while he could no longer tell whether the perfume of rot hung everywhere or whether his airways and faltering lungs were simply permanently tainted unto themselves.

They crossed south into Texas and made their way to the Cana-dian River. They began to kill bison.

They hadn't been in the country a week before a scout galloped in from the nearest trading post to announce that the place was under siege by several hundred Comanch', and God knows what-all war parties were afoot otherwise, but anyways another waddie already hotfooted for Dodge to get the army on down, and you gents best get on in and duck and cover . . .

By the time Lachlan's outfit made the post most of the action had abated, as the day before a young dead-eye named Dixon, armed with a twin to Lachlan's own Juno, scored a direct hit on a mounted warrior at a range of what other witnesses swore to be "damn near a mile."

It was largely luck, of course, and Dixon would say so himself until the day he died, but it had the desired effect. Several hundred festooned Comanches fell even farther into the distance, and through a spyglass appeared to be loading their dead onto ponies and pulling out even while other buffalo hunting parties trickled in.

By the time Roy became old enough to absorb the wild old stories a couple of decades hence, every red-blooded boy from El Paso to Glen Rose knew the name Billy Dixon, knew about that legendary rifle shot, same as they knew Davy Crockett and Jim Bowie and the Alamo, or Captain Hays and the Texas Rangers. And by the time of his fifth birthday, living with his father in Somervell County, Roy knew that the colossal rifle in the corner was itself the stuff of legend.

Young Roy already had a fascination with mechanisms, with bicycles and train engines and of course firearms, this one in particular. Even before he'd achieved the stature or strength to hoist and balance the big rifle, his father would brace it across the porch rail and instruct him to lever the action and drop the block, just to marvel at the timed and regulated genius of the thing. The forged and lathed and puzzlelike pieces toggled and locked in a unison not unlike magic.

Ammunition was no longer manufactured for the Big Fifty. No need, because nothing remained to shoot with it. Roy would peer into the tunnel of the bore anyway, like looking back through the spirals of history itself. He could imagine what it must have been like to slide a brass cartridge the size of a cigar into that beautifully machined chamber, lever the block closed with the unassailable authority of a bank door. With his father still balancing the gun, he muscled the hammer back to its cocked position, heard the fine click of the sear.

Still too small to shoulder the buttstock, he instead tucked the comb under the pit of his arm and aligned the sights at some imaginary mark across a span as much of time as of distance. In addition to the standard buckhorn affixed to the rear of the barrel, this particular specimen—what his father called Juno—also had a folding-ladder sight attached to the tang of the grip, with demarcations out to nine hundred yards. Roy could imagine himself on that great lost frontier, dodging tomahawks and arrows, riding and hunting and shooting. Free as the wind.

He held the sights steady, the notch on the ladder set to its extreme range, noted the way this forced the gun muzzle to elevate in a manner that hardly made sense. He imagined the path of the bullet exiting the bore at such an angle, up and up and into the very sky itself, in a rainbowlike trajectory, until the pull of the earth forced it back down in a scribed steady arc, and a fateful intersection with the intended target. But at nine hundred yards or better, how high must that bullet climb at its apex to remain airborne long enough to cross such a straight-ahead span? Two hundred feet in the air? Three hundred? A mystery that probably cannae be solved.

He pulled the trigger-set and heard the pawl click minutely into place, the timing of those fitted internal parts still regulated like a Swiss watch, even after all these years.

"Ye sneeze on 'er no', and aff she goose, lake Judgment Day."

Young Gilroy barely touched the trigger. The big hammer dropped on the hollow chamber with a railcar clank. He imagined anyway the roar and blast, the cinder and smoke out front, imagined the speck of a painted and feathered warrior blown off his pony a full five seconds later. He levered the big action open, could practically smell the fire and brimstone.

"How I wish ye could've seen it, lad," Lachlan mused. "Naught a greater sight on airth 'an 'at broad wild land and 'ose endless beasts a-roomin' it. How I wish . . ."

Years later Roy would come to understand the spiraling circular-
ity of the whole business. The great engine-driven line shafts of tool
and machine works in Europe and the East remained nonetheless
totally reliant on buffalo hides, for the long leather belts that powered
lathes and drills and shapers and power hammers and cotton looms,
and on and on. Those roaring industrial cauldrons would produce in
turn such magnificent alchemical wonders as sewing machines and
cash registers, typewriters and well pumps. Iron Horse locomotive
engines. Mile upon mile of steel rail.

Those same belt-driven works enabled the meticulous forgings
and spiraled barrels of the big buffalo rifles themselves, which would
in turn slay with such supreme efficiency the very source of the heavy
leather turning the wheels of all that ingenious industry in the first
place. Progress and cargo could chug ever forward, even across the
unsettled West, on a suturelike line of tracks and rails.

By the same token, in the first years of such enterprise a siz-
able buffalo herd migrating across the rail line might wreck a train's
schedule by a day or more. Or worse, wreck the integrity of the
railbed itself.

But eventually, that very train would make its eastward trek packed
engine to stern with green hides, to create in turn the leather for the
belts that powered the factories and tools and machines. Round and
round and round, two birds with one six-hundred grain, screaming
lead stone.

Or three birds, if you counted the U.S. Army's shrewd calculation that the demise of the buffalo herds directly correlated to the
containment and eventual vanquishment of the free western tribes.

By the middle eighties the bison had been shot out. Millions of
them, even tens of millions, steadily and systematically and finally
precipitously annihilated, in large majority by a mere few thousand
rifles specific to the task. Springfields, Remingtons, Ballards, and a
few others, but most famously and effectively the old reliable Sharps.
And clear to the Pacific, the trains ran on time.

Roy came to understand that for Lachlan, the math simply boggled. The rivers of bison seemed as vast and as endless as the empty land they inhabited, and the individual beasts themselves were such titans of irascible surliness. *How on airth could a handful of hell-raisers in buckboards just blot 'em, in haif a young man's lifetime? The aboriginals bin runnin' 'em beasties off th' cliffs by the score, f'r tame immemorial, withoat makin' so much as a scraitch . . .*

The bison were largely gone from the southern Plains by 1877, and Lachlan followed the trade north to the Yellowstone River country in '78. He killed a fair number of buffs—nothing like the old days, but fair—before the frigid winter air nearly caved his lungs for keeps. Guys were hunting on heavy wooden skis across great blankets of snow, packing fifty pounds of gear on their backs. He had no way to compensate. He got himself slightly recuperated at Milestown and took a paddle wheeler from Fort Keogh east and then south.

He'd taken to choking up blood on an alarming basis, was terrified to see a doctor about it. But he knew the Texas air had eased his lungs, and any fool could see his days as a professional hide hunter were no more. Probably time to settle down anyway—he'd saved a good bit from that mountain of skins he produced. He could buy a house, dream up some business. Maybe find a girl and marry.

Roy for his part had never not known the ratcheting cough, the ever-present handkerchief to capture the expulsion, so the incremental deterioration in his father's health largely escaped him. Then in his ninth year the decline went from gradual to obvious, characterized as much by waking nightmares and fevered ramblings as any scurvied gauntness or killing cough.

Lachlan had long regaled the boy with stories. The times the gun smoke would get so thick in front of him on a windless day, he'd lose all sight of the herd and have to crawl for another shooting position altogether. The times he played cards in a saloon with Wild Bill, first in Hays City and then again later in Abilene.

The time he stumbled on an ambushed wagon train a day or so west of Laramie, most of the wagons half charred and smoldering yet, men and women both scalped and bristling like arrowed pincushions and otherwise mutilated and outraged in unspeakable ways, a single dead and stripped and scalped little girl as well, but most of the kids evidently carted off with the stock.

And in like contrast, the times he rode through routed and shelled and burned-out Indian encampments after attacks by the U.S. Army. Shot-up and sabered bodies there, too. All ages, all sizes.

"Aye, it's true, the' were savage and dangerous times. But lucky was I to have had 'em, me lad. Lucky was I indeed."

The tales owned a persistent theme: Lachlan's wish that Roy could have seen it all, too. The land the way it was, of course, undeeded and unplowed and unfenced, but also the sight of a migrating Indian band, or the smoke out of a hundred paint-bedizened lodges marked with arcane geometry and totemlike silhouettes on an otherwise pacific night. Above all, the seemingly endless black herds that accompanied those old and lost ways.

But as the air in his lungs truly began to seize, the stories and the memories became more like phantasms, daylight nightmares from which he could never fully revive. He could hardly shamble to the outhouse, had no frequent urgency anyway because for that matter he could hardly eat, even water a thing to choke down.

"Aye, lad," he gargled, like talking with his head in a trough. "Y'aught to see 'em. Some. 'Ows. B'lieve Goodnight keeps a few. Or Montana . . . b'lieve the' migh not. Be. Full gone. Saddle 'at . . . wee gray. Take ye 'at Juno . . ."

The nearer the approach of death, the further this fantasy took him, until in his final hours, spent not in the house but at a small hospital in town, he flat begged the boy through spasms and chills, mind-fog and hacked blood and tears, and as near to frenzy as might be possible in such a state of absolute debilitation. "Pack ye 'at Juno, laddie . . ."

Roy did indeed own a lithe gray mare to match his father's stock-inged black. The two had ridden since before Roy could scrabble into the saddle on his own, potting jackrabbits and cottontails with a .32-20 Winchester, a pipsqueak of a gun compared with the thunder-stick Sharps. In later years he would remember those pale-pink bodies with their muscles and tendons and fading warmth, and the almost loving manner in which his father would handle or prepare them. It would dawn on him how little went wasted.

Pack ye 'at, Juno, lad . . .

Two days after the funeral and now totally alone in the world, young Gilroy rode out in the dawn, mounted on the gray and lead-ing the black. The women's auxiliary at the Episcopal church in town was already taking an active interest and Roy had the distinct sense he was bound for an orphanage. He parceled his father's stash of coin and cash in different hideaways in his gear and on himself and on the two horses—some in each boot, some in the toe of the rifle slip with the .32-20—and as much hardtack and jerked beef and dried fruit as the larder provided. He balanced Juno across the pommel and lit out.

Two weeks later he rode into the breaks of the Canadian in Hutchinson County and on out through the greened-up spring grass to the headquarters of the Turkey Track Ranch. A number of hands gathered at the sight of this pint-size kid setting in the yard with a Big Fifty Sharps across his lap. He told them he'd come to find old Fort Adobe, to see for himself the place where Billy Dixon made his famous shot twenty-two years earlier.

To his utter astonishment Dixon was living right at the ruins of the old trading post, on a good piece of watered ground with an orchard established and a new young bride and a log house dou-bling as the local post office. Roy rode in past the melting footings of the original ruins and straight up to a woman hanging laundry on a line, shielding her eyes the better to see him as he approached. From inside the house, an infant squalled.

He stayed most of a week, Dixon himself more than congenial, enamored with and probably somewhat bemused by this unusual visitor in such an otherwise empty and lonely locale. And Mrs. Dixon equally so—according to the two of them, she was the only woman yet residing in the entire county. They had just the one child, a girl baby not quite six months old. Mrs. Dixon for that matter was much younger than her legendary husband, only an infant herself back when the famed shot was fired.

"It was scratch, pure and simple," to hear Dixon tell it. They stood inside the molten remains of the old Hanrahan saloon, at the point of the very window ledge he'd used as a rifle rest. "Pure luck. I just shot at the whole bunched-up mess of them out there at the base of the bluff." Juno leaned against the wall at the moment, and Dixon took up the heavy rifle and sighted it the way he once had.

"I didn't hit a thing with the first two shells. They were so far out, I'm not sure they had a notion I was lobbing at all. Or if they did, I reckon they figured I was just burning powder and ball, at that crazy range.

"Like they say, third one's a charm. Had a bunch of spotters with spyglasses, and they watched that poor cuss sail off his horse like God Almighty hit him with a lightning bolt." He grinned at the kid. "Should have heard the holler go up then, tell you what."

He cranked the breech open, peered into that vast empty chamber. "Do hate to think of the hole in the guy who caught it. Like a whack with a dern cannonball. Prob'ly drive a six-team freighter right on through."

He looked out at that faraway bluff, across the broad emerald shimmer of prairie grass. A cow bellowed somewhere over toward the house. "They were a proud people. Vicious as the day is long, no doubt. But proud. You ever shoot this brute?"

He made no presumption, or at least voiced none, about the kid's sure inability to handle the recoil. Roy shook his head. "Pa had some empty brass for it, and bullet molds. I packed 'em along with me.

But he never had no live cartridges around." He thought a minute. "Told me this gun kicked like three mules, though. Even as stout as she is."

"They kill on both ends, all right."

"He was mighty sick, for a real long time. Now that I look back. I don't think he had the lead for it anymore." Roy clawed for some other identifier. "He was a Scotchman. Spake lake it, too, raight t' th' end."

Dixon grinned again and shook his head. "Like I said, it was a madhouse of a week. Time it ended we was all pretty near out of our minds ourselves, and a whole passel of guys had come in off the country by then. I wish I remembered him, I truly do. But it's a safe bet he and I never so much as helloed each other."

Roy gandered at the crumbling mud walls, at the open sapphire sky where the roof used to be. He looked out across the plain. Grass as far as the eye could see. A big bunch of the Turkey Track's Herefords out by the bluff.

"Thinking you'll ride on to Goodnight's?"

Roy pondered. "Ain't sure. From what you told me, I think I'd just be disappointed. They sound about like them cows out there."

"Well, they ain't wild like they were, that's for sure. But Montana . . . that's a sight down the trail, son, and outside what dregs is left around Yellowstone, I don't think you'll find what you want up thataway, either."

"Well, failin' means yer playin'." One of Pa's standards. "Anyways, Yellowstone's something."

Dixon nodded. "I myself was any less, uh, domesticated, I'd saddle up and ride right ahead with you." He gave a wry look. "Truth be told, I envy you. Wouldn't mind seeing them old shaggies myself one more time."

Roy had his birthday a couple of weeks later, the day after passing out of Kansas and into Colorado. He'd been told to stay near the railbeds or the drovers' roads, where they existed, that they'd keep him near to ranch houses and settlements and out of trouble with the stock thieves and outlaws who pretty much replaced the war parties of old as the most immediate threat to travelers.

He slept in bunkhouses and barns and sometimes in the homes of ranch families if they had the room, and one evening while taking his supper with such, the actual date and day of the week came up.

He looked down at his plate. "I just realized something. Reckon tomorrow's my birthday."

They insisted he stay another day so the lady of the house could bake him a cake. They sang to him in the evening, presented him with a pair of buckskin gauntlet gloves outgrown by the family's boys. He very nearly cried.

Attention from ladies was new to him and on this trek he got a heap of it, much of it a combination of astonishment at the mere idea of what he'd undertaken and also what he eventually understood as basic maternal worry. Nigh on to everyone practically tried to adopt him. He certainly never had to worry about feed for the horses.

A newspaperman happened to be in the area, reporting on the ongoing dustup between nesters and the established open-range cattle spreads. Roy proved enough of a distraction to merit an interview. His story and sketch made the Denver daily. Afterward, more often than not, the ladies in the ranch yards acted as though they'd actually been expecting him. Some kissed his cheeks upon arrival.

He missed his father and thought a lot about him, had a lot of time to think about him, riding day after day with the big empty Sharps balanced across the horse. Roy's mother did not long survive his birth, and his father had spoken of her often and with fondness, and of an evening now Roy would unwrap the gilt-framed wedding picture of the pair of them and study it. As with the Dixons, his father was a good bit the senior of the two.

For the first time in his life he felt the weight of responsibility. Pa clearly never blamed him, though, never raised a hand or uttered an unkind word. But in the wedding portrait her hand lay upon his shoulder, and despite the formality of the pose, Roy had to consider that his old man looked happy.

He rode up through Johnson County, Wyoming, into a town actually named Buffalo. Four years earlier an entire army of Texas mercenaries had descended on the place at the behest of powerful cattle interests, killing a number of homesteaders and igniting an all-out war. Roy recalled the episode well, as it had made national headlines. Tensions clearly still ran high.

For weeks he'd seen nothing but cattle and sheep, and the occasional skittish band of pronghorn. Despite the namesake of this particular hamlet, no one had seen an actual live buffalo anywhere close in twelve or maybe fifteen years. An outfit from the Smithsonian Institution in the East had a hell of a time finding any for a taxidermy exhibit, and that was ten years ago already.

There remained, however, at least a couple of dozen in the Yellowstone interior, as more than one local had actually witnessed. They told him he could book passage for himself and the horses on the new rail line out of Sheridan, thirty miles to the north, then catch a transfer to Livingston, Montana, and take the tourist train into the park. He could be at Fort Yellowstone by Wednesday. A few of them asked how he stood for money, offered to help with fare for the horses. He declined. Nobody treated him like a fool.

In the end he did not catch the train in Sheridan but rode instead along the tracks north into Montana and then west to Livingston and beyond, this last through river-bottom ranchland in the lee of the most spectacular sawtooth cordillera he could imagine. Eight days after departing Buffalo, he rode down the tourist stage road and up the Gardner River to the fort.

To his surprise and even disappointment, the installation was not a classically barricaded frontier outpost but rather a stately collection of wood-frame cottages and groomed grounds. He caught a tinge of sulfur on the warm air and spied curls of smoke along the bluff in the distance, and wondered despite the absence of audible gunfire whether he'd just missed regimental rifle practice.

The two soldiers manning the guardhouse at the fort's entry hardly knew what to make of him. In addition to the birthday gauntlets, he'd by now acquired from others along the way an entire outfit of castoff and hand-me-down regalia, including a fringed buckskin jacket and two-toned duck saddle trousers tucked at the moment to the inside of his boots. He looked like a dime-novel scout from the seventies, in miniature. And while the guardsmen were accustomed to checking visitors' guns as a matter of course, this particular visitor with this particular piece of hardware was plainly a new one.

"Well, dang it all, General Thumb," said the taller of the pair, a real podunk despite his natty forager's cap and smart blue tunic. His apple bulged in his throat like a frog in a bull snake. "That thing looks to be taller'n you are. Best hand 'er on down."

Roy sat his horse and kept Juno at rest. "What all you aim to do with her?"

"Well, we got two choices. Check 'er here at the fort fer the duration of the sightseein', or we can seal the trigger now 'til yer leaves for home. Depends on the itinerary."

"Seal her with what?"

"A big ol' fat gob of wax is just about exactly what." He eyed the horses, the bedroll tied behind the cantle, and the minimal camping equipment lashed to the sawbuck on Pa's black. He frowned. "Whereabouts *is* home, exactly? You ride up the valley from Livingston or something?"

"No, from Rainbow."

He looked at his partner, who shrugged. "Ain't heard of it, but I only been here two months. How fur a piece is it?"

Roy puzzled a moment. "Don't really know, milewise. It's down near the Brazos. In Texas."

Again it was their turn for puzzlement. Finally the shorter of the two spoke up, and Roy felt something not unlike the breath of a ghost at the nape of his neck. "Air we to ken ye correct, laddie? Ye clip-clopped all the way fro' the *state* o' Texas?"

Roy nodded. After a bit of a search he found his voice. "Ain't taken so long as I expected, neither. This here's what, August?"

They nodded too, all three of them, nodding as though they could at least agree on the month and the feat, and maybe those were enough. The tall one looked again to his fellow. "Reckon that would beat pedalin' here on them dern bicycles—I wouldn't trade places with them boys fer love or money."

"Air' whiskey," said the other.

As it turned out, his unusual arrival coincided with another, equally notable event a day or so earlier. An experimental Army bicycle unit had rolled in from a fort somewhere farther west, after covering something like three hundred miles in a matter of days. Arduous ones, too, to hear these two tell it, with rain and mud and mechanical breakdowns galore.

Roy was keen with interest. He and one other boy back home had their own bicycles, bought off a wizened old traveling peddler who'd himself acquired them on trade and seemed to regard them as mere novelty, if not an outright insult to the Texas character. He practically gave them away, even while letting them know he wasn't at all sure he was doing the boys' moral backbone any favors.

But still, so long as there were decent roads to follow, the bicycles were almost unimaginably liberating. They were up-to-date safety models, with wheels of a uniform size and a chain drive to the rear. Roy and his buddy could be miles out of town in a matter of minutes, setting trotlines on the Brazos or potting squirrels out of a pecan grove with a gallery rifle. No saddling horses, no leisurely pace to and fro. Just on and away, fast as the legs could pump, fishing rod or rifle strapped to the handlebars.

Then again, had he set out on that novel contraption instead of his trusty gray, he doubted he'd have made fifty miles before the chain broke or a tire burst. Rather than sitting his horse here in Mammoth,

Montana, he might even now be gritting his teeth in the tedium of an orphanage.

By this point the soldiers had coaxed out his mission, and they remarked on something at least as curious as the mere fact of bicycling soldiers.

"Beats all to Christmas you done made yer ride tryin' for some sorter truce with these buffs up here," Podunk told him, "only to show right about the time this particular unit rolls in."

Roy failed to see the connection.

"These fellers is Twenty-Fifth Infantry. Buffalo soldiers."

So nominated by the tribes, back about the time Pa plunked down the shekels for the Big Fifty. Roy knew of some colored cavalrymen down in Texas, but he never had yet witnessed any such himself. He still couldn't quite see a clear pattern between his own paladin's quest and this revelation, but something did indeed seem spooky about the timing. Pa always had a superstition about such things, a more than faint conviction that the world possessed mysteries wholly beyond any sphere of logic or chance.

"Well," he said, "I reckon that is a deuce of a thing."

A day later he rode with both rifles sealed out of the fort and east down the tourist road to the Lamar Valley, where a group of bison had been summering. He was already agog at the spectacles encountered at the fort, mainly around the vaporous hot pools and otherworldly mineral formations on the slope.

What he'd taken for gun smoke upon arrival turned out to be the steam of thermal cauldrons, bubbling and flowing out of rifts and pores in earth and stone. Weird water flowed and pooled in hues and shades he could not have predicted, blues like some inexplicable hot ice and greens deep as jewels, oranges and reds run together like blood through the yolk of an egg. And those oddly formed crystal terraces all around, like cataracts transmogrified into stone steps up into heaven. Or maybe down into hell, with its own steaming sulfur.

Out on the tourist road he began to see animals. Dappled elk
in small bands back in the shade of the trees, deer flaring out of the
creek bottom with their tails flashing. A badger shimmied through
the grass, stopping to look back at him at the edge of a stand of
white-barked trees. He knew there were bears about and thought
ruefully of the seal on the .32-20, hardly a realistic concern, as that
particular rifle qualified more as a peashooter than reasonable bear
medicine.

He camped for the night at another Army station and stage stop,
taking his meal in the mess for two bits and talking shyly with a pair
of English girls on tour with their well-to-do parents. The soldiers at
the guardhouse checked again the seals on his arms, made a notation
in their ledger.

In the morning he rode out again ahead of the tourist stage and
within two hours came into the broad valley, a bowl of deep grass
with dots of pale sage stretching off to the north and then rising into
rolling foothills and rising again into a formidable mountain wall,
steep slopes purple with pines.

He topped a swell in the land and sat his horse over this view, so
taken with the panorama he failed at first to spy the object of his long
quest not seventy yards off in the river bottom. Then his little gray
shied and jumped at the snootful she took on the breeze, and Pa's
normally unflappable black started to pull and shy, too. Roy nearly
lost Juno off the saddle in the same instant the big brutes became
manifest within his astonished mind.

Four of them bedded in the grass, plus one gangly calf already on
its feet. Its mother rose, too, looking squarely at him with eyes that
appeared at once dully disinterested and utterly menacing within the
broad hulk of her skull. The great hump atop her spine jutted like its
own unassailable wall, akin to the permanent mountain behind her.

Finally he goaded his rubber arms to move, reined the gray's head
around, and heeled the horse back over the rise and down below the
line of sight. The horses had gone nervy as deer, and he felt his hands

both wet and weak on the precarious Sharps and the slippery braided reins.

He tied the horses off at the nearest grove of trees, a little better than shouting distance back up the road. He contemplated loosening the cinches, then thought better of it. If another of those imposing beasts showed up and spooked them, the last thing he needed was saddle or sawbuck swinging under their panicked bellies.

He was suddenly uncertain what his plan should be exactly. He'd come all this way with no other thing in mind, and now here he was. He took the big empty Sharps and started back for the rise, and he'd barely moved ten steps before the horses began to stir and snort once more. He turned with his knees going weak all over again.

He anticipated another jarringly close-in bison encounter but saw nothing. The horses craned their heads back down the road, ears trained forward, and after a moment Roy heard it, too. A metallic clatter, not exactly what he would describe as mechanical but certainly not the sound of a horse-drawn coach or wagon. He tried to put his finger on it as the din drew nearer.

The bicycles emerged where the road wound back through the trees, two at first and then four more in loose formation and finally nine in total, their blue-bloused and campaign-hatted riders coasting and then pedaling and coasting again on the level grade. Bouncing a bit over the hardpan, too, their gear-laden cycles raucous with the jolts.

The horses got even jumpier as the soldiers approached, and Roy found himself moving toward the animals and whoaing them with his voice. The lead rider lifted a hand at the sight of him and began to slow. The unit wheeled to a stop and dismounted up the road a spell. Roy steadied the horses.

The lone white rider left his bike and approached on foot. He had a holstered revolver at his waist, while several of the others were armed with rifles. The horses calmed a bit with the clatter down.

"You must be the Texican," he said. "We heard about you at the fort yesterday."

Roy nodded.

The soldier patted Pa's black, introduced himself as Lieutenant Moss. He eyed Juno, at parade rest with the butt in the dirt and Roy's grip on the barrel. "They tell me you rode all this way to get a look at a buffalo."

Roy nodded again.

"You and me both, sir." The lieutenant looked out across the valley, scanning the broad reaches to the slope of the foothills. He looked back to the boy, then down to the great rifle. He gave a gentle smile. "Guess you brought the right hardware for it, too. Twenty years late, of course."

Roy looked him dead in the eye. "I don't intend to shoot any."

Still with that smile. "No, I didn't gather. They even make shells for that cannon anymore?"

"Not that I know of." Roy took in the scenery himself, thought how odd it was that there were in fact three or four tons of heavily muscled bison alive and dangerous on the hoof not two hundred yards away, if totally invisible from this vantage.

"Beginning to wonder if we're going to see any at all at this point," Moss told him.

Roy turned his head back from the view. "I can show you some right now."

Five minutes later he and Moss and the entire retinue of soldiers crawled up over the rise and peered down on the unsuspecting beasts. All except one were on their feet now, the last kicking and rolling nearly onto its great back in a wild churn of earth. Finally it stood, too, loose dirt coloring its flank like cinnamon on a cake. Roy saw flies buzzing around the lot of them.

"Ain't it something," breathed the soldier to Roy's right. He looked over and grinned. "Just ain't none left, and now here we are. Ain't it something."

They stayed low on the rise, and the bison did not appear to be aware of them. Roy watched and kept his hand on the sun-warmed gun barrel. He imagined what it must have been like for his father to settle into a position like this and unleash the unified forces of chemistry and lead and rifled steel upon hide and muscle and bone. He wondered if the animals would flee at the first shot or dimly hear only thunder, dimly cast their eyes on the first to fall, then the second, and so on. He wondered if any would run before none were able to any longer. For a long time he watched with the others and simply wondered.

Later he took lunch with the men back by the horses, watched the designated mechanic make minor services and repairs to the bicycles. He tightened chains, replaced a tire. His name was Findley. He kept his tools in a hard-sided metal box mounted ahead of his handlebars.

He told Roy that he used to work in a bicycle factory in Chicago and that the devices were all the rage in the East. Even the ladies were climbing aboard and whizzing away, ditching their cumbersome bustles and dresses for knee socks and trim split bloomers. He said the bicycle was the way of the future. Even the Army seemed to think so.

The soldiers' rifles spoke to the future as well. Roy had read about the newer European arms designs in *Forest and Stream*, which Pa had delivered to the house. Patents by German or Austrian makers that relied on curious turn-bolt actions and newfangled smokeless gunpowder similar to what the very latest Winchesters used.

"These rifles is Krags," Findley informed him. He pincered a shell out of a cartridge belt and handed it over. It had the same sleek bottle-neck shape as the new Winchester rounds, the same small-diameter projectile. "From Denmark. Or they pattern is, anyway."

He called for one of the others to unlimber a rifle and trot it over. Findley thumbed open the curious hinged magazine on the side of the receiver, spilled the shells into his hand. He opened the action and handed the rifle to the boy.

Roy worked the bolt a few times, studied the way it and the receiver fit and functioned in slick unison, the one sliding into the other with no more friction than a bead of water down a window-pane. "So this front hub here locks it into battery? When you turn the bolt down?"

Findley nodded. "Called a lug, though. Not a hub."

Roy eyed again the unusual stepped cartridge with its long pro-jectile, considered the degree of technical sophistication required to mirror that shape with reamer and die inside the Krag's chamber. Sixty years ago they were still igniting patched-ball long rifles with a hunk of flint clamped into the lock. This high-toned contraption left even the advancements of the Sharps cross-eyed in the dust.

"There sure enough no smoke when these things go off?"

Findley, for his part, had taken up Juno, studying the workings of the ladder sight mounted to the tang. "Barely any. Modern miracle. Smell ain't the same, sound ain't the same—more a crack than a hard boom. Like lightnin' smackin' a tree. Or lake ice comin' apart. You know 'at sound?"

Roy shook his head. "I know about ice-skating. Never seen a lake you could do it on, though. Shoot, I only seen snow once or twice, other than what's up on the mountains while I been traveling."

Findley slid the notch to the top of the ladder, put the Sharps to his shoulder at that extreme cant. "They flat-shootin', too, next to this ol' boss—reach out three, four hundred yards, with hardly no lift. My, this thing's a brute."

He lowered the Big Fifty and snapped the tang sight down, turned her over and traced the dish in the forearm. "You keep her 'crost the saddle, all 'at way?"

Roy nodded. "Every step. How my pa used to pack her, too. The wear was already pretty far along." He opened the bolt again on the Krag, felt again the smooth stroke of machined steel. Silk thread through a needle's eye.

"They had guns like 'at Krag twenty year back, I doubt even 'em buffs over the hill be here."

By the trees, one of Roy's horses snorted and stamped a hoof. He heard the buzz of flies, the swat of a tail. He gave Findley a nod. "Reckon it's a good thing they didn't, then."

A year later found him working as a ranch hand outside the eastern edge of the park, at an outfit at least as reliant on paying guests from New York and Philadelphia as beef and sheep on the range. Dudes, in the local parlance. He mainly worked with the chief wrangler, mucking stalls and maintaining tack and sometimes taking guests on trail rides and pack trips.

He also worked in the ranch's blacksmith shop, learning so quickly that by his second year he'd become a full apprentice to the head smith. By the time he turned seventeen, he'd taken over the shop himself.

In September 1911, while walking down Main Street in Red Lodge, a flyer with the bold print DIXON caught his eye. It turned out to be an advertisement for the third annual state fair in Helena, featuring a demonstration of one of the newfangled flying machines, flown by the youngest licensed aviator in the land. Cromwell Dixon. With a ten-thousand-dollar purse proffered to the first daredevil to fly successfully across the Continental Divide, Dixon seemed a sure bet.

Roy caught the train to the capital and attended the fair. Young Dixon performed several acrobatic demonstrations in his airplane, really little more than an enormous kite with a motor and prop and a couple of spindly wheels. But the display was impressive—all Roy could think of was his pa, hacking around the wild plains in a buckboard barely forty years ago, dodging hostiles and shooting shaggies by the score. Now it was all this.

Two days later, Dixon did indeed corkscrew to some preposterous elevation and flew across the crags to the other slope of the continent. He collected his ten thousand dollars.

A week after that, back on the ranch, Roy sat down to breakfast in the mess and spied a photograph of the young flier's airplane on the front page of a three-day-old newspaper. Seems Cromwell Dixon's next engagement was at a county fair in Spokane, where he came down like a stone in that same history-making kite and died an hour later from the injuries. Nineteen years old. The hell.

"I almost moved on right there. Handed my walking papers, saddled up with Juno across the pommel, and just rode south again for Texas. See if that other Dixon might still be around. Not even sure why, exactly."

"The Lord had a different plan, though," said Huck's ma, studying the contents of her plate. "By the name of Houston."

Roy reached over and rubbed her back a moment, right there at the table. He took in Annelise, then McKee. "Yeah, I reckon that's so. Because I didn't ride on, I stayed on. Right at the ranch." His gaze stopped on Huck. "And that's where I met your mama."

Cousins

1

He'd spent little more than a single afternoon three weeks earlier mulling the pros and cons of McKee's offer to help. Truth be told, there really were no cons, other than the risk of letting too many people in on the secret, and as Annelise put it, that cat was out of the bag.

As it turned out, McKee spent a fair bit of time on the project even while Huck and Annelise were across town at school, so much so that Huck began to wonder whether Pop hadn't hired him for exactly that reason. It wouldn't have surprised him, really.

Whatever the case, the airplane was progressing by previously inconceivable bounds. The wing and tail were now assembled, save for the cloth covering, with the thirty-foot wing frame squirreled away under a strategic pile of sheet tin behind the shop. The landing gear was nearly assembled as well.

McKee worked incredibly quickly, Huck had to admit. He was actually a little intimidated at first at how exacting the man was relative to his rate of production. Not to mention the amount of Highlander he put down in the process.

"A lot of guys can make a job come together," McKee told him. "What separates the men from the boys is how fast they can get 'er done."

Annelise for her part was certainly willing to pitch in. Eager, even. Granted, she had no shop experience, but she was a quick study and not afraid to get her hands dirty.

She could be moody, though. Huck often found himself on pins and needles around her, although when he thought about it, he guessed he really couldn't blame her. They'd spent a lot of time together in the past weeks, with Annelise staying at the bungalow during the school week and heading—teeth gritted, he knew—out to the ranch on Friday afternoon and then back for church with Mother on Sunday. Huck had given up his little bedroom for her here. He slept on a pallet in the front room.

Pop had an unclaimed electric sewing machine he'd taken in as a repair at some point, and they set it up on the desk in the office so they could hear the radio while they worked. McKee kept at the landing gear in the main shop. They could hear him out there, cutting and clanking and occasionally swearing, although with McKee even the worst of the curse words sounded like part of a comedy act.

Annelise had learned to sew a bit in home economics, which she'd regarded at the time as drudgery if not actual enslavement. Still, she made a few practice runs on scrap muslin now, got her sea legs back under her and before long formed a reasonably true run of seam. Huck tried it too, kept practicing until he was at least in the ballpark. They fetched the cutout panels from the fabrication bay and carted them back to the office.

Out in the shop, McKee popped a torch. Through the half-open office door they heard the hot-static sizzle of melting alloy, saw the white-blue surge and steady pulse of electricity, fusing metal unto metal.

"You should be out there learning that," Annelise told him.

Huck shrugged it off. "I already know how, a little. Plus he won't be at it long. He's only tacking things together."

They got to work pinning the muslin panels along the seams. The radio played a *Lone Ranger* chapter with a lot of dramatic background music and clopping horse hooves and dropped *g*'s in the dialogue. Pidgin English out of Tonto. Annelise strode over and spun the dial to a dance band before sitting down in front of the Singer. "Sorry," she said.

"It's okay." Huck watched her position the edge of the pinned sheets beneath the needle. "You know I thought you were fixing to have a . . . baby? When you first got here?"

She fixed that blue-gray gaze at him. "Obviously I'm not."

"I know. I just . . . wondered."

She made the first run of stitching, then stopped mid-seam. "Nobody said anything otherwise?"

He shook his head. "Figured you must've gotten into some other trouble. Way they're keeping you out on the ranch and all."

"I slept with a boy. A man, actually. Is that what you thought?"

Huck nodded. "I guess so."

"Well, now you know." She finished out the run and repositioned the cloth panels. "Are you shocked?"

He wasn't, though he knew he was supposed to be. He shook his head. "I've seen the movies. I know the world's different than they make out in church. I know people are just . . . different."

"It was books, for me. At first anyway. Then I got in with some much more worldly people than I was raised around, and I really started to see some light through the cracks. Then it just"—she shrugged her shoulders, made a singular gesture with her head and eyes—"happened to me, too."

"Weren't you afraid, though?"

"Of getting in a predicament, you mean? Maybe a little. There are ways around that, though."

"But weren't you . . . afraid of *God*?" Huck himself felt that old familiar flare of guilt, the conviction that He was listening even now, and certainly not amused. But he also cringed to think that his cousin, right here in front of him, might simply find him ridiculous.

She didn't laugh at him, though. "That I'd be judged, you mean? Or that I'd be punished."

"Some of both, I guess." He considered. "Aren't they the same thing?"

"Sort of like, was I afraid God would punish me by interfering with my own . . . precautions? I'm assuming you know what a rubber is."

"Why yes, I do," McKee said from out in the shop. Not exactly the disembodied voice of the eternal Father, but more than enough to turn Huck's face beet red.

"Not talking to you," Annelise said loudly. Huck could see the grin at her mouth.

"Oh. Too late for that." They heard him shuffle around a bit before he actually stuck his head in the door. His dark welder's goggles made him look sort of charmingly deranged. "Since we're on topic here at the Junior Aviators' Club, I'd like to impart this important safety tip: never, *ever*, jump without a chute on." He gave them a jaunty salute.

"And how about you, Enos? Flown at all lately?"

Huck was curious about this himself. For all McKee's efforts on the airplane project, the topic had never come up.

"Oh, hell yes. I'm a grade-A barnstormer, missy," he said. "A real wing-walking, barrel-rolling son of a gun."

"Yeah, I bet. I'm sure you're just up all the time."

He struck a fast, funny pose with his head, fixed his goggles at some imaginary point in the far-off yonder. "And always with my chute snugly in place, young lady." He turned his head back and held up his hand, three fingers in the air like a Boy Scout. "Honest Injun. Oh wait—you're talking about airplanes."

She smirked at him, and Huck felt like a dern wet-behind-the-ears kid. Raleigh would've caught on—why couldn't he?

"Maybe I actually am," she said. "Talking about airplanes."

"I wouldn't climb into one of those gravity traps for love or money. Mother McKee raised landlubbers. Smart ones."

"You do what Mommy tells you, then."

McKee worked the goggles up onto his forehead. He had creases in his cheeks from the pressure of the elastic strap. "Not always. But let's not kid ourselves. That Charlie Darwin is one cold son of a bitch."

Annelise shrugged. "At this point, flying's no more risky or foolhardy than most anything."

"Fun and games, I'm sure. Right until somebody puts an eye out."

Huck saw again the windows of the New Deal, barreling toward him out of the night. He had to admit, that little episode could well be described as foolhardy. Absolutely worth it, too. Still, the mere mention of the name Darwin put his nerves on edge.

"Lots of people said Charles Lindbergh was foolhardy," he offered. "Look at how that worked out."

"Oh, risk can have its rewards, no argument." McKee looked at Annelise. "To return to an earlier theme."

"At least we agree on that," she answered. "Run along now. You said it yourself—standing around jawing won't get the airplane off the ground. Even if you yourself don't want a ride."

"I may get up with you yet, darlin'." He'd already exited, his voice disembodied again but loud and clear on the air.

"I'm only talking about flying," she said loudly. But Huck saw the grin on her plain as day.

"Have you ever kissed a girl?"

They were walking to school, finally resuming the conversation from the evening before. Annelise saw him swallow, knew she was putting him on the spot. "There's no wrong answer, buddy."

"Reckon I never had the chance."

And would no doubt be terrified out of his wits if presented with one. Of course he was pretty young yet in any case, despite his deceptive height. He still caught her off guard when he opened his mouth and a cracking, irregular falsetto squeaked out.

"You will, probably pretty quickly. Girls like tall boys."

"Oh. I guess I ain't in any real hurry."

They walked a little farther. "You're blushing," she told him. "Girls like that, too."

"I can never tell what they like. I just get the notion they're pretty dern hard to please. No offense."

He really was pretty cute, she had to say. She hoped he'd figure it out for himself. After three Saturdays on the ranch in the company of her aunt, she knew he had to be even more puzzled about the general mystery between the sexes than any benighted Victorian virgin. Uncle Roy was certainly an asset and obviously no prude, but even he seemed to mainly step aside where Huck and Aunt Gloria were concerned. Choosing his battles, she supposed.

She shrugged up her sleeve and checked the time.

"That's a Lindbergh watch," said Houston. "If I'm not mistaken."

She let the thing slip back away. "You are not."

She'd seen him eyeing it in the previous weeks, which in and of itself was hardly unusual—it looked nearly like a wall clock on the inside of her wrist. But she'd wondered if he had a sense of what it was. They heard the school bell half a block off. "I'll show it to you once school's out. It's pretty amazing."

"Do you know how it works?"

"Not entirely." They turned up the walk, into the trickle of kids. "Do you?"

He saw Raleigh coming toward them. "No. I mean, sort of, in theory. But I've never really played with one or anything."

"Well, I guess not. I'd be shocked if there's another in a thousand miles."

Raleigh was nearly in speaking distance. Annelise watched him angle toward them, aware he had a sort of clumsy fascination with her the way pretty much all the boys at school did. The girls, too, although that was marked not by clumsiness but a nearly palpable territorialism. She caught Houston's eye with her own and she knew she must have seemed serious, because his gaze dashed right away. "Don't tell anyone what I've told you, all right? About my beau?"

"I won't."

"Thank you. I'm sure they're curious."

"They are," he said.

They were nearly to the school steps. She said, "Of course they are."

"So why's she have the watch?" Raleigh asked. They each manned a urinal in the boys' room. "Telling her about it's one thing, but letting her waltz around with it? Ain't that a heck of a risk?"

"It ain't the same dern watch." He finished and cinched his belt back up. "I never have told her about the one we took off the reverend."

"She's got one too? I thought you said it was some rare deal."

"It is. Believe me, I like to fell over when I saw it on her. She just said it herself not two hours ago, there probably ain't another in a thousand miles."

The bell rang in the hall, and they heard the clamor of lockers and feet. Raleigh zipped up. "You get a call from that detective last night?"

Huck looked at him.

"From Billings?"

"I didn't get a call from anybody. Like what, a private eye?"

"No, a police dick. Wanting to know if there was anything we'd noticed unusual on the body, and whether Cy or Junior or anyone else 'removed any effects' at the scene."

"What effects?"

"That's what I asked him. He says, 'Oh, just anything—a gun, a wallet. Or a watch.'"

"Hoo boy."

"Yeah. Hoo boy."

They collected their books and went out, just in time to see Annelise and a couple of other girls disappear up the stairwell to the second floor. "So I take it she ain't, you know, studying abroad," said Raleigh. "In the euphemistic sense."

"Nope. Not in any sense actually."

"Huh. Why'd she come here, then?"

Huck looked at him. "Who cares? What did you tell the detective?"

"Exactly what we told Cy. But how in the heck does he know about the dern watch?"

They stopped outside the open door to English class and watched a paper airplane sail across the room while Mrs. Hall rummaged in her desk. "Coincidence?" said Huck, admittedly with no conviction.

"Better dern sure hope so."

A little later, with Mrs. Hall diagramming a sentence on the blackboard, Raleigh passed a note forward. *If I'd known our innocent abroad planned to show up with the same lousy watch, I never would've told you to steal the good rev's.*

Huck crumpled the note and thought, *And I never would've listened to you.*

2

April 1, 1937

Blix—

God, I hardly know where to start, except to tell you I'm fine, and nobody knows a thing. Or at least, nobody knows about you.

Oh—for the record, I'm not in any so-called "trouble." I'm guessing this has crossed your mind if not caused you to sweat actual bullets. But don't worry, I've already fallen off the roof right into the red roses, same as it ever was. So whatever else might be said, the situation is at least not as dire as all that.

My mother did however sniff out the basic fact of a dalliance. I'm honestly not sure how—Lord knows I'm a gold-star sneak. A loyal one, too, you'll be glad to know . . . despite the Inquisition's best efforts to beat, flog, or otherwise blackmail a name out of me, my fellow conspirator remains a mystery. Exaggerating on the beating and flogging, but not by much.

I am however packed off to my aunt's, in Montana, the town of Big Coulee, which may as well be Devil's Island. No shark-infested waters, but anyway an impossible swim to the mainland for this girl.

Do you know any of this already? Golly, it must seem as though I simply vanished into thin air, and in a way that's the worst part of this whole mess. I wanted to get word to you somehow before they shipped me off, but the whole thing happened so fast and I was practically under armed guard, and the last thing I could risk was getting you even hotter in the drink than I am myself. But I know it must have seemed either awfully cold or awfully dire, just to up and disappear.

One bright note. My uncle has turned out curiously on my side, so far as I can tell. He's what you might call a salt-of-the-earth sort, a farmer (rancher??) but also (even more??) a mechanic or machinist or some such combination, and definitely no Mrs. Grundy like the rest of the family. And my little cousin Houston (actually six inches taller than me, but a frosh kid) not only has Lindy fever in spades, but I swear the ingenuity of the Wright brothers and G. Curtiss put together.

He's building his own airplane, Blix. I'm not joking, it's a real ship, from published plans. Two-seater, mono wing, but otherwise looks a bit like Bill's Gipsy, or a Stearman, or will anyway when he's got it all together. Called an "Air Camper," evidently? Have you seen any of these things? They use a Ford car motor, which he needs to wrangle yet, but I have little doubt he'll finish and fly it. He's that kind of kid.

Of course I'd blouse out of here this very minute if I could, but even so I halfway hope I'm still around when he gets her up and off the ground. He's doing this right under my aunt's nose and she doesn't have a clue or she'd put the kibosh in a second, and I would love, love, LOVE to watch him pull the whole thing off just to see the look on her face—or maybe even lift off and fly straight out of exile myself, how rich would that be? A fantasy, I know. And I know I am probably pasting my mother onto my aunt, but how can I feel otherwise? They're two sides of a coin, and it's hard to be any less furious at either of them for this whole nonsensical business . . . when what have I done, really, except behave as though I'm glad to be alive, with a glorious hunger, and happy to know I can be swept away? Didn't you feel that way, too?

I guess I should tell you I'm sorry I took your watch that last time, but I'm not, if you want the whole selfish truth. I wear it when I sleep so I can feel it hum in the dark, like a pulse I imagine to be yours. I hope you like the sound of that, hope it takes some of the rub out of letting it slip for the time being off your wrist, and on to mine, and then away.

Did you know the times I would wrap my fingers around your wrist, just to feel your real heart race? Did you? Bet you didn't, not in those particular moments.

Anyway, I will be a proper guardian, I can promise that. I don't exactly know when I'll get a reprieve, but when I do, and I will, your lovely watch will return with me. In the meantime, I know it's ridiculous to ask you to wait for me. I know how you flyboys are (she writes, with a wink and a glare). But you know me too, and I am no canceled stamp. If the charms of some other girl have your attention when I return, I will merely set my trap and lure you right back. It will be easy.

Write to me at this address to let me know I've indeed reached you, and also so I know how you are. But for the love of God, write only as my flight instructor, not with any hint or suggestion you might be what you actually are. I doubt highly my aunt could get to my mail before I do, but I have no guarantee. And as much as I want to read about how you would like to take me apart and see what makes me run, well, you know the stakes.

Isn't it a drag about Amelia in Hawaii? I still have not been able to gather exactly what glitched, but evidently it wasn't small potatoes. Have you seen photos or newsreel? Let me know, it's like the GOBI DESERT up here for the otherwise free in spirit and curious of mind. That is no April Fool.

Yours,

The other A.E.

3

"Any line yet on an engine for this baby?" McKee asked.

They had the muslin-sheathed fuselage and also the wing ele-vated on horses on the main floor of the shop, the welders and lathe and compressor pushed back by the forge, which left little room to work on much else. Huck had doped the edges and seams before school, then walked around with his head in a nitrate fog until third period.

Now Pop and McKee had the big bay doors rolled back to ven-tilate the place, with the REO and McKee's panel truck strategi-cally parked to block the view from the street. Huck, in his jumpsuit and rubber gloves, dipped a brush into an Arbuckles' can to get the first coat applied everyplace else. Annelise helped for a bit, until the fumes drove her back to the house with her eyes crossed and her stomach churning.

"We don't," Pop answered. "This is more a nickel-and-dime operation. Catch-as-catch-can." He winked at Huck. "I got a wrecker down in Billings keeping an eye out, though. Something'll come up."

"Better hope for sooner rather than later," said McKee. "By my figuring, we're right close to running out of things to do here."

Huck knew he was right. Hard to believe, really, that the build had come so far so fast, but McKee did indeed work like lightning. The way things were going, and assuming they came up with a motor, they might even have the thing ready for trials by July. Which led to the next obvious conundrum, one that in a way made the feat of the actual build seem a mere trifle. Mother.

The phone rang in the office and Huck jumped like he'd been forked. Two shorts and a long, the house cadence. He'd had a dread of the sound for two days now, ever since Raleigh brought up the police detective in the restroom at school. The phone rang again. He swallowed hard against his leaping gorge.

Pop kept on with his brush. "Dern phone's making me crazy. Ringing all day long and then nobody there when I pick up. Your turn, kid. The one time we ignore it, we'll miss a line on your engine."

Huck peeled off his right glove heading through the office door. The blaring receiver jumped in its cradle, made his heart jump in his chest. He accidentally dropped the glove to the floor. He thought, *Please, God, please*, and lifted the handset.

"Finn Metalworks." His voice squeaked back to him in the earpiece the way it always did, like a panicked mouse floundering in a bucket trap. Otherwise just the usual hollow crackling in the line, and a long-enough silence at the other end to suggest that Pop's persistent irritant might well prove his own answered prayer.

No such luck. "Houston Finn, please." A man's voice but barely audible, as though he were unusually soft-spoken or maybe not very proximate to his own handset.

"Yes?"

"You're him?"

"This is Houston." Huck felt his sweat rise. "Who's this?"

The man seemed fond of disconcerting pauses. "This is Detective Blank, with the Billings police. Do you know what this is about?"

"Uh, I guess?"

"Why don't you tell me, then."

He could feel the watch in his pocket, like a combination scorching cinder and five-hundred-pound millstone. "The body?" He sounded piss-scared and could literally hear it, his voice quavering up and down like a drunk sawing at a warped violin. His mind raced again to *Please, God, please*, and then it occurred to him that surely God was not on his side but on the detective's.

"You guess the body. What else, besides the body?"

The whole truth wobbled on the tip of his tongue, poised like any dark secret to claw for the bright light of day through the first available crack and finally reveal itself in a moment of both unavoidable judgment and sweet honest release. Salvation by confession. Besides, Annelise had the identical watch, right there on her wrist.

Then he remembered Cy. The second that hard case knew he'd been had, he'd descend on the shop like Attila the Hun, no two ways about it. If the stolen watch had come to seem like a tar baby, the airplane absolutely remained the last thing Huck intended to put on the block. What did Pop always say? Cross the high creek when you get there?

"Hang on," he said, "my pop wants to talk to you."

Finally the distinct lack of a pause. "Hold on, hold on," the man said, the voice now much less distant as well. "You're a straight shooter, right? A real straight shooter. You want to help the police, right?"

"Yes, sir." His voice cracked again, squeaked again like that drowning mouse, that cracked violin.

"The thing is, that gunshot stiff you boys found had some items on him that could help round up the rest of the gang, and we're talking about a bad bunch here."

Huck cut right to the chase, and to his surprise, his pitch somehow bottomed to a previously unknown depth in the earpiece, dropping an octave and into some steady, unflappable timbre. "What sort of items?"

His voice had changed, just that quick. He spoke again, mainly out of auditory wonder. "Who is this, again?"

He waited for an answer. None came.

"Hello? Hello? Are you there?" He didn't sound like himself at all, and certainly not like some green kid. He sounded like a movie star. "Hello?"

He heard the static in the line, the pop and crackle like the dead space at the end of a phonograph record. Then the distinct sound of a telephone receiver settling into its cradle, cutting off the call. What on earth.

Huck went back to the shop floor. McKee had taken up for Huck on the fuselage. Pop brushed away on the wing. Despite the ventilation from the shop door and an oscillating fan on the workbench, the fumes sliced the air like mustard gas.

"Anybody worth knowing?" Pop asked.

"Billings police."

Their heads swiveled as though managed by a single brain.

He chose his words. "I think it was just routine. Like a follow-through? He didn't stay on long."

They were still looking at him, each with the same grin. "Say something," McKee told him.

Huck felt himself redden. "Uh, *something*?"

McKee looked at Pop. "Reckon Miz Gloria won't be looking to change any britches now."

"Reckon you're right." Pop wagged a finger at Huck. "But with a baritone like that, I wouldn't be surprised if she tries to put you to saving souls over the radio. Brace yourself."

McKee turned back to Huck. "So, cowboy. Want a beer?"

"My ma said the same thing," Raleigh mused. They were eating lunch in a corner of the schoolyard. "Phone like to ring off the hook all afternoon, and nobody there when she'd answer. Finally my old man got up from dinner to pick up, and that seemed to put an end to it. They figured it was kids, playing a prank."

"It's got to be related, though, right? Every time one of us answers, it's the Billings police. Otherwise nobody's there."

Raleigh shook his head. "Yeah, but it don't add up."

Two girls angled across the yard in their direction. Pastor White's daughter Sharon and Katie Calhoun, who always made Huck a little tongue-tied. The breeze out of the west blew her skirt tight against her legs and he thought of the lissome showgirls in *Footlight Parade*. Katie was the tallest girl in school. She'd have fit right in.

"Ladies," said Raleigh. "To what do we owe the honor?"

Sharon glanced at Katie with a tight little smile that seemed to advertise its own slyness, as though half the fun of knowing a secret involved letting on that a secret existed in the first place. Meanwhile Raleigh was not only girl-crazy in general, but also still basking in his brush with fame from the newspaper story a few weeks back, a precarious combination indeed. Huck wished he'd never laid eyes on that dern watch.

Sharon pointed at Huck. "Say something."

This was getting ridiculous. He'd been called on earlier to read a paragraph in English class, and the reaction had been swift—a general murmur, punctuated by a catcall or two. Even Mrs. Hall had declared the delivery "very stentorian," whatever that meant.

He felt himself redden. "Uh, like what?"

Now both girls had that sly little smile. "Told you," said Sharon.

An odd silence fell over the bunch of them, even Raleigh apparently stricken dumb for once. The class bell saved them all.

Voice change or no, he was still sweating bullets over the watch and the phone call. Then sixth period rolled around, and to his undeniable elation but also complete horror he was paired in gym class with Katie Calhoun, to learn the basics of ballroom dancing.

Huck sat behind her in homeroom, but he generally lacked the courage to speak to her. Mostly he paid attention to the back of her pale neck, on account of the contrasting color of her hair—black as an obsidian arrowhead, worn straight on top with a neat part to the side, a short wreath of permanent waves along the sharp line of her jaw.

She always smelled like some fancy bar of soap, and he'd always been sort of slightly aware of it. They squared off in the gymnasium and, following instructions, moved to put their hands on each other. Her palm felt hot as a pistol.

"Did you hear what she said, Houston? You have to be firm, or I can't follow along. You have to hold me tighter."

Katie had always been a little standoffish, honestly. Now it seemed she had a bossy streak as well. Another Annelise. He had to admit he sort of liked it.

"It's okay," she said. "You won't hurt me."

He went ahead and pressed his hand to her side. He felt the lean run of her ribs beneath her dress. They reminded him of the riffled waves in her hair. He could feel the bottom edge of her brassiere. He caught the scent of her again, and she was listening to Mrs. Hall over by the phonograph, whom he couldn't seem to hear at all, and Katie was looking full-on at him with something like expectation. He noticed for the first time that her eyes were two slightly different colors, one blue and one green, the pupil in the latter slightly larger than its twin.

He began to stir, and also panic. His eyes darted around at the other squared-off couples.

Katie tightened her grip and shook his hand. "Firmer. Don't be a limp noodle."

Unfortunately he was anything but. Luckily he was wearing an old sweater of Pop's, which he wore partly to conceal the usual belted cinch-job at the waist of his pants. He tried to think about white paper, cold water, arithmetic. Bible verses. Anything to get himself under control.

"You're blushing," Katie informed him. Unnecessarily, to be sure—his neck was hot as a stovepipe. She said, "It's really cute."

This did nothing to subdue either the blush or his infernal pecker. By the time they began the first run-through of the basic step—slow, slow quick-quick—he was mainly concentrating on not bumping into or otherwise poking her, because he doubted she'd find anything cute about that indignity at all. He found himself torn between badly wishing he were anywhere but here and badly not wanting his hands to be anyplace but where they were.

* * *

He walked home after the school day and tried to busy himself with the airplane. He could still smell the soap on her, still feel the heat of her hand. The stir in his trousers. He couldn't get that line out of his head, about being cute.

"You are one lucky bastard," Raleigh had cracked after gym class, wit fully restored. "All over Lady Brett in there like a dern picador." No doubt a reference to some book he'd read, which like many of Raleigh's musings went right over Huck's head.

Pop and McKee and the REO were nowhere about, and Annelise had gone to the school library. So he was there in the shop by himself when the blare of the telephone jolted his attention right back to the watch in his pocket. He lowered the file in his hand and forced himself to walk to the office.

The phone's jangle seemed to course through the dern watch. He swore he could feel every piercing ring, zapping like voltage right into his leg.

The ringing had stopped by the time he made the office door. He could still feel the watch, like a live wire in his pocket. Lindy brushed up against his legs and started purring.

He turned to head back to the fabrication bay. The shriek of the phone again stopped him short. He stood there with his back to it, let the thing keep right on ringing.

4

"You have to go, Houston. It's mandatory, unless you have a note from a parent. Which, come to think of it, your mother would love to provide, given her aversion to anything resembling normal fun."

Big Coulee Central had its first-ever Spring Ball scheduled for the coming Friday, largely as an extension of the ballroom dance instruction. Annelise was right, attendance was required—otherwise all the boys would predictably skip, and the girls would be stuck dancing with one another.

"Also assuming you stoop so low as to ask, which is tantamount to saying the both of us will wind up stuck out on the farm all weekend. Bore. Ring."

"Ranch," said Huck. "I keep telling you."

"Whatever," said Annelise. "A yawn by any other name is still a big fat yawn."

They were on opposite sides of the kitchen table in the bungalow, Huck with the new issue of *Modern Mechanics*. Roy had been out at the ranch all day and likely wouldn't return until morning.

She narrowed her glare at him. "Besides, if we're stuck out there, we won't be able to work on the airplane."

This struck a chord—she could see it in the way he flinched. He looked so worried all the time, it practically made her furious. Even furious at him, even when she knew full well this was hardly reasonable. She wished she could pump some of her own cold blood straight into his veins.

He kept his eyes pinned to the open page. "I'll just get Pop to write one. Then we can stay in town, and you can go to the dance if you want."

"I'll tell him not to. He'll listen to me, too." His eyes remained in place, but she saw him react. "Why on earth are you so stubborn about this? I thought the only thing boys wanted was to get their grubby paws on a girl. Are you just scared of it?"

Now he did look at her, just a glance and down once again. "I don't like to dance, is all."

Annelise crossed her forearms on the tabletop and set her chin atop and tried to catch his eye. "But girls love it, Houston. If you get any good at it, we'll fight like cats over you. Besides, you're the only one tall enough to dance with Katie Calhoun. I already heard her talking about it."

He began to redden. "I already danced with her. In class. She's kind of snippy."

"That's not a bad thing, necessarily. Do you like her?"

Now he was a beet. "I guess so. I like the . . . way she smells."

God that new voice of his. Basso profundo. "Do you want to kiss her?"

He looked everywhere and nowhere at once.

"I'd kiss her," said Annelise. "If I were you. She's gorgeous."

She shoved off and went out through the door, and when she elbowed back through a moment later with the shop Zenith in her arms, he was right at the table where she'd left him.

He began to shake his head again. "Uh-uh. I don't want to."

She went past him and into the little front parlor. "I'm not asking. Get in here." She set the radio on the stand beside the room's one lamp and plugged it in. She dialed the tuner to a ballroom broadcast. "I'm waiting."

Even the slide of his chair had the skid of resignation. He appeared in the doorway. "I can't dance to this. It's too fast."

She beckoned with a finger. "It's a jitterbug, it's supposed to be fast." She held her hands out and fluttered her fingers. He rolled his eyes but stepped forward and took her hands. "Did you learn the basic step to this?"

He nodded. "I wasn't any good at it, though."

"Well, let's fix that. First things first: Speaking of grubby paws, we've got to scrub these mitts of yours before the real dance Friday. With Ajax, and a Fuller brush or something. You're a regular grease monkey. Okay, I'm going to lead, at first. Just the basic box step."

He proved a fast learner. By the time "Sugar Foot Stomp" came on half an hour later, she had him whirling through a series of basic inside and outside turns and breakaways, also a more complicated wrap step.

Or he had her whirling. She could feel the flush in her face from motion and speed, and when he began to spin her of his own impulse, she felt that delicious, half-chilling jolt, right through her spine and then way down deep. He pulled her tight into a closed position as though she were not his family at all but someone entirely different. Katie Calhoun, maybe.

Her face came to his collarbone. He was hot as a new brick and she could not only see but also scent his own flush, like a twin to hers. The damp salt on his skin, she swore she could smell it and she knew she was piqued more than she should be. She put it on loneliness. She could feel the hinge of his shoulder through the thin cloth of his shirt.

She quit and curtsied when the song ended. She didn't really want to stop, and she was laughing and giddy, but also just one plaintive note or wistful lyric from tears.

Houston had his own smile, with a goofy sort of wonder she wished she could get back for herself.

"It's fun, right?"

"More than I remembered," he admitted. She'd never yet called him Huck and knew now she'd never think of him as such, not with that new voice. "So what now?"

"That's enough, for tonight. I've got to catch my breath. But we've got three more nights before the dance. If you keep on like this, Katie's going to have to fight *me* to get out on the floor with you."

By the time the big day rolled around he had indeed developed into a pretty capable hand. Annelise taught him a series of more complicated swing steps and coached him through the foxtrot and the waltz as well.

Pop seemed to get a real charge out of the two of them. He waltzed with Annelise himself a couple of times, but pleaded out of the jitterbug. "You'll be calling for the ambulance in one minute," he told her. "I was already old when the Highland fling was invented."

Friday after school she did indeed set out a scrub brush and a box of Borax. "Get that water as hot as you can. We're going to make you look like a gentleman, not some troglodyte."

"What's a troglodyte?"

"A cretin. Now get to it. I'm heading for the bath. You're next."

He didn't know what a cretin was either, but figured he got the general picture. By the time she reappeared, his fingers were as wrinkled and eerily white as the lifeless digits on the corpse in the river. Most of the grease was gone.

"Congratulations." She pointed to the little bathroom. "Now for the rest of you. And wash your hair."

He heard Pop come in a little later, heard him talking and laughing with Annelise, and knew she'd been dead right about any fanciful idea to get out of the Spring Ball with the help of that turncoat. If anything Pop was as eager to please her as anyone, and that included McKee who at least wasn't a total stooge about it. In fact, when he thought about it, Yak alone had the sidewise charm to get her to do his bidding, and not the other way around.

Pop on the other hand seemed downright in cahoots with her. He'd shown up with a jacket and tie and a pair of two-toned spectator shoes. Huck looked at him.

"Borrowed some duds from Lou Candles," he said with a beam. "He's about your size, hey?"

Mr. Candles owned the local real estate office. He was known by the local standards as a snappy dresser. "Yeah, plus about thirty pounds," said Huck.

"I thought of that. But your cousin here told me all the young guys these days are wearing bigger suits anyway."

"It's true," she said. "Out on the coast, at least."

"I don't know how to put on a tie."

"That's why you have us." She waved him toward the bedroom. "In there."

An hour later the two of them left to walk back to the school. The unfamiliar necktie felt like a leghold trap around his throat and the jacket was indeed generous for his frame, but once outfitted he'd taken a gander in the mirror and had to admit he looked pretty stylish. At least Mr. Candles had the same size feet.

"You look like a grown-up," Annelise told him. Springtime had fully arrived, the trees overhead in full leaf and the young neighborhood kids pedaling bicycles and playing baseball into the evening.

"I feel like a detective. Or maybe a gangster, in a movie."

"No, you know who you really look like? Tall as you are?"

"Abraham Lincoln?"

She gave him a shove. "Don't be ridiculous. You look like Charles Lindbergh."

He felt even taller than usual. "Are you just saying that?"

She took hold of his arm. "I would never just say that. Now start acting like him, Colonel."

The sun had dropped behind the far rim of the coulee, and dusk came on. A block from the school they walked into a streetlamp's cone of light. Raleigh popped out of the shadows.

"Whoa, if it ain't Dashiell Hammett," he said to Huck. "Nice tie." Raleigh himself had somehow come up with a pair of golf knickers and argyle socks with a matching sweater.

"You're one to talk," said Annelise.

"Shirley and some of the kids are out by the bleachers. Shirley's got a jug of the good stuff."

"Oh really," said Annelise. "Point the way."

Huck as usual was a little slow to catch on. "You mean hooch?"

"I don't mean soda pop."

Huck's nerves were already humming like overloaded wires and this new turn jumped through him like an additional surge of juice. "Jeez, you think this is a good idea?"

"Of course not," said Annelise cheerfully.

"What if we get caught?"

"We run like hell," said Raleigh. "Live a little, Huckleberry. What would Tom Sawyer do?"

"He'd get caught, is what he'd do. And thrashed."

Annelise stopped and pulled back her sleeve. Tilted her wrist toward the light behind them. "We've got a half hour before we've even got to be there." She looked at Huck. "Just a nip or two, Houston. Alcohol exists for a reason. You're nervous as a bat already and this might help."

"That's the spirit," Raleigh chimed in. Another rank stooge. God, this girl.

"Besides, Katie might be there." Annelise put her watch away.

"That's *not* helping," said Huck, but he walked along beside her with at least a bubble of curiosity rising through the dread.

Katie wasn't there, as it turned out. The only girl other than Annelise was Sharon White, the last person Huck expected to see. Otherwise just Shirley and a pair of football-addled senior lunkheads, Royce Mitchell and Bobby Duane Boyd. Bobby Duane was even now doing chin-ups off the back of the bleachers.

"Houston," said Shirley. He took a pull on the bottle in his hand. "You look like Errol Flynn's dog Spot."

Royce let out a guffaw, reached over and took the bottle from Shirley. "Suave and de-boner."

"Ignore these imbeciles," said Annelise. "Wouldn't you say, Sharon?"

"You look nice, Houston," Sharon said. She herself was not in any sort of special outfit, just her plain school clothes. "Gosh, I'm surprised your mother's letting you go. You're lucky."

"Not to change the subject," said Annelise, "but what exactly do we have for cocktail hour in this establishment?"

Bobby Duane dropped down from his chin-ups and took the bottle from Royce. "Old Quaker."

"Appropriate." She extended her arm. "May I?"

Bobby pulled the bottle to his chest with both hands, like a football he'd just intercepted. "Well, let's just see. What's in it for ol' Hero?"

"Not a thing, unless you have trouble with your homework or something. I'm sure I can get Raleigh to help."

"How 'bout you show us your bobbers?"

Royce guffawed again. Shirley slapped his leg. Even in the low light Huck could see the bottle was already half gone.

"Fat chance," said Annelise. "And for future reference, it's best to ply a girl with booze *before* you cut to the chase."

Huck turned to Sharon. "I'm surprised your dad's letting *you* go tonight."

Shirley did an exaggerated double take. "Dang, son. Suave is right." He took the hooch from Bobby and held it out. "Welcome to the men's club."

He realized Shirley hadn't seen him since his voice dropped. He glanced at the bottle and waved it along to Annelise. She took a delicate swig and passed it to Raleigh.

"He's not," Sharon told him. "Remember, I had to sit out in class? I'm pretty mad about it, actually."

"Whoa," Raleigh cut in. His own voice still hadn't made the shift and Huck found it almost impossible that he himself had sounded so young and squeaky not a week before. "What in tarnation are you doing out here, then?"

To Huck's surprise, Sharon received the bottle from Raleigh and took a very healthy pull. He could practically see the stuff burn its way down her throat, watched it light right up in her face. "He had to make a visit somewhere, and my mother took supper over to Mrs. Muldoon." She took another drink. "So I left my brothers to themselves for a while."

Shirley took the Old Quaker back. "I'll drink to that. Better be careful those brats don't rat you out, though."

"I don't care if they do. If I'm going to be grounded in advance, I may as well earn it."

"Well, if it's any help," said Huck, "my mother is sort of in the dark about it."

"You're lucky," she said again.

Shirley again offered the bottle to Huck, and Huck again declined. He and Raleigh had sneaked a cigarette of Pop's back in the winter, and the thing had lifted his head like a bottle rocket. Any similar sensation was the last thing he needed going into this dance.

"It'll put hair on your chest, son," Shirley told him. "Suit yourself, though."

Annelise and Raleigh each had another moderate slosh apiece, and they started for the gym.

"We'll be along," Royce bellowed after Annelise. "Hope you're ready to cut a rug."

Annelise did not look back. "Hope you can keep up."

"He is around the bend," said Raleigh. "I'll dance with you, though. If you don't mind a younger, slightly shorter gent." He picked that precise moment to catch his toe on a crack in the walk. He stumbled but stayed on his feet. "Who put that there?"

"Your chances are rapidly waning," she told him.

He didn't have a retort, but he did manage to hold a level line until they turned up the front walk to the school. A throng waited in the lamplight. Huck scanned the sea of heads and spotted Katie halfway up the granite steps with a couple of girls.

Her hair was slicked back, with a red flower tucked above her left ear. She glanced down and her eyes seemed to fix right on him for a split second before she looked away. No expression on her face at all, the set of her mouth like a flat horizon. He didn't know if he should feel disappointed, or let off the hook. Then her head ratcheted back, and her eyes clearly met his. She smiled. He felt his mouth move, form the word *hi*, although no sound came out.

She rolled her fingers at him and again looked away.

Annelise dug in her purse. "You're in the door, Colonel." She fished out a pack of gum and offered him a stick. "Don't blow it. And ditch the gum before you ask her to dance."

She folded a piece into her own mouth and handed one to Raleigh as well. "I can practically see the fumes on your breath," she informed him. "Like a Bunsen burner."

From inside they could hear clarinet doodles and the plucking of a bass, the shimmer of cymbals. A live dance band had come clear from Billings. Huck wondered why they weren't letting anyone through the door yet.

Raleigh folded his gum into his mouth. "You are one swell dame, California."

She patted him on the head. "If you say so, Dick Tracy." She moved away a few steps to the base of the nearest lamp. Huck watched her flip a silver compact open and tilt it into the light. She ran a lipstick around her parted mouth.

Raleigh looked at Huck. "Speaking of detectives. We need to talk."

"He call you again?"

"No, I called him."

"What?" He realized he'd just yiped for the first time since his voice deepened.

"I called him. Or tried to, anyway. I got to thinking, after you said he hung up on you that night."

"Yeah?"

Raleigh pantomimed a pipe to his lips. "Elementary, Watson. Think about it: Why would the Billings police have a dick on this? Bank jobs go to the G-men, and beyond that the good rev got himself shot in Musselshell County, not Yellowstone. Plus, what the heck kind of a name is Detective Blank? The whole thing just smelled like fish Friday. So I called up the station and asked for the guy."

"Are you nutty as a dern fruitcake?"

"Houston, you ain't getting the dern point."

Huck hardly heard him. "I ought to turn the stupid thing in and be done with it. Take the hit, and be *done* with it. The last thing we need is to go out of our way to have the police—"

"Houston. There is no Detective Blank in Billings."

Huck clammed up and glanced around. A couple of nearby kids looked on curiously. A horn blasted a few bars inside the school. He looked back to Raleigh, jerked his head out toward the darkened terrain of the lawn and started walking. Raleigh chewed his gum and followed.

"What do you mean, no Detective Blank?"

"That's what I'm telling you. Some desk sergeant answered the phone, and I told him I was returning Detective Blank's call, and he said it was no joke to waste his time with pranks. I told him I was serious, and he said somebody was pranking me, then. No Detective Blank. That wasn't a cop on the phone, Houston."

"Who the heck was it, then?"

Raleigh let his jaw drop. "Do I have to draw a picture?"

"Shit."

"Yeah. Shit."

"*Shit*. Should we just tell Cy? Turn the blasted thing over?"

"Take the hit?" Raleigh shook his head. "I don't know. Maybe?" He stared off into the darkness. His brain, the biggest thing on him, was clearly throttling like a racing engine, Old Quaker or not. "Thing is, why do they want to know what happened to the dang watch? I get that it's rare and all, but rare enough to risk getting nabbed nosing around after it? That don't make a lick of sense. These guys are crooks, for Pete's sake. Just go steal another one, right?"

A collective stir rippled in the throng at the main entrance. Kids began to move up the stairs and into the building. Huck didn't know what he should be more nervous about, Katie Calhoun or a gang of desperadoes sniffing around and impersonating the police. "Guess we're on," he said.

Raleigh belched. "Guess so."

"You drunk?"

"I don't think so. About like I had a dose of the Tincture 23, maybe."

They caught up with Annelise at the base of the steps, rejoined now by Bobby Duane and Royce who were both clearly beyond the influence of anything like cough syrup.

"Evening, ladies," said Bobby Duane. He elbowed Royce for effect and nearly knocked him over.

"Class act," said Raleigh. He offered his arm to Annelise. "Lady Ashley?"

To Huck's astonishment, Annelise stepped over and took Raleigh's arm. He felt a stab of something close to anger, then realized what it actually was. Jealousy. He looked up the steps for Katie, just in time to see her disappear into the building. Raleigh and Annelise started up, too.

She looked back at Huck. "Gum."

He walked over and spit into the bushes along the stairs, then stepped up after her. Royce and Bobby lurched along behind. The band inside started up for real now, a rendition of "Stardust," the clarinet echoing out of the gym at the far end of the hall.

"Darn," said Annelise. "I love this song."

"This song loves you, darlin'," said Bobby Duane. "You know I'm captain of the football team? Oughta lose the runt, step inside with a local legend." He hiccupped. Huck caught the fumes from two feet away.

"Sorry," said Annelise. She tightened her grip on Raleigh with a bit of theater. Huck could tell he was trying to stand as straight as possible. "I think I'll stick with someone who can actually pronounce *debonair.*"

"Suit yourself."

"I always do."

They moved up the stairs and into the foyer. The overheads were off but strings of paper lanterns crisscrossed the length of the hall, throwing a mute orange haze around the ceiling. Huck looked across the mass of heads, watched Katie and a couple of other girls enter the gym. Through the maw of the far doorway he saw other lights, spectral lights, revolving in splashed projections across the one dancing couple he could see, gliding in orbs against the slick wax on the floor. Stardust.

They neared the entry and Huck saw the reason for the slow-going. Mr. Jenkins, the school principal, stood at the double doors, admitting kids on an orderly basis. Not only that, but worse—Junior Joe Candy was right there with him. Huck glanced back, saw Bobby Duane weave. He wished he'd been up ahead with Katie when she'd gone in.

The clarinet in the gym drifted to the song's close. From this position in the hallway, the whole thing sounded remarkably like a live radio broadcast out of an actual ballroom in Chicago or Denver. Somebody onstage started talking through a microphone. He leaned forward and put his head near Annelise's. "We need to lose these dunderheads behind us."

She stood on tiptoe to look ahead. Mr. Jenkins let another batch of students through, and the dwindling line moved forward. She looked back. He felt her peppermint breath against his ear. "It'll look too obvious. Besides, we're not really with them," and she got no further because the kids just ahead went in and there they were.

Junior Joe took in Raleigh. "Nice bloomers."

Raleigh did a little pivot. His voice sounded even more wobbly at volume. "Why thanks, Officer. I somehow lost track of my caddy, though."

Mr. Jenkins cut in. "Miss Clutterbuck. I've been expecting you." He shifted to Huck. "I hope you're keeping your cousin out of trouble, Houston."

Huck was looking past him, scanning through the low spotted light for Katie. He saw her with a few other girls near the refreshment table, graceful as a greyhound. He pried his eyes back to Mr. Jenkins. "We just want to go to the dance."

One of the lunkheads behind him picked that precise moment to let off a belch, which Huck fully heard despite the amplified chatter of the emcee. He caught another whiff of alcohol, fumes that could peel paint. So did Mr. Jenkins.

"Houston, I'm going to ask you one time. Have you been drinking?"

Huck realized he had three inches at least on Mr. Jenkins. "Drinking? Let's see . . . I guess I had water with supper, 'cause we were out of milk. Oh wait, is that what you mean?"

The emcee's amplifier let out with some violent, piercing shriek, then clarified again.

"Why don't you go ahead and tell me what I mean. You aren't that sheltered."

"Are you talking about, you know, strong drink?" He glanced past Mr. Jenkins's head, saw Katie looking over her shoulder at the door.

"Quit stalling, squirt." Junior Candy had sidled shoulder-to-shoulder with the principal to completely block the doorway. "You smell what I smell?"

"Answer the question, Huck," said Mr. Jenkins. "Tell me the truth."

Please, God, please. "I've never had a drop of anything in my life. That is the truth."

"Well, somebody here has. And Miss Clutterbuck does come to us as a bit of a known quantity."

Annelise still had Raleigh's arm. By chance or for all Huck knew actual magic, the prattle out of the microphone ceased at that precise moment. "Actually," she said, "you don't know the slightest thing about me."

Annelise had the remarkable ability to seem utterly aloof and rapier-sharp in the same breath. She hadn't spoken loudly at all, but something about that flat, poised delivery sent a chill even through Huck. Junior Joe was clearly a little unnerved, too, shifting back and forth on his feet, eyeballs scanning up and down over his cousin's outfit. It occurred to Huck that the deputy's head was probably swamped with dirty thoughts. His cousin wasn't the only known quantity.

"Be that as it may," Mr. Jenkins allowed, "somebody's been drinking. I can smell it."

"We can smell it," Junior echoed. "Loud and clear."

The band started up again, a slower song with a prominent piano line. Huck had heard it before, although he couldn't conjure the name now. Duke Ellington, he was pretty sure. Katie was still with her girlfriends, still at the punch table. Still looking this way.

Annelise unhooked herself from Raleigh. She leaned toward Junior.

"Smell it loud and clear is a mixed metaphor," she said, "or something," and put her painted mouth into a defiant ring. Huck knew her eyes must be locked right on to the deputy's, because Junior Joe looked instead straight to Huck, then to the lanterns on the ceiling, then anyplace at all except back to the gaze of this beautiful, brazen, ice-cold and incalculable little minx.

She blew a long breath of air at him. "Satisfied?"

Junior may have been unnerved, but Mr. Jenkins actually laughed. "What about these two behind you?"

"They're on their own."

His gaze shifted past her to Bobby and Royce. Huck heard some minor commotion at his back. "All right then. You three can head on in."

"They most certainly cannot."

The voice came seemingly disembodied out of the hallway, and for a moment Huck wondered if it were merely a figment of his imagination. But no. Right at the eleventh hour, things truly were awry. He knew because Annelise had whipped around at the sound and confirmed with the look on her face exactly what Huck feared. Mother.

With Pastor White, it turned out. She pushed past Royce and Bobby Duane and took hold of Huck's arm, and for the first time it was all he could do not to wrench it away. "Not these two, anyway. Raleigh is not under my roof."

"You can't do this," Annelise said.

"I certainly can, my dear." She nearly had to yell above the piano number's rising finale. "I have a responsibility." She turned to Mr. Jenkins. "You, sir, are running a dance hall for children. Thank God Pastor White brought it to my attention, since nobody else had the courtesy to. I suppose you're offering them liquor, to boot?"

Now this was rich. "Mrs. Finn, I can assure you this function is completely chaperoned and entirely in the students' best interest—"

"*Best interest?*"

Applause rippled once more from the gym as the song finished.

"Mr. Jenkins, do you mean to tell me it's any more than a hop, skip, and jump from the dance hall to the saloon to that house of ill fame out on the tracks? Do you genuinely not see a connection?"

This was not Mr. Jenkins's first encounter with Mother, Huck knew that. Huck again looked toward the punch table. Katie was no longer there.

"Mrs. Finn," said Mr. Jenkins, "we prefer to think of this in an educational way, as a formal experience. A way to teach social skills to young adults. Like it or not, couples have been dancing together since the beginning of time."

"That may well be, but you're not turning any son of mine into some dance hall lecher. Or my niece into Salome."

The band launched into another swing number. Pastor White was shaking his head at Bobby and Royce, both of whom looked, despite jackets and ties, like they'd fallen off a turnip truck. "Garbage in," he said, "garbage out."

"Children," said Mother, "Pastor White has offered to drive us home."

"I'm not going anywhere," said Annelise.

Mother still had her grip on Huck. She looked at Mr. Jenkins. "I am this girl's guardian, and I forbid her to participate. On moral grounds. Do I make myself clear?"

Mr. Jenkins turned to Annelise, this time with something like a change of tune. Or a shift of allegiance. "I'm sorry, miss. You'd better go."

Annelise turned to Raleigh and gave him a little curtsy. "I hate to run. Go cut a rug." She pushed past Huck and started down the hall.

Huck took one last look into the revolving light of the gym. He couldn't see her, though. He reckoned he should've known something like this would happen.

Mother began to pull him into motion but stopped up short with barely a step taken. She leaned toward Bobby and Royce. "You boys should be ashamed. You smell like a distillery."

"Sorry, ma'am," Royce mumbled. Bobby actually looked green to Huck, at least in the low light from the paper lanterns.

Mother turned back to the gymnasium door. Both Raleigh and Junior Joe had seized the moment and made themselves scarce, but Mr. Jenkins evidently didn't have the option. Mother looked right at him. "I rest my case."

5

"Is there really a brothel in town?"

Huck was no longer surprised by anything to come out of her mouth. They each held a piece of linkage in place on the front end of the tractor. "Sort of. A little way out of town, really. I'm pretty sure Shirley's been."

"Wow. Guess it still is the Wild West out here. I'm surprised your mother and Pastor White don't lead the charge down there, too."

Pop came out of the barn with a socket box. "If they tried that they'd have a riot on their hands and they know it. Too many ornery young bucks working in the coal seam. Without the cathouse to take the edge off, there'd be a fistfight on every corner."

"So it's a necessary evil, then."

"It's a necessary something. Pressure valve, I guess."

"And the bluenoses just look the other way? After last night, I have a hard time believing that."

"Oh, they'll harp about it, no question." Pop ran a nut down onto the spindle. "Like any vice. But push comes to shove, they'd have to pretty much eliminate erections to make it go away completely."

"Heaven forbid," said Annelise brightly.

Huck felt that old flush in his face. "Guess we should've figured where Pastor White got himself off to last night. When we saw Sharon, I mean."

"I'd have run interference if I'd known," Pop told him. He slid a cotter pin through the castle and reached for a screwdriver. "I reckon they guessed I wouldn't play along on this one, though, because they sure kept me out of the sewing circle."

Pastor White had driven them out here to the ranch the night before, then went back to town to let Pop know not to expect them. Pop wasn't usually one to rock the boat where Mother was concerned, but he may well have gotten his dander up with the pastor alone.

"All right, I'm going to fire this thing. Why don't you two drive over to the hay yard with a couple of poles and restring the gate before the cows get in."

"I think Aunt Gloria wanted me to come back inside after I helped you here," Annelise said.

Pop looked at her. "That what you want to do?"

"Well, no. But I'm supposed to be choosing my battles."

"I'll fight this one for you. High time somebody stood up for normal life around here."

Ten minutes later Huck steered the truck down the two-track toward the base of the bluff at the east end of the ranch. "Hang on," he said, and put his foot hard into the pedal before hitting the grade to the table. The track was dry as chalk even now in the second week of May and the dust rolled behind them like ash. Tools and general ranch equipage bounced in the back.

He drove down the edge of the wheat field along the lip of the bluff. Pigweed had already sprouted across the open expanse, with very little sign that grain had ever grown here at all. "Mormon crickets got the crop last year," he told her. "That's why there ain't much stubble out there."

"What are Mormon crickets?"

"Like locusts, in the Bible? Giant hoppers, millions of them. They ate this whole dern wheat crop, eighty acres, in less than a day. The field was just black with them."

Annelise looked across the field, out to where the far side of the table tilted slightly with the contour of the land. "Why on earth do you keep this place? It just seems like so much . . . trouble, I guess."

Huck had never considered this. "I'm not sure. Habit?"

She laughed and he realized it *was* a funny answer, even if he hadn't intended it as such. He liked that he could make her laugh, especially after last night's sour conclusion. She'd ridden out to the ranch in Pastor White's car in withering silence, despite the pastor's initial attempts to engage the both of them with a sort of forced camaraderie.

Huck had at least tried to be polite, for both their sakes. He'd been disappointed, to a degree, but the truth of it was, Raleigh's news about the fraudulent Detective Blank scraped at his nerves like a cocklebur. It was pretty difficult to worry about much else.

Annelise on the other hand fairly steamed, and in the end she prevailed. Most of the drive had elapsed in uncomfortable quiet.

He steered down off the table at the far side of the field, then stopped again on the lower ground. The lip of the bluff unfurled to the south with the plunge of a cliff. Huck set the brake. "Want to see something really wild?"

They walked down the base of the wall to a stone lid thirty feet overhead, a shelflike protrusion telegraphing into space six feet off the vertical plane of the bluff. He pointed straight ahead at the carvings, etched into the flat about eye level.

"They're shield figures."

"Where?" Annelise asked, then her eyes put the faint images into her mind. "Oh my."

Huck picked his way across the jumbled ground to the most prominent figure and ran his finger around the scribe of the circle, an image two feet across and containing a starlike etching within. A smaller circle, obviously meant to be the head of a man with a bonnet or sheaf of hair, perched above the upper edge, and another oblong shape jutted at about ten o'clock from the main circle. He pointed out a few others, similar in pattern but fainter, muted by time.

"From Indians, I guess," she said softly.

"Really old ones. Before white people and horses. And guns." He pointed to the stone lip above. "This was a buffalo jump."

She squinted overhead, the jut of the stone sharp and strikingly three-dimensional against the blue sky beyond. She laughed and looked back down. "It's making me dizzy." She stepped forward and put one delicate finger on the groove in the stone. "What's a buffalo jump?"

"They used to stampede a bison herd toward a cliff like that. Because of the way the ground is up there, you can't see it's about to drop off until you're right up on it. By then it's too late."

She looked up again, then back to the ground at their feet. "Back in them wild old days?"

He heard the sputter of the tractor winding along on the table above. "That's the truth. Them *really* wild days."

"What did you call these? Shield figures?"

He ran his finger partway around the rim of the large circle. "It's a warrior, behind a shield. This is his club." He pointed to the oblong shape. "We can come out and dig around later—the ground's full of bones. Parts of buffalo skulls."

Annelise looked around at the ground. The tractor idled up, then down. "You've dug up bones before? Where are they now?"

"The skulls I have down at the barn. Most of the others just disappear. I guess animals drag them off. I've found arrowheads, too."

Ten or a dozen points in the past few years, most of them not much larger than the leaf of an ash tree, but once he found what had to be a spearhead, pecked out of pink chert and fully five inches long even with the tip broken off. His history teacher at school, Mr. Dyson, told him it might be many thousands of years old.

"You know a road crew found mammoth skeletons not too long ago?" he'd said. "With big points like this one still stuck in the bones?"

"Mammoths? Like elephants? In Montana?"

"New Mexico. But they lived here, too."

Huck had never much thought about mammoths, but he knew plenty of dinosaur bones had been found in Montana. He'd somewhat averted his eyes from the subject—Mother believed the big femurs and giant petrified eggs had been planted in the earth by the devil himself to confuse people about the age of the world.

"Remember what Yak said about Charles Darwin?" he said to Annelise.

"One cold son of a bitch, I believe."

He looked away from the most intact glyph to one of the fainter remnants nearby, an image nearly ghostlike now after eons of wind and weather licking at the sandstone wall. He wondered in the moment how much time had passed between the first etching and the second. A thousand years? Two thousand?

"Ma's locked horns with the school before, you know. About evolution." The very word still made him nervous.

"Small surprise. But forget that. The real question is, how are *you* going to live your life in the here and now? You may be building your airplane on the sly, but the second you lift off and fly, the secret's out. Everyone's going to know. Including your mother."

He nodded. "I try not to think about it."

"That doesn't change anything. Clock's ticking."

She held up the big watch on her wrist for emphasis, and he felt a stab of guilt, the watch in his pocket jabbing yet again. It flashed in his mind just to haul it out and show it to her, get at least that guilty secret partly in the light of day. Except that would make Annelise a part of it, too. What she didn't know couldn't hurt her.

A little later they walked back over the rough ground to the REO. The wind was coming up out of the west, strong enough to blow loose grit through the air and start dead, spindly vegetation rolling and bouncing across the earth. "Are those tumbleweeds?" she asked.

He told her they were.

She turned suddenly and looked back once more at the cliff. Now with the wind, he realized they could no longer hear the tractor up above, and the air currents carried the rising dust in the other direction.

"A buffalo jump." She looked at him with a crinkle at her eye. "It's an odd name. Sounds like something more fun than it actually would've been."

"Probably was fun, for the Indians. Exciting, anyway. More fun than tackling a dern mammoth, I bet."

"This is a spooky place," she said. "You know that?"

He told her he did.

"You know what else?" She made a theatrical wave at the cliff, a wave that seemed to take in the endless expanse of broken, rolling ground in every direction. "I never thought I'd see it this way, but this is magnificent. Truly."

He knew what she meant about the eerie energy of the jump, as though the shields and the bones and the very rocks themselves still whispered and hummed with skulking spirits, actors from the past that couldn't leave and never slept. But he'd never much thought about the endless land beyond. From this vantage he could see the jagged, snowbound teeth of the Absarokas to the west, rising in the haze.

"Are we really going to fly over all this?"

"Yes," she told him. "We really are."

Juno I

1

By the last week of May the ship had largely come together, right down to the gauges in the cockpit. The stick already controlled the flaps in the tail, although wing and fuselage were not yet mated given the confines of the shop. But they'd added aluminum pigment to the last batch of dope and colored the whole ship silver, in the manner of Colonel Lindbergh's famous plane.

Or Miss Earhart's latest Lockheed, as Annelise pointed out. Huck knew she was right—he'd seen a Movietone reel in the Rialto about the Honolulu crash and she was definitely flying an aluminum-bodied Electra, a state-of-the-art ship indeed. Just two days ago, the radio in the shop reported that she planned to resume her attempt around the equator, departing this time not from California but from Miami, Florida. But in Big Coulee, Montana, there wasn't much left to do until an engine appeared.

McKee turned his attention to the Big Fifty Sharps. He'd badgered Pop for two months for the gun's original kit, and Pop finally sent him out to the ranch to rummage through some crates stored in the barn. Sure enough, he came back with a bullet mold and forty empty brass cases.

"We're in business."

Huck was sharpening saw blades at the workbench. He jerked a thumb at the fuselage, angled jauntily on its front axle and taking up most of the shop floor. "Unlike that there old mothballed crate."

"We're on temporary hiatus, is all. Let's get your mind off it."

One thing not on his mind lately was the mysterious Detective Blank, or whoever he really was. Frustrating as the absence of an engine might be, that other fraught situation had tempered considerably when the calls to the shop ended. Raleigh hadn't gotten any either since the day after the Spring Ball. That was nearly two weeks ago already.

Now the phone happened to sound in the office, where Annelise was listening for a radio update on Miss Earhart, and his blue mood seemed to revive that dormant dread, the folly of assuming they were totally in the clear simply because the guy had laid off calling for a spell. He heard her pick up.

McKee was at the scrap-lead bin, sorting through cutoff battery terminals and discarded wheel weights.

Huck shuffled over, just a hop and a skip now from the office door. He strained to hear Annelise on the phone, but her voice was a mere murmur and he couldn't make out what she said. She went silent a moment and his heart hiccupped, then beat on when she started back up. Then she laughed, a real peal echoing out into the shop, and her voice became more animated. Evidently someone familiar on the line.

McKee was still rifling through the scrap.

"Did you really work for John Browning down in Utah?" said Huck.

"John Moses? Yeah, you bet. Right about your age when I started. We had power hammers, milling machines, lathes—the whole shootin' match, so to speak."

"So what was he like? John Browning?"

McKee gave him a sly look. "Truth of it? Dead, by the time I got there."

"Oh. So you didn't *know him*, know him."

"I did not. Ain't above letting people think so, though—makes a better story." He rattled the scrap in the can. "Let's hit it."

They melted the soft metal down in the forge out back. They tried casting a handful of bullets straight out of the pot, but the composition was so soft that the sprue cutter damaged the formed slugs before they were even out of the mold.

"What now?"

"Trial and error."

They were back at the bench weighing a ratio of lead to tin when Annelise came in.

"That somebody calling with an engine?" McKee said.

"Nope. Totally unrelated."

"Care to join our metallurgy tutorial?"

"Is it for the airplane?"

"Not directly." McKee pincered an empty brass cartridge from the block on the bench. "We've gone into the ammo business."

"Oh, brother. I'd rather do homework. And that's saying something."

"Now come on. You might learn something."

She looked back and forth between the two of them. "Life's short. Why spend it dabbling in the past?"

"Because you might stumble onto something that helps you in the here and now. Just stick around."

They started with a one-to-sixteen ratio of lead to tin, which still proved too soft. McKee kept at it, working up the mix a bit at a time. Finally, with dusk starting to settle and sparks leaping above the forge, he got the hardness to cut a proper sprue.

"Progress," he said. He set the still-warm slug in her palm.

"Holy moly. It's like a railroad spike."

"With a hell of a charge behind it. Designed to drop a one-ton buff at a thousand yards. A bit of an exaggeration, but not by much."

She shook her head. "I still don't get it."

* * *

The next day he bought a hundred rifle primers and a pound of coarse-grain Hercules gunpowder in the hardware store. After school he showed Houston how a paper-patched bullet went together and set him on wrapping the big projectiles while he primed the brass cases.

He worked up a spread of test loads, starting with a ninety-grain charge and increasing in five-grain increments to the one-ten maximum. Five rounds per sample. He seated a patched bullet into the mouth of the last case and asked Huck how the breeze looked outside.

Houston ran out and right back in again. "Dead calm."

McKee pointed to the ceiling. "Somebody likes us."

They drove out to the little homegrown rifle range by the town dump. "Ain't the Butte Schuetzen house," McKee said, "but I reckon she'll suffice."

He sent Huck downrange to the backer board with a sheet of paper and a stapler while he set a sandbag and assorted other gear on the bench. Houston jogged back and McKee handed him a wad of cotton. He gave one to Annelise as well. "Tear that in half and plug your ears. Then clamp your hands over that."

Houston looked at him. "How loud is this thing?"

McKee was stuffing his own ears. "Like a stick of dynamite. Stay behind me."

He started with the heaviest load first. Slid the big brass cartridge into the chamber and cranked the breech closed. He flipped the ladder off the tang, rested the forearm across the sandbag, and pulled the big hammer back. He settled into the rifle and peered through the aperture, set the trigger and seemed to sit and hold his breath a moment.

The roar of the rifle hit her in the body as though the actual air rippled with some reactionary, concussive force. She jumped like a puppet with its strings yanked, watched McKee undulate hard with the recoil. Heavy white smoke drifted like a fallen cloud.

McKee came up out of the gun. He rolled his shoulder around. "Anybody says this rifle kicks has lace on his underpants." He looked at Houston. "Your turn."

"How bad is it?"

"One big thump. You'll find out, but not right now—actually better to figure out the group with one shooter."

He worked through the first three five-shot clusters, swamping the bore after each round with a cleaning rod, then left the last two loads for a different session altogether. He rubbed his shoulder.

They walked out to the paper. None of the groups looked bad, but the one-hundred-grain load showed the most promise—three holes in a cloverleaf, with the other two off by about an inch. He forked two fingers and put one each on the fliers. "That's why I'm quitting. Could be the load, but more probably old-fashioned shooter's fatigue."

The next afternoon had a stiff wind off the plains, so they loaded more ammo and came back on the third morning with the breeze settled. McKee fired two more one-hundreds at the original group and clover-leafed those as well, then got slightly bigger spreads with the next two loads.

"One century it is." He pointed at Annelise. "Want to learn how to shoot?"

She snorted. "Not with that cannon."

McKee laughed. "Good answer." He handed the big Sharps to Huck. "Brace yourself."

School let out the first week of June, just in time for the carnival to arrive. Also the tent revival.

"Golly," Annelise whispered to Huck when Pastor White first made the announcement from the pulpit. "What a coinkydink."

Aunt Gloria heard her and glared.

Later, out in front of the bungalow, she said, "God doesn't have time for coincidence, Annelise." She had that disconnected glaze over her eyes that Annelise had come to recognize, even squinting as she was against the light. "But He does work in mysterious ways. This carnival will no doubt bring people from miles around, and the Good News will be right there to battle temptation and debauchery."

"Temptation and debauchery," McKee echoed. He shook his head like a matron at a temperance convention.

Aunt Gloria paused at the front door and looked back. "That is what I said, Mr. McKee. I'm sure you've seen a carnival before. Temptation and debauchery. The devil's playground. It's already giving me a headache." She pulled the screen door shut behind her.

McKee lifted his eyebrows at Annelise. "The devil's playground. I can hardly wait."

The rides and booths and assorted personnel arrived in a regular caravan of stenciled and colored and festooned trucks and trailers, two days before the start of festivities. By Thursday evening the Ferris wheel and carousel were nearly together, along with another ride featuring miniature airplanes. Annelise and Huck walked down and took a gander when they finished dinner.

"Oooo, Houston. Gonna earn your wings with the kiddies?"

"Nope. I have a real airplane. Provided a dern motor ever turns up." He saw her absently clicking the outer bezel of her watch around. "I'm glad you decided to stay on a little longer, even though you don't really have to—wouldn't feel right to get up in the air without you. If we ever get to that point."

She'd done the high school graduation walk last Saturday, and when Huck saw her in her cap and gown he had the sobering realization that she probably wasn't long for Big Coulee. But surprisingly, after three months in the boondocks, his cousin wasn't as inspired to beat a hasty departure as they'd all expected—including her bemused parents. She'd already talked to Pop about staying on at least through the end of summer.

Now she looked up. "There's no *if* about it. And *when* it happens, I wouldn't miss it."

"Well, it's sure going to make it easier to, you know, earn my wings."

He saw a grin tug at her mouth. "I'm sure you'd have figured it out somehow. Happy to help, though."

"I thought you'd want to get back to your beau as soon as you could."

"Oh, I'm still struggling over that, a bit. But time and distance, you know . . ." She held up the watch at her wrist. "I do wish I could get this back to him, but I'm sure not going to risk losing it in the mail. He knows it's in good hands. Knows we have an airplane to launch, too."

She shifted her eyes to him, and he saw that crystal-hard glint. "Besides, my mother may have been able to ship me off on a whim, but she can't just order me back on another. She can't *make me* do much of anything anymore."

They'd kept walking on past the New Deal, could see the Four-square church against the evening sky up ahead. He said, "Your own ma might not be able to make you do much, but I reckon mine'll pretty much *make* the both of us go to the revival."

The timing of which, it turned out, proved to be neither coincidence nor miracle. The meeting's star attraction had gone to Bible school with Pastor White in Kentucky and answered the call to arms in direct response to the invading carnival. By Friday afternoon a great white tent had gone up on the ball field adjacent to the church, a bit of a controversy because the Miners' Union team had planned to play a franchise out of Billings over the weekend and now had to reschedule. But the church owned the ball diamond, so that was the beginning and the end of it.

Mother ushered the lot of them across town at four o'clock, including McKee. In typical fashion, he seemed mainly amused about the whole thing.

"I haven't had a dose of religion in a thousand years," he said. He was walking just behind Pop and Mother and just ahead of Huck and Annelise. They could hear chortling from the rides and the looping, dizzy whirl of a calliope trickling up to Main Street from the fairgrounds.

"I have been praying for you, Mr. McKee," Mother told him.

"Oh, I need it, ma'am."

The joint attractions had indeed pulled throngs from the outlands. Main Street was lined nose to tail with vehicles, a few later-model sedans and coupes but mainly rickety farm trucks and workaday jalopies that had clearly been bouncing over the county roads for years. Huck found himself clenching his fists over every Model A they passed, practically praying one would crack up on somebody's dark ride home and thus provide him with a cheap motor.

They came level to the Rialto and heard the first sounds of wailing go up from the ball diamond, the voices blending at first with the fainter shrieks off the rides back at the fairground. Then what sounded like the dramatic flourish of an organ, also somehow bleeding into and back out of the calliope's piping swirl.

"Is that an echo off the buildings or something?" Annelise asked.

The sounds from the fairground further receded a few steps along, and the wailing and blast of the voices ahead came on stronger. She looked sideways at Houston and whispered. "Steel yourself."

Mother had Pop's arm as they walked, and she did not look back, but her hearing could at times seem nothing short of supernatural. "You steel yourself, Annelise. God's calling to you, too."

Now she didn't whisper at all. "I wasn't talking to you, actually."

Huck felt some constriction at his throat, like the anxious rise of his own gorge. He kept his eyes on Pop, who patted Mother's hand on his arm but otherwise seemed to be looking at a banged-up Model A Tudor at the curb. Maybe he was praying for a wreck himself.

Mother kept her pace ahead now, as though she hadn't heard after all, which somehow made Huck even more nervous. Worse, Annelise didn't let it go.

"I said, I wasn't talking to you."

"Well, now that you are," said Mother, "I'd like to remind you that you have a choice to make, Annelise. We all do."

"None of this is my choice, actually. If you want to get right to brass, people like Houston and me? We're hostages." Huck couldn't disagree with her, but now his gorge really rose.

"*Train up a child in the way he should go*," Mother quoted. "That is my job, and I will not be caught sleeping."

"By all means," said Annelise, "give it a rest."

McKee looked back at her, shaking his head with what Huck assumed was actual shock. "My, you're a snippy thing this evening."

She *was* mouthier than usual, maybe in simple reaction to the hue and cry coming off the ball field. The racket from the tent had supplanted the din of the carnival altogether. McKee was still in his stride but still looking at her.

"What?" she said. "I'm just trying to paint a picture."

"I'll paint you a picture," McKee told her. "A portrait. Called *Still Life, with Brat*."

Pop practically roared, which made Huck practically jump. But nervous or not, he felt his mouth twist into a grin. Annelise sneered, though he got the sense even this was a mask for a laugh.

"Why thank you, Mr. McKee," Mother told him. "There may be hope for you yet."

"Do you think, brothers and sisters, that the *depression* besetting this nation, that these dark and dire straits we have *allowed* ourselves to sail into, blind on bootleg booze and wanton lust, do you think these are unconnected one to another? Do you think our actions, our thoughts and our deeds and even our very national character, do you think these things play out with no *consequence?*"

"*NO,*" roared the crowd in response, with a few *Amens* and *Tell it, brothers* bursting up here and there like small geysers in the sea of congregants.

"*NO!*" the minister roared back, throwing a violent uppercut at the air as though breaking the insolent jaw of Lucifer himself. "*And all God's people said?*"

"*AMEN,*" thundered the crowd.

They'd been in the tent for an hour now, and while it was full when they'd arrived, it had become increasingly so in the meantime. Annelise could feel the pressure of the throng at her back as much as she could see the density of the mass before her. More women than men but plenty of the latter, too, the former in tattered farmhouse shifts and some in their Sunday frocks, and most of the men in coveralls rather than town clothes. The air outside had the swelter of summer, but here in these packed confines with the pitch and agitation of the crowd and the utter lack of air, she felt as though she'd plunged right into the spuming heart of a caldera.

The preacher on the stage had a microphone on a stand. An organist off to the side blasted dramatic flourishes. Annelise hadn't caught the evangelist's name but he was a firebrand in the usual manner, with a mop of flying hair and rolled shirtsleeves and a necktie that had come loose in the course of his jumping and slashing, sweat running into his eyes like blood from the brow of Christ in Gethsemane.

He paced like a lion and dragged the microphone stand along with him. O, that mane. "Let me tell you, brothers and sisters, let me tell you. Our ship of state was once piloted by God Almighty, and our seas were calm . . ."

People had their hands in the air, heads bowed or wrenched upward toward the sailcloth's soaring peak, eyes screwed shut on some and pried ecstatically wide on others, the gush and babble and staccato yammering of eerie syllables surging and responding and subsiding again into the murmur of raptured bliss, or the hum of some dreamlike state. Aunt Gloria kept her hands raised. A little earlier, her mouth had issued its own odd torrent, and like the language itself, the voice flowing forth was not entirely hers.

". . . our passage tranquil, as we sowed the seeds of righteousness and reaped the great rewards of placing the Lord at the tiller. Our nation was *buoyant* . . ."

"Amen . . ."

". . . our fields were *fertile* . . ."

"*Amen* . . ."

". . . our coffers were *full*. FULL, brothers and sisters, because we knew the *FEAR* of God, and we felt the love of Christ, and we earned the *FULLNESS* of the Spirit. Amen?"

The crowd roared in response. The organ blared. Annelise felt herself swoon, and she knew the broiling density of the air and the packed-in closeness of the crowd had begun to fog her senses like ether. McKee and Houston stood on either side, hemmed right against her. She could feel the heat off both of them, practically taste their trickling sweat. She shook her head hard. She looked straight up and tried to find some oxygen.

"But, ladies and gentlemen. Brothers and sisters. This nation of ours has chosen a different course."

The organ again.

"We have chosen a different *captain*. This *nation* of ours has gone from a ship of righteousness to a ship of *fools*.

"*FOOLS*, my friends, on a *SINKING VESSEL*, a vessel not known by the fruitful yields of the blessed but by the *BARREN SOIL* of a dust bowl. By *PLAGUES* of locust and drought, ushered by the *HANGOVER* of debauchery, in *DEFIANCE* of the laws of God and what was once a Christian land."

The organ blasted, the *Amen*s sounded, and a general stir rippled in the crowd, a roil of anguish and agreement. Annelise shut her eyes and pleaded for air. Amelia's silver Electra flashed in her mind, Amelia and her smelling salts. That's what she needed now.

"We did not need repeal. We did not need repeal. No. We needed *repentance*." The firebrand's voice had dropped now to what might as well have been a whisper, and he hunched over his microphone like a monk atop a candle stub.

"My friends, the ripe fruit of sin does not appear as poison, not at first. When Eve took that bite from her own apple that fateful day, six thousand long years ago, that ripe perfect apple, well. The first flavor on the tongue did not appear bitter. And *sweet* it may have been, but *poison* it surely was, and we've been writhing in the grip of that pollution ever since."

With his voice ratcheted down and the crowd supplicant and the sweltering compression of the tent pushing at her hazy brain, Annelise swore she heard running rivulets of sweat, trickling like groundwater in the depths of a cave. Then in a moment of both stupefaction and clarity she realized she was hearing again the hushed whisper of tongues, like the flickering presence of spirits.

"WE HAVE DECOMMISSIONED ALMIGHTY GOD AND HANDED THE TILLER TO THE DEVIL," the lion roared, and a piercing squall out of the microphone stabbed like a shriek out of hell. *"WE HAVE CONVERTED OUR MISSION SHIP TO A PLEASURE LINER, A PARTY BOAT SO HEAVILY LADEN WITH GOD-HATING, SOUL-CRIPPLING, WHISKEY-SOAKED WASTRELS, SO TOTALLY FREIGHTED WITH DOGS AND SORCERERS AND WHOREMONGERS, SO BLIND TO OUR OWN SELFISH COURSE, WE HAVE FAILED TO SEE LIGHTHOUSE OR BUOY OR HAZARD, AND WHEN THE SHIP RAN AGROUND AND THE PARTY ENDED, WE REALIZED THAT GOD was no longer on board."*

The fever in the crowd spiked again, and now people were not only crying out in agreement or in tongues but also actually crying out, sobbing and wailing in guilt or repentance or maybe pure divine passion. Packed in as the throng was, a sudden surge rolled through the lines, and Annelise felt herself somehow lifted and then set down again three or four feet back, along with everyone around her.

The preacher jumped off the stage and away from the microphone, and though he was still yelling somewhere up front, the general din made it impossible to catch what he was saying. Some of the people around her craned their necks to see what was going on, but Annelise wasn't nearly tall enough. She looked at Huck. Even he was on his tiptoes. She nudged him in the ribs.

He leaned and put his mouth near her ear. "Somebody fell over and started thrashing."

People started singing in the forward ranks, then clapping along, and the organist joined in. *"Give me that old-time religion. Give me that old-time religion . . ."*

Soon the entire throng sang, the collective voice drowning even the ardor of the organ. Annelise felt her hands clap together and she observed them as though they were from some far-off place, watched them clap in time to the hymn. Her mouth moved with the words as well, although she couldn't say whether she truly sang along.

"Give me that old-time religion. It's good enough for me . . ."

The lion was back on the stage, back to his microphone, leading the song. Annelise felt the sting of sweat in her eyes. She was going to pass out if she didn't get into open air. She turned to McKee but McKee had vanished, as though he and he alone had been snatched away.

She turned back to Houston. Aunt Gloria was on the other side of him, both hands in the hot air above her head. She couldn't see Uncle Roy at all. Annelise reached up and put her arm around her cousin's flushed neck, and he put his head down near her mouth. "I need air."

She felt his arm circle and hold her beneath her ribs, and they were pushing their way through the crowd.

3

"I'm actually pretty furious at myself," she told him. They were at the lunch counter in the café drinking Cokes, listening to Bing Crosby on the radio. *Pennies from Heaven.*

"What for?"

"Getting so dizzy in the head, like some complete twit."

"Jeepers, you weren't the only one. I saw 'em carry five or six people out. Suffocating, probably. I dern near was."

"Still. I'd like to think of myself as a little tougher stock." She rattled her ice cubes around. "The sugar's helping."

They'd emerged from the dense air of the revival into full twilight, which meant they'd been inside the tent a few hours at least. She'd lost track of time, she knew that, and uncharacteristically hadn't ever thought to keep an eye on Blix's watch. Now the fragments of the whole thing kept reeling through her mind.

"Do you want some food? Pop's got credit here."

She shook her head. "I'm still a little woozy."

Something else occurred to her. She spoke around an ice cube, her own teeth like a painful miracle. "What happened to Yak?"

"Not sure. I didn't notice he was gone myself, until we went to leave."

She pivoted on her stool. "What on earth does your dad make of it all? I can't help wondering."

Even Houston seemed to speculate. "He's in a weird spot, I guess. He wants to do right by my ma, and she needs a lot of help, but . . ." He shook the ice in his glass, stared at the ceiling as though the right words might appear. Finally he turned his head to her. "Pop moved me into town to get me off the ranch. Into normal life, I guess."

Annelise nodded, slow as the melt in her mouth. She was beginning to see the light. "Guess I should've known."

"Well, my ma likes it out there, besides anything else."

"I'm sorry, Houston."

He started a little. "Sorry for what?"

Even her smile felt apologetic. "Just that it's so complicated."

Bing Crosby faded away, and Houston stood up from the counter. "Tell you what," he said, "we don't get some real pennies from heaven around these parts, we won't be keeping anybody out on the ranch." He shook the ice around in his glass again. "I don't think Pop prays for much, but I bet he does pray for rain."

They went out into the blue dusk and down the backstreets toward the fairgrounds. They could hear the calliope, but fainter somehow, in and out of the strains of some other music, which grew louder and louder the closer they got.

"They're having a dance," Annelise said. A band had set up on the little gazebo at the center of the grounds, playing a jitterbug that must have been original, or maybe too new to have reached her ears through the local radio stations. She took him by the arm. "Don't even try to talk your way out of it."

A couple of songs later the band took a break, and they walked with the other dancing couples off the portable floor and back to the lawn. He'd whirled and spun and rotated her as though they were two parts of a gyro, and she'd gone from blearily dissipated to blissfully dizzy in no time. He had the sense to keep right with it.

They started off down the line of game booths heading for the Ferris wheel and ran smack into Shirley and Raleigh. "Well, if it ain't Fred and Ginger," said Raleigh. "Darling, how are you?"

"I'm just fine, Raleigh."

"You two cut a rug like nobody's business," said Shirley. "Hope it don't get back to Mrs. Finn and the good reverend."

"Oh, they're indisposed." She glanced at Houston. "Back at that other carnival. I don't think they'll be leaving anytime soon."

Shirley flashed a bottle. "That's what we want to hear."

They walked out through the dark toward the train depot. She and Shirley and Raleigh passed the whiskey between them a few times. Houston, as ever, declined. They headed toward the back of the grain elevator, where a bunch of kids were already drinking. Annelise spotted Katie Calhoun. Evidently Houston did as well, because the next thing she knew he was seizing the bottle from Raleigh and pulling down way too big a hit.

He came out of it sputtering.

Shirley hooted. "Easy there, chief. They don't call it firewater for nothing."

Annelise knew he'd been avoiding Katie since the Spring Ball. "Just enough for courage," she told him, and they went ahead to join the others.

Half an hour later he still hadn't screwed up any courage, although it wasn't for lack of alcohol. He'd gone off with Raleigh, and by the time they ambled back her cousin was clearly well along in his cups. He leaned against her.

"I don't know why I never did this before." He already had a slur.

"Those sound like famous last words." She herself was a little tipsy, as much from missing dinner as actual drink. She realized now that they should've eaten in the café. She should have hit the water closet, too—all the Coca-Cola and melted ice and now hooch had her pressurized like a dirigible.

"We need to get you some food."

"Nuh-uh," he said. "I'm going to talk to Katie."

Hoo boy. "Houston, there's sort of a fine line here—"

"What? You were right. What's there to be afraid of? I see it now. She'll know I'm no Goody Two-shoes, okay? I mean, I'm not at the revival, am I? I'm right here." He hiccupped a little. "Drinking."

Lawdy she had to pee. She looked around for Raleigh. "Wait right here. *Don't* drink anything else."

She dragged Raleigh back a moment later. "He's already half in the bag, and I have to run back to the carnival for a bit. I'll get him some food, but I'm *ordering* you to keep him on the straight and narrow till I get back."

"Aye, aye, Captain," Raleigh said, and Annelise couldn't help but think of that wild-eyed sermonizer back at the ball field. The devil at the helm.

"Don't disappoint me," she said. "That means both of you." She started for the racket and lights.

"She's a pistol, all right," Raleigh said as soon as she was out of earshot.

Huck could not believe how quickly this lightning had gone to his head. He stole a look at Katie in the dim light off the elevator. She was talking to Bobby Duane, that lunkhead. "What?"

"I said, she's a heck of a pistol," Raleigh repeated.

It occurred to him that he needed a motorcycle, a big V-twin with a real roar to it. Lindbergh had ridden one all over the place back in his barnstorming days, an Excelsior to be exact, a very fast bike indeed. "Boy, I'll say," he muttered. "She's a dish and a half."

"Uh, yeah," said Raleigh. "Are we talking about the same thing?"

Excelsior was out of business, though. He guessed it would have to be a Harley, or an Indian. Not the 45 or the Scout, of course—he was six-two already, for crying out loud. He needed the big 74 or the Indian Chief. *That* would get her attention. "We're talking about exactly the same thing. She's a damn rocket."

"Well. I guess it's probably the liquor talking, but you may as well call it like you see it. I mean, at least she ain't your sister."

That damn Bobby had her laughing now and Huck knew he had to step in before things really went south. Why in the hell had he waited so long? "What?" he said. "Who's not my sister?"

"Uh, your cousin?" said Raleigh. "Your rocket cousin?"

Another voice cut in from behind him. "I'd like to ride that rocket. I'd like to fly her straight to the dern moon."

The words took a long pause to register, but once they did, they hit like a fist. Who the hell had that kind of gall? Huck turned and squared off like a gunfighter. Royce, standing there with Shirley.

"What did you say?"

Royce looked at him. "I said I hear you, brother. That ice-queen cousin of yours is one hot little rocket." He shook his head. "You are one lucky doggie, having that little darlin' around all the time." Royce held a can of beer and took a swig. He eyed Huck again. "How's she look oh-natur-*al*?"

Huck clenched and unclenched his fists. "How's she look *what*?"

Another long swig. "You know—how's she look in her birthday suit? How's she look *naked*?"

Shirley fixed on Huck. "Might want to let this one go, hoss."

"I ain't letting it go," Huck shot back. Liquid courage was right. Or righteous liquid fury maybe. He felt like Attila the Hun.

"I don't mean you, son," Shirley told him.

Huck barely heard him. "None of your damn business, you dern . . . troglodyte."

"Oh, come on. You just owned it with all that rocket talk, so don't go all Mrs. Grundy on us now. I had a cousin looked like that, I'd sure have my eye to the keyhole every chance I got. What's a troglodyte?"

"A cretin."

"Hey, Huck," Raleigh said cautiously.

"You shouldn't have dropped out of school, Shirl," Royce was saying. "I mean, the gams on that little filly, in gym class? I'd have bent her right over the tennis net before you could say—"

Maybe he would've gone on, but Huck had already launched like a stone from a catapult. Neither Royce nor anyone else had time to react. Two fast steps forward, and he socked Royce square in the kisser.

"Interesting watch, miss."

She'd nearly reached the line to the ladies' room on the far side of the fairgrounds, could hear the dance band playing again over at the gazebo, hear the dizzy calliope and kids shouting from the rides. She looked at the man who'd fallen in beside her. Cream-colored fedora with a darker band, light summer suit with no tie. Twice her age at least, but then she doubted he'd figured that out yet.

"Thank you." She kept walking.

So did he. "I couldn't help but notice. It's one big watch."

"It is that." She held it up in the blaze from the bulbs. Nearly ten o'clock already. "It belongs to my beau."

He grinned. "Just head it right off at the pass, eh?"

He was closer to her than she'd like or even consider normal, and the alcoholic lightness in her head shifted to a sort of half-wary intuition. "Fair's fair, right?"

"Fair's reasonable enough. Your beau's a flyboy, I take it."

"He is. Guess you are, too, or maybe just a watch salesman?" They'd made the tail of the line now. She shifted away from him.

"Something like that." He held out his hand. "May I? See the watch, that is?"

A woman with a little girl in tow emerged from the squat water closet, and the line advanced. She stepped forward but held up her wrist. She tried to find his eyes beneath the shadow of the hat brim.

He was about to say something, but thank God another voice beat him to it.

"Darling. Where have you been all my life?"

McKee moved up alongside her and she took his arm. She turned her face into his neck. "Right here waiting."

"Would you like to introduce me to your friend?"

Annelise lifted her head back up but kept her grip on his arm. "I can't. He hasn't exactly introduced himself to me."

The mystery man was backing away, touching the brim of his hat. "You're a very lucky man," he said to McKee.

"She's right, you really don't know her," McKee answered, and the guy gave a curious little laugh and moved along in the flow of the crowd.

"Forgive me for butting in," he said. "I can spot a guy who can't take no for an answer from a mile away."

"Oh, I'm glad you showed up. He was a little too interested in my watch. Among other things, I'm sure." She still had his arm. "Anyway, I was wondering what became of you. At the tent earlier?"

"Well, you know. All that carrying on about temperance worked up a powerful thirst." He tilted his head toward her and gave an exaggerated sniff, like a hound on a trail. "Speaking of which, young lady. What exactly have *you* gotten into?"

She disengaged and stepped for the jakes. "Don't go anywhere."

"Roy told me the ranch is pretty leveraged," McKee said. "I don't know how aware Huck is, or even Miz Gloria."

They'd left the fairgrounds and turned down First, heading for the little attic apartment McKee rented in a house half a block from Main. Annelise had never been there. She'd never been alone with him at all, actually.

"I'm guessing they both have at least a sense. Houston may be a kid, but he's not dumb." She struggled with her next thought but finally let herself say it. "Neither's my aunt, if you want to get right to basic brain power."

"No, I wouldn't call her dumb," McKee said. "That would be a mistake. Maybe a little crazy, but that's different. How sickly is she, exactly?"

Annelise had puzzled over this herself. "She gets bad headaches, and fairly often from what I can tell. According to my mother she was always pretty frail." The night had cooled down and the breeze had picked up, moving the leaves in the trees. "She's younger than she looks, with that white hair. A lot younger than my uncle."

They reached the house and went around to the stairs on the back. "Speaking of Aunt Gloria, it better not get back to her that I'm here."

"If it's any comfort, the old gent who lives downstairs, Mr. Neuman, is of French extraction."

She couldn't help laughing. "Funny, but no. It's not much comfort."

"More to the point then, he's deaf as a post."

"Now *that's* what I want to hear."

The door opened into a galley kitchen. Otherwise the apartment consisted of one narrow room not unlike Houston's attic quarters at the ranch, with a single table and chair and a twin bed down at the far end. Also a line of guns leaning against one wall. Spartan but neat as a pin, the way the tools in Yak's panel truck were. He opened the icebox and pulled out two beers.

They clinked bottle necks. "Here's to sin."

"Hallelujah." She tipped her brown bottle, let the cold slosh rush across her tongue and down her throat, felt it wash through her empty insides like that first evening breeze. She took in the line of firearms against the wall. "So. Still want to teach me to shoot?"

Royce went down and his beer went flying, but he came back to his feet as though the hardpack had turned to rubber. He dispensed with fisticuffs and simply charged like the football tackle he was, and Huck in his inebriated fury lacked the wit to dodge. Instead he swung, and Royce caught another good one on the ear but also knocked Huck ass-over-teakettle.

Huck felt the bite of gravel, felt his left arm go numb elbow to wrist. He started to get up, then heard as much as felt a tooth-rattling blow to his head, and for a spell saw only comets and meteors, heard a gong ringing in his ears.

By the time lights and sound diminished the entire gang was around him in a circle, including Royce, with Raleigh on one knee in the gravel. Shirley had Royce by the arm. Royce bled from the lip.

"Just let it go," Shirley was saying, "and I'll let you go."

"He busted my damn lip."

"Yeah, well, I guess chivalry ain't dead."

The entire right side of Huck's face throbbed steadily, and though the stars were nearly gone, his vision remained weirdly distorted, like he was looking through a fish-eyed optical lens.

"You all right?" said Raleigh.

He tried to move his left arm and couldn't. He lifted his right hand instead and brought it to his cheekbone. Another wave of pain.

"You're going to need some ice. He clocked you good."

"Can somebody run up to the soda fountain and get some ice?" said Shirley.

"I will."

Katie Calhoun. Huck couldn't see her from flat on his back but was pretty sure the voice was hers.

"I need to stand up." He couldn't tell where the alcoholic fog in his head ended and the effects of the wallop began. The other kids were mostly quiet, just watching.

Royce had moved off a few feet with Bobby Duane and Shirley. He took a pull from a bottle and winced when the stuff hit his lip. He looked at Huck and shook his head. "That was a hell of a jab, Galahad."

Huck collected himself and managed to get fully if not steadily to his feet. He wobbled off a few steps, felt the wash of whiskey in his gut like a drowning green wave. He bent at the waist and heaved right into the gravel.

* * *

"You've got the prettiest teeth I've ever seen."

McKee leaned against the little run of counter by the sink. He wasn't as tall as Huck, but he was lanky in his own way, with the shoulders and forearms of his trade. Blue eyes and dark hair, too.

Now she really bared them. "They didn't come cheap." She felt her eyes shift to his own mouth, felt herself go into motion as though drawn across the floor by a lodestone.

They kissed awhile in the kitchen, kissed and talked and drank and kissed again.

"How'd you get to be such a firecracker?" He had his hand in the small of her back, his fingers just down across the swell of her bottom.

"Born that way, I guess." She was pressed up tight against him, could feel his apparently unabashed arousal against the plane of her belly. She pressed herself even tighter, and his hand at her back pressed tighter yet. "It takes one to know one. You're not exactly any kind of a dud yourself."

"Raised the way you were, I mean."

She pulled her head back to look up at him. Her hand cupped the back of his neck. "That's only one part of anything. I'm still my own person. With my own mind."

He shook his head and his mouth had a little set to it, but she couldn't tell whether it qualified as mirth or something else.

"What?" she goaded.

"You, is what. Most people wouldn't know their own mind if it walked up and punched 'em right in the mouth. I know what I'm talking about, too. You think you got it with both barrels, you ought to see how I grew up."

She had a vague sense he'd come up Mormon, although they'd never talked about it. She was curious, but that could wait.

"Are you planning to ravish me?"

He slid his hand up her back and cupped her neck. Then he slid the same hand up into her hair, grown out over the last three months and no trick at all for him to seize a fistful close in to her skull. He pulled and then pulled harder, until she gave in and tilted her head back. "My goodness, miss," he said. "It never crossed my mind."

"I'll take my leave, then." She stuck her lip at the ceiling in a pout. "Boo."

He steered her to his bed. Though the window was open, the room hadn't cooled with the night and he left the taut covers in place, pushed her down on the quilt and settled half on top of her, and with his lean weight constricting the draw of her own breath in a half-painful, half-delicious way, she went ahead and got completely lost on his tongue, at first on his last cold blast of beer, and then on their shared inquisitive hunger and finally, when he pulled back from her mouth and moved to her neck, the crazy electric currency of being wholly and gloriously alive.

He put his tongue down her ear and she practically convulsed.

"You are one big romantic, aren't you?"

He didn't answer, just seemed uncannily able to read her body. She felt his hand cup her breast through the fitted fabric of her dress, felt him glide the ball of his thumb exactly across the invisible bull's-eye beneath. She wanted to sit up and reach around behind her back, run the zipper down her spine and shed her clothing like a skin, but before she could rouse herself, he'd already slid down the span of her belly. He hiked the hem of her dress.

He put her legs akimbo, and the next thing she knew, his mouth nuzzled the inside of her thigh, very close to the bridge of her underpants, and she was startled by this and stiffened with irrational panic, and he shushed her and had one ankle in his grip and the flat of his other hand pressing down on the opposite thigh. He put his mouth right to that white cotton saddle. Right *there*.

She recoiled again involuntarily, felt herself half against her own will flinch away from him farther up the bed, bumping her head into the wall in the process, but he lunged along like that same hound on the same hot trail and got his mouth on her again, and now there was no place to go, and she felt the circular pressure of his tongue and felt herself relax. She whimpered like a bunny.

She had never heard of this, had never even imagined it. Blix had certainly never—

Blix. Oh God, no, not now, plenty of time to think that through later, and oh God, yes, he was doing something else down there, pushing the line of her panties aside, and she felt his silken tongue *actually* against her tremoring wet flesh, and mind and body both caromed into places with no room for guilt at all, both her hands in his hair, both hands pulling at his hair—

She tripped and tumbled, down and down, bouncing over stair steps in the firmament, an endless invisible flight, each launching jolt and plunging drop like the thump and fall of some sweet giddy turbulence, sky and ground and round and round, so far below and *so* far above—

He clapped his hand over her mouth, and she came slightly back, heard herself crying out like one of those wringing ecstatics at the tent revival. She clamped her teeth.

"I'm glad I'm bad," she murmured.

She was naked now or nearly so, her shoulders and arms free and her unzipped dress bunched around her middle like an empty life preserver. Underpants and brassiere tossed God knew where. He was still inside her, and she could feel him twitch from time to time. She stroked the skin of his back.

He laughed. "I'm pretty glad myself."

"Where did you learn that?"

"Too much to get into. But I started off with a good teacher."

"Well, God love her. Here I thought I was quite the cosmopolitan." She shifted, looked down with her eyes and then back to his face. "Pull that out of me before you lose your 'chute. How's your hand?"

He flexed his fingers. "Just fine. No blood." He reached down and eased back into the world. "I hate that part," he said.

She laughed.

"Want a beer?"

"Always."

He fetched two more from the icebox and pulled the door half open to let the night air flow. He padded naked back to the bed. She'd fully shed her dress now and lay there propped on the pillow, splayed in the lick of the breeze. Belly flat as a pancake. "You're a doll," he told her.

She draped a leg over his. Checked her watch, the only piece of apparel left on her. "I hope Houston's okay. He finally ditched his halo and decided to live a little."

"What'd he do, hold a girl's hand?"

"No, but he wants to. So he chugged half a bottle of rotgut with that in mind. Right before I ran into you."

"Liquid courage?"

"More or less."

She tipped her beer to her lips, and he teasingly reached over and pushed to hold the tilt of the bottle, until the flow came faster than she could swallow. She started to laugh and beer sloshed down her chin and across her chest. He let up and she sputtered and laughed some more and finally slapped him a ringer across the cheek. "You are an ass."

He licked beer from the flush of her clavicle. "I'm just the way God made me." He listed on an elbow. "You feeling okay about this? I know you've got a real beau . . ."

"Oh, I'll feel bad in the morning, I'm sure. I'm not that heartless. I think this was a foregone conclusion, though." She pointed at the artillery along the wall. "We've been packing loaded guns around each other for three months now."

"Glad it wasn't just me."

She looked at her watch again. "I should get dressed. I told Houston I'd bring him food, and that was hours ago already."

He could still feel the bilious scorch in his gullet, but he was indeed more sober.

Katie and her friends returned with two cups of ice. Somebody came up with a clean handkerchief, and he'd parked himself on a loading dock alongside the elevator and held a dripping compress to the side of his face. His mouth tasted awful and his head still throbbed, and he hardly noticed either because Katie sat there with him.

"I think it's dreamy, the way you defended your cousin's honor."

In truth, he had a feeling he'd reacted at least as much out of basic possessiveness as anything else. He mixed Annelise up in his head with dancing chorus girls, with the actress Jean Harlow, even with Katie herself. Couldn't exactly bring that up, though.

"It's one thing to think a girl's pretty, but that ain't a free pass for poor behavior." This last was one of Mother's lines.

"She is pretty." Katie was looking off into space. "All the boys are smitten by her."

"Most of the men, too. Seems like."

"Well. She does seem sort of older. You know? Poised, or something. With her beret, and her . . . attitude, I guess. To tell you the truth, she's intimidating."

"I know. But she's not as cold as she seems sometimes." Another thing struck him. "She ain't as bulletproof as she seems, either."

How much to tell her? He'd promised a long time ago to keep mum about why Annelise was here in the first place, and God knew he was no stranger to keeping a secret. "Shoot, she nearly passed out at the tent meeting earlier—"

He really couldn't win. He'd been so intent on preserving his cousin's privacy about her beau, he just uttered the first thing to pop into his head. He never had spoken to Katie about the Spring Ball.

"Passed out?"

"Yeah. From the heat. I practically had to carry her outside."

"I wondered if you were over there tonight." The other kids were a little way off in a cluster, and the lot of them let out a raucous laugh at some joke or goof or something.

"Me and Annelise both." He looked at her with his one eye. "I wish I hadn't told you."

"Oh. How come?"

"It's a little embarrassing, I guess. My ma, though—she's really strict about that stuff." His mouth felt like a hay bale, and he could feel the fire yet in his throat and even through his airways. He took the cup of ice and drank a good bit of melt out of the bottom, then sucked in a shard and spoke around it. "Probably sounds crazy, I know."

"It doesn't matter. My family's Catholic, although we haven't been to Mass since we left Butte." She put her elbows on her knees and her sharp little chin in her hands. "Have you ever been to Mass? That might seem strange to somebody from the outside."

Pretty and nerve-racking as Katie was, and despite the dripping hanky and the heat around his eye, he couldn't help considering what a muddle religion truly seemed to be.

At one point that fire-breather at the revival delivered a scorching aside about the prophecies ushered in by President Roosevelt and the recovery programs, even suggesting that the president himself might be the Antichrist, here and living among us. Huck had wondered what Mother thought of that one—despite the thrall of the meeting, she generally subscribed to Sister Aimee's sense that the president was only trying to help in plainly dire times. His repeal of Prohibition, though—that she blamed on the Catholics.

"Houston? Did you really fly down the street that night?"

He came right back. "Yes. I sure did."

"What was it like?"

The ice disappeared on his tongue. "Not exactly a pure D success. I smashed out the window in the New Deal and cracked up altogether when I put down in the ball field." His mind had gone back to that night again and again, and he always came around to one thing. "But for a few seconds there, I felt like the king of the whole dern world. Even after I crashed, I knew I'd just had the finest one minute of my life."

"How high up were you?"

"Thirty feet, I guess. I hit the sign out front of the Deal, and that was way before I got to my ceiling."

"Thirty feet," she said. She looked up at the elevator, as though trying to calculate how tall it might be. "With a plane you built yourself."

"Glider. Glider Number One is what I called her."

"Glider Number One. Gosh. I wish I'd seen it." She turned her head to him. "Weren't you scared?"

He remembered in a jealous flash how Bobby Duane had been making her laugh earlier, and he wished he could think of something funny, too. "Not when I was in the air. I almost turned it over in the middle of the street when I was trying to test the controls, and that was pretty scary. Raleigh and me sort of stole this big Buick to tow with, and he had me going almost forty, just on these chintzy little buggy wheels. But I thought about it a lot beforehand. I had a pretty good idea it was all going to work."

He lifted the handkerchief from his face and squeezed the sopping melt into the dirt. "On the other hand, the trouble with putting two and two together is sometimes you get four, and sometimes you get twenty-two."

Raleigh's pinched line, but it got a laugh out of Katie.

He tried another. "To put it another way, that ol' Charlie Darwin can be one cold son of a bitch."

Now she let out a real peal and Huck cracked a grin back, felt webs of pain jolt out of his cheekbone. He didn't even care. "You're funny," she told him.

"Ow," he winced. He still didn't care.

"It's a doozy," she said. "Your eye, I mean. Can you see out of it?"

He tilted his head toward the bulb on the elevator and covered his good eye. "Not really. That light up there's like looking at the crack under a door."

They sat in silence, listening to the other kids laugh and drink fifty feet away. Now that he'd made her laugh, he had no idea what to do next. Under ordinary circumstances this might be his moment to steal a kiss, but his face was no doubt a sight and his mouth tasted like a slop bucket. His effort to make a bold statement with a whiskey bottle had turned out to be his downfall.

She reached into her little purse. "Do you want some gum?"

Maybe her mysterious eyes could look right into the corners of his mind. "Gosh, yes."

She passed a piece over and he folded it into his mouth. "Sorta hurts to chew."

She laughed again and this time he hadn't even meant to be funny. "So," she said. "Glider Number One."

"It was kind of a prototype. That's why I called it that."

"Do you still have it?"

"Nope. Burned it."

"I'm sorry?"

"I burned it. It didn't work."

"But you flew it, right?"

"Yeah. Long enough to know it wasn't right. And no way it ever would be. Plus I was in hot water with Cy Gleason, not to mention my ma. So I gave it a proper send-off."

"But surely that's not the end of it. Surely there's Glider Number Two?"

"Glider Number Two would probably be even crappier." He gave her a little sidewise look. "Get it?"

"Yes, I get it," she said, though this time she didn't laugh. "You boys really are all the same."

He had a sudden flash of panic, and following that, an impulse to get her back where he thought he'd just had her. It occurred to him to lead her over to the shop. He didn't have a motorcycle, but something that would really separate him from the boys—an honest-to-God airplane, which would rock-paper-scissors the bejesus out of anything Bobby Duane Boyd might come up with.

He'd have to swear her to secrecy of course, but not for long. Once they had a motor in hand, the whole town would know. He imagined taking Katie up in the passenger seat, flying out over the sage steppes and along the sandstone rims, across the patchwork hay-ground in the bottoms and the golden grain higher up on the tables, climbing the updrafts along the slopes and finally banking right over the spine of the Bull Mountains, showing her the world as neither of them had ever seen it—

Another voice, a girl's, snapped him back. "Who all's the same?"

Sharon White. Huck hadn't noticed her before. Surely she must have been at the revival, too. She walked up to them.

"Boys in general," Katie told her.

"Houston's a little different from the average," said Sharon. "In a good way."

"You're right. On the other hand, we've been sitting here alone for an hour and the fool hasn't kissed me. I even gave him chewing gum."

Huck felt a hot glow travel through him like lava. One part embarrassment, one part incredulousness. One part thrill. "Must be that hit I took to the noggin," he offered.

Katie started to say something else just as the throng of kids in the lot broke into a scatter like billiard balls. Headlights came at a fast approach, then two red flashers and the growl of a siren. Sharon bolted, and he and Katie were up and flying too.

She kissed McKee and let herself out, made her way down the back staircase in the dark. She'd checked her watch again in the light of the little kitchen. Nearly three hours since she'd left Houston down by the grain elevator.

She debated simply walking on her woozy legs back to the cottage and actually went a few steps in that direction, before thinking better of it and turning on her heel. Maybe he'd gone home already himself, in which case he was no doubt sleeping off the prelude to his first official hangover. But if he happened to linger at the carnival, he was no doubt lingering for her.

The rush of motion behind her at first made her think of McKee and his endless pranks, her beer bottle tipped and held in place and fed by relentless gravity, faster than she could swallow.

She realized the folly of this the instant she lost her chance either to flee or to scream. A hot hand clapped to her mouth, and her right arm was wrenched in a blast of pain behind her back, and something hit her in the backs of the knees. She went down as though dropped through a trap in a floor. Her head bounced on the walk.

Freeze or fight. She feared them both but she feared the first more, and her legs started kicking and striking like they had their own reactive brain. The hem of her dress was back up around her hips but not at all like earlier. She connected hard with something not attached to whoever pushed her down from the back and heard a rough grunt, and she knew there was more than one.

The hand pushed hard at her mouth, pushed her head into the ground. She felt screaming tracers in her wrenched right arm, and the second her mind went to that, some weighted black bulk pinned her kicking legs down. She swung her left fist as the last untrapped thing, and a grip like a vise seized that, too.

This was a crazy place to rape a girl, with houses all around, and almost simultaneously she considered the sheer oddness that her mind could even go to such an objective place in such a moment. Then her left thumb bent back sharply in the wrong direction, bent like it might snap off at the base. She froze like a plank.

Something worried at her wrist. Undoing the band of her watch. *I couldn't help but notice. It's one big watch . . .*

An hour ago she bit McKee to keep from crying out and now she sunk her teeth into this other evil hand for exactly the opposite reason, pincered what meat she could and clamped like a terrified dog. She heard a gargled reaction, half gibberish and half curse, and the instant the hand ripped away, she went to shrieking with a pitch to smash glass.

Her arm was still pinned behind her, but her legs had come free again and she started kicking and lashing and kept on screaming and now flinging her head from side to side like a madwoman, screaming and screaming and flinging and flinging, until she flung it right into some wallop that seemed to detonate like dynamite, way down deep in her ears . . .

She swam back from some deep black suspension. Fleeing footsteps and a pan of headlights. Car doors slamming, tires angrily squealing. She heard the rising sputter and diminishing fade of a departing vehicle.

New footfalls pounded and she rose up swinging. She landed a blow on a bare chest and another alongside a head with her opposite hand, and he flinched but took the hits and said over and over, "You're okay, you're okay," and she recognized him then and clutched him and put her face into him, and panted and sobbed at the same time. Her heart wanted to drum right out of her chest.

McKee had a club or a bat or something in one hand, but he managed to get an arm under her knees and the other beneath her shoulder blades. He carried her to the steps behind the house.

"I knew the old boy was hard of hearing but I had no idea he was that deaf." He eased her down. "You have to walk, honey. I can't carry you uphill."

"We need to go to the shop and call the police. There's no phone here." He was looking at the side of her face in the light of the kitchen. "Bastards smacked you good. You're gonna have a black eye, miss."

He'd given her another beer, but she was unsettled to the edge of nausea and couldn't drink it. She placed the cold glass against her blazing cheek. McKee was barefoot and shirtless, trousers buttoned but not zipped. It wasn't a club he'd held but a short-barreled shotgun, lying now atop the counter.

She looked at him. "Oh my God."

"I know . . ."

I couldn't help but notice. It's one big—

Her wrist shot into the light. "Oh my *God.* They took my watch."

Huck skirted the fairgrounds and got over to Second and walked in the shadows, heading home.

The carnival was winding down for the night, the dance band gone and the calliope quiet, although he could still hear laughter and the occasional bark of a huckster. He could see the top of the Ferris wheel with its bulb-described spokes and rim, still turning away. Up ahead, the headlamps of cars departing down Main.

His right eye had fused totally closed and either that or the shock of the originating blow gave him the distinct sensation of balancing on a catwalk, even on level ground. Somehow despite this he'd run like an ace sprinter with Katie around the other side of the elevator, then down the tracks to the darkened platform in front of the depot.

She'd cut right and gone up under the veranda and stopped in the dark. He nearly ran right over her. "What now?" she'd hissed.

He looked back and saw the bob and pan of a flashlight. "This way," he said, and hustled down the length of the platform and just around the corner of the building. They flattened against the wall in the dark.

She leaned in close. "What if somebody's coming around this side?"

Huck peeped back around the corner. The flashlight traveled in the other direction, down toward a line of dormant rail cars. "Pretty sure it's just Junior and he's gone the other direction. We ought to scoot," and the words were no sooner out than his mouth went straight to hers as though it had a mind all its own.

Or maybe she really could read right into his thoughts, and liked what she saw. Her mouth opened and his did too. For months he had dreaded looking like an amateur in the moment of truth, but now their tongues practically collided with this identical urgency, and all his concern went straight out the window.

She tasted like wet electric peppermint. That's all he could think about for the longest time. Her tongue was a hot inquisitive mystery, exclamation point and question mark and magic charm all in one. A teasing pink miracle. A temptation he'd never dream to resist.

When they came up for air, he was actually light-headed. He peeped around the corner again. The flashlight was coming up the tracks, nearly level to the platform. He took her wrist, pulled her through the wedge of shadow along the building and peeped around the front corner toward the elevator. He couldn't see the county cruiser from here.

He pulled her around to the front and looked back the way they'd come. The flashlight beam waved around.

"Stay in the shadow," he said, and they held hands and went at a fast walk up the street to the newspaper office and into the alley out back.

"Are we safe?" she said, and they were kissing each other again.

*   *   *

"Can I give you advice?"

"Sure."

"You won't be offended?"

"No."

"Don't be offended."

"I *won't*."

"Promise?"

He had one working eye and the alley was dark but he could see her, even the glint in her own mysterious eyes. He said, "I hope I don't taste like puke . . ."

She laughed and shook her head. "You taste like gum."

"Am I doing it wrong?"

"No, no, not wrong, just . . . go slow. Trust me. Slow *down*."

He didn't know how long they had been here, because he couldn't keep track of seconds or minutes at all. Maybe the knock to the head had something to do with it, but mostly the delicate maze of her mouth seemed to have some time-dilation effect, some catalytic ability to make him feel on the one hand permanently frozen between the jump and stall of a ticking watch and on the other hand, soaring through particles and waves like a gravity-defying ray of light. He didn't know how to slow down, because he had no idea whether they'd been kissing each other for thirty seconds or two hours.

Finally the dots connected. "You mean my tongue?"

She kissed his cheek. "Yes, Houston. Just a little slower . . ."

They parted a couple of streets over, half a block from Katie's house. She had a one o'clock curfew and would barely make it, which Huck found stupefying. For all he could tell it was five in the morning, the hours passing in a flash.

He came up on Main Street and looked down toward the shop-fronts. The two taverns were still lit up, with a handful of vehicles clustered in front of each, but most of the street had cleared. He passed under the streetlamp and walked for the shop.

He hoped that Mother was asleep, although he doubted she would be. She slept poorly to begin with, and otherwise would surely not appreciate the unauthorized departure from the revival. Maybe the black eye would prove a blessing in disguise—he could tell her he'd been elbowed by a guy shouting in tongues. How on earth had she missed it, she'd been right there when it happened . . .

It was a good idea actually and brought him back to Annelise. Hopefully he'd cross paths with her before he encountered Mother, so they could get on the same page. More to the point, he was dying to tell her about Katie. He knew she'd say something clever, something teasing but still a seal of approval.

Things began to look up as he approached the shop. McKee's panel truck was parked out front and the office light was on, but the REO was nowhere to be seen. Surely the tent meeting couldn't still be going on. He peered through the pane in the office door. McKee and Annelise sat next to each other on the front edge of the desk, Annelise shaking her head dramatically and yammering away.

He'd been so heady to tell her but he hesitated now because she wasn't alone, felt a self-conscious flicker when his eye caught McKee's through the glass and that was enough to derail him altogether. He shifted to his cousin and saw he wasn't the only one to have taken a shot to the face. He flung the door open.

"What happened to you?" he blurted.

"What happened to *you?*" McKee and Annelise in unison, syllable for syllable.

Then his cousin only, rising to her feet and coming toward him, putting her hands on his shoulders but looking to McKee. "Good night— they got him, too. Okay, you're right. We need to call the police."

"Cripes, don't do *that* already, I just spent an hour *running* from the dern police." He frowned, took in her swelling eye. "Who attacked who?"

"Some passel of thugs jumped her on First," said McKee. "We are . . . what is it we're doing again?"

She winced, and not because of her eye. "We're trying to come up with a story."

This was beginning to sound familiar. "For what?"

She let out a breath. "For why I just happened to be leaving this jack Mormon Romeo's apartment alone at midnight." She gave him another wince, a truly exaggerated one. "Get it?"

"Oh." He *was* starting to get it. "Who attacked you?"

"I don't know. More than one man, though, and I think one of them had already approached me at the carnival earlier, right after I left you and Raleigh. He . . . wait. That eye looks *terrible*. Why were you running from the police?"

"Junior Joe showed up down at the depot and we all had to bolt. That was way after the fight, though."

"What fight?" Annelise and McKee, again one voice.

"I took a swing at Royce. Busted his lip actually." He put his hand to his hot balloon of a cheek. "He did me one better, though."

"Royce is an ass," said Annelise. "I've wanted to hit him myself, more than once." She glanced at McKee. "Back to square one, I guess."

McKee took a pull off the usual Highlander. "I think we need to make the call. At least get it on record, in case these bozos wind up jumping some other poor girl. Plus it's the only chance of getting your watch back."

Huck saw his life flash before his one good eye.

McKee went on. "Here's what you tell them. You lost track of Huck and figured he either went to my place or back here. So you decided to head home, but check in with me first."

"Not bad," Annelise said.

The swollen eye of course had a throbbing burn, but now Huck's entire face flushed hot as a skillet. "They took your watch?"

She held up her bare wrist. "Fucking bastards. The guy at the carnival earlier? That's what he was badgering me about."

Huck stalled. "You think he was in on it?"

McKee's bark of a laugh said it all.

Annelise was shaking her head, and to Huck's own grief she started to cry. "Fucking bastards," she said again. Her voice wobbled like a sparrow's.

Huck wanted to cry himself. He reached into his pocket. "They weren't after your watch. They were after this one." He let it dangle by the strap from his fingers.

"Oh my God," she said. "How did you—"

"We took this . . . *I* took this. Off the dead man. The guy we found in the river."

McKee groaned. Annelise was still perplexed.

"They saw your watch, I guess. Thought it was this one."

"Wait," she said. She shut her eyes tight and scraped at her face with her hands and looked in the moment stunningly like Mother with a headache mounting. "You've had that same watch all this time?"

The words spilled out like a dam had broken. "I should've told you, I know, but then they started calling Raleigh, and they started calling me, fishing around for the dern watch, and I just got more and more scared, and Raleigh called down to Billings and found out—"

"*Wait*," she barked, a contrast indeed to the swiped shine on her cheeks. "Wait. You mean the *police* were calling around looking for that?"

He couldn't stop shaking his head. "That's what we thought, but it wasn't the police. Raleigh figured it out. It was the rest of the gang. Or one of them, anyway."

McKee groaned again.

"And you've known about this for how long."

He could hardly bear to hold her eyes, so precise a combination of ice and flame. But he swallowed hard, and he blinked his one working eyelid, and he dutifully observed her glare. "Since the dance. The Spring Ball."

She started to heave air in great tortured gasps. Her whole body quivered like a willow switch, raised and about to come down.

The next thing Huck knew, she'd taken two steps in a flash across the room. She slapped him hard across the good side of his face.

Later, and not much so, she felt awful for hitting him. He looked as stunned as she felt to ignite with that sort of fury, as though some demon had gotten into her and propelled her body outside her actual will.

The rage went out of her quickly at least. Houston, standing there fighting tears, couldn't even look at her. His cheek was livid where her palm had landed. For once McKee didn't say a word.

Finally she broke the silence. The steadiness in her voice surprised even her. "All right. We're not calling the police, at least not yet."

McKee cautiously tipped his bottle. "What are you thinking?"

She reached over and gently took the watch out of Houston's grasp. "It's opening Pandora's box, because at this point we're going to have to tell them the whole unvarnished truth."

"So what? Houston lifting a watch off some dead stiff pales next to a bunch of goons jumping a girl to get the dern thing back." McKee frowned. "Wonder what's so special about it. Seems like a lot to risk for a lousy watch."

Houston tried to say something and choked like he was gagging on a raw egg. He looked back at the ceiling.

Annelise knew he was still fighting tears. She felt sick in her belly, guilty as sin for hitting him, but her voice remained calm. "If we call the police and begin at the beginning, they're going to start snooping."

"This is a bad thing? Your eye's already half black, Annelise. Let 'em snoop."

"If that happens, they will find the airplane."

Huck finally looked at her. "You're right," he croaked. "Maybe that's what I've got coming to me."

"Shush," she told him. "Don't be ridiculous. What's done is done, but that airplane in there is too big to hide. And we're way too close to give it up over a stolen watch."

McKee blew out a breath. "I can't argue with you."

Annelise studied the dead man's Longines. It was indeed indistinguishable from Blix's. Huck had told her how the corpse had looked surfacing through the depths, coalescing gradually and then instantly into what he described as a ghoul, and she tried to resist the image when she buckled the strap to her wrist. She looked at him. "Is this okay?"

"Gosh, of course." His lip quavered. His poor face, thanks in part to her. "I'm really sorry, Annie."

"Shush." She had the watch fastened now. "I'm the one who should be sorry." She stepped forward and pulled him into her, guided his throbbing face down along her own battered mug. "Listen to me. I love you very much. Okay?"

She felt him tense against her, finally heard him snort back a real wellspring. "Okay," he mumbled.

"Too bad we can't track them goons down ourselves," McKee said behind her.

Annelise rocked Houston a bit, listened to McKee finish off his beer. "Like vigilantes, or something?"

"More like car thieves. When they hauled on out of civilization a while back, they hauled out in a Model A Ford."

Huck could hear Annelise turn from time to time in his bed in the other room. He lay there awake on the pallet for a long while, feeling the hot throb around his eye. Pop had left them a note on the kitchen counter saying that Mother was exhausted from the tent meeting and wanted to go back out to the ranch.

He wanted to think about kissing Katie but he couldn't, not with any sense of swagger, because at the exact moment he'd lost himself on her peppermint tongue, Annelise had been jumped and pulled down and punched in the face. The thought of her being hurt because of his stupid mistakes made him want to beat his own back with a razor strop.

Or track the bastards down like McKee said, and not simply to steal any Model A. More like to fill each and every one so full of holes, they wouldn't hold a pint of water between them. The more he imagined it, the more he wanted to throw up all over again.

Finally the solace of sleep did creep in, and in the half-light of consciousness he remembered something that did actually make him understand atonement, something that felt akin to what baptism or even salvation was made out to be.

Listen to me. I love you very much.

Annelise had said those words to him, after all the rest of it had passed. Her loss, her fury, his confession. She loved him anyway. Very much.

No one had ever told him that before, or anything like it. He didn't even know it was a thing people might say, and didn't know whether he could bring himself to say so in return. But now that she'd said it, he could at least think it.

He loved her, too. He loved her very much.

4

She made her way back to McKee's a few times over the next couple of weeks, always in the evenings with Houston at the Rialto and Roy out at the place with Aunt Gloria. Her uncle figured something was up, though. One afternoon when she and Houston were at the ranch, he saddled the horses and asked her to ride out with him to move the lease cows from one section to another.

"I don't mean to pry, but I'll sleep better at night if I ask you this. You know about Merry Widows and whatnot?"

She looked at him from the easy sway of Houston's little bay. "Umm . . . like, Peacocks?"

"Okay, that's out of the way." He fished out a Lucky Strike pack, lit a cigarette and handed it to her, then lit one for himself. "One more thing. You need help buying them, or does McKee already have a handle on it?"

She felt herself redden. "Umm . . ."

"Don't worry, it ain't that obvious. But I'm around you two enough to see that if it ain't happened yet, it's probably about to."

"McKee won't get me into trouble."

"Good enough," he said. "I got enough keeping me awake at night. I don't need that worry on top of everything else."

She felt a spasm of guilt in the moment, not for their current conversation but for lying to him about the origin of her blackened eye the night of the revival. She and McKee and Houston simply worked her into the fistfight story, with a fish tale of how she'd caught Houston's elbow while trying to pull him away from Royce.

She knew from experience the way a lie could roll off her tongue, sweet and gold as pure clover honey. Sometimes she felt perfectly fine about it and sometimes not, and this fell into the second category for sure. But as McKee had pointed out, it really wouldn't do to put her uncle in the position of keeping a secret of that scale from the police even if he did agree to it, and both of them doubted he would.

"Roy?"

He'd risen up in the stirrups, looking at something through the screen of junipers. "Yeah, darlin'."

"Thank you."

"Just being practical." He blew out smoke. "Reckon the world would turn a little easier in general if people were just more practical."

She rode a few steps in quiet satisfaction, feeling the sway of the bay's gait and hearing the creak of the saddle and realizing how much she'd missed having her own horse, missed having all that harnessed power beneath her. Finally she came back to herself. "Practical as opposed to what?"

"Practical as opposed to pining, for some lost place in the past that was never there to begin with. I've done a fair bit of figuring over the years, and I've come to see it like this: the notion of the good old days may not be the worst thing anybody's come up with, but it ain't far off from it, either."

She listened to the soft thud of the horses' hooves in the sand of the wash. "The Garden of Eden," she mused.

"Yeah, that's what they're all in a panic over. Some crystal palace where nobody ever farts or dies, and the babies fly in on a stork. Nothing changes, nobody misbehaves, and the bread just bakes its own self."

"Paradise lost."

"Reality lost, is more like it. Here, follow me to the top." He clucked and tapped his horse out ahead and angled up a ribbon of trail, threading the junipers to the flat of the low table, where he reined to a stop. Annelise came up alongside. The table gradually declined into an open bowl with a handful of black cows grazing in the sun. "How'd you get into airplanes anyway?"

"My eighth-grade English teacher sort of took me under her wing." She laughed at her own accidental wit. "Miss Callenby. She was still a really young woman herself, I'm sure a complete *garçonne* out of the classroom—"

She caught his sidewise look.

"Flapper," she said. "Or would have been, back in the day. Anyway, she saw some of the same bratty independence in me, I'm sure. Loaned me a few books, stories and novels that she'd really loved when she was in college, and also another one that maybe was the best gift anyone ever gave me. *The Fun of It*, by Amelia Earhart. That set the hook."

Roy leaned over and put out his Lucky against the heel of his boot, tossed the butt into the sand. "You like being alive, don't you."

"I guess so. From all appearances." She snuffed her cigarette and straightened up again. "I get the sense that all the puritans you're talking about really don't, though. And so their whole purpose comes down to *boring* the rest of us into submission along with them."

She thought for a moment. "One thing I will say about Aimee McPherson—she at least brings some spectacle to the endeavor. I mean, Angelus Temple may as well be called Angelus *Theater*. It's like a cross between a Roman circus and that tent revival we all endured. How long did you stay with it that night, by the way? I've been wondering."

"Quite a while, after you and the kid ducked out." He waved a fly away, pulled his hat off and wiped the sweat from his hairline. Gave her that sidewise, gold-toothed grin. "Tell you the truth, it was all I could do not to bolt on out of there with you."

"I had to. Bolt, I mean. My legs were about to go out from under me."

"Oh, I'm sure the preacher would've gladly laid hands on you, if they had."

"And the lame would have instantly walked, I suppose."

He chuckled. "Aunt Gloria went forward to get herself healed. No more headaches, no more ailments."

"I wondered. How's that working out?"

"Time will tell."

"You know," she told him, "I think it's amazing, you covering for Houston so he can reach for something big in the here and now. He's lucky to have you."

"Yeah, well. I raised myself, for the most part. Rode from the bottom of the country to the top when I was ten years old, mainly because I didn't have a mother to tell me no." He looked out at the expanse of sun-curing grass and black cows. "Houston tell you why I moved him into town?"

"Only that you wanted him to have a normal life, or something to that effect." She gave a little laugh. "Although I'm not sure flying a glider down the street in the middle of the night qualifies as normal, exactly."

He snorted. "That's downright ordinary, compared to what he didn't tell you." He waved at another fly, but shook his head at some other irritant buzzing not in the air but evidently inside his own skull. When he finally spoke again, she had the sense he was swatting at whatever that was for the first time in a while.

"A few years back some radio preacher out of Oregon started predicting the Second Coming, on a certain day and time."

"I remember. October, I think it was. And he thought Adolf Hitler and who's it, in Italy? Mussolini? He thought they were predicted in Revelation."

He gave her a single giant nod. "That's exactly right. Anyway, they took it all pretty serious at the church here in town. Now mind you, people in these parts are primed for it—you've seen a bit of the despair by now. No need to feel guilty, but a lot of the country ain't so well situated moneywise as what you're used to."

"Obviously."

"Right. So Pastor White got pretty caught up and started preaching on Armageddon and how the pieces are already in place, and at one point he invited another preacher up from Billings for a debate on whether the Rapture happens before or during the Great Tribulation. White's a before man, but this was about a week after the Italians invaded Africa, which they at least agreed to be a sign that the end was indeed on the approach."

"I've sat through a bunch of this stuff, too—" Annelise started.

"Well, hang on. I have a feeling I got you beat." He shook out another smoke and offered her one, but this time she declined. She could still feel the dizzy lift in her head. He lit up and went ahead. "Like I said, Pastor White and the whole dern congregation got pretty single-minded on the topic, but I'm sure you can guess who *really* went above and beyond."

"What did she do?"

He looked rueful. "Like you say, it was in October. Houston and me were still mainly living out at the ranch then, with him going to the rural school down the road. And I guess you probably remember the prediction was pretty specific. High noon on the appointed date."

"What I remember is thinking, Okay, noon. Noon where? Greenwich, England? Jerusalem? Rome?"

He chuckled. "You're quick, I'll admit. That sure never occurred to most. Anyway, the day rolls around, and Gloria keeps Houston home from school."

"Uh-oh."

He was nodding and talking. "I took him out that morning, up to the wheat table with a shotgun, and the two of us kicked around the edge trying to scare up a pheasant." He turned his head to her briefly but couldn't seem to hold her eyes.

"You have to understand something. For years I'd been lonely as hell. Never had a mother myself, then I lost my father, too. Not even ten years old. So when I met your aunt and saw this mix of—not weakness, exactly, and not illness, either . . ."

"Fragility?"

"Yeah, fragility. Mixed all inside out with faith. Some kind of suf-fering perseverance. Not so unlike my own pa, comes down to it. But I saw something else in her, too, those first days she'd come west."

He looked down the slope at the cows, then out beyond where the land rose up again, tables and buttes fainter and fainter with the hopscotch of distance.

"It's majestic, down in those parts. Like paintings you see, railroad posters. Mountains and waterfalls. Not so spare the way it is here. She was bewitched, I guess, and the wonder of it all just came off her like a shine on a coin. First time she'd been on a horse, on a trail; first time she'd done anything at all just for the fun of it. Possibility—the world as a bigger place. But right at the edge of it, fragility.

"And I guess I thought I could maybe keep that notion of possibil-ity alive for her, and that would keep some possibility alive for me, too." He still looked rueful. "We got married, and much as it pains me to put it to words, I stayed pretty lonely anyway. Watched her nearly die in 1918, that damn Spanish flu. She had the first miscar-riage then, and at least one other before Houston stuck. And after he was born, you could *really* see the fragility in her, and the *fear*, too. Taste it, almost."

She watched a single bead of sweat gather and form where his hat met his temple, then roll down toward his cheek and pause at the ridge of bone beneath the skin.

"I got to just going along with whatever took the sting out for her. Half believing, maybe, and half just . . . accepting what she needed to get by on."

Annelise found her voice and she let it murmur out. Water over stone. "Did you find any pheasants? With Houston, that day?"

He had never stopped nodding, that bead of sweat still in place, and she wanted to reach over and put her fingers to it. "We did. One giant rooster come right up at our feet, like a land mine going off. You ever had one spook you like that? It's the damnedest thing, this green-headed dragon, exploding out of nothing but dry dirt and thin grass, right there in front of you . . ."

"Did you kill it?"

His horse shook its head around against the reins, and Roy let it drop its neck to crop grass. Annelise slacked hers, too. "Nope. I shot but I missed. On purpose." He studied the smoldering tailor-made in his fingers, then cocked his head to look at her. "Figured it wasn't, you know, practical. On the off chance we *were* about to rise on up into the air.

"So about eleven we tromp back down to the house. Houston had a lot of those airplane models already, and always one under construction. He went up to his bedroom, I figured just to kill time and maybe put on his Sunday clothes or something. But when I went up to get him, I found him sitting there at his little worktable with a pin-striping brush, painting on one of the models." Now he did look away from her, and she could see he was actually choking a little.

But he kept on. "He asked. He asked me. If he held on to it when Jesus came, did I think he could take his airplane too."

"Oh Lord. What did you tell him?"

"That I didn't know. Because I didn't." He was shaking his head again, and she knew he was either dumbfounded by the memory or flogged by guilt, or both. "I wanted to tell him he could try. But I didn't."

"Because of Gloria."

"Yep. Because of Gloria. I knew it wouldn't go over." His cigarette had a ridiculously long ash, but he didn't tap it loose. "She'd already told him what would be left behind, crumpled on the ground when we went up. Clothes and shoes, wedding rings. Watches. The gold off my tooth. Cars wrecking on the roads, when their drivers disappeared. Trumpets blasting and the sky wide open, like the sea coming apart for the Israelites.

"Anyway. He left his airplane where it was. Cleaned his brush and came downstairs. We all went out into the yard, held hands in a circle. None of us talking, of course, just waiting. But finally the time's getting pretty close, and Mama's got her eyes closed, and Houston finally breaks the silence.

"'What'll happen to the horses?' he says. 'Who's going to feed the horses tonight?'"

"Wow," said Annelise, and it flared in her head that Houston had no doubt been keeping this from her. She guessed she knew why, but a pang went through her anyway. "What did she say?"

"She opened her eyes, but she didn't really look at him. She just looked up to the sky and said, 'It's not for us to worry about anymore.'"

They sat there in silence for a full minute, the horses even now cropping grass around the bits in their mouths. Finally she said, "Well. We're still here."

He laughed. "We sure are." He waved his hand at the horses.

Annelise frowned. "So how far past noon did you all stand there?"

"Ten minutes, maybe. Finally the kid speaks up again, says, 'How much longer do you think it will be? My hands are getting sweaty.' And they were—we were all still holding hands, and his was hot and clammy both, you know that feeling?

"Then I realized he was trying to prod it along, because he says, 'Do you really think we'll fly right on out of our clothes?' And finally I'd just had enough. I said, 'Not today I don't,' and I gave his hand a good squeeze and then let go of it. Gloria looked at me, and I told her I had work to do, and Houston was going with me."

"Did she say anything?"

"Yeah. She did. But not right off. She kept hold of Houston's hand a little longer—I'd already let go of hers, but she'd kept a grip on his—and looked back up to the sky for another spell. Like if she stood there long enough, it might happen yet.

"Finally, though, she gives Houston's hand a squeeze too, with the both of hers, and she says, 'Well, no man knoweth the day or the hour. The Word does say that.' And she let him go and went back to the house. I moved him into town a few days later."

She hinged in the moment on telling him the truth about her black eye, telling him the truth about all of it. He already knew she'd given herself to McKee, and he clearly didn't hold it against her, in fact seemed ready to help. If he could unload this festering secret now, shouldn't she do the same?

She saw exactly what was stopping her—spilling the beans with Roy would mean betraying Houston. Ironically, she had the sense she couldn't bring any of this up to her cousin, either, not without betraying some other confidence. Tangled webs, divided loyalties. The problem was, sometimes secrets and even lies seemed to exist mainly to protect the people you loved. Rules, too, she suddenly had to admit.

Her horse stamped underneath her, then shifted slightly to crib grass from a thatch nearer to Roy's sorrel, and the sorrel turned and bared its long yellow teeth. Her own horse shied away.

"Easy now." He patted his horse's neck.

Annelise kept waiting for him to go on, to try to make some sense of it, but evidently he didn't have much else to say. Or maybe he was waiting for her to put some logic to it, some redemptive conclusion. As the silence went on, she realized it was not an uncomfortable space but merely a shared one, its own patient form of solidarity. As though an answer to human confusion and human folly and human suffering in general surely existed out there somewhere, and if they sat there long enough, waited long enough, well. It might occur yet.

Finally something else flushed the whole tangle from her mind.

"Did my mother know about any of this?"

"I'd sure imagine so. Tell you the truth, I've been wondering for the last four months if you already knew yourself, had maybe gone through the same thing at the same time. Well, an hour later, anyway."

Annelise shook her head, but she didn't laugh. "No, but we're not living on a farm outside the general line of sight. And regardless of what my father believes in private, he's still in the professional class. In that life, appearances matter." She blew out a long breath, like a boiler bleeding pressure. "To be honest, I never could figure how people with so much money can have so little sense."

He laughed. "In my personal experience, the two have been equally hard to come by."

"Money's slippery. But you have plenty of sense. You absolutely did the right thing, with Houston."

"That one I stand by." He tightened the reins, put heels to his horse.

5

Annelise had struggled with the McKee situation, it was true. She wasn't as amoral as she put forward in theory, and she did have a deep sense of connection to Blix down in California. A gold-star sneak, but a loyal one. Sort of.

Down in California, though. That was the trouble. The ethics of the thing became situational, and this was the situation, and she had to admit that McKee, while certainly convenient, nevertheless owned a part of her heart as well, and had before she'd ever climbed those stairs to his room. So she kept going to him like that same old lodestone.

He had a real way with her, too. A charm.

"You know this is my favorite part of a woman's body?" He'd only be talking about the inside of her wrist, the words running around an emery kiss of taut skin and delicate bones. Then later he'd say the same thing about her collarbone with his mouth against that, rough and gentle at once, or the flutes of her ribs.

"Look at our hands," he'd say, and hold his beautiful working-man's mitt wide against her own fine fingers. "Who *thought* of that?"

The contrast *was* irresistible, and she loved him for noticing. It almost made her not want to broach this other thing. "Can you get into trouble for this? I don't think I'm regarded as a grown-up in Montana until I'm twenty-one."

"Miz Gloria'd have my head, I'm sure. But trouble, with the law? Uh-uh. You may not be able to decide for yourself about the school dance, but otherwise you're a woman at sixteen in these parts. We could get married today if we wanted."

"Put *that* out of your head right now," she told him.

He only laughed. "Here's another curveball. Fella I worked with over in Butte went and got hitched to his high school sweetheart right after they graduated. Both eighteen, but get this—his wife automatically became a legal adult the second they said the I do's, and he still had to wait until he hit twenty-one. When they bought a house, only she could sign the contract."

She frowned. "So you can legally hop into bed at sixteen, but you don't get to be an actual adult for five more years?"

"That's about the size of it."

"It's eighteen for both, in California."

She wasn't sure how much to tell him, how much he'd even want to know. Then again, lying there naked in his bed, it occurred to her that he was the only one she *could* tell. Solidarity by secrecy.

"I seduced Blix, you know, not the other way around. He's about your age, and he'd have gone to prison if we'd gotten caught. Could have, anyway. I was still seventeen at the time."

"Risk does have its rewards."

"Maybe so, but I think he was pretty nervous about it. He's much shyer than you are. Wouldn't have touched me if I hadn't gone out of my way to make resistance totally futile. But part of me always felt guilty as sin for putting him in that position."

He put his finger to the tip of her nose. "What do you know? There is a conscience in there."

A joke, of course, but he was more right than he probably knew. She couldn't evade the haunting feeling that she'd brought the theft of the watch upon herself, although she couldn't decide whether this stemmed from two-timing Blix or carnal behavior in general. She tried to dispense with all of it as, in Roy's words, impractical, but the ghosts of her upbringing hovered nevertheless. And despite her running internal monologue, she could never quite jettison the terror that God was in fact watching and ready to pounce. At least none of McKee's rubbers had broken.

And weirdly enough, the watch business turned out to be not quite finished. She was in the office at the shop, waiting for her parents' weekly check-in, when the call came.

She lifted the receiver. "Hul-loh," she said.

"Miss Clutterbuck." Not her father's voice, and somewhat distant.

"Yes?"

"First off, apologies for our previous encounter. But it's come to our attention we have something that belongs to you. Or your beau, at least. Your flyboy."

"*We.*" Oddly, it struck her that this was the title of Lindbergh's account of the flight to Paris, a reference to the way he'd come to think of himself and his plane. A perfect, almost spiritual fusion of man and machine. Why was this occurring to her now? "Who's *we*?"

"Doesn't matter. You have something that belongs to us."

Already she felt herself shaking.

"So what are *we* going to do about it?" Her voice was also shaking, which she resented even as she heard it. Her chest had gone tight as a steel band. "All I know is, I'm missing my watch."

He paused again. "And now you're wearing another one exactly like it."

"I don't know what you're talking about."

"Don't kid yourself. We've got it on good faith."

She had the unsettling feeling she was being peered upon. She heard the creak of the swivel chair beneath her, realized she was actually on the edge of her seat. She forced herself to lean back.

He went on. "Let's keep this simple. We have something of yours, you have something of ours."

"My eye was black for a week."

"That wasn't part of the plan and I apologize. We don't want anything like that happening again."

"You almost got yourself shot."

"As I said, we don't want anything like what happened last time. Let's just make this work for all of us. You get yours, we get ours."

"A simple exchange?"

"As you said. You're missing your watch, I'm missing mine. Easy math."

"Where and when?"

"Good girl. I'll call you back. Same time tomorrow. And, miss?"

Her brain wanted to scream through this whole thing, was trying to see it from every angle. "Yes?"

"We know you never called the police last time. By all means, keep it that way."

She heard the gentle return of a handset into its receiver, heard the line go cold. She hung up her own phone. She stared at the watch on her wrist.

"Now this beats all," said McKee. "Back for the original watch. You can't make this stuff up."

He and Houston had been out shoeing horses all day at a ranch north of town, had rolled back in not long after the call. Houston was now sitting in the cockpit of the airplane in the shop, for no real reason other than the possibility of it. He looked mighty worried, though.

"What do I do?" she said. "I'm out of ideas here."

McKee shrugged. "Seems like you've got three choices."

She looked at him. "You are way further ahead on this than I am."

"What are they?" said Houston from the cockpit. "The three choices, I mean."

"Number one: Do nothing. You've got a replacement watch, miraculous as it is. Tell 'em to pound sand."

"They won't," said Houston. "Not if they're still nosing around for the dern thing."

Annelise held out her hand for McKee's beer. "He's right."

"Of course he's right. So, number two: Go ahead and make a straight-up trade, if it means getting them down the road once and for all. Also if you're really attached to having your beau's original watch back."

"I'd prefer to think of myself as more practical than sentimental, but it is sort of that way. He used to say the watch gave him his special powers. He trusted me with it."

"A fool and his watch are easily parted," said McKee cheerily. She stuck her tongue out at him.

Huck cut in. "What's the third choice?"

"Go back to square one and call the police. Tell the straight-up truth." McKee shrugged. "If they can connect the dots to set up a pinch, there might be a reward. Might be a means to an engine."

"Yeah, *might*," Houston replied. He thumped the stretched skin of the fuselage. "Might be a means to never getting this thing off the ground, too, 'cause Cy's gonna kill me for taking that dern watch. Not to mention building an airplane in the first place."

McKee shook his head at Annelise. "Would you talk some sense into him?"

"Actually he's making perfect sense. We go to the police, they will at the very least confiscate the one watch we do have." She shook her head. "No way am I losing both."

She tossed around half the night, trying to figure it out. She'd slide into rough sleep and jerk right back out again. She felt like a spider's prey, even her old reliable stinger wound in sticky silk. Yak was right, of course—under normal circumstances they'd have gone straight to the police. But not unlike her cousin, she wished she'd never taken that other watch in the first place.

Normal circumstances, that was the kicker. She was pulled between poles. Wishing for the solace of McKee's bed in one moment, then in the next practically sick with the position she could put people in. Could she be in love with more than one person at the same time?

Maybe everyone could. What did they make you say, on betrothal? Forsaking all others? As though the fork in the road were bound to come up eventually, and nothing good would come of the detour. Maybe that *was* the original sin.

She returned to her own first plunge. Blix had gotten his mitts on a Lockheed Vega, the same model Amelia soloed across the Atlantic and so, like Lindbergh, secured her fame. Yellow not red, but otherwise a gleaming totem, fairly screaming speed with its blunt taper and comet-shaped fairings at the wheels.

She showed up for her lesson, and he told her he had something to show her.

My God, Blix, is it real? Can I sit in it?

He let her twist his arm.

Sit in it? For like a minute, you mean? Guess I pretty much have to cave to that . . .

The Vega belonged to some South American millionaire who'd left it while he hunted sheep out in the desert, or something to that effect. She could barely hear Blix and barely contain herself either, had already squeezed through the door and threaded her way to the little trapezoidal cockpit.

No dual controls, just a single stick and pedals. She looked overhead at the sliding hatch that allowed the model's more illustrious pilots—Wiley Post, Ruth Nichols, Amelia, of course—to stand up out of the cockpit for the flashbulbs and crowds. Blix peered in.

Barely room for one in here, let alone two.

Oh, I think we could fit. Don't you want to try?

One thing led to another. She squeezed over to the side, and he got up into the pilot's chair. Worked the controls around.

I tell you I met Wiley Post once? Right after he set that eight-day record.

You did. Now tell me you don't want to fly this thing.

Oh, I'd love to fly this thing. That big Wasp out front? Four hundred horses and then some. We could shoot this baby to Mexico and back, still have time to run for lunch.

Let's do it then.

He'd only laughed, at first. But one thing did lead to another.

They didn't get anywhere close to Mexico, and he didn't ever offer the controls and she didn't ever ask, but for twenty glorious minutes she sat wedged right alongside him while he climbed and dove and chandelled, maneuvering like the plane was a cross between a roller coaster and a flaming javelin. Her heart and her belly both dropped and rose and dropped again, and every so often he'd bank hard so that she'd have to lean into him with gravitational force, and they were both laughing and laughing, pressing and pressing against each other, and she felt like they were some giddy airborne version of Bonnie and Clyde.

They didn't venture far from the airfield, maybe five miles or so, but with the throttle wide open they reached even that limit in what seemed like seconds. He made one flat run at 180 miles an hour, and she could feel the thrum of the engine in the seat of her underpants. She got to thinking.

Finally he dropped for the runway as though the airplane itself had a parachute attached. He nosed up at the last possible second, set her down light as a feather. They taxied back over and powered down outside the hangar. A grinning moment of silence.

She is one hot little tamale.

Speaking of which. *Guess we didn't quite make Mexico. But you were right, we do have time to grab lunch.* Legs still pressed together in the cockpit, faces just this close. *Or, um, something . . .*

That was the day she'd pounced. One thing leading quite to another. Somehow that was a year ago already.

Now it was all this. She'd kept him safe, kept him out of it. Let herself be sent off just to keep him out of it. And then she wore his watch—straight into someone else's bed. And now it was *all this*.

But there was only one person she knew to conspire with—the same one she'd already shed everything for *besides* the watch. She was aware of the irony.

She rode out of town in McKee's Stude, first thing in the morning. His own wheels had been turning, scheming up an exchange on a backroad proximate to the ranch.

She felt a creeping dread. "Doesn't it make way more sense to meet in a public place? Like the café? I could sit at the counter, and one guy could come in and sit next to me, and we trade watches, he leaves, no one the wiser. And I'm safe in the process."

"Uh-huh. They'll go right for that."

"How do you know they won't?"

"Because for all they know, the two guys in the booth behind you and the cook in the kitchen and maybe even the waitress are undercover law."

He had a point. She flashed back to the slam of the sidewalk and the choke of terror, and she could hardly believe she was entertaining any of this. "What, then?"

"Way I see it, the element of surprise is key. You tell them you'll meet on a backroad, just you and your cousin. What you don't tell them is that you'll be on horseback, and they never will get a glimpse of old Huckleberry.

"They set the watch in the road in front of the car, you drop theirs behind and keep a good berth riding back around. Nothing that lets them anywhere close to you. The second you've got what you're after, you hit the spurs and get hell-for-election out of there."

Something else struck her. "I'm assuming you'll be with Houston."

"I will be about."

"You'd better."

"Oh, I wouldn't miss it."

Later in the office she watched the steady jump of the second hand at her wrist, and someone was evidently watching the identical hand on the identical watch, because the telephone did indeed jangle exactly on time.

"Miss Clutterbuck." Same detached voice. "I take it you're ready to deal."

She told him she'd meet no more than one of them at the county junction near Horsethief Creek. "If there's more than one, I won't even show myself."

McKee nodded at her from across the office.

"You be alone as well, then."

"No. No way. I'd have to be out of my mind, and I can assure you, I am not." The words sounded laughably ironic even as they left her mouth.

"I understand your concern, but I myself am not a fool. I'm not going to show up solo only to have half the high school football team come out of the weeds. Or your redneck uncle, or your gun-toting boyfriend. Never mind the police."

"Now that's pretty rich, coming from a grown man who helped two other grown men jump a lone girl on a dark street." She couldn't stop herself. McKee pointed at her with one hand, raised his middle finger at the telephone with the other. She said, "It'll just be my cousin. Houston."

A long pause.

"All I want is my watch back, with as little trouble as possible. But I don't trust you."

The pause again. "Just your cousin, then. Believe me, I get it. When can you do this?"

Monday, McKee mouthed.

"Monday," she said. "Eight in the morning."

"Early, okay. Early is good."

"What will you be driving, so I know it's you?"

"Ford sedan. Green."

McKee gave her a thumbs-up.

"No guns."

"All right."

"That I don't believe for a minute," she retorted, and hung up the phone. She looked at McKee. "I'm scared."

He nodded. "I know, but we've got this figured. And unbeknownst to them, I will be hovering."

She rubbed her eyes with the heels of her hands. "You damn well better be."

"Who are you, anyway?" She yawned into his neck, burrowed into his blankets and wrapped around him. She wanted to go to sleep and knew she couldn't.

"What do you mean?" He riffled the curls at the back of her head.

"I feel like I know you, and I don't know you. You're some mechanical genius or something, but how? How do you know all this stuff? Motors, metal. Guns." She loved the feel of his fingers, the throb in his chest against her cheek. She yawned again.

He laughed. "Have a knack, I guess. Even as a kid. Dodged a big-ass bullet and wound up in the right place at the right time."

"Tell me then. You told me you would."

He spoke against the top of her head. "Guess I do have you where I want you."

McKee

*I want you to understand I shall not hold you to any midaevil code of
faithfulness to me nor shall I consider myself bound to you similarly.*
          —A.E., letter to George Putnam before their wedding

By the time of his birth in 1914, the holy writ of celestial marriage
had been running against simple math for decades.

His great-grandparents on his mother's side joined the burgeon-
ing faith clear back in New York, although McKee knew little more
than the skeletal details. He could imagine them young, caught in
the countryside fervor of revivals and awakenings, seeking piety and
ecstasy and truth in a unified impulse against the workaday knocks of
weather and season and crops.

They must have been ripe for the picking, in that time of seer
stones and painted hexes. He imagined them falling under the magic
vision of a spell-wrought seeker, a visionary with conviction coming
out his very pores, lightning in his eyes and a trance in his head and
the wreath of his hair like the flaming bush itself. At the prophet's
decree they would migrate or pilgrimage or flee with him, Ohio to
Missouri to Illinois, where McKee's father's line came into the fold.

This required less in the way of speculation, as the facts were sol-
idly anchored in the foundational lore of the Church. Lemuel McKee
had also been a young seeker, but with a hot head and righteous
indignation clear to the marrow, the twelfth of fourteen boys born
to a mash-stilling, mash-swilling, rifle-making Kentuckian. Lemuel
was the only one of the clan whose customary baptism in the river
seemed to endow a principled aversion to both drink and general

helling around—he was saved before he ever sinned. His siblings called him Parson before he could shave.

He'd heard of the Saints and their troubles down in Missouri and held already a keen interest in persecution, in the suffering for faith. More yet in the lashing back against it.

So when he encountered a pair of roving missionaries on the wharf in Paducah, he unleashed a font of questions. Was it true the red Indians were in fact the Lost Tribes of Israel? Did the revelations of the prophet indicate the coming of the Great Rapture? How many presently belonged to this newest manifestation of the faith?

The number was nothing short of stunning. Ten thousand and more were at that very moment building a citadel up in Illinois, with fresh converts trickling in by the day, some from as far away as England. One thing really pricked his ears—after the routings in Ohio and Missouri, the prophet organized and trained a massive armed militia, the Nauvoo Legion, at least half the size of the U.S. Army. Never again would the faithful flee, submit, or otherwise take a drubbing.

This was exactly the kind of conviction young Lemuel could get behind. He left the wharf's smudge pots and its clanging, belching commerce with a wagonload of barrel blanks for his pappy's smithy and *Another Testament of Jesus Christ* for himself. Three months after that, he took himself and his apprenticed skills north to see Nauvoo firsthand. He never laid eyes on Kentucky again.

Fifty-two years later he died at Provo Bench, Utah, mourned by a quorum of wives and thirty-nine living sons and daughters.

Animosity toward the faith in general and plural marriage in particular had even then reached the level of congressional edicts and federal raids and mass incarcerations. With the patriarch dead and persecution coming down like Gentile brimstone, most of the clan migrated south to Cottonwoods, a stronghold in the wild canyon lands for those clinging to the prophet's original condemnation of the cosmic evil called monogamy.

So the marriages and endless birthings went on for another generation in relative solitude, beyond the scrutiny if not the rumor mill of the Gentile world outside.

It was all just life by the time young Enos McKee came along, his mother's first child but then she herself was only thirteen years old at his birthing, and the nineteenth wife of Lemuel's eldest surviving son. Other babies followed in more or less annual succession, and two additional young sister-wives by his sixth birthday. With his child-bride mother perpetually either pregnant or nursing a new baby, Enos was weaned and shooed out early from the petticoats, tended in part by the combined efforts of half-siblings and sister-wives but raised in any real sense by himself alone. His father remained a distant figure, an elder in more ways than one and the progenitor of dozens of offspring, busy with the affairs of the church and a collection of business interests ranging from a cattle ranch to a stone quarry to a water mill.

Young Enos gravitated to the town smithy as though his very blood held magnetic particles, and the blacksmith for whatever reason let him loiter and learn. By the age of eight he was already a capable hand fitting horseshoes and smithing tin, and had as well a rudimentary intuition for the way mechanical parts regulate and time—the lock of a gun, or the arms and wheels of a stationary engine. He learned to temper springs, to hammer and file a knife blade from a billet.

"Make yourself useful, sonny," the smith told him many times. "If you learn anything, learn that."

The smith also taught him to shoot. Rifles at first, but as soon as he'd grown enough to fit a sixteen-gauge Parker built for a lady, live pigeons and trap as well. These last were the smith's real passion, his one extravagance, and he traveled to competitive meets down in Arizona and up in Salt Lake two or three times a year. The kid longed to go with him, to see for himself and to keep learning, but the elders held a tight rein on travel outside the community, in an almost total sense for women and girls but nearly with the same stringency for young males.

Until they were no longer so young.

He saw the math earlier than most. His own sprawling enclave of siblings and half-siblings lacked even a one-to-one ratio, on account of his father's tendency to sire more boys than girls. Otherwise, even at roughly one-to-one, the community at large simply could not reconcile the vexing overflow of virile young males to the celestial doctrine of plural marriage. Eternal godhead could be achieved only through an obedient man's union with no fewer than two wives, and a quorum of at least seven as the actual goal. And only sister-wives could attain the status of goddess for all eternity. Such was the principle, handed down to the prophet by Christ Himself.

McKee watched his half-sisters married off as fourth and fifth wives to elders and bishops three times their age. He saw widows with an existing brood sealed to a new marriage covenant, and budding daughters betrothed in turn to the same demigod.

And he watched the boys depart, cast out at sixteen or seventeen into a world they'd never known, as missionaries to Mexico or conscripted laborers hither and yon, advised to find a bride on the outside before returning to Cottonwoods. But they never seemed to reappear.

Just after McKee's twelfth birthday, his half-brother Samuel took a fourteen-year-old bride from a community even farther south, in Arizona, a supreme blonde beauty named Sara, and two years after that, Sara's younger sister Eleanor became Samuel's second wife.

Samuel owned a special place in the family. The youngest child by their father's first bride, and the direct subject of a specific prophecy about the future leadership of God's elect, he would never, like so many of his brothers, be quietly if summarily ushered from the community.

So when Sara failed to conceive, month after month, whispers and murmurs rippled through the houses and gables. With Eleanor by contrast visibly pregnant within half a year of her own marriage, the expected order of things, the *proper* order, seemed to have gone awry. With the station of a celestial wife wholly dependent upon her creation of new life in the present, it was simply unthinkable that the Almighty might so ordain a barren woman.

By the time Eleanor delivered twins, Sara was no longer the subject of mere whispers. She remained as lithe as ever and so represented at minimum a failure and very possibly a deceiver, right in their midst. She tended to her sister and her sister's babes, but was otherwise kept at arm's length from the general circle of women.

Which was how she came by the freedom of solitude, with solitude's natural outfall—loneliness. Until she began to encounter the community's other outlier, her husband's young and restlessly curious half-brother.

McKee had been around her in a general sense, but the two had barely exchanged a word in the three years since her marriage. He was hunting down in the creek bottom outside town the first time he encountered her alone, rambling along with the Parker 16 and making his way toward a snag at the mouth of a drainage that drew mourning doves on September afternoons. He could see the little gray rockets fairly far out on his approach, whistling down the draw out of the milo field on the flat up above. But he saw as well that they flared right back out again, most of them not even fully settling before flaring away with that panicked, erratic whistle.

He understood why a few steps along, at the glint of lemon sunlight on her blonde hair as she stooped and bobbed at the base of the tree.

Sara, his brother's first betrothed, was hunting herself, after a fashion. Everybody knew she had a knack for plants and wild herbs and their healing properties, that she could make nostrums to cure morning sickness and poultices to ward off infection. Barren or not, this nonetheless made her grudgingly useful. He stopped to watch her pull handfuls of some plant near the base of the dead cottonwood, that golden hair like a late-summer halo.

Her beautiful head. He saw this now, felt the tight bud of such a knowledge bloom inside his consciousness, as though the dead cottonwood behind her were the biblical tree of good and evil. He did not want to scare her by skulking, and he heard himself say her name.

He watched her flinch and straighten bolt up, watched her put a hand to her eyes against the sun. He broke the Parker and started toward her.

"Hello," she called. "You must be hunting."

"This is my dove tree," he told her, when he strode within speaking range.

"They have been flying in the last little while." She smiled when he drew nearer. "You have very blue eyes. I never noticed before."

He gestured at her shock of plants. "Some kind of daisy?"

She took in her own yield as though seeing it for the first time. "It's feverfew. I guess you don't know it?"

He shook his head. "Never paid much attention. What do you do with it?"

"It prevents headaches, for one thing." She held out her hand so he could smell them. White flowers and featherlike leaves, the scent of which brought to mind the lemonade he'd once had at a wedding. Sara breathed them in herself, watching him over the flowers. "It also helps with certain girl troubles."

"Plenty of that around here, I guess." The words just popped out.

She chewed her bottom lip. "You aren't shy, are you?"

He didn't know whether he was or not, but now that she'd brought it up, he did wonder if he hadn't just put his foot into something. But his mouth again ran ahead. "Seems like there aren't enough of you to go around, is all. Can't be, really. Unless you know some plant makes more girls than boys."

Two more doves fluttered into the limbs overhead, and they both watched the birds startle and cry their way into flight again. She turned back to him and said, "Funnily enough, feverfew is also called bachelor's button. But that's not the sort of girl trouble I'm talking about. Do you want me to leave, so you can hunt?"

He did not want her to leave, actually. She had the prettiest teeth he'd ever seen and he wanted her to smile again. "You were here first. I sure don't mind moving on."

"How old are you, Enos?"

"Fifteen. For a few more weeks, anyway."

There, that smile, and thank God. "Well. How about this—do you mind if I just sit with you awhile? Watch you shoot? Or I can maybe be your retriever, if you kill anything."

"You don't have to retrieve nothing," he told her. "But maybe you can just help me watch for incomers. Two sets of eyes, you know."

"I would like that." She breathed in her flowers again. "But, Enos? You know we aren't supposed to be out here like this. Alone, I mean."

He did know, and he realized right then he didn't give a tinker's damn whether he was supposed to be alone with her or not. He just wanted to see her smile. "I can keep a secret." He pointed again at her sheaf of flowers. "Tell me what kind of girl trouble."

She didn't, on that particular outing, but they met again at the same spot a few days along and again after that, and he shot very few doves because mostly what they did was sit by the creek and talk. And eventually she did explain.

She was the first assigned wife for one of the elect and she couldn't conceive a child, or hadn't yet at least, and this had raised not only eyebrows but also suspicions, like hot embers blown up out of a fire. Quietly among the council of elders, but pointedly and even triumphantly within the circle of women.

There was so much competitive henpecking anyway, so many household rivalries. There was solidarity as well, out of both necessity and genuine sisterhood, but by the same turn, jealousy and envy and injury in spades. Condescension, criticism. Gossip wielded like a weapon. The curse of proximity, and the endless cycle of fleeting possession and mandated sharing. And in that, this particular barren beauty—a principal wife no less—may as well have had a target on her back.

"Think about it," she told him. "Put yourself in my place. I was named to an exalted position and I couldn't fulfill my husband's destiny. Oh, and we tried, too—more than the rules even allow. Tried when we weren't supposed to try—do you have any idea what that means?

"No matter. Let's just say we got to trying all manner of things after a while, just caught up in our own frustration, and our own impulse, and praying something would work, and at the same time scared sick that we were dooming our own chances the more we strayed from the rules—that God was watching, and letting out more rope for us to hang ourselves with.

"But we tried anyway, and it didn't happen, and didn't happen, until the shine wore off, and then it got to be like trying at gunpoint." She reached over and patted the stock of the Parker.

"Samuel was afraid it was him. That's why he took my sister so soon." She drew a deep breath. "And he proved it wasn't him, in barely any time at all."

She wasn't able to look at him, eyes scanning the sky as though she hoped for some sign, or maybe just winging doves. "Once he knew it wasn't him, everybody else did, too."

He could smell her, sitting there on the log, literally scent her like a flower, and he studied the taut symmetrical braid in her hair and realized she'd bathed that morning. Lavender, that's what she smelled like. Purple lavender grew in the community's gardens and by the door stoops, hung dried in bunches in the houses. Flavored the honey out of the bee boxes. She herself actually looked like honey. Smelled like lavender, but looked like honey.

She said, "You know I've heard of wives—met them, even—who've only mated nine or ten times in their whole lives, with nine or ten children to show for it?"

He thought about that a moment. He'd been around animals his whole life.

"I don't think the math works. Even with critters that only come into cycle once or twice a year, it's not always a one-shot shebang."

She looked at him. "It's possible, though."

"Yeah, I guess. It's also possible they're lying."

She frowned. "But they're supposed to be the purest of all. The most exalted."

He tilted his eyes at her. "You know you can lead a horse to water, but you can't make it think?" One of the smith's lines.

She blinked at him, and for a second he almost regretted having said it. But she put her head back and laughed at the sky.

They sat just looking at each other, as though both were aware of some puzzle they didn't quite have the code to decipher. Finally she said, "You know a lot of them think I've got something figured out, some special plant or concoction, to give myself an abortion. Do you know what that word means?"

He nodded. "There's things that can make a cow abort a calf, I know that." Still looking at her. "You don't, though. Do you?"

She shook her head. "No. Like I said. We tried and tried."

Two doves streaked in, braked in the air and fluttered into the tree. McKee looked up at them but didn't move to raise the Parker.

"The thing is, E. When we were doing all the trying, Sam and me, before my sister came along? I got to liking it. Part of me did, anyway."

He shifted his eyes to her, caught her own glance and looked back to the doves in the tree. "Why wouldn't you? Horses obviously do. Rabbits. Don't even get me started on goats."

"You know the tenets. We're supposed to be the opposite of animals. We're supposed to keep the lamps out and our underthings on. We're supposed to be without lust, or at least above lust. Pure, I guess. And in this little world you and I live in, in the middle of this desert? Purity is everything. At least for a woman."

The doves still hadn't exited the tree. One of them preened itself with its beak, evidently totally unthreatened. Sara seemed very fixed on them. She shielded her eyes to watch them in the light.

"They really are lying, aren't they?"

"About nine or ten babies? In nine or ten tries?"

She shrugged. "Might only be the tip of the whole thing, but that's a start." She chewed her lower lip, that habit of hers. Those pretty white teeth.

"The math just flat doesn't work. In more ways than one, I reckon."

"But you know how it does work," she said, "in this order. Every triumph, every blessing, every misfortune, and every tragedy—all of it gets explained by God's judgment, or God's approval. If the crop fails, the farmer must have done something to bring down wrath. If a woman delivers a healthy baby every year and her husband prospers, she's in favor.

"But if another of his wives bears a crippled child, or loses a baby in delivery, surely that's the outcome of her own behavior, her own mischief. Her own rebellion."

McKee had begun to think of his future. He knew of boys sent off hither and yon for this infraction or that. Talking to a girl unsupervised was a standard one. Another dove came winging down the draw only to panic and flare in the usual fashion, and the lingering pair in the tree up and departed as well.

"I had my patriarchal blessing when I was twelve," Sara said. "Five years ago already, with Uncle Lehigh, one of the elders in the southern sect. He laid his hands on my head and told me the blood of Jesus Christ flowed in my veins. That I had been a royal spirit in preexistence and that my children would serve as trainers to the ten tribes when they return to earth."

She had her long braid in her fingers, seemed to study the taut plait as though it represented the woven strands of fate itself. "That's why they sealed me to Samuel—his own blessing twined with mine."

McKee had yet to receive a blessing. He knew many young people who had, certainly all the girls by the time they reached eleven or twelve. Usually they did not speak of the details the way Sara was, for fear of tainting its power. It struck him in the moment to wonder whether any of the boys who were ushered out of the community ever received any such blessing. He truly didn't know. He also wondered whether he had in fact been making himself as useful as he might.

"Uncle Lehigh told me that I was destined to go through the veil as a goddess and that my children would achieve great and necessary things. So long as I lived the true faith and honored my husband." She studied her braid. "I was always a good girl, too. Honestly, I was just relieved to go to a young husband and not become the nineteenth wife of somebody my grandfather's age. So the only thing I can think of that would bring down God's wrath? I turned out to be not above lust." She had a tight little smile. "It's the only mark against me, so far as I can tell."

He didn't quite know what to say, but he could only think that this honey-colored woman—girl, really—sitting next to him on a fallen log could not possibly be guilty of anything beyond having a mind.

"Why are we set up to fall this way?" she said. "Commanded to fulfill a destiny, but punished for the pleasure of it?"

He thought for a moment. "You know how in the Bible, when Jesus goes to his first Passover? He's just a kid, maybe twelve or so."

"Yes, it's in the gospel of Luke."

"His parents lose his whereabouts for a few days, right? And when they find him, he's in with the Pharisees or whoever, and they're all amazed he knows just as much as they do. Am I getting it right?"

"I think that's the gist of it."

"And a long time later he winds up crosswise with the same bunch, and now they're certain he knows more than they do, and then what?"

"They kill him."

"Right. Lynch him basically. Well, maybe the people who spout the rules the loudest ain't the ones have any business spouting them in the first place. Maybe that's just as true now as it was then."

"You are bold." She flashed her eyes around. "Better hope the trees don't have ears."

"I know it." He'd wanted to touch her for days now, just something as simple as putting his hand over hers or pressing his palm to her cheek. Anything to connect. But so far, they'd had this small space between them, this silent frontier. The words just popped out, quick as a thought. "We're playing with fire, aren't we."

"Is that a revelation? It's not a bad one."

"It's not one at all. That math is easy as it gets."

She reached over and pinched his arm, and he felt that one small contact go through him like lightning. "Want to hear my revelation?"

"Heck yeah."

"I'm sealed to Samuel, but something's obviously wrong. And you and I, well . . . we're drawn to each other. Am I getting it right?"

"Heck yeah."

"Have you stolen a kiss from a girl? Tell me the truth."

He shook his head.

"Would you like to learn how?"

Surprisingly he felt less anxious than he would have expected. It occurred to him he'd been half hoping for this, maybe even anticipated it. He looked at her with one eye wide, the other clamped shut. "We *are* playing with fire. Aren't we."

"Yes, we are. And we might well get burned. Right at the stake, for all I know. Then maybe in hell."

He let his clamped eyelid loose, took her fully in. "I don't care."

* * *

For the next few months they met as often as they could, in the creek bottom with a blanket while Indian summer lingered and later at an empty granary he knew about by a fallow field outside Cottonwoods.

He marveled at her naked body, the small swell of her pale breasts and the delicate sculpting of her throat. Though he'd never seen so much as a depiction of a naked girl previously, much less a fully developed one, he had assumed the latter would have a thatch between her legs the way males of a certain age did.

To his surprise her entire form was bare as ivory and nearly as smooth, although some degree of pelage did grow not only between but also down the length of her legs, as well as beneath her arms the way it did on a man. When she laid her wrist on the blanket above her head that first time, his eyes went straight to the exposed cup beneath her shoulder and he could see the stippled skin. When he moved his hand up the length of her calf, he felt the same faint rasp he recalled from his very early childhood, the few times he got close enough to his father's face to feel the barb of shaven jowls. When he entered Sara that first time, he felt a similar slight prickle.

Despite a good bit of trepidation he finished in a jiffy, startled at the yielding clench of her flesh and then stunned by instantaneous white fire flashing into and through and out of him. But before he could even see straight, his general academic impulse had the better of him.

He ran a thumb through the swale beneath her arm and asked whether this was the usual habit of women.

"Hush a minute," she whispered. She pulled him down again to the heave of her ribs and held him. She kept him in place and said, "Shortly before I married Samuel, my mother took me aside to explain what I'd need to know. Not all of it was about pain and sacrifice and duty—some of it had more to do with staying ahead, once there were other wives in the picture. For my own survival, I guess.

"She told me the best way to lock up a man's attention, once there was competition, was to shave everything but my eyebrows."

McKee raised his own, because this did beat all.

"Then she swore me to silence, which at the moment seems like a lot of water under the bridge."

He hoisted himself back up to see her face. "What's the difference, hair or no, if you're only supposed to do this lamps-off and bloomers-on in the first place?"

"I imagine that's why she swore me to silence. She must know full well herself that nine or ten babies in nine or ten tries is, um . . ."

"Hogwash," he said.

He hoped to make her laugh, but she suddenly had a faraway look in her eyes. "Of course," she said, "when my mother gave me that advice, I don't think she had any notion my own sister would be next in line."

She could go from babbling, mind-bent bliss to gales of grief in minutes, as though her heart were a pendulum with a wrecking ball's swing. The first time she did this was the third time they sated each other, and contrarily, the first time he found himself fully able to fall out of his own head and into the moment, with its tumbling plunge.

One minute she panted and seethed into his ear, clawing the bare skin of his back, and the next she was curled into a ball, sobbing. His own warm wave curdled.

He was afraid to touch her then but he did anyway. With her back to him he saw the red flush from the scratch of the woolen blanket, felt the heat of it when he placed his hand there. "Did I do something?" He could barely get the words out, his heart lodged in his throat.

She gulped at the air like a fish dragged to shore. Finally settled a little. "No, no . . . shhh. It's nothing. Not you. I promise."

And though she wouldn't say more, he knew that whatever did ail her, it couldn't amount to nothing.

*   *   *

Late in the fall with the leaves blown from the cottonwoods and the doves long winged south, the smith took him with a freight wagon over to the coal operation a couple of miles out of the village. His normally jocular mentor had gone oddly grim over the past few days, and they were barely into the red desert before he started talking. The low tone of his voice held a grimness all its own.

"Been needing to talk to you, hoss."

McKee studied the yaw of sky from the sway of the wagon. Hazy clouds a-smudge across the blue yonder, the sun low and mute. He crossed his fingers that this was about some bungle or other in the smithy. He very much feared otherwise.

"They're onto you, kid. Or think they are anyway, and in these parts there ain't much difference between the two."

McKee risked a glance. "I guess this is where I'm supposed to ask what in tarnation you're talking about."

The smith shifted his own eyes right back, a look that said everything.

"All right, then. Yeah. I been at her, hammer and tongs. Guilty as charged. Or we've been at each other, if you want the whole untarnished truth of it."

"Jehoshaphat, kid. Your brother's own wife?"

McKee let the wind blast from his lungs like a gust through a canyon. "She's pretty lonely, comes right down to it. Anyhow, Samuel and I mainly just share the same pappy."

"Reckon that ain't all you're sharing." He nudged McKee in the ribs, and they both did laugh a little. "She is about as pert as they come, I'll give you that. Good work, if you can get it." He ribbed the kid again. "*While* you can get it, anyway."

"How bad's it liable to be?"

"They gonna run you out, I expect. What I been trying to save you from." Another sidelong look. "Maybe not my smartest play, come to think of it."

McKee shook his head. "Ain't talking about me. I mean how bad for her."

The smith squinted up through the haze, at the pale disk of the sun. "They'll keep it under the rug, I reckon. Keep her under the rug, too." That sideways glance again. "This sorter thing ain't exactly unheard of. Which ain't to say it'll much get talked about either, at least not in the wide-out open."

"But they'll keep her in the fold?"

The smith nodded his great beard. "She's done sealed. After this I doubt anybody much lets her out of sight, though."

"They never do run the girls out, do they? Even the barren, untrue ones."

The smith snorted. He had no wives at all, save the one buried in the ground years ago, along with his first and only child. That's about how much McKee knew. "Heck, kid. They don't even run out the homely ones."

McKee looked out at the towering features of the desert. Red rock and thin snow, slashing and slashing up the parapets and reefs. A beautiful waste. "They'd have run me off eventually anyway. Useful or not."

"You got clan up around Ogden, right? Manifesto people?"

"That's the story. I ain't met any of 'em." Ogden may as well be the Orient.

The smith thought a minute. "All right." He slapped the reins, and the horses' ears tilted back and they quickened their step. "There's a trap meet up thataway at the end of the month. I got an idea."

They rode along in silence, McKee calculating for himself what exactly this plan might entail. Finally he said, "Truth be told, I'd have bolted on out anyway of my own free election. One of these days."

Sure enough, when he next went to the granary at their appointed time, Sara failed to arrive. He gave it a lonely hour and made his way back.

She came in like a ghost from the dusk at the end of the day, the embers in the forge still glowing. She had a shawl around her head and another around her shoulders, and framed the way she was in the doorway and bathed in the glow of a lantern, she looked for all the world like some Madonna of the desert. McKee knew already he'd never see her again.

One week later, at a trap range outside Ogden, he registered for the first time as a competitive shooter with the Parker 16. To his surprise, the meet was not a purely staid affair—there were plenty of churchmen, to be sure, but an even greater number of Gentiles from as far away as Denver and Cheyenne. An entire tent city sprang up with a carnival-like atmosphere of betting and drinking, the smell of gunpowder heavy in the air.

A lull in the competition brought sporting girls in a pair of gleaming touring cars. He'd never seen anything like them, never seen lips that were actually red and cheeks with a blush that wouldn't fade. He found himself staring at first, his mind amok with the possibilities of what might be going on behind the flaps of tents.

Then he thought of Sara with her honey-colored hair, her honey-colored skin. Even her lips had a golden hue. In an unexpected flash he considered what she might look like painted up the way these girls were and he quickly roused inside his trousers, but for the first time in a way that made him feel not only unsettled but actually ashamed. A boom from the trap field rolled through the chill, bright air. He hurried away from the tents and tried to force her false painted image from his head.

He hadn't quite managed a total purge by the time his round came up on the line, and he found himself so rattled by his own conflicted brain or the disorienting strangeness of the setting that he shot right over his first three targets.

The smith walked up behind him. "Gotta take your time, but you've also *got* to hurry up. Shoot quicker, before they start to drop."

"Think I got too used to incoming doves." The smith knew full well he'd barely shot any of those lately, either.

"None of the rest of this may look familiar, but I've thrown you plenty of targets just like these the past few years. Swing up through 'em and smash the daylights out of 'em." He put his massive hand on the kid's slim shoulder, as though to impart some insight beyond the utility of words.

McKee chipped the following two targets, then settled in and got his head straight and proceeded to inkball ninety-five straight disks in a row. He walked off the line to hoots and applause.

The smith grinned like a happy dog. He pointed to a cluster of well-dressed gents nearby. "That young fella over there, on the left? He just won a thousand dollars on you. Wants to talk to you."

"Me?" The fellow in question was not much older than his brother Samuel, but with an air about him even young McKee could see in a glance. Straight as a ramrod, with a haircut and suit that may as well have been commissioned by God the Father.

"Know who it is?"

McKee shook his head, wondered if it could possibly be one of his supposed Ogden relations.

"That's Val Browning. John Moses's son."

For the first time possibly ever, or at least that he could remember, Enos McKee went weak in the knees, because he may as well have just won the match on behalf of God the Father's only begotten Son. Every sturdy boy in Utah and many in the rest of the world knew the name and the legend of John Moses Browning, the most ascendant arms designer in the history of the world. Inventor of about half of Winchester's current sporting line and nearly every practical automatic weapon in existence, holder of hundreds of patents and a certified titan in the pantheon of Franklin and Edison and Ford. Ogden native, Latter-day Saint. Died at his design bench just about three years ago to the day, still innovating at seventy or thereabouts.

"John Moses's son," said McKee. He looked off to the towering wall of the Wasatch, let his eyes scan upward from the blushing bleed of sage and snow across the foothills, through white bands and whipped drifts on the granite above. "Thought Val lived in Belgium."

"He does. Mostly. But they keep a shop here in Ogden, too. That's why he wants to talk to you."

McKee clutched the barrels of the Parker like the rail of a ship in a heaving chop. Despite the brisk autumn air, he felt the lingering warmth from a hundred exploded shells. "This all part of your big plan?"

The smith again put his big mitt on the kid's slim shoulder. Gave the usual shake. "Got a few tricks up my old sleeve yet, little hoss."

"I apprenticed in that Ogden shop for four years. That's where I really learned guns, same time I was learning machine work. We had lathes, milling machines, power hammers . . ."

"You are so lucky that's the way it went for you. All things considered. It could have gone so much worse."

He brooded for a moment, breathing there against her, and when he finally spoke, she realized he was circling back into his own tale, after the missing and fractured parts, the parts he'd avoided or misplaced in the original telling. "She knew I had to go, is the thing. Of course she did. She knew I had to go, and she never could."

Annelise held him tight, stroked the muscle of his arm, kissed his hair, his cheek. His voice had choked and cracked more than once, and more than once he'd had to stop and collect himself, and she could sense the gale of old grief, racking inside him yet. "All it was, was circumstances. She didn't choose them, any more than you did. Otherwise, she'd have chosen differently."

When he had his voice, he said, "I tried to talk her into leaving with me. That last time I saw her, in the smithy. Guess it sounds ridiculous, but it seemed reasonable at the time. Seemed possible."

"Oh Lord, honey. I can't imagine that would have ended well. They would've tracked you both down."

He sort of shrugged, wound up as he was in her arms. "Don't know if they would have or not. But yeah, probably. That ain't what stopped her, though." He took a deep breath. "She didn't only come to say goodbye. She come to tell me she finally had a baby inside her."

"Oh. Oh my." She stared at the bulb in the ceiling, the hammering moths. "So she—passed it off as your brother's, I guess?"

He didn't even bother to answer.

"None of that was easy on her, I promise you. Those circumstances were not easy on her."

"Well. She did have some fire to her, I can say that. I got to glimpse it, at least."

"Do you still love her?"

"Always. Never won't. That okay?"

"God, of course. How could it not be?"

They lay there in silence.

"Do you know what happened to her?" she finally asked, and an eerie shiver passed through her even as the words came from her lips, the fine down on her forearms standing straight up like hoarfrost.

He eyed her sudden gooseflesh, ran a finger up her arm where it lay on the sheet. "No. Not beyond what I can imagine, and I imagine she's still right where I left her." He shifted around a little. "But once you're gone from a place like that, there really ain't a way to go back. Not if you leave the way I did. It's like being cast out of the garden, or something."

She looked at him aslant. "Yak. That was no Eden in the first place."

Juno II

Huck settled back with his spyglass in the limber pines atop the rim above the county road and scanned the country in the rising light. Horsethief Creek burbled yet, although barely, little more than a drought-choked trifle on the other side of the roadway. He panned the reef on the far side of the creek. Yak was forted up in there somewhere, although Huck couldn't pick him out after twenty minutes of glassing.

He'd saddled the horses out back of the barn at five o'clock, and he and Annelise had cantered down the two-track and along the greened-up wheat in the rising light. The moon floated like an apparition in the west, mysterious as a silent veiled girl.

He moved up alongside her. "Think Yak's already set?"

"I'm sure he is." He'd wanted to get into position early, in case the other conniving bastards had the same idea.

They clipped fast where the track leveled south across the sage flat, past an old impoundment that hadn't held a good reserve of water in ten years. The light came up steadily while they rode, the tattered edges of clouds limned with coral a half hour ahead of the strike of the sun.

They came up on the boundary fence and cut back to where the two-track exited the ranch through a poor man's gate. Huck swung down and handed the reins to his cousin. He put his shoulder into the stave and took the tension off the keeper. He looked up at her. "This is a stupid idea, isn't it?"

Her mouth twisted into a grimace, as though to acknowledge that he was only saying what she herself was thinking. She prodded the bay and passed through the gate with both horses. "Yeah, probably. Yak can be sort of . . . *persuasive*, I guess."

"Maybe because he's such a hand," Huck mused. He left the gate open and swung back onto Pop's sorrel. "I mean, the guy can do *anything*. He's good at *everything*. Like some crazy genius."

To his shock, Annelise leaned right off the starboard side of the bay and heaved a gush, straight at the ground. Mostly water, it looked like. She spat a few times, still leaning and also gripping the saddle horn. "Ugh," she said, then retched and hacked again. Nothing else came up.

"Whoa. You okay?"

She nodded and gulped air. Finally she looked up at him. "He may be a genius, but that is no marker for basic good sense." She spat again. "We should probably all have our heads examined."

An hour later Huck found himself automatically reverting to the old *Please, God, please* from his perch on the rim. *Please, God, please keep Annie safe. Please, God, please let this work.* He hardly cared about the watch or the plane or anything else at the moment.

With the hour upon them he realized he'd had a sort of swash-buckling bravado over the past few days—like Annelise said, McKee's general devil-may-care personality was nothing if not persuasive. Contagious, even. All that vanished like money once he watched her vomit from Wilbur's back.

He wished he could at least see her now, but she was down off the rim and up the road, around some calved-off boulders where McKee had stashed his rig earlier. Or not his rig exactly, but the REO.

"Shoot," Huck had said. "Don't tell me Pop's here too."

"I can't imagine."

"Wonder why Yak brought the tow truck then."

She leaned off the side of the horse and screwed her eyes shut against the ground. "There is no telling with him. I think I'm going to be sick again."

She wasn't, though, at least not while he was still there with her. He glassed the reef again, thought he caught movement back in the dappled light where the sun filtered through the trees. Maybe McKee, maybe just a jay or a dern chipmunk.

He heard the unmistakable sputter of a Model A Ford, carrying up the rim like the buzz of an insect. He trained his jittery spyglass down the county road. The roof of a sedan rose into view over the swell of the terrain, sunlight flashing like a strobe against the windshield.

The Ford downshifted and coasted to a stop. Huck couldn't make out the interior with the sun on the glass, couldn't see the driver or tell if he was alone. He yanked his eye from the telescope and whipped his head the other direction. Annelise clipped out to the roadway from the jumbled rocks.

She walked the horse toward the car and hadn't gone far before Pop's sorrel neighed out after her, tethered back in the boulders. Wilbur jerked his own head around and neighed in response, and Annelise reined him a bit and nudged him with her heels and loped forward.

She reined Houston's little bay to a standstill fifty feet ahead of the car. At this span she could see the driver's indeterminate form through the windscreen, and he did appear to be alone. She heard the pop of the door.

The same bastard from the fair, she was sure of it, even if she hadn't gotten a great look at him that night. Same light-colored fedora, though, tipped almost jauntily on his head. He stood on the running board, looking at her above the V of the open door, forearm atop the window frame. "Howdy. Nice horse."

"May I see my watch."

He put his hand into the air. Blix's Longines dangled like a military pendant. "And mine."

She held up her left wrist. "I'm going to ride around you. Keep your distance."

She tapped heels to Wilbur and steered him down off the roadway and along the creek bed. Fedora came around from the driver's door and leaned casually against the grille between the headlamps. When she came alongside he said, "So where's your cousin?"

"He's watching you, through a telescoped rifle." She forced and held a tight little smile.

He laughed. "Hold your fire, kid," he shouted. "I already owe you one."

"That was a really low play you all made," she told him, swiveling her head to watch him while the horse gained ground. "You ought to be ashamed."

"Oh, I ain't proud exactly. There's still honor among thieves. Sort of."

"Could've fooled me. What would your mother think, I wonder."

"She'd beat my ass. Send me to my room."

"Good for her." She held up her wrist again. "What's so special about this particular watch?"

"It's sentimental. You wouldn't understand."

"Oh, Yak was right, you really don't know me. I might not put sentiment above practicality, but I would put it above honor, in the right situation."

He laughed again. "You are a pistol, darlin'. You ever want a life of crime, come find me."

"Don't tempt me. You can walk down the road now. Take twenty steps and stop."

"You're the boss." He straightened up and stepped forward.

She cleared the sedan and turned Wilbur back up onto the road and went another couple of car lengths before wheeling around. Fedora had stopped where she'd told him to and was looking at her now with the watch trailing from his fingers. Annelise undid the buckle at her wrist. "I'm going to drop this. Put mine down at the same time."

"Don't break it."

"You either." She gripped the saddle horn and leaned off Wilbur's side as far as she could. The watch dangled within two feet of the gravel. She kept her eyes on him. "Put it on the ground."

He set the watch down. "Now you."

Annelise let hers go as well. She straightened up. "Walk forward."

She let him get five steps from the watch and put Wilbur back off the shoulder and into a trot. She got ahead of the sedan and steered back onto the road and whoaed the horse above Blix's watch, glinting in the dust. Key to a kingdom. She turned Wilbur again so she could watch Fedora. He'd just cleared the tail of the car.

McKee had given her a horseshoe magnet on a length of cord, coiled now like a miniature lariat from a latigo on the saddle. She freed it and lowered the magnet on its tether, prodded the horse a step forward and felt the irresistible pull of the thing seize the watch with a thud. She reeled it like a trotline and shoved watch and magnet and all right down the front of her shirt.

"Adios, amigo."

Fedora looked back. He wasn't quite to his watch. Annelise slapped the reins and launched like a cannonball.

The drumbeat of Wilbur's hooves vanished, although the dust from his haste wafted like gun smoke. Huck snapped back to himself and looked to the opposing reef, just in time to see the flash and white bloom of actual gun smoke at the tree line, and not at all where he'd figured McKee to be earlier. He knew only one gun with such a belch.

He'd shot enough game animals to know the *kugelschlag*, the almost pneumatic *thh-wapp!* of a bullet searing through flesh, an instant behind the blast of the rifle itself.

From his vantage on the rim he heard a reverse of the phenomenon. The great lead slug ripped through the Ford's iron wheel with the shriek of a train wreck, and the rear of the car collapsed in a burst of dust. The echoing boom rolled like thunder.

The goon jumped like a jabbed cat and bolted back for the Ford, apparently on impulse. He couldn't have driven the thing in any case, but no matter—just about the time he had a hand on the latch, McKee let another one rip. The glass in both rear doors exploded in a hail of diamonds.

The goon hit the deck and covered his head, his fedora flipped into the dirt. Huck heard a mad whine and saw a second car coming fast over the rise, a newer five-window coupe hurtling through a comet of dust. The goon scrambled up again and tried to paw around inside the Ford while still crouching behind it, and yet another billow opened from McKee's position on the reef.

The Ford rocked like a boat on a swell, though none of the remaining glass seemed to break. The man had evidently had enough, as he scrambled back out empty-handed and lit on a dead run for the coupe, which careened to a ragged halt.

The now-bareheaded goon jumped around like Harpo Marx out front of the second car. He appeared to be trying to communicate with the driver through the windshield, pointing underneath and waving his arms and gesticulating wildly toward the reef and its waft of highland haze.

Huck figured it out. The coupe had come to a stop directly atop the Lindbergh watch. McKee either reckoned the same thing himself or maybe just felt it best to keep slinging lead so long as these honyocks were inclined to stick around and present a target. He let another one fly at the idling coupe, a can opener of a bullet that tore a long gash across the convexity of the roof and also spiderwebbed the windshield. The man *was* a sharpshooter. Juno's report rolled again.

The hatless goon let out a yelp and scrambled for the passenger door as the car lurched into reverse and started back the way it had come. He managed to get the door flung open and himself flung inside, and the driver poured the coals. Huck heard the laboring whine of the transmission. The open door bounced like a busted wing.

The coupe went into a skidding radius well up the way and jerked to a hard stop crosswise to the road. The door slammed shut. Huck watched the car steer around the way it had come and roar back over the rise.

Now this was a turn. He realized he'd already jumped to his feet, spyglass dangling from his hand. He looked toward the reef and watched McKee emerge from the trees and start down toward the crippled Model A.

Five minutes later Huck came out of the limber pines and scrabbled down off the rim to the REO. Annelise still sat atop Wilbur, the reins to Pop's sorrel in her right hand. She looked like she'd just heard a homicide through a hotel wall.

"What just happened? Is he all right?"

"He got us an engine, is what happened." Huck opened the driver's door and tossed his spyglass onto the seat. "He shot up the Ford with Juno. Gotta be why he brought the truck instead of his own rig."

"Tell me you weren't in on this."

"No clue. Honest."

"Please tell me the guy's not dead."

"They had another car over the hill, came and picked him up." He hit the starter and the REO churned to life. "You all right?"

She let out a breath. "Remember what I said about common sense and genius?"

"Set tight. I'll honk if it's still clear."

He drove up onto the road and around the bend. The Ford slumped on its rear fender, the wheel at a totally incoherent cant. McKee had come down from the reef with the Sharps.

Huck rolled up even with him and stopped while he picked his way across the creek and to the roadside. "Nice shootin', Tex."

"That last one was a hell of a gamble, I'll admit. She okay?"

Huck blasted the REO's horn. "Well, she ain't hurt. A little dazed, maybe."

Yak looked down the road to its vanishing point at the crest of the rise. "Wait right here a minute. Keep your eyes peeled."

"You think they'll be back after all that?"

McKee swiveled his head the other direction. Annelise had come into view with the horses. "If I got it figured, that dern albatross of a watch is right there where she dropped it."

He kept the Sharps in the crook of his arm and walked up the road, then sure enough knelt down and recovered the second Longines. He took another glance at the rise, then motioned Huck forward.

Annelise arrived with the horses about the time Huck had the REO backed to the tail of the crippled Ford. She took in the damage to the wheel and hub, the blown-out glass. She looked down at McKee. "I have half a mind to wring your neck."

He struck a theatrical pose with Juno. "That'll have to wait. We have an airplane to power."

An hour later they had the Ford backed into the barn. McKee hung a chain hoist from an overhead beam, and after another hour of wrenching, he and Houston nearly had the engine free.

Annelise paced around with her belly half in a roil. She was supposed to be keeping an eye out for her aunt. She'd look out the barn door at the chickens pecking in the yard and the horses in the corral and the long summer light across the contour of the land, then turn back to the bullet-riddled Ford and feel herself upend all over again. The other two seemed infuriatingly cavalier, or at least single-minded on the task. Why on earth were they worried about Houston's mother when they'd just double-crossed a bunch of outright criminals?

Finally she put her head through the shot-out window. The back of the sedan fairly glittered with shattered glass, and the door panel had a gaping exit hole. The same bullet had also ripped through the back seat, white stuffing blooming like cauliflower. "What are we going to do with the rest of this heap?"

"Dump it down a ravine," McKee told her. "I've got one picked out. With any luck, nobody'll find it for a couple of decades."

She pulled her head back out. "I don't like it that they didn't get their watch back."

"Hell with 'em. Serves 'em right."

"I don't care. I'd just as soon know they were long gone and never coming back."

She reached for the handle on the front passenger door and turned the latch and swung the door on its hinges. A flat leather satchel fell out and landed on the running board with a thud. "Uh-oh."

Houston wriggled out from under the car. "What?"

She pointed. "That. Evidently it slipped down between the seat and the door."

"Huh. Wonder if that's what the guy was trying to get once the shooting started. I figured it was probably a heater." He held up his grease-blackened mitts. "You gonna pick it up?"

Yak straightened from the engine. "Pick what up?"

"This here pouch. Just fell out of the car."

McKee glanced at it. "These guys are like the Keystone Krooks. What's in it?"

She lifted the satchel with two fingers and held it out away from her, with the distinct feeling that drawing the zipper might unleash some genie that couldn't be put back. Finally she resigned herself and drew out a small leather-bound book.

"The Good Book?" said McKee. He shifted to her cousin. "Maybe the guy in the river really *was* a reverend."

"It's not a Bible. It's a diary."

"Oh, like girls keep, you mean. For all their secret thoughts."

"More or less."

"These are some mighty demure criminals, I'll say that."

She flipped through it. "Mostly seems like a ledger, in some kind of shorthand." She went to the front flap. "Here's a name, though. Charles H. Angle. And a Billings address."

"Huh," said Houston. "Wonder if that's the guy you just shot at."

McKee tested the chain coming down from the rafters. "Who knows? Could be the stiff in the river, or their dern accountant for all we know. Just stow it for now, we'll check it out when we've got more time. We need to pluck this thing and ditch the evidence."

"Hello? Houston?" Aunt Gloria, and evidently not far off.

Houston froze like a salt pillar.

"Annelise? Where are you two?"

"Scoot," said McKee. "Be quick."

Annelise shoved the book back into the satchel and tossed it over toward the saddles on her way to the door. She felt sick to her stomach all over again.

The squall in her center became a blessing in disguise. Aunt Gloria was not far at all from the entry to the barn, and Annelise had barely begun to contrive some plausible excuse to turn her back to the house. Her stricken constitution handled it for her.

She veered slightly off course and bent at the waist and heaved once again into the dirt. She spat and gasped.

"My land, child. What's into you now?" Aunt Gloria started toward her.

She forced herself upright and wobbled ahead. "Can you help me get to the house?"

"My head is pounding." It wasn't, really, but she sat in the kitchen with her eyes clenched and rubbed her temples. She heard her aunt wring a cloth into the basin.

"I'm going to put this on the back of your neck. That always helps me. I get a weak stomach from those awful spells, too."

She felt the cool, delicate pressure on her skin, and headache or no, it did feel good. Her belly really was out of sorts, that at least was true.

"Have you had your back and hips checked?"

She thought back to that day in the shop when they were slathering airplane dope on the raw muslin of the fuselage. The searing fumes hit her right between the eyes. "I don't generally get headaches, is the thing. But the boys are using some chemical out in the barn. It burns just to breathe around it, it's so strong. I think the fumes got to me."

"Heavens to Betsy, stay away from that nonsense. Bad enough men have to work with it, but there's no reason in the world for a woman to. We are just not built the same."

She could hardly argue, given the bluff she'd just played. "I guess it is sort of impossible to imagine a girl riding a horse clear from Texas, like Uncle Roy did." And she had to admit, she actually meant it.

"Oh, men used to do that sort of thing. Even when I was a girl, the world was a different place. Why, we got to town in a buckboard wagon."

"Right, but he was only ten years old."

This seemed to stop her aunt cold. Annelise still had her eyes closed, the damp cloth at her neck, but the long silence could not be missed.

"I guess that's so," she finally said. "It's hard for me to imagine him that young. There are no pictures of him. So I tend to think of him as just . . . older. Always. The age he was when I met him, anyway. Which even then was nearly thirty."

Annelise cocked an eye open. Gloria appeared to be lost in thought. "He must have been pretty capable, though. At ten years old, I mean."

Her aunt seemed to consider this for the first time, too. "Well, yes. He must have been."

"Apple didn't fall far from that tree. With Houston."

"You know I . . . have to stop and remind myself he's even in high school now? Even as tall as he is, and now with this new voice he has?" She trailed off, then shook her head at the ceiling. "How on earth did it happen?"

"I could still wring your neck. Don't go thinking everything's hunky-dory, just because we made it through that ridiculous stunt in one piece."

They were in McKee's room, not for the usual reasons. She leaned against the countertop with her arms crossed, tight as a bar across a door. He'd tried to nuzzle his way in but finally gave up and sat at the table.

"You mean the stunt that got us a motor?"

"You could have at least told me."

"You never would've gone for it."

"You're right."

"Plus I didn't want you implicated. If things actually went south."

She tried to stare him down but his blue eyes never wavered, and she finally looked away herself. "If somebody wound up dead, you mean?"

"Or if Farmer Brown happened along, or the police came into it. Anything."

This was the problem with sleeping with someone. You started to fall for the whole nine yards. "It was still a hell of a risk."

"No doubt. But you said it before. Risk has its rewards."

"Actually you said that."

"And you believe it, same as me. You think Miss Earhart's not taking on risk, flying over the widest part of the dern ocean? You think the ol' Lone Eagle didn't take a hell of a risk? New York to Paris, in a flying gas tank? Come on. Sounds crazy even now, ten years down the road. Who's that other one you told me about, from last year? Beryl somebody?"

"Beryl Markham. Who crashed when she landed, by the way."

"Lived to tell, though. She set a record, right?"

She nodded. "True enough. First person east to west across the Atlantic."

"Took a risk."

She nodded, almost against her will. "A big one."

"Well. I took a risk, and here we are. With a motor."

She'd thrown up again once they'd gotten back to town. They'd hauled the husk of the Ford out on some rough winding road and up a grade, and he'd backed the thing off an inside bend and cut it loose. She could still hear the grate and screech as the car half rolled and half slid down the chute, still hear the rest of the glass coming out when it veered and tipped sideways and finally crashed into the brush.

Hunched over the commode in the bungalow later, it struck her that she might be pregnant. What an irony that would be. She'd heaved again, hard enough to start tears. That panic didn't last, thank God.

She crossed the floor and pushed him into the seatback and sat in his lap. "Don't get any ideas. My period just started." Nerves, all along.

He sat there and held her. "Great news."

She laughed. She was frayed, but she could laugh. And they had a motor.

Air Camper

1

According to letters received by the editors, interest in the conversion of the Model A Ford motor as applied to my little ship has been mighty hot.

　　　　　—B. H. Pietenpol, 1932 *Flying and Glider Manual*

"B. H. Pietenpol," said McKee. "Who *is* this cat?"

He had the motor plans pinned to the corkboard in the fabrication bay, the engine resting in a cradle. He'd studied the prints a lot in the past months, the way Huck had for the better part of a year. They were both stunned by the marvelous simplicity of the whole thing.

"Some farmer in Minnesota," Huck said.

"Yeah, I gathered that." He looked over at the motor and rapped his skull with his knuckles. "I'm no slouch at oddball engineering, but this makes me feel like a first-grade bedwetter. What in God's name made him think you could run a homemade crop duster with a full-size car engine? And how in the hell'd he survive the trial and error?"

Huck shrugged. "How'd Orville and Wilbur?"

McKee gave him a stumped look. "Good point."

They'd been at it two evenings and one full day and had already finished a lot of the modifications. Most of the major adaptions involved the lubricating system. Since the propeller bolted directly to the crankshaft, the motor mounted to the fuselage in reverse of its normal orientation. So in a climb, no provision in the original design could prevent the oil from pooling at the wrong end of the case rather than recirculating through the working system. Down she'd go, in a fatal tutorial on the nature of gravity—not to mention human folly.

Pietenpol had solved the problem with sheet-metal oil dams in the splash pan, plus a couple of quarter-inch copper lines to the crankcase to route the necessary lube to bearings and rods, regardless of the degree of climb. Simple but ingenious. The stock timing and valve covers were swapped out for lighter versions, and beyond that a handful of tweaks to manifolds or brackets made up the bulk of the reengineering. They had little to do now but replace the original distributor with a hotter magneto for ignition.

Pop sauntered into the bay. He shook out a cigarette, which he hardly ever did in the shop. He sat on a sawhorse. "That was Cy Gleason on the phone."

Huck looked at him. As far as his father knew, the engine came out of a totaled Ford McKee had caught wind of over in Golden Valley County. He tried to conjure a casual line of inquiry and came up instead with a guilt-ridden blank.

Not so McKee. "What's he want, donations for the stray-dog fund?"

Pop lit up and dragged. "Nope. He called to say the state police have a line on the rest of that holdup outfit. Or think they do, anyway."

"They catch 'em?"

Pop blew smoke through his nose. "Nope."

"Kill 'em?"

He snorted. "No, but evidently somebody tried to. Cy's calling every garage and grease monkey he can think of, telling them to be on the lookout for a gray Plymouth coupe with a cracked-up windshield and pretty serious damage to the roof."

Huck had the upper bolt for the magneto run down into the block, and he went to start the lower but couldn't for the life of him get the thing to thread. He stared at his hand, shaking like he had an attack of the ague. The ratchet in his other hand jumped like an eel and bounced off the floor.

Pop pulled in another drag. "Don't get ahead of yourself, sonny. Cy's calling everywhere, not just here."

"Seems like a long shot these guys would risk pulling into a local shop," said McKee.

"True, but he's got to start somewhere."

"What makes him think somebody other than Johnny Law's after them?"

Pop exhaled again, shifted to his hired hand. "According to Cy, somebody blew half their roof off. With a dern big gun."

McKee clucked like a mother hen. "Poor bad guys."

Pop laughed, but Huck had the sense it was half against his will. "Couldn't happen to a nicer bunch, all right." He turned to Huck. "Where's that cousin of yours?"

Huck left the ratchet on the floor and concentrated on the bolt. He held on to the solid anchor of the motor with his off hand and got the shakes under control. He started the threads. "She went up to the post office. I guess a package came for her."

Yak had again picked up the 1932 *Flying and Glider Manual*, flipped it open to the motor conversion. "So how'd Cy catch on that these bozos are still around?"

"That's the funny thing. Anonymous tip, to the Custer County Sheriff's Office. They put the word out, and sure enough, a deputy up in Garfield passed a gray Plymouth with cracked-up glass and some kind of gash in the roof. So now they're putting shops onto it, too."

"Anonymous tip," said McKee. "Sounds like something Raleigh would come up with."

Huck nodded. "I'm sure it wasn't Raleigh, though." He realized how incriminating this sounded as the words passed his lips. "I mean, he'd tell me if he caught wind of something. Anyway, he's been over in Oregon with his pa the past week."

"I mainly meant he seems well versed in detective lore."

"He does have a wild imagination." Pop studied the smoke curling off his cigarette, then looked between the two of them. "Kind of like some other fellers I can think of."

McKee's eyes never strayed. "Believe me, you don't want to know."

Roy rubbed his forehead. "I'll bet. You kids are gonna drive me to drink." He looked over to Huck. "How's that magneto shaping up?"

Huck was running the last bracket bolt down even then. He leaned back on his haunches. "I think we're just about ready to power an airplane."

Pop stubbed his cigarette on the sole of his work shoe. "Regardless of whatever else you daredevils have going on, brace yourselves. Cy's gonna steam like a clam the second you put this thing in the air."

"How are you thinking to plead?"

"Ignorant."

"Think he'll buy it?"

"Hell no." He stood up off the horse and unlocked one of the caster brakes on the cradle with his foot. "We cross that bridge when we get to it, I reckon." He looked at Huck, tapped the motor's long iron head. "You ready?"

Two nights later they towed the hay wagon in from the ranch and under the cover of full dark winched the fuselage onto the deck. They lowered the wing out of the rafters and lashed that on as well.

Roy towed with the REO while Huck and McKee rode on the wagon bed itself, holding on to the fuselage. Annelise tailed in the panel truck.

They took a backstreet parallel to Main until they cleared the last cluster of houses, then jogged over to the highway and went south a mile to Coal Camp Road. They bobbed and bounced up the gravel incline to what passed as the local airfield, in truth just a graded and graveled strip of sage flat with a tin-sided shed and a handful of petrol barrels. Occasionally some sport flier from Helena or Billings would drop in to refuel, but otherwise the strip mainly saw Forest Service planes or visiting coal executives, and those weren't exactly common, either.

Pop towed the wagon down near the shed. The full moon was only two nights past, and it hung now bright and barely gibbous over the butte to the east, throwing her cold white glow across the flat, throwing long shadows off the sagebrush along the runway. They'd brought carbide miner's lamps, but between the moon and the headlights of McKee's rig, Huck could see already they wouldn't need them.

They had the wing loose and stowed against the shed and the fuselage offloaded in a fast half hour. Huck studied the propeller in the moonlight, the glint along the lacquered blades and a pool of the same gleam on the silver shoulder of the cowling. He looked up at the sky, took in Arcturus and Vega through the blue-white glow. He took in Scorpio.

He realized Annelise had come up beside him, could suddenly actually scent her on the breeze. Soap like the soap that Katie used. She took his hand. "Nervous, Colonel?"

He put his other hand on the smooth gloss of the prop. They'd test-fired the engine back in the shop, with a temporary gas tank rigged and hanging from the rafters overhead, and she'd fluttered to life like an emergent moth. An unmuffled and noisy moth, to be sure, but a thing born for flight. The whirling prop blew dust and debris like a cyclone, flapped the pages of the *Flying and Glider Manual* like a shuffling deck of cards.

He squeezed her fingers with his own, and she squeezed right back. He said, "Ask me tomorrow."

2

The bunch of them drove back to the airfield at first light in McKee's rig and had the wing mounted and the gas line hooked to the carb by nine. They cabled the ailerons and ran through a basic safety check. Annelise went back to the panel truck and returned with a cardboard box.

She lifted the lid and brought out two leather flight helmets and two goggle sets. She handed one each to Huck. "May as well look official."

He turned them over in his hands. "Well. I was all set to wear a football helmet. Where'd these come from?"

"A little bird brought them." She batted her eyes at McKee. "Don't be jealous."

"That's a known risk." He pointed at Huck, then to the prop. "Do the honors, cowboy?"

They let her idle in place ten minutes to get the engine up to temp, then he wormed his lanky frame into the forward passenger seat. Annelise climbed in behind him and made one more check of the rudder bar and stick controls. Huck watched the ailerons lift and lower, lift and lower, on either side of him. The unmuffled engine clattered like an oversize typewriter, even through the grip of the helmet.

He felt her hand on his shoulder. "You ready?" she shouted.

He put his thumb to the air, looked over to see McKee's lank hair blowing straight sideways. Both he and Pop squinted against the blast. The engine wound higher.

She taxied the plane halfway down the runway and turned it in as tight a buttonhook as she could, and that still put them a little off the actual graveled lane and into the cropped weeds alongside, but she steered right back onto the grit and back the way they'd come. She made a little series of S curves, then straightened again, and Huck waved to Pop and McKee when they passed. Annelise buttonhooked again and this time taxied nearly the entire length of the strip.

She made a complete circle to the left, got back onto the runway, and made a tight circle to the right. She went back down to the starting point and again turned the plane about and let the motor idle down. She shouted to him from behind.

He looked back at her. "How's she feel?"

"Like an airplane. I'm going to hop her."

"Already?"

She nodded at him, eyes like blue sparks through the glass of her goggles.

"You want me to get out?"

"No," she shouted, "but I think you should. Till I know I've got it."

It was the last thing he wanted, too. Except for one other thing— for Annelise to worry about anything other than getting this dream of his off the ground. "How's her temp?"

Annelise's eyes tilted to the gauges. "One-fifty almost."

He gave her another thumbs-up, then wriggled his way out through the cables and cabanes. He slid to solid ground, peered into the cockpit at the panel. Oil pressure looked good and the tach hovered at 1,200, right where it was supposed to.

"Don't buy the dern farm," he yelled.

She put her own thumb in the air.

With only one passenger, and a light one at that, the plane got right to speed, and before Huck even quite expected it, the tail raised up to float along level with the ground. No sooner had he gotten his head around that than the wheels lifted and left the earth too, and she was twenty feet in the air, then setting back down again with plenty of runway still out ahead.

Pop and Yak were hooting and yelling, with Pop waving his fedora around like a racing flag. Huck started up with his own whoop, and they were looking at one another and shaking their heads, all three grinning like fools.

"I have to admit," said Yak, "I always thought this was a pretty half-cocked idea."

"That's saying something, coming from you. Watch her."

Annelise turned at the far end of the strip, and they heard her throttle back up, saw her start to taxi toward them and again make speed. Rudder and flank lifted and caught the morning sun like a signal mirror. The wheels floated up and away, and again the three of them whooped and chortled on the ground, slapped one another on the back as though even a repeat of what they'd already witnessed remained a singular miracle.

She touched back down and roared past and waved, made another buttonhook and went for it again.

She hopped the plane higher and longer a few times, back and forth on the runway, and finally touched down and steered toward them and backed off the throttle. The spinning prop slowed and by some trick of the eye appeared to reverse its own direction in a sort of rotational mirage. Then back to its correct swing, and back yet again to what he knew to be an illusion. A hypnotic one to be sure, like a watch on a fob.

Annelise killed the barking engine and the prop froze. The visual trickery evaporated into sudden, concomitant silence. Huck blinked and nearly tripped as he started toward her.

They spent an hour going over the cables and connections, tightened a turnbuckle here and there, and ran through a ground check of rudder and elevators and ailerons. Checked fluid levels, checked air pressure in the tires. Nothing had shifted and nothing had leaked, and the cables had stretched only barely, if at all. She was sound as the second she left the shop. Huck stood on the seat and topped off the gas tank.

They ate the sandwiches they'd packed in the shade of the wing. Then with the breeze just starting to lift out of the west, Huck spun the prop and refired the motor. Annelise pulled on her helmet and goggles and climbed back to the cockpit.

She taxied to the east end of the strip and pointed the little silver bird into the wind.

3

A life has to move or it stagnates.
> —Beryl Markham, *West with the Night*

She could feel the heat of the radiator from where it jutted out front and the rush of air off the prop, could hear the unmuffled sputter from the stacks.

So odd the way this whole exile-to-Siberia situation had worked out. She'd expected to remain at the confluence of murderous rage and suicidal boredom for the duration, round and round in a vortex of her own colliding polarities.

But that's not what happened. She hadn't been stuck in the middle of nowhere, hadn't been isolated even within her own head. She'd found instead another tribe, all boys to a man and all pulling for their girl, right over there. Still here, when she didn't have to be, and flying again, thank God. Blix's lucky watch back and on her wrist even now, thank God.

She looked ahead, through the warren of cables and struts, triangles and trapezoids exactly equal and exactly opposite, starboard to port, like a cross between a blueprint and a Rorschach pattern. Downfield she saw the lift of the wind sock.

She pushed the throttle forward and heard the motor ramp up, glanced at the tach to watch the needle climb past 1,200. She looked again across the cowling as the ship started forward. She advanced the knob and felt her speed increase, felt the tail rise up behind her.

The sagebrush along the runway appeared to glide, the way telephone poles appeared to slide by the glass of a train car, or the way the sun seemed to drag across the sky. Bodies fixed and bodies in motion, and which was which.

With a headwind now the initial lift came on even more rapidly. She felt as much as saw the drop of the ground below, well before the runway's midpoint. She eased the stick back and felt the elevators tilt and the nose of the plane instantly climb in reaction. She was two hundred feet in the air in no time, with the terminus of the runway behind her. She leveled off.

She throttled to 1,600 and flew out over the sage and across Coal Camp Road, light as a bubble and, according to the speed indicator, clipping along already at nearly seventy. She could see the rail tracks and the plunge of the highway into Big Coulee to the north, and badly wanted to bank out across the great pine-studded rim at the edge of the bowl and over the plunge and right out above the buildings and trees of the little town itself.

But she restrained herself. That was for Houston to do. She instead banked left and turned south, straightened out and crossed the road again and flew back toward the flat.

She couldn't see dead ahead because of the jut of the radiator. She eased the stick left again and steered just north of the airfield, leveled above the dotted sagebrush and peered over the leather padding. McKee's panel truck looked like a kid's toy, the metal-sided shed no bigger than a Log Cabin syrup can and the boys in a line like tin soldiers. Even from here she could see them waving, each with both arms overhead in the same calisthenic flagging. She put her own arm up and hoped they could see her too.

She buzzed way out over the east end of the runway, to where the natural sage flat abutted this country's usual fan of triangular breaks and ravines, standing like a line of Egyptian pyramids and from a distance looking not so unlike one of Sister Aimee's theatrical painted backdrops. Valley of the Kings. She felt the natural lift of an air current when she soared over, put the ship into a right bank and came around into the wind.

The runway stretched before her like a surgical scar, a wound of unnatural precision. She throttled back and watched the altimeter. She was nearly to three hundred feet and the needle dropped off only slightly. She throttled down again and started to descend.

She hadn't landed an airplane in what—four months now? Nearly five? But evidently it was like riding a bike. She hit a turbulent patch and bucked around a little but compensated with the stick and leveled, decelerated as she approached the edge of the runway. She cut her speed barely to forty, her elevation within a hundred feet of ground and the plane still dropping.

One quick glance around the radiator, and she saw her champions out ahead at the edge of the strip, McKee with his hands on his knees like a home plate umpire. The altimeter was almost to ground level as she crossed the end of the runway. She throttled back again and heard the engine tune down. The wheels and rear skid kissed the earth so gently she hardly felt the contact.

Annelise steered toward them, and they ran out across the strip as though she'd not only won a race but also set a record. She taxied until the distance closed and they had to shield their eyes against the blast of the prop, then killed the motor and looked at them across the cowling. Huck had a beam on his face like the wink of a coin. She wriggled her goggles up and grinned at him.

McKee of course broke the silence. He thrust both arms in the air and conjured Peter Lorre: *"Eat ease a GREAT SUCCESS!"*

She gave a bow.

They safety-checked again and this time left the fuel tank within the wing partially empty. Lighter that way, with two of them to consider. The wind had become a little stronger, but that was more a help than a hindrance. Huck again wormed his lanky self into the passenger seat.

He kept expecting to wake up from a dream and find his handiwork well back in the middling stages, say about where he was before his cousin and McKee came along. But the two of them were sure enough real, real as the heat he could feel even now off the radiator.

And as real as the motion of the forward stick, jutting from the floor in front of him and moving in tandem with Annelise's steerage in the seat behind. She told him to keep an eye on that and also on the rudder pedals at his feet, to start to get a sense of what to do and when to do it, and he watched both as she taxied to the east end of the strip and turned into the wind. He saw the throttle knob move forward, heard the spike of the engine out front.

They gathered speed. He felt the leveling tilt as the tail came up. Annelise poured more gas, and he had the uncanny sensation he was back in Glider Number One that crisp October night, anticipating the cold plunge of his innards even as the ship around him defied gravity and departed earth.

They were already afloat above the runway. Somehow he'd missed the moment altogether. He looked over the leather padding and watched his own shadow sail atop the silhouette of a moving airplane. He forgot the past entirely, forgot everything but the rush of wind in the here and now. His belly was not dropping after all.

Her plan had been to hop a few times with the both of them aboard, to get a feel for the ship with the weight of another passenger. So when the stick in front of him moved straight back, and the nose of the plane angled in response, he fully expected her to shift forward again, fully expected to touch back down and land.

Instead she held the climb and held it some more, and even with a good hundred feet of altitude, it hadn't totally sunk in that his cousin simply intended to fly. He twisted around and saw the grin on her face. He let himself believe.

They sailed back out across Coal Camp Road, and again he looked over the cowling to catch their shadow, threading and blinking through the sage maybe two hundred feet below. He looked out across the sweep of the prairie and the plains and caught sunlight on the silos beyond the river, and from this vantage even that appeared a downright stone's throw. He could see the entire top half of the Absarokas out on the wide rim of the world, a solid three-hour journey by car. He never had seen them up close.

The stick between his knees tilted to the side and the airplane tilted too, banked in a slow sweep that finally did make his stomach drop, in a way that reminded him of sledding in winter as a youngster, or sticking tight to Wilbur when the horse hooked hard to cut a cow. A way that reminded a body of its own blindsided capability for wonder, or the capacity for thrill. A way that reminded him it was okay to do something for the fun of it.

He'd intended to keep his attention on the controls as she flew back beyond the runway and banked around again, but he found in the moment that he simply couldn't. He watched Pop and McKee leaning against the fender of Yak's pint-size panel truck as they passed, then looked over the other side to see the ship's smooth shadow gliding across the ground.

He was faintly aware of the throttle knob moving back when Annelise brought the motor down. Otherwise he just sat there and felt the rush of air, took in the magic sight of the runway coming, a ways off at first and then in no time right out in front. The motor dropped again and he felt the wheels bump the earth, with no more thump than a hop off a milk crate. He looked up at the wing above his head, this thing that could bend the flow of air and so defeat the very law of gravity.

Please, God, please never entered his head.

They parked the sleek little ship along the runway not far from the shed and tied it to a spread of stakes against the wind. They'd come back tomorrow, and he would begin to learn.

They took turns with Annelise's little camera, snapping photos of each other leaning against the ship, and of Huck and Annelise sitting in the cockpit with helmets and goggles. Pop was getting a shot of the rest of them lined against the fuselage when they heard the drone of another plane above the breeze across the flat.

A Ford Tri-Motor. Huck predicted it by the sound, confirmed it by the oncoming profile. They watched the big silver bird make a pass over the runway to check the wind sock, bank back the way it had come, and make a sweeping return way out over the sage.

The pilot brought her in so subtly at the far end of the strip that Huck couldn't discern the actual touchdown, a feat like sleight of hand. He watched the slow, deceptive crank of those three oncoming props out front—one on each wing, one on the nose—as she went from clearly airborne to clearly not, rolling on her tires down the straightaway.

The plane's corrugated flank bore the legend JOHNSON'S FLYING SERVICE, a commercial outfit out of Missoula that Huck knew to specialize in backcountry flying. The pilot taxied over and came to a stop, cut his motors and slid a window shut in the cockpit. A moment later he hunched his way through the door aft of the wing and stretched his back a bit. He wore a sweatshirt and sneakers, which for some reason Huck hadn't expected. He sauntered over.

"You all heading out or showing up?"

"Heading out," Roy told him. He hooked a thumb. "The kids here just had 'em a successful test run."

The pilot looked past them, and Huck watched his eyebrows lift. "Built you a Piet, did you?" He fished out a pack of smokes, shook one loose, angled against the breeze, and fired it. He looked over the cup of his hands at Annelise, still in her flying helmet. "You the resident barnstormer, miss?"

"Only because I've had some lessons." She thumbed at Huck. "This guy's the up-and-comer."

The pilot clapped him on the shoulder. "No offense, sonny, but she's a sight better-looking."

He strode past them and leaned into the cockpit, thumped the heel of his smoking hand on the turtle deck a time or two, and stepped back to scan the length of the whole ship. "Seen a few of these here and there. Midwest, mostly. Some of 'em pretty raggedy, but this here's a good build. A really good build."

"You out of Missoula?" Huck asked him.

"Last I checked. Supposedly. Ain't been there in a month, though." He was looking at the landing gear, a split-axle rig that deviated from the original fixed strut of the standard blueprint. "You're smart to set her up thisaway—most don't take the old Rocky Mountain forced landing into account. Pretty much asking for a crack-up."

Annelise made a theatrical gesture at Huck. "This is my cousin, Houston. He's a genius."

The pilot looked at him. "Your build?"

Huck could feel the flush inside his own skin. "Well, I had a sight of help."

The pilot stubbed his cigarette with his sneaker. "How long she take to put together?"

Huck turned to Roy. "Ten months, I guess?"

"Not even that. Started her in October."

"Fast work."

Huck was red, but hoping he didn't come off as merely green. "Couldn't have done it by myself."

"Expect you're wrong about that. This really the first day you've flown her?"

"First day Annie's flown her. I don't have my wings yet."

The pilot looked at him and back to Annelise. Another gust slapped in off the flat, stronger all the time, making the sagebrush out across the strip flicker like some stiff green fire. The wings of the little two-seater bobbed and rocked in the stir—even the clouds above dashed across the sky. "Been following the equator flight, I guess? A.E.?"

"Oh, yes."

"Guess you know she's been grounded for a week. Some Dutch field in Indonesia."

"Java, I think," Annelise said. "Last I heard on the radio, anyway."

"Yeah, that's right. West Java. Here's the thing about the radio, and the newspapers—they want it both ways with this whole show. They want it to look like the feat it sure enough is, for the publicity and the endorsements and what all, but they're downplaying like hell what a hairball slog she's taken on out there."

"Hairball or harebrained?" said McKee.

Annelise shot him a look. "What's that line of yours again? No risk, no reward?"

The pilot's eyes shifted back and forth between them, and he smirked a little, as though he knew already the tale between the lines.

"Look, I'm not saying a thing against her. She's no slouch and she's proved it, many times. But you have to wonder where calculated ends and fool's errand begins. I'm guilty myself—I fly into some rough-ass spots in some rough-ass weather, with a hell of a lot of weight at my back, crate bucking like a saddle bronc because the wind's blasting ten ways from Sunday. And at the end of all that, some backcountry strip in the middle of nowhere that makes even this here look like God's golden runway.

"Every time you pull one of those trips off, you feel like you can walk on water, and that's its own drunk thrill. So you keep looking for it, and keep trying for it, and it takes more and more to get to that spot in your own head, until you can't tell luck from skill anymore. That's a risky place to be."

For a minute nobody said anything, nobody except the wind. Huck leaned against the fuselage right at the cockpit, and even staked down, he could feel the ship tensing and flexing like a live thing. He imagined what it must be like in the bottleneck of a mountain pass, nothing below but miles of rough rock and dark forest and water like a silver ribbon, way down in some backcountry canyon. All he knew was, he wanted to be good enough to do it too.

He shifted to Annelise. "She's on the home stretch now, though. Or will be."

"Oh, she's on it," the pilot answered. He was looking at her himself. "I heard the report right before I pulled out of Denver. She got back in the air day before yesterday, heading for Australia. But what I mean to say is, she's been through the wringer, more than meets the eye. Hence six days on the ground in Timbuktu."

"She's said she'll retire after this," Annelise said. She had to practically shout now, her curls blowing around her face in the wind. "From the first-attempt and record-chasing stuff, anyway."

"I know it. We'll see if she can. Walking on water, you know."

"Well, I guess you're never more alive than when you're cheating death almighty."

Huck wasn't sure he'd heard her correctly in the rush of air off the sage. *Death almighty.* That was a new one.

The pilot pointed at Annelise but looked at Roy. The wind had risen to a near roar and he had to shout. "Best keep an eye on this one."

4

The two of them spent the next four days up Coal Camp Road, with Houston in the front passenger seat that first day learning how to taxi around the airstrip and how to make a hop and touch back to ground.

He learned quickly, she had to say. An easy touch and no trepidation. Then again, he knew airplane engineering inside and out, the same way he had a prodigy's sense for how to make a car run like a top. She herself was a very good driver, one of the first in her class to get her license. Another of her father's indulgences, similar to flying lessons. She'd taken both for granted at the time.

Fifteen minutes in and he was already steering around the runway as easy as riding a bike and before long had the ship turning in full circles in place as though the cowling rotated on a spindle. He hopped on his own after watching her demonstrate the exercise a mere handful of times—just as with the dance instruction. By lunchtime their first day out she was already tempted to let him take it up and make a circuit.

She knew the jig was about to be up, and she was honestly curious what the reaction might be. Cy Gleason was hardly a concern from where she stood. Houston was worried about him, but that was more congenital than practical. In fact, the airplane was not against the law, and she'd already sent off for the forms to register it with the aeronautics bureau.

Aunt Gloria, though—there was a wild card of a different sort. It wasn't that she could really do much once the spotlight beamed its inevitable truth. Annelise could see that even now, as clearly as she saw Cy Gleason's jurisdictional limits. Anybody who could build his own honest-to-God airplane was definitively too big to spank.

But there was the rub. The airplane was not merely a lie of omission but a declaration of independence. Gloria had been kept in the dark, by her and by Houston and by everyone. They'd deceived her to break away from her, and that was going to hurt her, and Annelise knew it. She wondered if the others had considered this, too. Roy, probably. Yak definitely, but he was on the outside, looking in.

She tried to shove it out of her mind. Aunt Gloria was a grown-up. The lanky kid at the controls just wanted to fly. And she could help him.

"You sure you're ready?" she asked.

They sat against the shed with their sandwiches, watching the airplane glint like a jewel. Still practically no breeze with the temperature north of eighty, and no doubt fixing to climb higher yet with the arc of the sun. Huck didn't quite know how the ship would handle on a hot day, especially with two people. He needed to cross this other bridge first, and quickly.

"Sure you're not asking if it's *you* who's ready?"

"No, I'm not sure, actually." She swiveled her head to him. "No offense, but it is a homemade crate, with a first-time pilot. Not to mention an unlicensed instructor."

"Pot, meet kettle."

"Pretty much." He anticipated what she was going to say next before the words were actually out, because the thought was in his head, too. "Honestly? Compared with everything else lately? Going up in the air with you at the stick is the last thing I'm worried about."

Huck examined the dregs of his sandwich. "So it's not just me."

She winced. "This has all been wonderfully distracting the last few days, I'll admit—I mean, in one way I'm in *heaven*, getting back up.

"But then I'll check the time, and all I can hear are feet rushing up behind me in the dark, or the crazy sound that Ford made when we rolled it down the mountain." She held up her wrist with her beau's watch. "Maybe this thing's not such a good-luck charm after all."

"Oh, I don't know. It got us where we are right now, I guess. I just wish Yak had left the other one right there where you dropped it." He paused. "Or at least had that plan B of his come together."

Annelise cocked her head at him. "Plan B? What plan B?"

"You know that supposedly anonymous tip to the police?"

"That was Yak?"

Maybe he'd said too much. "Who else would've known about it?"

She slapped herself in the forehead. "Do you have the other watch now?"

"Hell no. I haven't touched that thing since we tried to get rid of it."

She looked at him. "Because it's the opposite of a good-luck charm?"

"I don't want that albatross anywhere near me." He pointed for the sky. "Especially five hundred feet up."

A little later he got hold of his nerves and took the rear cockpit for the first time, with Annelise up front. He taxied out to the far end of the runway, powered up, and flew a wide loop around the flat.

He banked back toward the strip and powered down, and as the ground floated up toward the belly of the plane, he had a flash in his brain to the night he'd crashed the glider last fall. A flare of both familiarity and slight panic, triggering the merest hesitation of his hand on the throttle. He looked at the back of Annelise's helmet-clad head, then glanced at the gauges.

His attitude indicator showed a perfect level. He glanced back at the ground and watched the last of the sagebrush skim along thirty feet below, and now when he looked ahead he saw not a baseline on a ball diamond coming at him in the dark, but the wide flat threshold of a runway. The doubt diminished. He eased back again on the throttle, watched the ground lift again. He set down with no more jolt than the bounce of a rubber ball.

Out in front, Annelise raised both arms in the air, like a kid on a roller coaster.

The next day in the cool of the morning, he flew her a thousand feet above ground level, out across Coal Camp Road and over toward the long flat spine of the Bulls. He kept one eye on the temperature gauge.

The ship had an oversize radiator in relation to the original design—a standard Chevrolet core split down the middle and stacked in tandem, a trick he'd picked up from other gents who'd tweaked Pietenpol's specs for higher-elevation flying. She ran at a steady one-fifty, well below the point of a vapor lock or boil-over. He ran up beyond eighty, thirty miles an hour faster than he'd ever gone in a car, and watched the straight-on smooth approach of the mountains.

He'd thought to bank back around before he'd gotten much above the foothills, but the sloping red soil and scattered firs came on in such short order that he caved to giddy impulse and stayed right on tack. Dunn Mountain rose up high and pyramidlike through the haze to the east, but here the flat-topped spine ran long and tree-studded and many hundreds of feet below, even at the highest knobs and rims.

They passed across the southern slope and saw the character of the land totally shift. Sagebrush and squat black juniper, clear to the horizon. Dry washes, cutting and forking like arteries of sand and wind. He banked west along the base, saw the white dot of a wagon canvas far below, saw minuscule grazing sheep.

The terrain reeled almost slowly along from this elevated vantage, although he'd never yet throttled below seventy. They crossed a weird expanse of sculpted sandstone formations, an army of gnomes frozen for all eternity. The north-side coulees with their snarls of wild plum and buffalo berry may as well have been an ocean away.

He banked north and crossed back over the line of mountains. Annelise had her elbows on the leather pad around the cowling, torquing back at him to grin or make a silly face now and then, but mostly looking out at the endless geography below. Off to the east he could see the ribbon of highway, see the parallel run of rail tracks a little way off, and when his eye followed to where the trestle crossed the river, he caught the boiling clouds of smoke out of the 12:20 coal train. He banked toward it, throttled up and closed the gap.

He flew down the line of empty cars, the first few of them nearly invisible beneath the billows out of the stack until coalescing like a ghost train through the vapor, then finally a full reveal a dozen or twenty cars back. It struck him as odd to see a roaring freight engine with all its scissoring locomotion and volcanic plumes but hear nothing above the rush of his own soaring bird. He flew over the caboose and banked around once more.

He caught the train again and flew alongside, steadily gaining until he came up to the roiling exhaust and that frenetic working engine, and just as steadily moved out ahead to leave the long train behind. Now he followed the curve of the empty track toward the highway and the pines and the wide stone rim above Big Coulee.

Annelise looked back at him again, grinned again. He tried to lift his eyebrows through his goggles. The steeple of the church on the far side of town came into view, and the ball diamond and the New Deal and the tops of the big eastern elms. They cleared the plunge and the entire town slid into the bowl before them, no larger than a Lionel train village at Christmastime.

He could identify everything in the coulee in little more than a glance. The hospital and the high school, and over here the long roof of the machine shop and the bungalow next door. The REO and McKee's panel wagon parked out front. The Rialto with its neon marquee set just back from the sidewalk. The rail depot where he'd fought Royce and run from Junior Joe and kissed Katie Calhoun, all in a single night. Even the very street where Yak's little apartment was, where the girl in the front bay had taken her drubbing and somehow paid in advance for this very view.

It all looked so gol dern small.

5

She had that woozy flush in her languid arms and lazy legs and right to the roots of her curls. Warm water through slim copper pipes. "Can I ask you something?"

"Well, you do have me where you want me."

"Were you the anonymous caller? About the car, with the bullet through the roof?"

He gave her a mock *Who, me?*

She thumped his shoulder. "Can't you at least tell me *that*? You told Houston."

"No, I did not tell Houston. But I can see how he figured it out." He studied the missing contents of his bottle. "That day Cy called the shop. I basically told Roy he was better off not knowing."

"Surely you didn't make the call from there, though."

"No. I went clear to Ryegate and used the phone at the depot."

"Smart."

He tapped his skull.

She handed him her own beer and he took a pull. "But they still haven't caught them."

"Nope. Roy talked to Cy again today, when you and the kid were with the plane."

She took her bottle back. "We should've left that watch right there in the road."

"Yeah, I've been kicking myself. At the time, though—poetic justice, and all."

She sucked in a breath, blew it back out. "Every time a car's headlights shine across the wall in the middle of the night, I sit straight up
in a panic. Maybe we *should* get married. Then I could stay here, with
this arsenal you keep around."

"I do. For better or worse." He banked his hand like an airplane.
"Sorry, flyboy."

She laughed a little. "It would fix my mother's wagon, I'll tell you
that much."

"Especially after we convert back to the faith of Moroni."

"Ho. Even I'm not that vengeful." She bit a nail, caught herself
and stopped. "Do you think they'll be back?"

"Hell, who knows. We're idiots if we don't consider the possibility. That's why I dropped the dime so quick, hoping the police would
pick 'em up in a day or two and put an end to the whole business."

She thought it through. "That could've been a problem in its own
right. What if they'd spilled the whole thing? You did shoot up two
cars, after all."

He got up and made a trip to the icebox, sauntered back in the
usual unabashed fashion. "I thought about that too. Singing to the
cops means admitting to jumping you, which would put them in an
even worse fix."

"Okay. That may be true."

"It's pure D true. But there's more to it even. Has to be. Otherwise, why go out on a limb that flimsy, just for a watch? Even a rare
one?"

"Right."

"You bet I'm right. Whatever they need that thing for, they don't
want Johnny Law to know one solitary thing about it. So yeah, we
probably haven't heard the last of them."

"You're getting me worried all over again. You know Houston
walks home after his shift by himself? What if they ambush him the
way they did me?"

"I can't imagine they'll get that bold again." He swung his legs to the floor. "Plus, he doesn't wear the watch, so it's not such a sure thing as it was with you. Get dressed, though."

She looked at him.

He shrugged. "I've been wrong before."

"I still don't get it with this flipping watch," said Huck. He sat behind the desk in the office with Lindy in his lap, held the dead ghoul's Longines into the lamp's glow.

Annelise and McKee had been waiting for him out front of the Rialto, sitting there on the running board of McKee's Stude. Huck instantly assumed something had gone wrong, both parents flashing in his mind.

Nothing of the sort, it turned out. Pop had stayed out at the ranch with Mother, and all was quiet so far as anyone knew. But the giddy buzz of the past few days with the airplane had begun to subside. Other business remained.

"Nobody gets the flipping watch. It's a dern puzzle, and we need to put it together."

"Maybe it *is* just sentimental," Annelise said. "Or personal. I can sort of see it. I sure wanted mine back. Or Blix's, rather."

"I'm not buying it. How the hell would they even know they swiped the wrong one? There's no difference between them. Even the straps are the same."

Huck thumb-nailed the hinged cover on the back of the watch-case and studied the intricate assemblage of gears and wheels. Minuscule ratcheting pawls and golden cogs, like a glimpse under the hood of the universe itself. "Only difference I can see is the serial numbers."

"You ever memorized a serial number in your life?" said McKee. "On anything? A gun? A motor?"

Huck drew a blank.

"Neither have I. Besides, with a watch this unusual, why would it even cross their minds it might not be the right one?" He looked at Annelise. "You still have that satchel?"

She shook her head. "I sort of forgot about it in all the excitement with the airplane."

"Is it here or at the ranch?"

"I don't think I took it out of the barn. It's probably still sitting there with the saddles."

"We need to get it. They might want that back even worse than the watch."

Her mouth had that taut little set. "Maybe it's time we spilled this whole thing. It's not like anyone can stop the airplane at this point."

"You're probably right," said McKee. "Can't do much until morning, though."

"I'm worried about my ma," Huck said. "She spends a lot of time out there by herself."

Now that the words were out, he felt a flash of guilt along with the queasiness of dread. The airplane had been such a supreme distraction the past few days, he'd cheerfully forgotten everything else.

McKee at least tried to come to the rescue. "Well, your pop's out there with her now, so don't fret on it. We'll come up with something."

6

"Are you totally sure she won't overheat? It's supposed to hit nearly a hundred today."

They'd come back to the airstrip after breakfast, delivered by McKee, who then immediately left to fetch the satchel from the ranch.

"Totally sure?" He stood on the captain's chair, tilting a fuel can. "Or just sure enough?"

"I said *totally*."

The gasoline crept toward the inlet and he eased off. "It's a mechanical device. There is no *totally*."

She wrinkled her nose. "You're starting to sound like McKee."

Who wouldn't, it occurred to him, go up in the plane himself. Probably better not to bring that up. "We haven't had a lick of trouble so far. And if we do, I've been scoping out landing spots for six months now. I know this country like the back of my hand."

"McKee," she repeated. "He's created a monster."

"You're starting to sound like my ma."

She rubbed her eyes. "I barely slept a wink last night. I'm a little frayed."

Huck hopped to the ground. "You want the controls? I know I've been hogging them."

"You've earned it. Forget about this other stuff." She fought back a yawn—he saw it in the flare of her nostrils. "Especially today. I'm too tired."

He had been trying to forget the other stuff, not entirely successfully. They had an engine, hence a full-fledged bird, but at what risk?
He didn't want his mother to stand in the way of his airplane, nor did
he want the secrecy to put her in actual danger. Even Pop was in the
dark about half of it, and Huck was pretty sure even Pop would blow
his stack at the whole unvarnished truth.

"Okay," he said. He looked at the sun, still well in the east and
blushing the long lower edges of the stratus clouds. "We'll be back
before the real heat sets in. Besides, it's not like we're way out over
an ocean or something."

They flew across Haystack Butte, and a few minutes after that saw
the barn and the house and shelterbelts of the ranch.

Huck backed off the throttle and buzzed the wheat table and the
buffalo jump, then circled and took her straight over the yard. No
sign of the REO or McKee's rig, either—evidently he'd already been
here and departed again. But even at five hundred feet they could
see the chickens pecking about outside their run, the horses in the
pasture east of the barn.

Then he spotted the lady of the place herself, working away at
the well pump, which made him feel a little sad, because she always
struggled with the whining thing more than a taller or stronger person would. She straightened at the drone of the engine, and Huck
was pretty sure she was shielding her eyes to take in the unusual sight
of a low-flying crate.

He could set down on the access road at the edge of the wheat
table, and it crossed his mind just to go on and be done with it. Let
the secret out. Maybe she'd even be proud.

He needed the whole business off his conscience, and soon.
Needed to talk to Pop, needed to spill it with Cy. Take whatever
medicine he had coming, which he was increasingly certain would
not entail losing his airplane. Maybe they'd make him take real lessons

down in Billings and get a real license or something, but nobody could call him a harebrained dreamer anymore.

The thing to do was to take Cy and Mother up to the airfield and give them a proper demonstration. That was the grown-up solution. Landing in a wheat field out of the blue would be exactly the sort of dern-fool stunt they all equated with dern-fool kids.

He banked around and buzzed over again and saw Mother with her water pail, shuffling toward the chicken house. He had to admit he felt more relief than he could have predicted to see for himself that she was indeed still safe from the hazards of the actual dern-fool shenanigans. The guilt stuck in his gorge all over again.

He leveled out and throttled up. He pointed the prop toward town.

He brought her down over the strip and kissed the ground with his roughest bump yet, nothing too severe but a blow to his pride all the same. Annelise didn't seem to react.

Yak was waiting for them. He climbed out of his rig as Huck taxied over, hooked his thumbs into his pockets. Something about that stance alone triggered another flare of anxiety, and Huck realized that worry over his mother's well-being had overshadowed other possibilities. The goons could just as easily pay a visit to Raleigh, and even Katie. The implications went outward in ever-expanding circles, like rings in a pond, and here he was, the plopping stone at the center of the whole rippling mess.

Evidently Annelise had the same premonition, because when he got near McKee and killed the clattering motor, she tore her goggles and helmet loose as though trying to escape a trapped hornet. McKee took a couple of hesitant steps. "What is it?" she said.

McKee came up and crouched beneath the wing and set his hands on the leather trim. "It may be a false alarm, keep that in mind. Too soon to know."

"Is it Pop? Or Rolly?" Huck said.

"Huh? No, no, it's not the crooks, the watch, none of that."

Annelise came out of her seat so fast that she bonked her head on the underside of the wing and sat right back down. "Something with my parents?"

He had his hand on her shoulder now, almost as though he wanted to hold her in place. "They're fine, they're all fine. Listen to me. It's Miss Earhart. She's gone missing."

Annelise looked as though she couldn't decide whether she'd heard him correctly. "What do you mean, missing? *Crashed?*"

McKee shook his head. "No word yet. The news broadcasts are all abuzz, though. She went out of radio contact and never made it wherever she was heading—"

"Howland Island." She looked up at the wing and let out a breath. Her head swiveled back to McKee with the speed of an owl's. "This better not be some stupid joke of yours . . ."

He shook his head. "You know me better than that."

She nodded now, her mouth little more than a smudge across her face. She raised herself out of the seat more carefully this time. "I need to get to a radio."

Zeniths

1

You will find that patriotism is close akin to religion and that love of country and love of God go hand in hand for the success of the land and glory of the Kingdom of the Lord.

—Aimee Semple McPherson

"I saw an airplane just yesterday," Mother told them. "Right out over the house." She clutched Huck's arm even tighter. "I wondered whether *it* was about to crash, as low as it seemed to be. Then not five minutes later they interrupted *The Gospel Hour* with a report about that poor foolish woman vanishing halfway over the ocean."

Under normal circumstances Huck couldn't imagine Annelise letting this last slip by without a barrage of retaliatory lip, but these weren't ordinary circumstances. Even Pastor White had taken time out from his Independence Day sermon to address the news, which pretty much demolished Huck's plan to ease Mother into the existence of the airplane anytime soon. An example of pride going before a fall, no less, although at the close of the service the pastor had at least offered a prayer for Miss Earhart's safety and recovery.

Huck wondered whether he should have filed a prayer request for his cousin, too. She'd taken to her room with the radio the day before, and when he jerked awake in the middle of the night to the shred of firecrackers down the street, he could hear its low hum yet through the crack beneath the door. She looked so frazzled now he doubted she'd slept at all. Even Mother on first glance asked if she might be coming down with something.

They stopped off at the New Deal for groceries. Annelise found a quarter in her purse and bought a newspaper. Not the *Big Coulee Dispatch* but the Sunday *Billings Gazette*, which was twice the size. She took the paper out front and sat on the bench beneath the patriotic bunting draped overhead. Huck went out after her.

"Hey."

She was scanning the front page. "Hey."

"Anything?"

"Nothing we don't already know. CHANCES FOR EARHART RESCUE FADE. NAVY PRESSES WIDE HUNT FOR MISSING FLYER." She gave the paper a brusque fold and started fanning herself. Tilted her blue-gray eyes at him and bobbed her head like a person about to nod off.

"I know it. Don't think I've ever been this dern hot." Even in the shade he could feel the sweat rising through his hair like oil from a seep.

"It's fucking sweltering."

Down the street a riot of laughter went up from the guys in front of the tavern. "I think they heard you."

"Who cares."

He was only joking, which of course she knew. Didn't she? "Can I sit down?"

She tried to smile at him.

He eased to the far end of the bench. "Gonna be a record, I guess. The heat, I mean. Wheat's gonna have a tough time next spring, we don't get some moisture in the ground."

She nodded and fanned.

Huck ran his fingers through his hair, felt the slipperiness of his own scalp. He flicked sweat toward the road. "I had it in mind to buzz the parade tomorrow, just right down the middle of the street, with the old Stars and Stripes flying off the wing. Make a big bank out over the ball diamond and come back over again."

Annelise chewed her lip. "That isn't a bad idea, Houston. Or wouldn't have been, if it wasn't for all this." She flapped her folded paper around.

"Thing is, Independence Day is the only regular holiday my ma really gets excited about. Almost like it's Christmas. She comes in for the parade every year, even in the middle of the week. That's how much she likes it. I thought maybe I could fly over with the flag, and she'd think it was really patriotic, and Pop could take her up to the airstrip so she'd know it was me all along."

"Oh, Houston. I wish it were all different." Now she did force a smile. "At least you've got the airplane to begin with."

He watched Junior Joe Candy slow to a stop in the police cruiser in front of the tavern, talk to the gents out front. Across the street, another burst of firecrackers ripped out of the alley. Despite the heat, everything seemed pretty amiable.

He eyed the door on the New Deal. "I guess it's like Yak says. If it ain't one damn thing, it's some other damn thing."

They ate cold sandwiches for Sunday supper to avoid firing the stove.

Pop dragged the fans in from the shop and cranked them full bore, which helped a little but also dampened the Independence Day broadcast out of Great Falls. Mother and Annelise each dragged a chair to either side of the little Zenith and sat there like a pair of unlikely peas in the same steaming pod, right down to the tendrils rising around their ears in the sweep of the fans.

The truce didn't last. A rendition of "The Yankee Doodle Boy" closed out the hour, and Huck saw Annelise tense up. He picked up the words *tragedy* and *South Pacific* amid the rush of the blades and leaned closer to the radio.

"*. . . have steamed from Hawaii to join the U.S. cutter* Itasca *in the search, including the battleship U.S.S.* Colorado, *with three small scouting planes on board . . .*"

"Now this is hardly——" Mother began, but Annelise stopped her with a sound like a stab and a glare as frigid as the day was hot. Huck looked across the table. Pop gave him a stoic wink.

The report went on. Several weak radio signals had been picked up that were believed to be from the missing aviatrix in the hours after her last verified dispatch. It was not known whether her eighty-thousand-dollar flying laboratory had gone down over land or sea. Other naval vessels stood by, expected to join the search as well. *"And now a return to our holiday revue, brought to you this hot hot Fourth of July by the cool cool cool Crystal Creamery Company . . ."*

Mother shook her head. "Eighty thousand dollars. What did they call it? A 'flying laboratory'? Now imagine the cost of these rescue shenanigans, and to the American taxpayer, no less. I'm praying for her of course, but do you see where folly leads? Straight to the bottom of the ocean."

Huck watched the flush rise in Annelise's face, and he knew it wasn't from the heat.

"The flying lab, as they called it, had gigantic custom fuel tanks. Has them, I mean. If she ran out of gas and was forced down on the water, the empty tanks alone would float her like a bobber."

Huck remembered what the Missoula pilot had said, about walking on water. Despite the swelter he felt a chill up his spine, felt the hairs stand on his arms.

His mother nodded. "I hope you're right. I don't wish the poor woman any harm. But modern people keep forgetting that Almighty God did not put us here to chase our own glory. He gave us these brains we have, this curiosity, to seek and know *Him*."

To Huck's shock, Pop spoke. "Well. There might be more than one way to skin that cat, comes right down to it."

Mother looked less surprised than Huck would have figured. "Have your cake and eat it too, you mean? Serve Christ by serving yourself? How do you explain this missing airplane, then?"

Pop shrugged. "Don't feel any need to. Life ain't safe, never has been. And whatever confounded reason there is to the world, toiling in boredom because boredom is safe ain't much of a way to honor the life we've got. Seems to me."

"Oh, I understand, maybe more than you realize. I'm glad Christopher Columbus raised his sails when he did. I'm even glad Orville and Wilbur Wright learned to fly."

She looked at Huck. "It's true. Minister's sons, with exemplary lives. And yes, more souls can be saved because of airplanes. God has a mission for everyone, and every age has its own opportunities. But God doesn't change with the age. He still wants us to put our faith in Him, even now, not in our own newfangled Babels. Give the glory to *Him*, rather than boast of it for ourselves."

She glanced to her niece. "I don't know what's in Miss Earhart's heart, whether she knows Jesus or not. But we live in a country that's fighting for its soul, and she's this new America's idea of a heroine. It's not Susan B. Anthony any longer, or Harriet Beecher Stowe. It's not even Annie Oakley.

"I have no doubt that Miss Earhart has some fine qualities. But the fact remains, she is a figure for an age that has lost its compass. And I choose my words carefully, for the hand of God does not dabble in mere coincidence."

To Huck's surprise, Mother reached across the space between the chairs and put her hand on Annelise's knee. Annelise looked at Mother's flushed face and said, "Do you believe God's watching out for her?"

Mother sat back in her chair. "I believe God hears whoever calls upon Him with an honest and open heart. But the heart can be hard, and God is not accountable to anyone. He will bless those who invite Him in, and He will curse those who don't, and I worry for the soul of our entire nation. Look at *this* curse, upon us even now—a great depression, and years of failed crops, years of locust plague, years of drought. We're like the Israelites in the wilderness.

"Did you know that this heat spell is a record? On the birthday of our country, and on a Sunday, no less. Is that coincidence?" She shook her head, and her fine white tendrils lifted again with the arc of the fan. "I don't believe it is."

Annelise's own curls settled in turn. "I refuse to believe there's anything wrong with trying to be good at something. With following your own dreams, and . . . okay, your own *heart*, if you want to get right to the center. She's showed a whole lot of us that we don't have to settle for what we're offered, or for somebody else's notion of our proper place. A *woman's* proper place. Obviously she inspired me. And okay—thank *God*."

"But, Annie, she's not done any of it for God, for His glory or His purpose. She's done it for what? The fun of it. By her own account. There's more at stake than that."

Pop started to say something, but Mother ran right on over top of him. At moments like this, it was easy to forget she was only five feet tall and generally not robust.

"I understand her allure to so many young women just like Annelise. I understand it and it worries me, because she's presented as the sunshiny model for the future—forward-thinking and sophisticated, next to the old fuddies in the Dark Ages. Out with the old, in with the new. But tell me, where's all that gotten her now?" She turned back to her niece. "On the birthday of our beautiful, suffering country even. Is that coincidence? I don't believe it is."

Huck kept expecting Annelise to find her stinger and strike, and he sat there with dread's big fist in his chest, wishing it didn't always have to come to this. But when he glanced back at his cousin, she simply seemed overheated and otherwise out of gas.

"Actually we don't know where it's gotten her, at the moment," she finally said. "That's the trouble. But she can float, for a long time."

Mother stood and went to the sink. She let the water run from the tap and delivered a glass to Annelise. "Drink this, Annie. I wish we had ice, but we don't. I hope you're right, and I hope they find her."

Annelise took swallow after swallow, and Huck could practically see the cold moisture on her breath when she lowered the emptied glass and blew the air from her lungs. Mother filled the glass again, and Annelise took it and this time pressed it to her cheek. "If they don't find her out there soon, even I'm going to start praying."

"That would be a start," Mother told her.

2

Shortly into the parade the next morning Huck realized he'd dodged a bullet, unfortunately at Miss Earhart's expense but then nothing ever did seem to happen anymore without some equal but opposite consequence. Just about the time you pinched a watch off a guy who had no further use for it, your cousin breezed in with the exact same model. Just about the time you screwed up the courage to ask a girl to dance, your mother swooped in like a brood hen and pecked you right back to the coop. He reckoned Pop had it about right—no such thing as a free lunch.

Still, buzzing the festivities would not have led to a heroic finale. Half the parade consisted as usual of either horseback riders or horse-drawn wagons, a few converted into rudimentary floats and others lugging flag-waving or confetti-throwing passengers.

By ten in the morning the mercury had already climbed toward ninety. The animals were dark with sweat around cinches and har-nesses, and skittish as mustangs from the strings of firecrackers that kept tearing off along the street. If he had flown overhead at seventy-five or a hundred feet, motor howling along the storefronts, the likely result would've been a stampede right down Main Street. He could already imagine Cy roaring up to the runway to punch him right in the mouth.

"Wish these fools would knock it off with the crackers," Pop said loudly. He glared at a couple of seventh-grade boys who'd already shown themselves to be the fools in question. They slunk away.

Pop had his hat kicked to the back of his head. "I was thinking to trailer Wilbur and Dixon in, so's you and Annie could ride too, but now I'm glad I didn't."

Annelise had pleaded out of the parade altogether, which even Mother seemed to take in stride. Then again, his cousin at this point looked a bit like a wrung-out dishrag.

Katie Calhoun, on the other hand. A dish, but definitely no rag. Huck spotted her in the parade and gave a start, part nervous shock and part thrill. She'd been gone nearly a month, spending time with relatives over in Butte. She'd sent him a couple of postcards, but he hadn't seen her since that crazy night at the carnival. Now she rode down Main Street in loose formation with the Big Coulee Girls' Bicycle Club, in fits and starts because of the pace of the hay wagon just ahead.

She spied Houston at a pause and waved, pretty enthusiastically. Huck gave a feeble wave back, feeling Mother's presence beside him as though she suddenly loomed ten feet tall. Katie blew him a kiss.

"Why, Gilroy. I think that was for Houston. I think this young man has an admirer." Mother shielded her eyes as the girls started forward again on their bikes. She turned to Huck. "My land, she's tall. What's her name, Houston?"

Huck could feel his blood come up. He forced his eyes from the bicycles. "Who, Katie?"

"Katie. Well. Maybe you could invite her to church, I'm sure I'd remember if I'd seen her there before."

"Oh. She hasn't been, she's"—he nearly blurted *Catholic* but luckily caught himself—"new in town." This hardly made sense, because how on earth would she be part of the school bicycle club? "Pretty new, anyway."

The hay wagon moved ahead, and Katie pumped her legs to get her bike zinging along again. "Those bicycles still make me nervous for young girls," Mother said. "I hope she's careful on that thing."

Pop gave him a wink, little more than a flick of one eyelid and that may well have been from sweat. He had rivulets seeping out from beneath his hat, the felt around the band already darkening like the damp streaks on the horses. He pointed down the street at the oncoming float, this one pulled by a Ford pickup. A young woman in a spangled gown waved from a throne bedecked with the red, white, and blue and situated atop a coal cart on a short length of track.

He swabbed his brow. "Speaking of pretty girls, here comes the new Coal Queen."

The parade ended shortly after eleven. The temperature had climbed above ninety.

Mother and Pop planned to head out for the ranch to feed and water the animals, then drive back in for the church picnic. On the walk back to the bungalow Huck spied a contingent of the bicycle club in front of the café across the street, including Katie. A throng of other kids stood around as well. Including Bobby Duane.

Katie straddled her bicycle. Bobby Duane straddled her front tire, with his grubby paws all over the handlebars. She was laughing again, and Huck felt the mercury surge in his blood again, and this time not from embarrassment. "I think I'll pass on the ranch."

Pop clapped him on the back. Mother fanned herself now with a church bulletin dredged up out of her purse. She didn't look wilted, though. In fact, she appeared more vibrant than Huck could remember in quite a while. She said, "Oh?"

Huck stepped off the curb. "Think I'll invite Katie to the church picnic."

"And *I* think that is a fine idea, Houston," she said behind him.

Which is how he wound up retrieving his own bicycle from the shop an hour later and pedaling with Katie Calhoun straight up Coal Camp Road.

3

There were times in an aeroplane when it seemed I had escaped mortality to look down on earth like a God.

—Charles A. Lindbergh, 1927

He knew within one minute he'd made a colossal mistake. His first time flying without Annelise, and already he was too big for his britches.

He'd barely gotten off the runway and into the thin hot air, and now with the sagebrush and drought-wrung ground crawling just beneath the belly of the plane, he bit the bullet and dove down into the valley near the river, below the elevation of the airfield. His temperature gauge had already edged beyond what he regarded as a comfortable operating range, and at a speed that would barely keep him in the air.

Keep *them* in the air, actually. That was the unfortunate irony. It was true he'd known to use a beefier radiator than Mr. Pietenpol called for in his original plan, on account of the elevation difference between Montana and Minnesota. He knew as well that even on a blistering day like this, he could probably fly the ship solo with little trouble.

That additional weight of the otherwise innocent girl in front, though—there was the kicker. He'd brought her to the plane purely to impress her, to put Bobby Duane Boyd in his knuckle-dragging place, and now his own evil pride might well be flying barely ahead of a very literal fall.

Katie appeared none the wiser, which made the whole grim circumstance all the more tragic. She craned around in the seat and peered at him through Annie's goggles, off-colored eyes bright as a hawk's and her teeth in a delirious grin. She blew him another kiss, and his fear came up like bile. He tried to grin back.

Holy cow, Houston. Her words came again to him now. *You* built *this?*

That's why there's no Glider Number Two, he'd told her. *I built Airplane Number One instead.*

She'd had one hand on a strut, the other on the padding around the cockpit as she peered in at the gauges, took in the controls. *Houston, it's beautiful.* She reached out and gave his shoulder a petulant little shove. *How come you never told me about it?*

You're the first who knows. I only put her in the air a week ago.

They'd kissed awhile there against the fuselage. He'd tried to go slow.

Finally she pulled back from him, her hands still around his neck. *She needs a different name, though. Airplane Number One's too . . . experimental, or something.*

Yeah, he said. *I thought about that.* The Spirit of Big Coulee *maybe?*

Katie looked past him out at the sky. *How about* Cloudmaker?

This girl. Turned out she was right on the first score, even if she didn't have a clue. Charming as the name she chose surely was—Cloudmaker—*experimental* was much closer to the truth. He'd managed to coax the ship to just under three hundred feet AGL, which probably seemed lofty enough to her but in terrifying reality was anything but, especially when his temp was already nearing 170 and the thought of pushing the motor any harder put God's own chokehold right around Huck's scrawny neck. And her lovely one, whether she knew it or not.

Height. What a stupid, stupid slap. On the street in front of the café he'd had this moment of jubilation when it dawned on him that not only was *he* taller than Bobby Duane but Katie was as well, by a solid two inches. He began right then to think of that pigskin-addled jackass as Shrimp, or Squirt. He'd gotten up on the walk and checked his posture in the café's glass, made sure nothing about him slouched. Katie kept grinning at him. Shorty let go of her handlebars. How pathetic it all seemed now.

The Bull Mountains shimmered out ahead, an apparition in a furnace. But above them, something else. Cumulus clouds, bunching over the ridge. Katie must have seen them back on the runway and so came up with the name. Now she peered over the cowling, watching the ground as it reeled below.

He had fog at the top of his goggles, a bead of sweat rolling down the right lens. Couldn't tell if it was inside or outside the glass. Must be inside, otherwise the push of air would surely splatter any droplet into a hundred tiny polliwogs. He was as hot as he'd ever been in his life, hot as the engine out front belching like a breath out of hell. All he'd wanted to do was impress a girl.

Now all he wanted was to bank around and head right back for the runway and he knew he couldn't, not at this speed that hardly kept him in the air to begin with, let alone climb back even to the altitude of the airfield. But he looked at those clouds and looked at those hills, creeping closer through the mirage, and he thought of something.

The clouds gathered out of the north. In the past he'd watched both raptors and scavengers harness the air currents beneath formations very much like these, watched them fix their wings and soar up and up, as though floating rather than flying.

At the same time, a good blast of wind could pluck a grounded airplane by the wing and toss it right on its back, hence the stakes and tie-downs. Despite the terrifying absence of climbing ability at this particular moment, the basic science was unavoidable—he and Katie were limping along in what amounted to a giant kite. All they needed was an updraft.

He had sweat in his eyebrows inside the goggles, then sweat running into his eyes inside the goggles, and finally he reached up and tore the goggles loose. The sudden lick of air felt like balm in Gilead. He swiped thumb and forefinger along each eyebrow, felt the salted moisture gather and drip and fly away with the wind. The stick in his other hand felt slick as a greased eel.

Katie looked back at him, gave another happy grin. She had no idea. She put her hand out over the cowling and pointed down. He looked and saw what she saw—a little band of pronghorn in the sage, heads lifted in curiosity but otherwise not particularly worried about this giant insect buzzing in a slow line overhead. Then they were past.

He hoped Annelise was right about Amelia, hoped she was out there at this very moment, floating in her buoyant Lockheed, flare gun in hand and rescue a matter of time. A silver speck on an endless sea. How amazing that her will to achieve could be taken so seriously that half the Pacific Fleet was even now steaming along in what might well go down as the biggest rescue operation in history.

He remembered Annelise's worry about the plane overheating, as though she'd had some premonition about this or about Amelia, or both. She'd probably slap his face all over again if she knew what he'd gotten himself into. What he'd gotten Katie into. He felt like slapping himself.

The line of mountains began to crystallize through the heat. He'd kept their speed at forty, and even at that hobbled pace the engine's temperature had crept another five degrees north. If he could keep on like this just a few more minutes, he'd have them to the base of the slope and almost certainly to a rising column beneath that billowing stack of clouds. Slow and steady. A matter of time.

Jump.

Stall. The seconds were beginning to feel like agonizing hours, as though he had flown into some madhouse warp of not simply time but calculation, and the unnerving potential for *mis*calculation, and somewhere in between the two, the unavoidable anxiety of the second-guess.

He realized his hand had gone of its own impulse to the throttle knob. The temptation to shove the thing forward and double his speed and close this infernal gap had become nearly more than he could resist. Surely he could risk another ten-degree spike.

His own head had begun to overheat, that was the problem. He thought to tear the leather helmet loose the way he'd torn away the goggles a moment ago, and let that roiling pressure bleed off with the wind. Maybe he'd have clarity then, an end to this foggy delirium of choice and counter-choice and damned dire consequence.

He forced his hand back from the throttle. He was being tested, that's what this was. What had Pastor White said the other morning, about pride going before a fall? That's exactly the trap he'd flown himself into, trying to impress Katie. What had Mother said, about Miss Earhart? *Look where such folly had led* . . .

It struck him that he was not in fact praying his way through this, hadn't fallen back on the old *Please, God, please* even one time, and didn't begin to now that the realization brought it to mind. He realized he wasn't at all certain whether God looked down in the first place, whether to help, or dish out doom, or any of it.

He didn't know if God existed. Just flat couldn't say one way or the other. Was this the panic and heat and delirium talking? Wasn't this the sort of circumstance that generally forced people in the other direction?

A foxhole conversion, is what Pastor White would call it. That moment under fire when a gent's looming demise made his own life flash through the machine gun strobes, and he'd pledge anything for a miracle.

Of course the opposite could also be true—the apostle Peter, say, denying his own faith before the rooster crowed. So where did that leave him, Houston Lachlan Finn, right here and now? Somewhere smack in the middle, he guessed, unable to tell where faith in God ended, and fear of his own mother began. It was the realization of a lifetime.

He felt the updraft the instant he flew into it. Or thought he did—maybe the physical sensation was actually just a trick of the mind, triggered by the cue that the sagebrush and undulations in the ground below had begun to shrink. He looked to the altimeter and watched the needle climb nearly a hundred feet in a matter of seconds, that great column of clouds almost directly overhead now. He looked at the temperature gauge, watched the needle there come slightly down.

The wall of the mountains jutted a half mile off. He pushed the throttle knob ahead, squinted against the surge of wind, and edged the stick back. The ship climbed like a rocket. He heard himself whoop like a war chief. Katie craned back with a grin as wide as the sky and whooped along with him.

He eyed his temperature and, when it appeared to hold steady, throttled up again. His altimeter gained three hundred feet in nearly the blink of an eye.

They were above the ridge of the Bulls now, still rising on the draft. He banked beneath the clouds, then leveled off to fly southwest down the spine of the mountains. He ran the throttle nearly fully forward and came back on the stick, took her up to five thousand feet and called it good. He backed his speed off and merely cruised for a stretch, until his heart settled.

He looked up at the bright billowing mass and instantly squinted and shied, as though a camera bulb had popped inside a darkened room. He shielded his eyes and looked again. The floor of the column seemed barely above them, dense enough to appear nearly calcified, and blinding indeed with that concentrated platinum light. He banked the plane again so Katie could see, too, out beyond the edge of the wing above her head. He looked over the low side and took in the haze from the heat across the land below, stagnant as murk on a pond.

The air beneath the cloud came on so cool he wished he could actually drink it, just gulp it down like water. He leveled again and watched his gauges and realized they were gaining altitude, as though the bright billows above pulled at them with an attractor beam right out of *Amazing Stories*, some mad inventor's ionic elevator.

He realized he could let the updraft carry him right up into the mist, and no sooner did the thought cross his mind than he shoved it back out again. He'd already gambled enough, and who knew what he might encounter within that blinding mass.

He banked back toward the landing field and throttled up, and in a few minutes he'd gotten beyond the reach of the clouds. He flew without a hitch across the sandstone and sage to the runway. He buzzed the limp sock once, made a wide sweep and set them flat on the ground, like a feather alighting on a cobweb.

He taxied to the tie-downs and cut the prop and just sat there. The engine ticked out front like a blazing stove. Was that the hiss of steam as well? Probably so. He tilted his wrist to read the big Longines, the first time he'd ever properly worn it, again to impress Katie. They'd been in the air barely twenty minutes. He felt as though he'd aged twenty years.

Katie tore her harness loose, tore helmet and goggles free as well. She pivoted up onto her knees and looked back at him, hair a tangle of damp black waves and teeth as white and blinding as those towering clouds.

"Houston," she breathed, "this is the best day of my whole entire life."

4

Annelise on the other hand seemed to descend ever deeper into the trench, even two days along. She'd barely left her bedroom, and never so much as got out of her pajamas. She just sat there with the radio, tuning through song after song after serial, one end of the bandwidth to the other and then back in the other direction, for fear she might miss something clear down where she'd started.

"She'll come around," Pop told him. They were in the shop with McKee, working on a waste-oil still they'd started last fall, then put on the back burner when the airplane began to take up space. "Quicker if they find Miss Earhart of course, but however it works out, she ain't going to stay in her pajammies forever."

"Think they might actually find her?" He himself had had nagging doubts from the get-go. He didn't let on to his cousin, but Pop did tend to see things with a broader view.

"I wouldn't put my last dollar on it, exactly. But this ain't the first time somebody went missing in the ocean only to turn back up again."

"Sister," said McKee.

Pop glanced at him, then back to Huck. "Yep. You remember it, I'm sure."

McKee shook his head. "Nope. Annelise does, I know that. But we didn't get much for news to speak of, where I was brought up."

"I remember it," Huck said. "A little, anyway."

"Do you? You were a little shaver, back then. Three, maybe? Even my memory's a little fuzzy."

"No, I do. Mostly because of Ma."

Pop nodded. "She took to her bed for a few days, too. Anyone with any sense just assumed the woman had drowned on the beach in California, when lo and behold here she is marching out of Mexico a thousand miles away. Nobody saw that one coming."

All three went quiet, each of them appearing to study some private aspect of the waste-oil contraption, but Huck at least mulling in his mind the likelihood of the missing Amelia pulling off an Aimee McPherson–style resurrection clear down in the watery South Pacific.

McKee was evidently thinking the same thing. "How long was it, between the time she up and vanished and the day she showed again?"

"A while. Six weeks? Point is, this thing with Miss Earhart may not look real promising, but that don't mean it's over. Hell, half the U.S. Navy's out there hunting for her."

"And working in one big bucket of water, don't forget." McKee stood from his haunches. "Not trying to be a half-empty guy myself, but I don't know what good it does to give our girl in the pajamas anything other than the straight dope."

Roy nodded. "Expect you're right. Anyway, anybody who mollycoddles Annelise does it at his own risk. And she will come back up, or I don't know her like I think I do."

She'd forgotten about the watches, the satchel, the shot-up cars, everything, in the shock and angst of the past few days. Also in her febrile race up and down the radio dial.

At night she'd slept fitfully, though deeply enough a time or two to descend into dreams. Not very good ones—in one she wound up corkscrewing toward the ground in a falling airplane, slamming awake with her heart in her throat at the moment of impact.

In another, she'd been kidnapped off the dark walk by the goons, spirited to a shack somewhere deep in the desert. Mexico, she was sure of it, although the passing of time from the abduction to the hideaway happened in an impossible blink.

What did drag on was the time she spent bound to a chair in an otherwise empty room. She could hear a steady conversation on the other side of the door, but make out only occasional words— *vanished, ocean, search party.* Eventually it dawned on her that she wasn't hearing the voices of her captors, she was hearing the persistent thrum of a radio broadcast. She began to work against the rope at her wrists.

She could feel the bind on her skin but mostly as a peripheral figment to the drone of the radio, which she strained to hear. Then somehow she was free and projected forward, crouched at the door, still trying to hear the finer details of the broadcast. Finally she cautioned a turn on the doorknob.

The door creaked. She peered in, left then right. Only the radio, with its little light glowing. An announcer prattled away about the rescue effort, how the offer of a twenty-five-thousand-dollar reward was now implicated in the drowning deaths of two searchers off Venice Beach, and how another ransom note from a self-declared kidnapper turned out to be yet another hoax.

Venice Beach? Ransom notes? Then it struck her—the news reporter was confusing Amelia with Aimee. This was old news indeed, the opposite of anything that could qualify as an update.

She spun the dial, screeched to a halt at the next broadcast.

. . . *meanwhile at Angelus Temple, mourners from across the country have gathered to . . .*

She spun again, this time landing on the voice of Sister herself, a performance of the old perennial "Heavenly Aeroplane." She spun again.

The airwaves were utterly dominated by Aimee McPherson, either wildly outdated news of her disappearance or evangelizing broadcasts from the woman herself. It was like Amelia Earhart had never existed, let alone vanished on a record-setting flight. She felt a flare of rage, pulled the infernal lying radio off the stand and hurled it across the room.

The radio hit the wall by a mirror she hadn't noticed before, knocking it askew, and when she started forward in the same righteous fury, intending to smash the fallen radio to smithereens, she caught a glimpse of herself in the silver glass and stopped cold. Not herself at all, but Sister Aimee, staring back from within the crooked gilded frame.

The hard suck of her own shocked breath wrenched her out of sleep. The Zenith from the shop glowed at her from the night table, crackling with static. This time she didn't reach for the dial.

By morning she'd finally tired of her own anxiety. In one way she hated to admit it, as though such a realization—not actual insight, not any sort of intuition or revelation, but abject boredom, of all things—constituted a betrayal against not only Amelia but also her own ideals.

She fought it for a while. Tried to will herself to keep on as though vigil itself were a rescue attempt. But her brain wasn't working anymore. Her thoughts and her feelings ricocheted like delirious bullets, fired by some artificially alert psychopath.

Part of the delirium and maybe the foggy acuity as well came down to simple lack of sustenance. A couple of days of privation and her stomach had begun to squawk like a gaping baby bird.

But what on earth was A.E. eating out there? Certainly not the steady procession of scrambled eggs or Texas hash that Roy kept carting in. She tried to steel herself out of solidarity, told herself she'd eat when Amelia could too.

It didn't last. She could smell bacon from the breakfast Roy had dutifully brought for her. She found herself peering over the cliff edge of the bed at the plate on the floor, the rashers gone cold but nevertheless a supreme distraction. Maybe even a temptation—she hadn't touched the radio dial in the better part of an hour, could hardly listen to anything besides her own petulant belly. Finally she reached for the plate.

She thought she'd stare a moment at the shriveled brown bacon in its glaze of grease and then leave it uneaten in moral triumph. She'd continue with her mission of solidarity, depriving herself for the cause. She never had lacked for willpower.

Then again, she'd never lacked for a square meal, either. Before she knew it the bacon crumbled in her mouth, then half the strip went down in a gulp. Her belly groaned, a sound with an almost carnal satisfaction. She didn't think about guilt and she didn't think about consequence, she just wolfed the glorious smoky remainder and scrambled over the edge for more.

She knelt on the floor in her pajamas and cleared the plate like a soup-line hobo, cold eggs and stale toast and all. She actually licked the empty porcelain, tongue lapping like a famished dog's, and finally, when there was nothing left, she set the thing woozily aside. She lowered herself on the floor, drawing great draughts of glorious air.

She stared at the ceiling, watching a spider track across the plaster. She wondered what was truly superior, a long life span or the ability to stomp around upside down.

Her head lolled sideways. The radio played on, a piano concerto that would no doubt go on awhile, but she didn't reach for the dial because she noticed something else. The slim satchel from the Model A, tucked under the bed with the dust motes and a stray sock and her collapsed travel valise.

McKee had brought it into town from the barn. Annelise couldn't remember carting it into the bedroom in all the panic over Amelia, but evidently she had. She reached over and pulled it to her. The concerto played on.

She dumped the diary into her lap and saw something she hadn't noticed before: a pair of keys on a length of cord, dangling out of the upended satchel. One appeared to be a simple padlock key, but the other looked more like the one that opened her father's safe-deposit box. She brought her palm up so the key lay flat. The number 1260 was stamped into the bow.

She set the satchel aside and took up the diary, leafed again through the pages. Most were blank from about the midpoint on, with notions in that inscrutable code or shorthand in the forward half. She flipped to the inside cover.

Chas. H. Angle
Box 1260
2310 Montana, Billings

The time had come to spill it to the police, now that they had an actual name. Just tell it like it happened. She'd been jumped in the dark and had her watch stolen, only it hadn't been the right watch, because, rare as the thing was and unbeknownst to anyone otherwise, Houston had pilfered an identical Hour Angle Lindbergh model from the dead guy in the riv—

There was no Chas. H. Angle. No Detective Blank, and no Charles Angle. A bulb flashed in her brain and she simply knew it, as surely as she knew her own name. She looked at the number on the key, same as the number on the page.

Centered at the bottom was an odd little legend: $X\_\_/\_\_/\_\_$.

Except for the X it almost looked like the standard format for a month/date/year notation, minus the actual numerals. Or the sequence for a high school locker combination, again without the numbers.

Chas. H. Angle. Charles Hour Angle. Charles's Hour Angle? She frowned at the watch on her wrist. The rotating bezel around the perimeter did indeed resemble a combination lock, numbers and all. Was there some trick to the alignment of the thing, to reveal a particular sequence? That wouldn't make sense, though, or they wouldn't have needed the goon's watch back when they had Blix's identical one.

The tumblers inside her brain fell into place. She clawed at the strap and got it unbuckled. She pried the hinged back open.

She was on her feet and heading for the garage. Behind her the concerto began to fade. Nobody was going to the police after all.

Pop barely predicted it and here she was, barreling back into the shop. Huck wished Pop hadn't just rolled out for the ranch, so he could see it, too.

"Back among the living," McKee said. "Still in your jammies, though. What's the news?"

"I don't know. I quit listening, in the interest of my own sanity." She had the diary from the goons' Ford in one hand, Blix's Longines in the other. "Do you have the other watch?"

"It's inside," Huck told her.

"Drag it out here." She held up the book and started for the office. "I think I know why they wanted it back. Come here."

When he returned from the bungalow, she and McKee had the diary open on the desk.

"Looks like a brand, there at the bottom," said Huck. "Not sure how to read it, though."

"It's no brand, and that's not a mailing address up above." She set her watch facedown on the page, its back cover still open. "I think it's a combination. Let me see yours."

Huck handed her the other watch. She set this one facedown as well, so the engraved legend on the back of the case faced up.

LONGINES LINDBERGH

INVENTED BY

Col. Chas. A. Lindbergh

HOUR ANGLE WATCH

"Look at the name in the diary. Chas. H. Angle. Charles, as in Lindbergh. H. as in *Hour*." She gave him a prodding look, chin down and her eyes angled dramatically. Despite their hawklike gleam, he could see how haggard she looked. Four days, no sleep.

"Charles's Hour Angle," he said.

"It's an inside joke. All it does is refer to the watch." She tapped the script on the page with the key. "This is the key to a safe-deposit box. Which means 2310 Montana is probably the address of a bank."

"If memory serves," said McKee, "that's the street number for the Billings depot." He pulled the telephone directory out of the desk and thumbed to the right page. "Bingo."

"Okay, there are security boxes in train stations, too. Look at the serial numbers. They're both seven digits long, and they both begin with the number five. Except for the other six numbers, these two watches are ringers. What if the X is meant to cancel out the first five and leave the other numbers as the integers to a combination lock? That would explain why my watch—Blix's watch—wouldn't stand in for theirs."

McKee chewed the corner of his mouth. "You have some notion of these bank boxes?"

"Yes, we have one. Or my father does. Some of them take two keys, one held by the bank, and one"—she flipped her fingers at the key on the thong—"by the box holder, who also sets a dial combination for himself."

Evidently she still had a pang at her heart, because he watched her well up and blink it back again.

"Last year, on my birthday, he showed me where he keeps the key. He made me . . . memorize the combination, in case something happened to him. I guess he trusted me."

Huck felt himself start, but he caught himself and managed to stay mum. Pop had sworn him to silence on his own birthday just last year, with an oddly similar secret. He'd taken Huck down into the root cellar at the ranch and worked a loose fieldstone out of the wall, pulled a quart Mason jar out of the cavity behind. The jar was about half full with gold coins. Pop dumped a few into his hand.

Reckon you know these aren't legal these days.

Huck remembered nodding, remembered people hauling eagles and gold notes down to the Farmers' Bank to turn them in for new

paper scrip when President Roosevelt outlawed private gold possession. But not Pop, evidently.

Ma know about these?

*Hell no. If it was up to her, she'd have turned them over faster than you
can say "render unto Caesar." That's why I'm letting you in, in case something
happens to me.*

In truth, at face value the coins in the jar amounted to only a
few hundred dollars, which hardly seemed to qualify as any kind of a
hoard. They were pretty neat, though, nearly like a pirate's treasure.
Two of them went back to the 1850s.

*What was the point of ordering people to give these up, anyway? Seems
kind of fishy.*

Pop snorted. *I wish I had an answer for you, other than never trust a
politician. Or the banker he works for.*

Now he bit his tongue and looked at McKee, and McKee was
not looking at Annelise. He studied instead the numbers inside Blix's
watch. "So if I'm following, our hapless bad guys have already tried
twenty-five-twelve-zero-nine."

She seemed to resurface. "What? Yes, assuming I'm right on this."

"It's a dial combination, like on the school lockers?"

She shrugged. "My father's is."

"They wanted this particular watch back pretty dern bad," said
McKee. "It's as good a theory as any."

Huck thought of something else. "Why would the guys in his own
gang not know the combo, though? Seems kinda shaky."

She wiped one of her eyes, but her voice had steadied again. "Oh, I don't
know. All that Tom Sawyer, blood-and-honor-among-thieves business?
That *is* the joke. I doubt a real gangster would trust his own grandmother."

"She's right," said Yak. "The less the hired help knows, the less
they have to sell him downriver with."

"Didn't work in this case. He done went downriver on his own."

Annelise laughed, even though she swiped at her eyes again. Her
hair had grown out since spring, and she twisted a curl around her

finger and stretched it like a tempered coil. She shifted her eyes to take it in. "I'm going to wash my hair and put myself together. I think we need to go for a drive."

Four hours later she walked alone across the marble floor of the Northern Pacific depot in Billings, Houston and McKee in the panel truck outside. She'd washed her curls and lined her eyes. She wore the best summer dress she'd brought from home, black-and-white patent leather heels tapping down below and the leather satchel tucked like a purse beneath her arm.

It struck her as she made her way for the ticket counter that she had not returned to Billings since Uncle Roy whisked her away from this very station back in the spring. The intervening four months may as well have been four years. She told the clerk she wanted to rent a security-deposit box. He pointed her to the U.S. Mail office at the other end of the building.

Two minutes later she stood before the postmaster, a shuffling old gent with a paper collar and sleeve garters straight out of the Gilded Nineties. He studied her through wire spectacles perched so far forward on the tip of his nose, he had to tilt his head back to take her in. "Do you have mail?"

"I do not," she told him. "I need to open my deposit box. Number twelve-sixty."

He shuffled off again into the back and returned a few moments later with a key and a ledger book, a fairly large one. He tilted his head back from that as well, flipped around a bit, and finally ran a knurled finger down a page. "And you are, Miss——?"

She had the name on her tongue, the only logical guess if it came down to it. Again she twisted a curl around a finger. "Angle. Charlotte H."

Despite the ridge of arthritic knuckles, he pincered the pencil from his ear as delicately as a florist might pluck an errant petal from an otherwise perfect rose.

"Popular box," he remarked.

She felt her pulse rise but he only made a little flourish with his wrist and with a slight tremor scribbled something in his book. It took him a couple of shaky tries to reposition the pencil above the arm of his spectacles. "Right this way."

He led her into the back, through a maze of crates and bulging canvas sacks stenciled U.S. MAIL, then around a sorting table to a vault door set in the wall. He told her to look the other way. She heard the dial turn and, when she stole a peek, saw his thin shoulder blades like folded wings beneath the black satin of his vest.

She heard the rotating whine of the lever, the nearly ominous muffled clank of the retracting bolts, and she let herself look again. The heavy door swung without a sound.

He beckoned her into the vault, which was tinier than she would have predicted from the formidable look of the door—only about the size of an average bathroom, with a small library table and a single chair. The three interior walls were lined with rows of numbered metal doors, each about the size of a dictionary's spine and each containing a single dial combination centered between a pair of keyholes.

The postmaster eased his way around the table and found the correct box on the back wall. Somebody dinged the service bell at the front desk. He jittered his way through several attempts to stab his key into one of the locks, mumbling in frustration but finally succeeding. He turned the key and stepped back. The bell dinged again.

"You may use the table," he informed her. "I'll be up front."

She waited until he'd shuffled out, then loosed the key from the thong and put the satchel on the table. She tried the other slot. The key wouldn't enter at all, and she saw then that a little metal barrier behind the portal blocked its passage. She looked to the combination lock.

She reached for the dial and saw that she herself had a shake, worse even than the elderly postmaster's. She looked up, sucked in and blew out a couple of giant breaths at the whitewashed ceiling.

Concrete, she could tell the longer she looked. She had gooseflesh on her bare arms despite the July heat. She was in a concrete room, a true vault, even the air somehow as still as death. She got herself settled and reached again for the lock.

With the initial 5 canceled out the remaining two-digit numbers were 33/19/17. She assumed the thing worked in the usual right-left-right fashion but was still shocked when she spun to a stop at the terminal integer and heard a slight shift inside the mechanism. She raised her key again and inserted it cleanly within the slot, turned it, cleared the hasp, and swung the little door.

The box felt so light she immediately wondered if the thing might actually be empty. What a slap that would be, if someone had beaten her to whatever was supposed to be inside. Or maybe there never had been anything to begin with, the whole cat-and-mouse charade more along the lines of a practical joke foisted by a dead man. She levered the hasp and raised the lid.

Not entirely empty, but nearly so. A single sealed envelope, unmarked on the outside, which she snatched up and thrust into the satchel. She wanted to run in a sort of eleventh-hour dread, a near certainty the whole jig was about to unravel after so many puzzles and so many doors, and she wanted nothing so much as to be *gone*, back with her prize and her boys in the Stude outside.

Again she collected herself, enough at least to return the box to its slot and clap the door closed. She wheeled for the exit with the key still in her grip, slipped past the postmaster and his customer at the counter, and forced herself to tap and not run through the marble and columns of the station.

"It's a map. Sort of." She was wedged between Houston and McKee, barely two blocks down from the depot. The torn envelope had fallen to her lap. She held the unfolded page in her hands.

"Of course it is." McKee slowed to a stop at the next light and looked over. "Sort of. Not much of one. What's New Breton?"

The words appeared in ink toward the top of the sheet, almost certainly in the same hand as the diary notations. A small and pretty artfully executed sketch of a Wild West street front crossed the page below, featuring a saloon with the usual bat-wing doors and hitching post, a false-fronted building marked "General Store," and another marked "Assay Office." A stylized arrow meandered down to a second sketch in the lower-right corner, labeled "Boot Hill" and consisting of a handful of grave markers. A single stone structure sat to the side, labeled "Pere DeMers" and emblazoned with an X.

"A town, I guess?" she said.

"It's a ghost town," said Houston. "I think."

"But you've heard of it?"

He racked his brain. "Yeah, seems like. Can't remember where, though."

"Where it is, you mean."

He shook his head. "Not exactly. What I mean is, I can't remember how I even know that. Maybe something Pop told me? Or Raleigh, probably. But I could be totally wrong."

The light turned and McKee let out the clutch. "It would make sense, just from the drawing. Boot Hill and a saloon and all. It's a starting point, anyway."

"Yeah," Raleigh told him, "New Breton. People used to call it Frenchville, too. Canuck settlement, been abandoned for years."

He'd been gone two weeks, and the water under the bridge in the meantime made his voice through the telephone sound all the more pipsqueak. He was as encyclopedic as ever, though. "It's up in Fergus County. One of those places the railroad passed by, so everybody up and moved."

"You know if there's a, uh, cemetery up there?" Huck asked. He was grappling with how much to spill. Raleigh had been in it at the outset, then drifted out of the line of fire without ever realizing it. Maybe the less he knew now, the better. Or maybe that wasn't Huck's call to make in the first place.

"Cemetery? Reckon there's got to be." Huck could practically hear Raleigh chewing on things through the line. "What all's afoot, Houston? This about the rev and the watch and Detective Blank again?"

Huck was at a loss. Never in his born days would he make a born liar. That was Annelise's department. "Something like that, yeah."

"Let me guess. Not over the phone?"

"Yeah. Something just like that."

"All right, I'll get over there soon as I can. Maybe not today, though. But if you really want to know about Frenchville? Old Man Neuman's the one to ask. He was born up thataway."

McKee and his landlord were in the habit of taking a nip of an evening anyway, so McKee did the honors. He came back to the shop the next morning greener than usual, eyes clamped as though the very light of day bored like a drill.

Huck watched him gimp to the sink. "What got into you?"

McKee cranked the water and thrust his entire head beneath the flow. He came up sputtering, then tilted back and stood there dripping. "Ol' Neuman's hooch is what got into me. Should've stuck to Highlander."

"He say anything?"

McKee swabbed his eyes and blew a breath. "Oh yeah. You get him going on Frenchville, he don't know the word *quit*." He looked at Huck, still with the squint. "But get this. There is a cemetery up there, with a crypt. A pretty roughshod one. Built to house the town founder, some old boy named Jacques DeMers."

"Whoa. Just like the map."

McKee yawned. "That ain't the half of it. He told me when they mothballed the old cuss back in the nineties, they put him to rest in a glass-topped casket."

5

"A glass-topped casket," said Annelise, for maybe the twentieth time. "That is so weird."

"Not exactly unheard of, forty or fifty years ago."

They were in the Stude the following Saturday, winding along the new U.S. highway north and then west into Fergus County. McKee was back to his usual devil-may-care deportment, although still vowing to "stick to the beer from now on."

He said, "I saw plenty of old funeral pictures as a kid down in Utah. Some of the crates for the big chiefs were downright cock-for-Dolly—black lacquer, silver trim, you name it. And yeah, glass windows on a few of them."

She shook her head. "I don't get it."

Raleigh was perched on an upended milk crate behind the seat, not yet totally up to speed but a regular font of information regardless.

"The Victorians had a real death fetish," he piped up. "They used to take family portraits with the deceased, like the body was still alive. Had these special contraptions to prop it in a chair, and everybody would sit around like it was just another day in the parlor."

"That is *so weird*."

"Know what's even weirder? Sometimes in those old pictures, the quick ones will look a little blurry and the dead 'un will be clear as day, 'cause the cadaver was the only one to keep perfectly still during the exposure."

"What you might call a dead giveaway," said McKee.

"Uh-*zackly*."

"They must have stepped pretty quick to catch the moment," Annelise mused. "From the deathbed straight to the sitting room. I mean, can you imagine if somebody keeled over in that heat a few days ago? He'd be ripe as a fish in no time."

"Oh, the Victorians had 'er figured pretty slick. They'd ice the body and siphon the blood right on out. Completely drain it. Then the undertaker would pump it full of arsenic and lead. Total preservation."

"How do you know this stuff?" asked McKee.

"Actually, I'm not sure. But I'm pretty curious to get a look— he's probably lying under glass like he kicked off yesterday."

"You're going to give me nightmares," Annelise said.

The land shifted as they drove. The rims and tables fell away, and they entered rolling grassland. Better ranches with better water, and ricks of hay like giant loaves in the bottoms. Mountain ranges rose in the distance, pine-green islands out of cured-straw sea, the Snowies to the south and the Judiths steadily approaching.

Old Man Neuman hadn't been home in years but he'd given McKee a pretty straightforward route into the place. Gilt Edge Road just up to the base of the hills, then south and west two miles on the old Lewistown stage road and due south from there on the New Breton cutoff. McKee called the county extension office and determined that the route in was still passable, at least within a half mile or so of the abandoned town site.

The end of the line turned out to be a collapsed bridge across what was now a sheer-sided if utterly chalk-dry creek bottom. They parked the rig in the withered grass and went forward on foot, packing a set of bolt cutters and a hacksaw as well as a one-inch cold chisel and a hand sledge. Annelise toted the carbide lamps and her Kodak Brownie, Raleigh a kerosene hurricane lamp.

They followed the trace up into a draw, a pair of mostly bare hills rising steeply left and right and a smaller dry drainage just down off the old road grade. The ravine curved around into an open bowl, and they saw the dregs of the town up ahead, mainly a couple of hollow-eyed stone buildings in steep disrepair and a handful of framed structures as well, sagging and slumping toward the ground in various stages of collapse.

McKee looked at Annelise. "Ever seen a ghost town before?"

She shook her head. "Uh-uh. Well, that's not true, either—we flew over one out in the desert once, during a lesson. But it just looked like a bunch of buildings from that perspective. How long has this place been abandoned?"

"Turn of the century or so. Ol' Neuman would probably have a heart attack if he saw the place now."

The brutal heat from the early part of the week had backed off considerably, but even so, Huck felt beads of sweat trickle down his ribs beneath his shirt. Despite this, he swore he saw Annelise shiver.

They walked through the scatter of derelict buildings on what had obviously been the town's central street, with the remains of other foundations visible in the grass on either side.

"All right," said McKee, "let's divide and conquer. I'm guessing the cemetery's a little way from town, as usual. Huck, you and Raleigh head over that way toward the trees. We'll walk up toward the top of the bowl on this side. Try to stay in earshot."

A little later Raleigh whistled Huck over to a low rise in the contour. They looked down on a fenced-in square of grave markers, some wooden and invariably weather-battered, others lichen-specked stone, and most of them askew this way or that. Ornate iron picketry bordered a few of the more elaborate stones, spindles and finials laced with overgrown grass. And sure enough, off to one side, a low-slung structure of masoned fieldstone.

"X marks the spot," said Raleigh. "How in the heck did you guys figure this out?"

Huck shielded his eyes and scanned the bowl. Annelise and McKee emerged around the upper end of a hawthorn draw. "Believe me, it's an epic. I'll tell you on the drive back."

Two deer exited the low side of the tangle into a patch of snow-berries, a sleek doe and her gangly fawn, white spots visible even from here. Huck cupped his hands around his mouth and hollered. The deer stopped and looked, and so did his cousin and McKee. Huck waved his arms overhead, and the other two started toward him. The deer bounded away.

By the time they made their way across the shallow bottom and back up again, Huck and Raleigh had examined the little stone crypt from all sides. The roof was made of granular concrete, maybe five feet above grade at the ridge and shallow-pitched. A set of iron shutters blocked the only entry, rusted and held fast with a crossbar that looked to have been peened into existence in some medieval torture pit. A padlock of newer vintage held the bar closed.

Annie and McKee came up through the grass. McKee rapped his knuckles on the iron door. "Anybody home?" He took hold of the padlock and rattled it around on the hasp. "Definitely not as old as the rest of this relic." He pointed at Annelise. "Crack the champagne, milady?"

She shook her head. "Nope."

"Hand 'er over, then."

She fished beneath her collar and produced the key, hung on a string around her neck. She lifted the loop over her head and held it out. Her mouth had that grim set to it, and Huck couldn't blame her a bit, because his own felt about as dry as that creek bottom back at the crippled bridge.

The shackle disengaged with a clank. The lock flopped open, and Yak slipped it from the hasp on the crossbar and popped the bar out of its saddle, then up and around with a rusted screech. McKee took up his flashlight and shot the beam into the doorway.

A short set of wooden steps ran to the floor, which appeared, like the roof, to be made of concrete. Then Huck let his eyes wander with the light, and he was looking at a casket. Part of one anyway, what could be seen through the frame of the portal.

McKee looked at Annelise. "Okay, then. You first."

She shook her head. "Nothing doing, bucko."

He laughed and hunched under the low transom to test the first step, then the second. He went down and disappeared into the vault. Huck sensed Annelise shift closer to him, sensed her but didn't actually see her, because he couldn't pry his eyes loose from the open maw. He watched the flicker and bob as the beam panned around, then felt the thump of his heart when the light cut out.

Then an actual thump, or maybe a thud, out of the eerie darkness of the vault, and the flinching stab of Annelise's grip.

McKee appeared in the doorway. "*Just kidding!*" He beckoned with the flashlight. "Come on, water's fine."

Still Annelise's grip. "I hate you," she said. "You never know when to quit."

"What's your legal term? Mea culpa?" He stuck his head up into the daylight. "But the thing is, nothing down here can hurt you. Just a bunch of stiffs."

"How many?" Raleigh asked.

McKee ducked back in, flashed the beam around. His voice came out of the hollow with a sort of tin-can projection. "Eight."

"Whoa."

"Yeah."

"All glass?"

"Only two."

"Whoa. Is it weird?"

McKee surfaced again. "Yeah, pretty weird. Come see for yourself." He hesitated. "Be warned, though. One of them's a kid."

Annelise still had Huck's arm, a grip like a trap. "I don't know if I can do it."

Raleigh already had a match to the hurricane lamp. "I'm game," he said. He looked over. "Huckleberry? Ready for the initiation? Sign the robbers' oath on a casket?" He shifted to Annelise. "No girls allowed, by the way."

She gave Huck's arm one last tight squeeze. "In this particular case I'm not going to argue."

McKee's tin-can chortle echoed out of the tomb. "Jackpot."

Raleigh took in a deep breath, held the lantern out ahead and stepped down into the vault. Huck saw the toe end of a casket again in the new throw of light. He looked once more at his cousin.

"Give me a report," she said. "I need to know what to expect."

"Ho-ly," said Raleigh, his voice as hollow as McKee's.

Huck held a miner's lamp but didn't spark it, what with the interior now plainly aglow. He could see the vague pulsing of shadow and light as the pair of them moved about, Raleigh no doubt waving the lantern around like a semaphore. He heard McKee say something that he couldn't quite make out. "You still on the fence?"

She puffed her cheeks and blew out air like a deflating balloon. "I'll probably do it. Nightmares or no."

"Okay. I'm doing it."

"Why am I so creeped out by this?"

"Because it's a dern creep-out," he told her, and ducked his head under.

The air inside the chamber was cool and stale, an inert density not so different from that in a mine shaft. Two steps down and he found himself surrounded by caskets. The concrete ceiling was hardly an inch or two above his head, and the unnerving nearness of all that hanging, crushing weight triggered a sort of fun-house confusion about his own equilibrium. He felt himself sway in place and quickly looked down, not sure if he was still on a step or totally descended to the floor.

Still on a step. He put a hand over his head and steadied himself against the ceiling. He stepped again. With the new margin between his head and the roof, he felt his balance more or less return.

McKee stood across from him like Bela Lugosi, flashlight turned under his chin. "Yeah, funny. Don't do that when Annelise comes in."

"Wouldn't dream of it." He turned the beam to the coffin beside him. "Papists."

Huck saw the glint of glass on the upper half of the lid. "That the head honcho?"

"Must be."

"What's a papist?"

"A feller of the Roman Catholic persuasion," Raleigh told him.

Huck felt some of the rubber return to his legs but willed himself forward. Even in the soft light of the lantern the wooden parts of the casket were clearly ornate, with carving and silver fixtures. The lid had not one but two glass panels, upper and lower, divided by a solid black sash. Some of the other boxes were stacked atop one another along the perimeter walls, but this one rested on its own velvet-draped stand.

The man inside wore a red satin shroud and matching cap, a contrast to the casket's billowing white lining. His enormous red beard descended from an otherwise wax-white mug. Garish red rouge on his cheeks, though. An elaborate crucifix lay on his chest, and his clasped hands held a rosary. Yellowed fingernails.

"Almost just looks asleep." Huck's own voice, coming back at him in the blank bottled air.

"Rip Van Winkle," said Raleigh.

"Where's the other? The kid?"

"Right this way."

The child's coffin sat atop a plainer box against the back wall, and it was sadly small indeed. White, with gold-washed handles and trim. He came up on the glass and saw to his shock that the enclosed was not a boy but a little girl, maybe five or six years old. She had the same rouged skin but hair dark as a raven's wing, stark against the white lace of her costume.

"Whoa. Didn't figure on a girl, for some reason."

"Me neither." For some reason they were both whispering. "You know the weirdest part, though? Her dern teeth."

Huck looked back through the glass. Her little lips were parted in what could nearly have passed for a smile. The bottom edge of her tiny white incisors showed in the aperture and it *was* sort of an eerie sight, although he had to admit she looked perfectly peaceful.

"Hello?" Annelise had mustered the nerve to crouch by the entrance. "It's mighty quiet down there."

"We're paying our respects," said McKee. "You want to come down?"

"I think so."

Huck found his normal voice. "It's not that bad. The kid ain't a boy, though. She's a girl."

"Okay, good to know. Does she look . . . I don't know, normal?"

"She looks like she could've been walking around yesterday," Raleigh said. "The arsenic-and-lead operation evidently worked."

"Houston?"

Huck was still looking at her delicate parted mouth. With Raleigh's lantern angled away, her skin looked less ghost-pale than nearly luminous. "She looks like an angel."

McKee went to the base of the steps. "The old guy's like a dead pope, no big deal. The little girl doesn't look old enough to be where she is, but the both of them could just as well be asleep."

Huck could practically hear the row inside her brain. He knew her nerves were still jangled from the unfortunate business with Miss Earhart, knew as well she'd hardly be able to live with herself if she didn't steel up and take a couple of embalmed cadavers right in stride. Which is exactly what Miss Earhart herself would have done.

"All right, I'm coming down. Hold the light on the steps."

Huck watched her descend, backlit by the daylight behind her and wary as that doe across the bowl a while ago with its guard up, and he thought how good it was just to be a live human being with your own people around to feel it too. McKee held out his hand to her.

She took in the caskets. "This just feels wrong."

"Oh, come now. Don't tell me you've never done this sort of thing."

She paused while holding McKee's hand, and Huck heard Raleigh clear his throat, only now doing the math. Usually Huck alone felt eternally in the dark. Odd as it was in the moment, he felt a small swell of pride, maybe even triumph, to be a step ahead for once.

"All right. Pope first."

McKee led her forward. Annelise peered through the glass. Her voice came on steady, nary a wobble nor a hitch. "O Bearded One. He looks like Saint Nick."

"Ho, ho, ho," said McKee.

"Not funny," she said. "Remember that part about paying respects? I take it that's the little girl?"

Huck stood aside for her, and she untethered from McKee. Raleigh held the lamp higher.

She walked up, appeared to dare herself to peek down, and let out a sound somewhere between a whimper and a sigh. "She can't be six years old. Or couldn't have been when they walled her up in here. I wonder how she died."

McKee moved in behind them. "Kids used to up and die all kinds of ways. Flu, pneumonia, dysentery, scarlet fever. Hell, a bad hangnail could probably do it. Even when I was a kid, down in the desert. I bet one in five was gone before they were out of diapers."

"I wonder how old she actually is," Raleigh mused.

"Like I said, I doubt she's six. Still with her front baby teeth."

"Right, but she didn't die yesterday. She's been in here for what, forty years? Maybe fifty?"

This was a startling thing to consider, that the child in the case was technically older than Mother and possibly even Pop. At the very least, she'd probably been right here in her dreamless sleep clear back when Pop made his long ride from Texas. The same dawning silence hung over the lot of them.

Finally Annelise broke the spell. "You missed it by that much, kiddo. I am so, so sorry."

"Are you talking to her?" Raleigh asked.

"Let's say she's been here forty years, like you said. That's 1897." She took in a breath, blew it audibly back out again. "That's also the year Amelia was born. So this little girl died never knowing what an airplane was, never knowing cars, never knowing the radio or even electricity, most likely. Never knowing she'd be able to vote someday, or maybe fly her own airplane. And now here she is, six years old forever—1897 forever. Think of what she missed. By *that much*."

Huck wondered if she was actually a little angry—this was as much of her usual fire as he'd heard in more than a week. When she'd first arrived in Montana those months ago, that edge she possessed put his nerves on an entirely different sort of edge. Now he was just relieved to hear her talk like herself again.

"Amelia will be forty, two weeks from today."

Huck started a little.

"Forty," said Raleigh. "I didn't realize. Would've guessed younger."

"I think that's why this was supposed to be the last big feat. Her gift to herself."

"July twenty-fourth?" Huck said.

"Yes. The twenty-fourth. Missed it by that much."

"That's my birthday."

Even in this light he saw her react. "How did I not know that?"

Huck shrugged. "Guess it just never came up."

"Well. That is curious." Annelise held her hand out, palm flat and fingers splayed above the little girl's folded hands, but careful not to touch the glass. "Guess we'll never know this one's birthday. Or her name, even."

She let her hand hover, then pulled it into a fist against her chest. She turned away. "Can't say this won't come back to haunt me, but it's out of the way for now. What was that about a jackpot?"

Huck had sort of forgotten why they were here in the first place.

McKee beamed his light into the front corner of the crypt, down the wall from the stairs. Another wooden box, but a crate rather than a coffin, maybe two feet long by a foot tall, made of no-nonsense unpainted wood.

"What's in it?"

"Ain't sure. The lid's nailed down."

"Then how do you know it's any kind of jackpot?"

"Try lifting the thing. It's got something solid in it. I mean really solid."

"Concrete?"

"Doubt it. I'll be right back." He went up the steps and out, returned with the hand sledge and chisel. He gave his flashlight to Annelise.

He drove the point between box and lid, enough to start the nails backing out, then dropped the hammer and put his weight into the shank. The nails wrenched with a squeal. The crate itself, solid as an anchor, barely moved. He worked the lid up and down until the last of the nails whimpered free.

They peered in at a flap of folded canvas. McKee grabbed the corner and pulled the covering back. They looked down on a crateful of gleaming gold ingots.

"Ay Chihuahua. There's a stash."

"Yeah, a stash of contraband," said Raleigh. "Wonder what in tarnation they planned on doing with that."

"They may not know themselves," McKee said. He lifted one of the bars, about the size of a brick but clearly much heavier. Another layer of ingots sat below. "Not everybody turned this stuff in when they were supposed to, though. Not even the honest people."

"True," said Annelise, "but this is actual bullion, and not a small amount. My dad had a bunch of coins and certificates that he exchanged, or said he did, but plenty of people hid that stuff away rather than just hand it over for less than it was worth." She seemed to consider. "I assume he did, too, even though he's usually as by-the-book as it gets."

Huck remembered Pop's stash of eagles, squirreled away in their Mason jar. He reached in and hefted one of the ingots but otherwise kept his word. "I saw an article last spring on the new depository in *Modern Mechanics*. Fort Knox. It's a dern fortress—granite walls two feet thick. The heaviest door ever built in all history. You know they're moving six billion dollars of this stuff into it? Right while we're standing here."

McKee set the bar back into the crate. "Our backwoods crypt may not be all that, but I reckon this stuff's safe enough for the time being."

"What do we do with it?" said Raleigh.

"We leave it right where it is, at least for now. Try to figure out some sort of game plan."

Annelise looked back and forth between Huck and McKee. "We have to spill this to the police. Now that we've seen this. Because they will almost certainly be back."

"Who'll be back?" said Raleigh. "Detective Blank?"

"In a manner of speaking. Along with Charles Angle."

"*Who*? I'm playing Heinz 57 here."

"It's a long ride home," she told him.

6

She beheld an oblong bulk, hovering within a fog, dark and indistinct but somehow, she sensed, dearly important. She both dreaded and desired the knowledge of whatever it was, like some deadly mythic apple. An answer to a mystery she was fated both to solve, and forevermore regret solving.

She wasn't peering through mist—she was peering through water. She realized it when she realized she was holding her breath, because she was underwater, too. The object swam toward her, or drifted at least, black and pliant as a half-deflated inner tube but increasingly taking on the loose-limbed countenance of a body, in half-buoyant suspension.

Houston's ghoul, coming right at her. He'd described the sight of its face rising through the murk, gradually and then suddenly coalescing from a wax-white smear into a fully distinct death mask—bruised-fruit eye sockets and purple parted lips, dark hair dancing with the action of the water. Though she warned her eyes away even now, she knew full well her morbid curiosity would prove the stronger. She knew she'd see it, and never in her born days find a way to unsee it.

The figure drifted nearer by the second. She couldn't hold her breath much longer, the sear of expiring oxygen burning in her lungs. But the ghoul was nearly distinct now, just a few more seconds, just a few more feet through the murk . . .

The golden halo threw her off. Houston and Raleigh were still talking months later about that dark wrack of hair, how utterly macabre it had been, but somehow he seemed now to shine right through the water. Maybe he really was a reverend, forgiven in the end of whatever misdeeds he'd committed.

The body bobbed ever forward and she saw in a flash it was not the ghoul at all but Amelia, half-lidded though blue-eyed yet and even smiling, with that famous gap between her teeth. Her head of copper curls seemed to generate its own numinous light through the distorted heave. Annelise gasped by reflex and felt her lungs flood—

She came awake sputtering, had evidently been holding her air even while she dreamed. She clawed for the lamp and turned it on, chasing out the dark.

7

Her dreams continued to torment her sleep for the next couple of nights, to the point where she was practically afraid to turn off the lamp, afraid to face her own mind in the sinister dark. She felt bone-weary during the day from lack of rest, caught herself more than once nodding off at the desk in the office, or even in the bathtub.

Finally she and Roy and Houston spent a night at the ranch. To her shock, she woke up very late in Houston's little attic bedroom, after her first solid night's sleep in weeks. No agonizing hours inside her own head, no fraught imperiled visions. She lay there looking at his models soaring beneath the tattered ceiling. She felt the calm of her own air.

Roy came into the kitchen while she was finishing the eggs her aunt had fried for her.

"There's the sleepyhead. I had half a mind to run back to town two hours ago and come back for you this afternoon." He winked. "You were sawing wood like a lumber camp."

"You do look rested," Aunt Gloria told her. The two of them had been sitting there while she ate, not even playing the radio, because her aunt for some reason had started to tell her about her own mother when they were girls, and how Annelise resembled her.

I don't mean looks, exactly, although there's that, too. I mean her spirit. She'd given a rueful smile. *Victoria. The right name exactly. I could tell you stories.*

I'd love to hear one.

Oh. She'd never forgive me.

Swear me to secrecy, then.

Her aunt chimed with a laugh like a rare bird, and something shimmered inside Annelise, too. *That is just what she would say. My land. It's like you're her, or she's here, right in my kitchen. You know she . . . also loved to dance when she was young. Your age or thereabouts. Had the beaux lined up for it, too, to speak the honest truth.*

By the time her uncle came in she was on to Victoria's first experience with the moving pictures, and how she'd come to idolize Mary Pickford. Gloria herself was as animated as Annelise had ever seen her, outside of that tent revival those long weeks ago.

Even Roy noticed. "Don't mean to bust the party, but we need to scoot. You close?"

She took in her empty plate, everything down to the runoff yolk mopped away with a piece of toast, and it struck her. Already she understood her mother better than she ever had. Meanwhile the goons and their watch and their coded ledger and those dark relentless dreams awaited back in town.

"I think I need to rest. Maybe I'll just stay another day?" She looked at her aunt. "If that's all right?"

Three days later she was still there. Still sleeping in near-dreamless bliss in the attic at night, still systematically forking down eggs or powder biscuits or chipped beef and, on the second evening, nearly half a chicken that Aunt Gloria roasted for her.

They set a table in the shade of the porch with the sun slanting, away from the infernal heat of the cookstove. They'd made a potato salad that morning and cooled it all day in a tub of water in the root cellar. Aunt Gloria as usual ate like a sparrow, but Annelise tore in like a pack of hyenas.

"Sorry," she said, with her mouth half full. "I guess I haven't been eating enough lately."

"That was my mother's recipe. The potatoes. She was of German stock."

"I wish I'd known her better, when I was little."

"She could cook, like a true farm lady. I don't hold any sort of candle."

"I have to disagree."

"Well, thank you. It's lovely to have someone to cook for again." She paused. "If I didn't know you'd been starving yourself lately, I'd almost worry you were eating for two."

Annelise practically choked but managed to swallow down the food in her mouth. "*Oh*. Definitely don't worry about that."

Aunt Gloria looked out at the shadows, stretching long across the folds in the land. She seemed very calm, even serene. "That's probably all it was, with your mother. All those months ago. Just . . . worry. Panic. I'm sure she saw her own life in it, if you want the truth. She had a wild spell herself when we were girls, put your poor grandmother through no amount of nerves." She looked back and smiled in the shade. "But Victoria can be a lot scarier than my mother ever was."

Annelise took another bite, considered how strange a conversation this was turning out to be. "She just . . . doesn't understand that she might be wrong. It doesn't seem to occur to her."

Her aunt looked up at the underside of the little overhang, where the points of roofing nails pierced through the sheathing. "Victoria was always headstrong. I admired it, to be honest. She had the certainty of a given moment. And the next day she could decide the exact opposite, and she'd be just as certain. I guess that's what you'd call conviction."

Annelise felt herself nodding. "Yep."

"You've got some of it, too, though maybe not with the same . . . unholy stubbornness."

They both laughed a little.

"It did startle me to see you so down the past couple of weeks. I almost picked up and moved into the cottage in town, in case you needed anything."

Annelise tried to imagine that one, with everything else that had gone on. "Well, I came out here. This is better."

"It's nice, isn't it? Nice and quiet. Just us. I do wish we had some lemonade—we had some at the Independence Day picnic back in town, and I couldn't get enough. Such a rare thing." Gloria studied the nails on one of her hands, and Annelise noticed for the first time that they were chewed to the nub. "I just wished you were there with Uncle and me, so that you could have some, too."

"That is . . . very kind. I wasn't in much of a place to appreciate it, unfortunately."

"It made me sad to see you in such a state. A girl with your spark. But I do understand, maybe more than you know. I could see some of myself, hovering over that radio with you." Aunt Gloria looked up from her poor bitten-down nails. "A heroine of mine once disappeared into the ocean, too."

"I got my monthly when I was nine years old. Did my mother ever tell you that?"

"Well, no. No, she didn't."

"I can't really blame her. She was probably as shocked as I was, in her own way." Annelise looked out into the dusk, the last light of the sun just a purple striation where the land scribed the sky. Somehow evening had passed into night.

"Not to mention I hid it for as long as I could. I was scared and confused, though. My mother's more about plain appearances."

"Even that can come from being scared and confused." Gloria had taken up her fork again. She spoke around a mouthful.

"That never occurred to me, but I guess you're right."

"Being a grown-up is just as frightful as growing up in the first place, in my experience. Especially once you have young of your own to keep after. How long were you able to hide it? Your moon, I mean."

"Four or five times, I guess? I didn't understand what it was, because nobody had ever talked to me about it, and I was afraid to say anything because of where the blood was coming from."

"My land. You must have been anguished."

"Terrified I was dying, and that's the truth. The first time it happened, I pulled the sheet off my bed and hid it in the neighbors' trash."

Gloria clucked her tongue. "Nine years old. Bless your heart."

Some detached part of herself considered even in the moment how she could not have predicted such an evening, with such a person as her aunt.

"What did you do in place of napkins? If you don't mind me snooping."

"Toilet paper. I'd just wad it in my underpants and pretend I had to go to the bathroom a lot."

Gloria clucked again.

"Finally, though, I bled through the back of my dress. First week of the fifth grade. My teacher sent me down to the school nurse and I remember just crying, partially out of shame but also maybe halfway in relief that someone else finally *knew* and could tell me it was normal. But I was begging her not to tell my mother, for reasons I didn't even quite get, and she was really, really nice to me about it, but of course she had to. Tell her, I mean.

"And of course, my mother took me straight to the family doctor. He's actually *still* the family doctor, and he seemed older than Methuselah even then.

"Anyway. That was my first full exam, lying there on my back, trying to reach these stirrups with my short little legs." That silver reflector, flashing like a moon across a bay, half revealed above the horizon of the gown she'd had to wear. A foreshadowing of what she'd dodged by confession later.

She didn't elaborate now, but the wisp of a thatch she'd developed had anguished her right along with the secret spells, and never more so than in that exact moment. The silk on her legs, too, blonde and usually hidden beneath stockings but glinting in the air like electrified filaments, her limbs angled in that punishing light. At least nobody looked beneath her arms.

"It may not be entirely his fault, or any of his fault even, but I've hated that doctor ever since."

They'd sent her to the waiting room afterward, with a nurse and a lollipop. What was he telling her mother behind the barrier of the door? She could hear the hushed murmur, hear the urgency even, but the message itself would remain a mystery. She never did unwrap the candy.

Her aunt was looking at her, she could tell even in the faded light. The moon had risen now, not much more than a crescent over the empty quiet. "Thank you for telling me, Annelise. I hope my sister cooked your favorite dinner, after all that."

"Oh. I can't even remember. I think she was averting her eyes, which I guess would be normal. She brought me a little book, called *Marjorie May's Twelfth Birthday*. I'm sure she'd rather it *was* my twelfth birthday.

"Otherwise, she gave me a safety razor and some soap. Proper napkins and a harness. As much of a hug as she was capable of, I guess? And that was that."

Her father had stayed totally out of it, and she guessed that must be normal too. He did treat her a little differently, from then on.

"The other girls my age still had a couple of years to go, and I didn't have older sisters or cousins around. So even once I knew better, I still felt like a bit of a sideshow freak. I was just a little girl, in spite of what my body was doing. Just completely sheltered, completely naive."

"I suppose I can relate to that, too." Gloria shifted in her chair. "I had some troubles myself, around that sort of thing. Not in quite the same way. Is it too cold out here? Or too late? We can go inside, or just call it enough for one night."

"No, I'm fine. Really. It's so good to talk."

"You've been so honest, and I know it's hard to be honest, with these secrets we think we're supposed to carry around."

"Do you want to tell me, Gloria? You can, if you want. I always could keep a secret. Even when I was nine."

Gloria

I

And it shall come to pass in the last days, saith God, I will pour out of my Spirit upon all flesh:

and your sons and your daughters shall prophesy, and your young men shall see visions, and your old men shall dream dreams:

And on my servants and on my handmaidens I will pour out in those days of my Spirit; and they shall prophesy . . .

—Acts of the Apostles

My sister was always the strong one, always the bright fire. Older than me by three years and rather haughtily precocious, I suppose, burning young with questions and convictions, skeptical in Sunday school and even challenging the minister on this point or that.

The doctrine of predestination against the necessity of free will to personal salvation.

The age of the earth as calculated through the Scriptures, versus the assertions of the geology we were taught in school. A mere girl then, and told to shush up and worry not over things beyond her ken.

Papa was a Methodist by heritage, a good man but a docile one, more consumed with his farm in Indiana than his future in eternity. Probably he could have used a few sons, but what he wound up with was a pair of girls. I still don't know what he actually believed, and I've come to understand that probably he did not know himself.

Mother on the other hand had long volunteered with the Salvation Army, and she raised Victoria and myself to answer that good Christian call. We worked right beside her in poor farms and orphanages, seeing firsthand the rotting fruits of strong drink and gambling and the dissipation of sin.

There was a distant sense that Jesus would one day return and that we must repent and be saved. And although good works alone were not enough to gain the Kingdom, we understood as well that by one's own fruits should a true Christian be known. We were instructed to be pious but also well-mannered, modest but stalwart servants, never raising an eyebrow with so much as an outburst of joy, let alone anything like the fullness of the Spirit.

The Good Book spoke of such fullness, though. Signs and wonders, and manifestations of the Holy Ghost. The speaking of strange tongues and the healing of the infirm. Though Jesus Himself instructed His disciples to heal the sick, cast out demons, and preach the Kingdom of God, we were encouraged in our staid little church only toward the latter. The age of miracles had passed. Now we occupied an age of faith, as the evidence of things no longer seen.

And it was true, none of us had ever seen a demon, at least not of the sort Christ cast into a pack of swine. We had seen no cripple made to walk, nor blind man to see.

I myself suffered mightily from what the doctors termed a twist in my spine. Pain like a tightening chain through my hip and back and shoulder, then on through the taut cords of my neck and finally agony in the region behind my left eye. Pain to make waves of sickness churn and convulse right through me. Pain to blind me with distortions of magnified light and arrays of agonizing color. Mother and sister held back my hair while I retched into a bedpan, or worked liniment into my back and neck. Pressed a cool damp rag to my aggrieved eyes. They prayed for comfort for me, but no one imagined that the bend in my back might actually straighten through supplication to the Spirit alone.

* * *

Victoria on the other hand fairly exuded what was known in those days as pulchritude. She had health and she had beauty, and a way about her in equal measures charming and headstrong, and that had suitors coming around early.

Probably she needed to slide a bit, as the Lord will sometimes allow. Needed to see the lure of the world for the false glitter it contained and so discover true conviction, in a way bland recited dogma could never match. His ways are indeed mysterious.

She trotted herself off to more than one dance at the community hall in our little hamlet. When the same hall featured a showing of one of the latest moving pictures, Victoria accepted an invitation to that, too. Mama could not rein her in, so imperious was Victoria's combined force of threat and will.

Her name is Mary Pickford. She is the latest sensation.

I was barely twelve and, I must confess, prey to a burning curiosity. Victoria was so . . . of the world now, positively a-brim with the forbidden knowledge of what lay outside the garden. I wanted to know, and yet I did not want to know.

I fear Mama does not approve.

Mama does not approve. Nor will she explain why.

She says it is a mere hop and a skip from the dance social to Sodom and Gomorrah.

But how can she know that if she hasn't experienced anything for herself?

She had a point, and anyway my curiosity got the better of me. *What does Mary Pickford do, in the moving picture?*

Well. It's a story, of course, so she is pretending to be someone else. Little Red Riding Hood, in this case.

Can you see the red riding hood? Its color, I mean.

No, silly. It's just in the shades of a regular photograph. Like the ones of us on the mantel.

But does it seem real?

This she had to consider. *Yes, and no. They are real people moving about, but they behave in a dramatic fashion. I suppose they have to, to get the story across, since you can't hear what they might be saying. Also, the wolf is clearly only a little shepherd dog, and seems a bit puzzled by the whole business. But anyway, it's somewhat mesmerizing to behold. Mary Pickford does have quite the head of ringlets.*

Why do you suppose they call it a riding hood?

Again, she had to think. *It must have been a horse-riding habit at one time?*

Were there places where girls rode horses? I'd seen men on saddle mounts of course, and farm boys a time or two up on the bare backs of plow horses on a whim, or playing at cowboys or knights, but no girl in her petticoats and skirts would ever dare to be caught astraddle such a creature. The newfangled bicycles could be deadly enough to a young lady's honor, as I myself had already had the misfortune to discover.

Victoria's knowledge extended even here.

There is a thing called a sidesaddle, you know. For aristocratic ladies to protect their virtue, as they ride about their estates. It's regarded as quite sophisticated.

A sidesaddle?

Yes. Mostly in England, I believe . . .

I could hardly imagine it, particularly in the pall of catastrophe that had hung over me those past few years.

Was I nine, or ten? No matter, except that it was ahead of Victoria's turn toward doubt. A boy from town, the mercantile keeper's son, with a raffish new bicycle, red and gleaming like nothing I'd ever seen. We were in the village with springtime all around, had ridden in with Papa and Mama in the wagon.

Victoria and I had dollies and teacup settings at home, but nothing more strenuous for play than hoops and sticks, and I was stunned and a little smitten at the speed of this bicycle, its proud owner zipping back and forth on the graded street out front of the mercantile.

His name was Otto, and Victoria and I made a rapt audience from the boardwalk while Mama did her procuring inside. Neither of us girls had seen a bicycle before, outside of sketches and advertisements in the broadsheets that Papa sometimes brought home. We had gathered even from that limited exposure that in far-off places such as Boston and Philadelphia, ladies and girls had also taken up the invigorating fad.

Otto's legs pumped like the treadle on Mama's sewing machine. He was in my grade at school and pretty boisterous, always climbing a tree or building a slingshot. Once he leaned across his desk and dropped a frog down Flossie Donnelly's collar and got himself properly thrashed, although he seemed to take it as a matter of course if not actual pride. He made me nervous and I usually tried to avoid him, but now I found that I simply could not peel my eyes away.

And somewhere in there, I guess I just wanted him to like me. So when he skidded to a stop at the edge of the sidewalk, I was already aware of not wanting, for just this one time, to slump in my sister's shadow.

Guess you can tell I had me a birthday.

Of course she beat me to the quick. *Looks like a happy one, too.*

Ain't she grand?

Oh, dashing. Faster than a racehorse, I'm sure.

I knew full well Victoria had never seen a racehorse, but why couldn't I come up with something to say? True or not?

She's an Iver Johnson. Same outfit makes the pistols?

For once even Victoria seemed stymied.

Anybody like a ride?

I certainly would, very much. The words just popped out, with no thought behind them.

Well, hop on down. Let's take a whirl.

And how on God's green earth do you intend to do that?

I couldn't tell whether my sister directed this at me, or at Otto. I didn't even know whether Otto had it in mind for us to somehow ride together or for me to try it alone, which struck me right in the moment as an even more preposterous notion. Either way, I had to admit, Victoria had a point.

Otto however was unperturbed, and how on God's green earth *that* could be was a whole separate mystery. He plunked a fist on the swale between his hand grips. *Easy as pie. You can set right here, even in your skirts. I gave Flossie and Myra a ride apiece yesterday. Works like a charm. So who's first?*

Part of me knew I should immediately go and ask Mama. But all of me knew, already, exactly what the answer would be.

Come on, Vicky. Never knew you to be the shy one.

I remembered Flossie squealing when the frog went down her back, and I remembered a flare of jealousy, too. Not that I wanted a frog down my own dress, but I was nevertheless not a bit surprised to hear that the victim of such had already allowed the offending prankster to pedal her about on his rakish cycle. There in my own moment, I certainly would not abide granting bold Victoria the first go-round.

Quick as a wink I hopped to the street. *I'm not shy, either. How do I do it?*

Well, there's the pioneer spirit. Otto straightened the gleaming device and steadied the handlebar. *Just step up on the tire and get yourself acquainted.*

Um, Gloria?

Already I was clambering, more unsteady than not, but Otto did a good job holding the tire. I managed to get my skirts underneath me and pivoted around to settle onto the swale.

Gloria.

Victoria's eyes were the size of walnuts. She shook her head at me. *Where do I hold?*

He showed me, right to the inside of his own hand grips, alongside each of my hips.

You have to keep your legs out straight, away from the wheel.

Gloria . . .

This time I didn't even look at her. *Go fast.*

The ride was a little wobbly at first, and I a little precarious in my perch, but in not much more than a moment Otto huffed and pumped his way to a rather thrilling speed and this seemed to smooth things right out. I found I could just sit and hold myself steady and sort of glide, all the way up to the end of the street.

Gonna turn now . . . keep yer balance . . .

I remember having my skirts tucked up between my knees to keep them from the spinning tire, remember this pure new fun of motion and balance and I guess daring risk with old devil-may-care Otto, taking me along with him and steering and tilting into a thrilling sweep of a turn that traveled through me like a sweet cold chill, a shiver to the tips of my outstretched toes and the roots of my hair, and I was simply overjoyed at how easy it was to keep perfectly poised even at a tilt on this thin little bar when you had your proper motion and already there we were, coming back straight again, just gliding forward in the other direction with the shop windows and the hitching rails and the rain barrels flying by, and I had just begun to think how I would be able to lift one hand and wave to Victoria—

Gloria Marie Comstock. YOUNG LADY . . .

Either Otto faltered at Mama's rile or I lost my confidence, or both. Whatever the case, my knees definitely lost hold of my skirts. The turn of the wheel snatched the hem and sucked me in a violent instant right off my perch and down hard, astraddle the tire.

A jolt of pain tore in my center and I remember shrieking, and I remember they had to shred my dress to get it out of the hub of the wheel. A man I didn't know carried me along the sidewalk. I remember Mama turning away white as a ghost and trying not to sob down in the doctor's office, my dress in tatters and blood indeed streaking my underthings.

But in almost no time it didn't hurt very badly anymore, certainly nothing like the excruciating throb of my headaches, and before long I found myself trying to comfort Mama from flat on my back on the doctor's table, telling her I was sorry I tore my dress, that it wasn't Otto's fault or Victoria's either, that I understood now it was dangerous but it was more of a shock than anything and really, it just didn't hurt very much anymore . . .

Victoria was right there with us, eyes still like globes.

The doctor took the briefest glimpse at my injury before testing uninvolved things like my ankles and wrists, then moving on to soothing Mama. He spoke in a low tone, although I could hear parts of it.

Not as uncommon as you think . . . a notion from the Dark Ages, really. It's just an adaptation—nature's way of keeping everything safe before the childbearing years . . . No moral weight to it at all . . .

A little later Mama collected herself and left me with Victoria. The doctor had some books for children that he took down for us, but in short order Mama returned with a new dress and underthings. I had a smudge here and there, dirt from the street and black from the tire, which she wiped clean with a washcloth.

She did not seem angry at me, even at the loss of my ruined dress. She was very gentle, but I knew anyway that something was not right. She could hardly look at me and Victoria may as well not have been there, although my sister did fix and adjust my hair.

Finally Mama summoned whatever she needed to summon to meet my eyes.

We've done what we can. It's in the Lord's hands now. Whatever you do, do not tell anyone where you were injured. But especially, do not tell your father. Her gaze shifted to my sister. *Victoria?*

Yes, Mama. I understand.

When Victoria was seventeen, she was still going to church with Mama and me, still badgering the minister and the Sunday-school teacher with questions and conundrums. She volunteered still at the orphanage and the old folks' home. But her evenings were her own.

We had heard the term *Pentecostal* and had a faint sense from rumor that the adherents believed in principle what we ourselves did, so far as sin and salvation went. But by the same rumor, they actually *felt* the approach of the Final Days, and felt as well the moving presence of the Spirit among and within them. Many people looked askance, called them Holy Rollers or Jumpers, and still others considered that their babbling exuberance had more to do with the devil than with blessed Jesus. But I'll admit, curiosity ran high.

So when an Apostolic revival came to the community hall, Victoria heeded the call. She returned with her answers, utterly baptized in the Spirit.

She shook me awake, and even in the dim glow of the lamp, I could see the transformation. Eyes like shining embers; hair, which had been bound in plaits, come loose and practically standing around her head, as though the power of the Spirit had run through her like voltage and blown her glowing curls into a halo. She'd sweated right through her dress.

You have to come tomorrow, Gloria. You have to feel it. It's the most real thing I've ever known. I mean, it's real, Gloria, it is REAL . . .

She told me she'd spoken in the language of the Holy Ghost, been anointed with that gift. She'd seen crutches cast aside, seen others healed, and she knew that I could be made whole too.

I knew by then she was not talking about the headaches or the twist to my spine, or at least not those alone. Not so long before, whole sermons were preached about the moral threat of bicycles upon the young, especially young ladies, the ones in the East who had shucked their proper skirts for split bloomers and mounted up and pedaled away, off to uncharted places.

I, of course, did not even have to do that. A single ill-informed passage, my very first naive attempt at a lark with a boy, and I broke my mama's heart.

Do you really believe so, Victoria? That I will be made whole again?
She was on her knees beside my little bed, eyes roving the shadows at the ceiling. That wild hair. *I felt things I've never even imagined. I believe that you will, too.*

We rode the three miles to the hall with some good, God-fearing neighbors, in their surrey. They hadn't attended the night before, but already they had heard, as half the county evidently had, of the transforming power of the thing. Mr. Perkins, the gentleman of the house, was a dairyman somewhat older than Papa, and suffering a rheumatism that made milking troublesome. He had walked for some time with a cane. Victoria told him she had already experienced a power greater than the afflictions of either the earth or the devil. She told him to make himself ready.

We were early to the service, but already the crowd was such that the meeting had been moved outside, with the hall's front porch serving as a stage. The piano had been rolled out, too, and I could hear it as we approached through waves of a general din and a chorus of both song and hallelujah-style shouting, heard it being played with a gusto I could associate only with the automatic player piano I once saw demonstrated at the county fair. This was no perforated roll of paper above the keys, though, but astonishingly enough a colored man, fingers flying and pounding as though he intended to reduce the device to splinters and sprung wire.

The hymn, if it may be called that, was nothing like "Rock of Ages" or "Amazing Grace," but a song with some other form altogether. A frantic man with a tambourine on the edge of the porch hollered, "My God is alive," to which the whole roaring crowd replied, "He has made me glad," over and over, emphasizing their enthusiasm with a loud, proud handclap at the end of each call-and-response. Then again not the whole crowd, because many of them were in a state outside the bounds of normal comportment, some in a kind of rapture or trance with their arms outstretched above their heads, others on their knees with their hair in their hands, and still others jerking and quaking as though stricken with the same palsied fit. The ones who could respond, though, were not only singing—many were also *dancing*.

I had heard of quadrilles, or the waltz. Those dances were most certainly not this. I recognized people I had known my entire life, stalwart farmers with their stalwart wives, staid townspeople who seemed born composed, bouncing and swaying and kicking up their heels in ways that reminded me of young colts, bucking and jumping in a spring pasture. What Papa called "feeling their oats."

Hands clapped and clapped and hands reached toward the sky, and suddenly I jolted back to myself with all of it gone, although I, too, had been shouting and clapping and swooning for some unknown time. When did the light fade? Just when I felt time had stopped, it had actually catapulted forward, full dark nearly upon us now, and a woman—*a woman*—preaching from the stage.

Could not be. But yes, she was right there, a Bible in one hand and the other splayed urgently against the air, speaking about the power of Jesus, the hunger and the thirst for righteousness that's come *so alive* in this present age, the way the Word declared that it would.

You will hear of wars and rumors of wars . . . and nation will rise against nation, and kingdom against kingdom. Look at Old Europe even now, brothers and sisters. Nation against nation, in those awful trenches and no-man's-land . . .

I had only a vague idea of the great conflict unfolding in Germany and France, from Papa's weekly newspaper and also from the cluster of boys around Victoria who seemed itching to get into the fight themselves.

Victoria beside me had tears streaming and her arms thrust in the air. I was crying, too, dizzy with the terror of it all.

I remembered the times the two of us peeked into the Book of Revelation, only to clamp our eyes shut again. Words to chill the very bone, passages about the whore of Babylon and the seven seals and the seven trumpets, and the number of the beast, which shall be six hundred and threescore and six—puzzling and horrible mysteries that nobody seemed to address, although they must be true. Surely they must be true, for they appeared *right there*, in the *very last book* of the eternal Word of God.

Do not despair, brothers and sisters. Do not worry long over this strife, but rejoice! Rejoice, for the end is nigh, and ye shall be with your Lord in Paradise—

Victoria took to crying out herself beside me, and a torrent of strange syllables gushed out, as though the cooing of doves and the gibberish of a baby and the yodeling of Papa at the cows and the war whoops of boys playing Indian had all run separately out of the wells of her limbs to converge in a righteous river from her babbling tongue, and she went to her knees with her hands clasped before her, going on and on and on—

Be diligent, brothers and sisters! Go forth and preach the Word, and be constant in your calling, for though no man knows the day or the hour, it is prophesied that YE SHALL KNOW THE SEASON, and that season is UPON US. Amen.

Sweat and tears ran out of me the way the crying and yelling ran through the dense mass all around, Victoria on her knees with her mouth still issuing its inscrutable torrent while other strange tongues came through the air in fits and waves, and my eyes darted and raced, and some of those lamplit faces were just plain people I'd known my whole life who were suddenly transformed, seized by an energy unlike anything I'd ever witnessed in Sunday school. And I wanted that energy to course through me the way it coursed through them, wanted to give myself over and *know* that the power of the Lord lived inside me, too.

Victoria was struck with a jolt and went to the ground on her back, as though she'd been swept by a palm and dropped flat. I felt that energy concentrate and pull me down like a reeled fish alongside, not to my back but to my knees, right there beside her.

She jerked and shuddered and writhed, her mouth still uttering with esoteric mania, and her eyes wide upon me now and with such absolute *joy* on her face that I began to sob and wail out myself. I seized her hand with both my own, and in that moment of contact the fire of the Spirit flashed through me, too. And I felt it, I did, the first overwhelming dawning of absolute righteousness.

The cries of the crowd subsided. The lady preacher appeared, hair blown around her head, the way Victoria's had been the night before and was again now. The preacher knelt down across from me and took my quaking sister's free hand in one of hers, laid her other palm across Victoria's forehead.

Slain in the Spirit, praise Jesus . . . Feel the power of Almighty God, feel the power within you over the enemy of the Lord's people. Slain in the Spirit, praise God . . .

Victoria's wide eyes rolled frantically toward me and caught my own, and I quivered, still feeling that mighty surge flow out of her and into me, but then she looked to the lady preacher and another babble came forth. Victoria squeezed my hand tightly, and I gripped back just as hard, and her eyes came to me again while she warbled and cried, then back to the lady preacher, whose own mouth moved in an utterance as well, a whispered one with an entirely different tenor than either Victoria's secret dialect or her own thunderous preaching from the stage.

You have travails, child. You have come tonight seeking deliverance.

She was talking to me. Victoria's stream had fallen to a ragged burble, and she merely lay there, whispering around great gasping breaths, her quaking otherwise stilled. I looked across her, at the lady preacher.

You have come to be made whole, in body and in spirit. This is manifest through your sister's gift, and in your own hunger and thirst for righteousness.

I nodded and cried, and she lifted her hand from Victoria's forehead to reach across for one of mine.

We all have come short, child, but I sense the power of the Holy Spirit within you, imploring you to cry out for Jesus, to receive Him fully, and to let the same Spirit that raised Him from the grave quicken your own mortal body, child. Let thee be healed . . .

Hands from all around settled now on my shoulders and my back and my head, and a mighty shaking came over me, not just in my body but within me as well, and a din of praying and tongues of the Spirit climbed into the night. I felt the energy of those sanctified believers, as though a fountain of pure water rose through my body and out to the tips of my fingers and toes and right into my dizzy head, rising and rising in a stirring pressure, until a gush of ecstatic speech shot from my mouth like a geyser.

I came back to myself flat on the ground, with no memory of how I'd gotten there. But Mr. Perkins cast his cane aside and walked unassisted that night, and I returned home in the surrey in the wee hours in an afterglow of pure bliss. The stars in the heavens seemed placed just for me. Victoria held my hand.

Mother awaited when we returned to the farm, there in the little parlor room in her nightgown. She looked back and forth between us, at our flowing hair and our mussed dresses.

I must confess. You do look like the Lord's own angels.

We have been filled with the Holy Ghost. Baptized, from the inside out. Both of us have spoken the evidence of it.

Now Mama took my shoulders in her hands, glanced in a flicker to Victoria, then back to me. *You look . . . taller, or something.*

I felt the power of Jesus, Mama. Really and truly, for the very first time. It is like I have been restored. Healed. If I am taller, maybe it is because my spine is straighter. The healer was a lady. She told me I will see signs and wonders, if only I am willing to look.

Mama still had her hands on my shoulders, and she glanced at Victoria again and pulled me to her, rubbed my back the way she had during so many of those agonized bouts.

I certainly hope you do, my dear.

I knew full well my back was no different than before, but on the way home in the surrey in the wake of all that terror and exuberance and unleashed power, while I watched the dreamy spray overhead and listened to the clop of the hooves on the road and felt dumb-struck or thunderstruck or just completely wrung inside out, even then I was aware of something happening, some stirring or transfor-mation, down there low in my belly, and yes, in the place where the bicycle took a part of me.

I'd been holding my water for hours now, and maybe it was only that, but a little later, out in the privy in the light of the lantern, I saw again the streaks of blood in my bloomers.

Mama and Victoria were still in the parlor when I came in, Mama in her rocker and Victoria kneeling on the floor with her wild head in Mama's lap. She raised up and they looked at me as though I really was a-glow.

I believe I have received my moon.

Meteors

1

"I can't believe she's still out there," said Huck. "What's it, four days already? It's like they've started some girls' club or something. You ought to see it."

They were back to work on the waste-oil still, installing fittings to connect the boiler to the condenser. Pop had run down to the mercantile to fill a grocery list for Mother and Annelise.

"Can't say I'm surprised," McKee told him. "Your ma's pretty starved for company in general, any fool could see that. And Annelise might have her legs back under her, but she's still worn to the nub. Probably just needs to sort things out."

"Couldn't have predicted she'd hole up at the ranch, though. With all the unfinished business, I mean."

"Yeah, well. Part of that may be worry over your mother. Leaving her out there alone. Not to mention in the dark." McKee shook his head. "My fault, comes down to it. I should've left that watch right there in the road. Mea culpa, and all that."

Huck had been trying to think his way through that one himself, had lain there at night considering from every angle how to get out of the maze. "They still wouldn't have the ledger, though. Or the keys that were with it."

"Nope."

"They'll be back, won't they?"

McKee looked at him. "I'm surprised they haven't showed already. Pains me to say."

He'd been somewhat less than his usual whimsical self the last few days, which Huck mainly put on the absence of his cousin. Of course there was more to it. "What do you think they're liable to do?"

"No idea. But for all they know, we've already called in the law, which is why they haven't shown."

"Shoot. Maybe we should, you know? Just go on and spill it already. We already sent the forms to register the plane, so I don't think there's much Cy can do on that score."

"Okay, but there's another side to it. I ain't a kid, far as the law goes. We tell the whole naked truth, they might clap my own sorry hide in jail. Which I'd just as soon avoid."

Huck started. "You? What on earth for?"

"That cockamamie ambush, for one thing. Your cousin's right, it ain't the Wild West anymore. Assault with a deadly weapon, endangering minors, failure to report a crime. That's off the top of my head."

Jail, when all he'd been worried about was having his toys taken away. He looked at Yak, and for the first time understood what his cousin meant that day, about how brilliance and basic sense were two different things. "I wish Annelise were here. She's good at this stuff."

"She can think ten steps ahead, no doubt. Impulsive as even she can be."

What would Annelise do? It was a natural question, in the absence of the actual brain to pick. Funny, when you considered that the oracle in consideration had lately taken refuge with exactly the person they'd all sworn to keep in the dark. "You know what I think she'd say?"

"Call the police and take our chances?"

"Nuh-uh. I think she'd say they're likely to do exactly what they did before. Try to feel us out without putting their necks on the block."

"Call, you mean. I will admit, every time that phone rings, I about have a heart attack."

Huck nodded. "And every time, turns out it's somebody needs a pump fixed or something. Shoot, who knows, maybe we're luckier than we think. Maybe they did just cut and run already."

"I hope you're right. But that was a hell of a stash of illegal gold down there with the stiffs." McKee started for the workbench after some tool or other, but he stopped himself midstride. "If they do call here looking for you or for Annelise, and if I'm around, do us all a favor. Put me on with them."

Later Huck would come to think of it as beyond coincidence and more along the lines of the prophetic. The phone did ring, not one full day later. He had that clench in his gut even before he recognized the voice on the other end.

"Houston Finn?"

"You got him."

"Is Mr. McKee available?"

Huck eased out to the shop. Yak looked at him like he already knew. He hooked a thumb at the office anyway. "Charles Angle. For you."

He listened from the doorway to McKee's side of it.

"Yeah . . . Damn straight, and you're lucky I tend to hit what I aim at . . . Well, you're welcome, but don't bet on my generosity twice . . . Yep . . . Yep . . . All right . . ."

McKee turned and sat against the edge of the desk, and his eyes flicked once to Huck in the doorway but otherwise seemed to rove around at nothing in particular while he listened to whatever case or threat or plea came at him through the line.

Finally he said, "Might be a little more complicated, but I follow you. And yeah, I want a written guarantee you chumps are down the road for good . . . I'll need some time, say a day or two . . . That'll work. One more thing—from now on, it's just me, or no dice. Leave women and kids out of it . . . I'm holding you to it. I'll be waiting."

He pivoted and set the receiver in the cradle. He turned back to Huck. "You have the watch on you?"

"It's in the house. Remember, I quit carrying it?"

"How about the satchel, ledger, map—where's that-all?"

Huck shrugged. "Probably Annie's room."

"Run in and take a look. Bring it out if you see it. And bring the watch."

Huck's legs felt cemented in place and he realized he was scared to move, not merely out of the doorway but out of the moment, regardless of what McKee had just contrived on the telephone. He'd rather never have heard from them at all, even if it meant looking over his shoulder for a lifetime. "What's going on?"

McKee shook his head. "I've got a day or two to think my way through this. Trust me, the less you know, the better."

2

Houston uncharacteristically chose of his own election to stay at the ranch one night, for no real reason, which surprised her. Usually he'd sleep over only if he and Roy had some necessary task at hand.

Once the daylight waned he insisted they walk up to the wheat table, to scan for meteors. He did carry a blanket to sit on, but they hadn't gotten past the barn before he came clean. "They're back. Charles Angle, Detective Blank. Whoever they really are."

"Well, of course. Just when I was allowing myself to be cautiously optimistic about one tiny thing. Did they call again?"

"Yesterday. Figured I'd better get you on the page."

She stopped in her gait and squared off to him. "Are we really going to the field? Are there really meteors, or was that just to get me out of earshot?"

"Actually there might be meteors. The Perseid showers should be starting up pretty quick. Moon's a little bright, though."

They kept trudging. "What's the upshot?"

"I only answered the phone. They wanted to talk to Yak."

"*Oh.* And what was that about?"

"I ain't really sure. I could only hear his side of it, and he wouldn't let me in on the rest. Told me I was better off not knowing."

She felt a bit of her old flare coming back, her stinger rising. "Well. You remember what happened last time he made his own plan."

"Yeah, I do. I remember it got the ship in the air."

"That is true. Opened Pandora's box, too."

They were on the grade already, angling toward the table. The moon was half full or better but at their backs, just up over the black silhouette of a rim. Whether they saw a comet or not, the spray of stars glittering in the velvet was a sight in its own right. A coyote yipped, not so far off.

"I'm pretty sure he's playing them while he figures out how to turn it all over to the police. I gave him the watch, and he's got the ledger, the map, all of it. I think he's trying to keep us out of the hot seat."

"That does sound like him. Noble, but impossible."

He chewed on that a moment. "He's trying to figure out how to spill it without getting locked up himself."

Bam, there it was, like a comet through the ink of her own distracted brain. She'd spent months agonizing over the jeopardy she'd engineered for Blix, yet somehow never really considered the implications of what McKee had engineered for himself.

"I should get back to town. I feel like a high-grade bitch at the moment."

"Shoot, I don't think Yak thinks that at all."

"That's not the point, Houston. I missed the ball on this one."

They reached the top and walked along the field and finally spread the blanket and sat with the moon at their backs. Even the amaranth that had taken over the field had not done much, bone-dry as the summer had been. Still, she could hear the breeze in the stunted stalks and fronds, coming through the dark like a whisper.

"I'm not trying to get you to come back, if you don't want. And Yak didn't put me up to it, either."

She reached over and thumped his knee. "That actually never occurred to me. Guess I really have been down the rabbit hole."

"Never expected the rabbit hole to be out here, I can tell you that much." She heard him hesitate and had some idea of what he'd say next, even as he tried out the words. "Is it going okay? With my ma?"

What to tell him, exactly? By now she and her aunt were in the midst of a days-long conversation, or monologue even, as though a stopper had finally exploded out of a fermenting bottle. "This might sound crazy, but there's more to her than you realize."

She knew about Gloria's silent envy of her headstrong sister, knew as well of the commensurate shame that skulked right along with it. She knew her aunt had feared herself a pariah long after the incident with the bicycle, terrified late into her teens that she'd end her days an old maid, unwanted and unloved.

Then the miscarriages, more than one, once she did meet Roy and marry, and no matter how hard Gloria tried and no matter how hard she prayed, she couldn't shake the gnawing fear that her child-hood curse brought those losses to bear as well.

Much as Annelise had come to wish for her cousin and her aunt to find some sort of honest peace, for both their sakes, she herself could see the possibility only because she'd been placed in the trust of each. For all the open confession with her aunt, Annelise never had let on about the airplane, and it was not for her to betray Glo-ria's confidence now. The same way she had shrewdly kept Roy in the dark on all manner of things, while dutifully keeping Roy's con-fidence on others—that dubious wait for the Rapture, for example, had never come up with either her aunt or her cousin. Tangled webs and divided loyalties, and for what? Surely not to abet these pointless family rifts.

They sat in silence and finally a fast streak bloomed and almost instantly split, a brief bright V that winked out again in an instant. She heard the catch of her own breath.

"That was a good one," he said. They watched a while longer. Again he broke the silence. "So what all have you been doing out here? Do you just argue, or what?"

She grinned at the stars. "It's actually been very peaceful. She's talkative, when she has an ear, and I don't mean lectures. And we listen to the radio."

She could practically hear him gnawing on that one. "Sister?"

"In the mornings, when she's on. But I play whatever I want when her programs are over. And she's pretty partial to symphonies. Knows a lot about them, actually."

He had no idea. "How did that happen?"

"Listening to the radio, most likely. She has a lot of time to herself, Houston."

"Symphonies," he said.

"Indeed."

"And she lets you play whatever? Dance music? Without harping?"

She'd been a little surprised herself, at first. Now, nearly a week in, she wasn't surprised at all. "She's very much like my mother—stuck in the routine of seeing a child where one no longer exists. Still wearing the same mask she did to talk to a five-year-old, in order to train us up in the way she thinks we're supposed to go. I don't think she's even conscious of it. I think it's part instinct, and part habit."

Just this morning Annelise had watched a sleek little doe run a lone coyote off across one of the pastures, while the doe's spotted fawn flag-tailed it for the trees in the other direction. The doe charged after the yipping and yet steadily retreating canine, lifting and kicking and slashing down with her front hooves, like a cross between a parade majorette and a knife fighter. They went fifty yards at least in this fashion, with the coyote weaving and scrambling to avoid a trouncing, and finally turning tail for the horizon. The doe circled back for her fawn.

It dawned on her then how motherhood and terror were simply manacled together like convicts on a chain gang, with one unable to so much as lift a leg without feeling the nagging jolt of the other. In the case of a person like Gloria, the necessary instinct took on even greater implications, and *there* was the rub. It was one thing to make sure a toddler didn't chase a ball into a street, but quite another to suffer the endless, foreboding panic of eternal judgment. That burden ceased to be something like a prisoner's weight, and more along the lines of a cross to bear.

She could tell he was hesitating, but finally he said it. "Was it Miss Earhart that made her come around? See herself in you? I can barely remember it, but Sister disappeared that time . . ."

"That was probably part of it. Also part of why I let my own guard down and told her some things, really private things. I think she saw she could let hers down, too."

"Or take the mask off."

Touché. "Yes, exactly. She realized she could drop the mask, and talk to me like a grown-up."

"You told her about Yak?"

She actually laughed. "Um, no. I think that would've had the opposite effect. But what I did tell her, she could relate to."

She herself had experienced flashes of an almost grown-up uncertainty in the past couple of weeks, even about her own raw impulses. If she'd simply stayed with Houston at the carnival that night, she doubted she'd have ever been jumped on a darkened street.

Then of course McKee had gone on his ridiculous rampage with the Sharps. Would the one have ever happened without the other? Almost certainly not, and now it sounded like he was having his own second thoughts. Why all these dire consequences, for the mere sin of lunging at something, just for the fun of it?

It was like her cousin could read her mind. "I'm sorry they haven't found her yet, Annie. Miss Earhart."

"That's all of us, buddy. Including your mother."

"Do you think she's still out there?"

She took it face-on. "No. I don't. She probably should have quit the whole show when she wiped out in Hawaii back in the spring. Taken it as a sign."

"A sign? You mean from God?"

"I don't know, Houston. But she took a big risk, and here we are." She sucked in the cooling air. "Now they're even calling off the search."

"Yeah, I heard. On the radio."

The low hoot of an owl sounded, from which direction she couldn't quite tell.

"You know they're talking about banning exploratory flights after this? 'Stunt flying' is what they're calling it." She snickered. "Somehow I doubt this would be the terminology, if it were a man."

"Well, I doubt they'd have thrown half the U.S. Navy at the search, if it hadn't been a woman."

She wanted to hit him, more so because he was probably right. If Lindbergh had gone down and vanished a decade ago, it would've been entirely on Lindbergh. How things had changed, the further the envelope got pushed.

"I haven't told anybody this, but I think you ought to know. You remember how hot it was, the day of the parade?"

"I'll never forget." She shifted her eyes to his long dark mass beside her. "What happened?"

He stalled, but not for long. "I . . . made a big mistake. Got too big for my britches, basically, and took Katie up in the ship. And I couldn't get the dern thing to climb, Annie. Had to dive into the valley, below even field elevation. Couldn't make three hundred feet clear to the Bulls, motor running so hot I couldn't get any speed. Just *stuck*. It was like flying in a casket. Most scared I've ever been in my life."

"Gulp," she said. "What did you do?"

"Kept a line for the mountains, hoping I'd hit an updraft if I could hold out. Tried not to crap my pants for what seemed like thirty-three hours, but was really only ten minutes maybe. Luckily this big bank of clouds rolled in at the same time, and I got us under 'em. Like hitting an elevator—altitude came way up, temperature came down. Pulled it out, I guess."

"Babe, I hate to say it. Your airplane is brilliant, but let's face it—it doesn't work well enough. It's more dangerous than it should be."

"I know it," he said, so automatically it surprised her. Evidently his jaunt with Katie really did scare the lights out of him. "To be fair to Mr. Pietenpol, it probably works better where he lives than it does out here. And it works fine here, too, if the weather's right."

"What's Yak's line? If you don't like the weather in Montana, give it ten minutes?"

"Right. I already thought of that." He went quiet again, and she could tell he had something else in his head. "You ever heard of this guy William Faulkner? Writes stories about the South, I guess? According to Rolly, anyway."

Now this was not what she could have predicted, God love him. "Yes, I read a novel by him, and it was really . . . unusual, I guess."

"Like dern near impossible to follow, you mean?"

"Well, *difficult* would be another way to put it."

As I Lay Dying. Her ninth-grade English teacher had told her about it after learning she'd already encountered Hemingway and Fitzgerald. She'd been totally put off at first, mainly because she'd loathed every trashy, malformed, bucktoothed and gap-toothed and no-toothed character in the book, and could not for the life of her imagine why such an unrepentant collection of knuckle-draggers merited such excruciatingly lofty language.

Now, in this exact moment, she had the sense she may have been wrong. "What does William Faulkner have to do with your airplane?"

"Thing is—this book? Raleigh gave it to me, because it's supposedly about barnstormers. It's called *Pylon*."

The night air had cooled considerably, and she grabbed the edge of the blanket and pulled as much around her as she could. "I don't know that one."

"It's just the way you said—sort of difficult. I got about thirty pages in and had no idea what was what, who was who, who was supposed to be talking, nothing. So I pretty much gave up.

"None of that's the point, though. I've been stewing over that Ford motor myself, and I think this book may have accidentally solved it for me. There's a part in the beginning where they're tearing an airplane down in a hangar, and he says something about a super-charger on the top end. You know what that is?"

She'd heard the term before, no doubt in one of those shop-talk conversations involving a lot of random numbers and codelike ter-minology. What had Houston just said about Faulkner? No idea what was what, and who was who . . .

"Not the faintest," she said, "other than I gather it makes an engine more powerful."

"You know what a Duesenberg is, though, or an Auburn Speedster?"

"Big, glamorous cars."

"For the last few years they've been supercharging Dueseys and Auburns, and Cords, too. The basic engine ain't any different, just outfitted with an impeller to increase the air and fuel going in. Bumps the power by a third or better. I've been studying up, and I'm pretty sure I can build a supercharger for the Ford."

If six months ago she had heard something along these lines from *any* not-quite-fifteen-year-old boy, she would've automatically rolled her eyes. "How complicated is it?"

"It's really not. You remember that busted Hoover vacuum in the back of the shop? I'm pretty sure I can convert the housing and impeller from that. Then I'll have to work up some brackets and whatnot. Nothing but a thing."

She smiled to herself in the dark. "Well, you've sure got to do something. I'm glad we at least agree on that."

The meteors had really started to fly, three or four of them in the last minute alone. She heard the owl again, from back toward the house and barn. He said, "Seems to me like I've got to do something just to get you back in the cockpit."

She ribbed him again. "Always thinking of me."

"It's true, though."

"I know it. Don't worry—I'm still me. Somewhere in here. I'll get back up again."

"I'll make you a deal. I'll build the charger, quick as I can, and put her to the test. If it solves the power issue, you've got to try her out for your own self."

"Okay," she told him. "That's an okay deal."

"Pinkie swear?"

She laughed but felt him shift, saw the dark lift of his hand in the air above her. She reached up and their fingers fumbled around a bit together before she found his own frailest digit. They hooked and held, and to her surprise, a pang came to her eyes. She blinked in the dark, felt him relax. She didn't want to let him go.

"I'm worried about Yak," she said. "I didn't mean to leave him holding the bag while I ran off and hid like an ostrich."

"He doesn't think that, but he ain't himself, either. I know he's scraping his brain trying to figure what you would do if you were there."

"Oh, Lord, no. I don't have the foggiest. What do you think drove me out here to begin with?"

"People tend to figure you have the answers, though. It's easy to think of you that way."

"You aren't the first to tell me that," she admitted. "It's an act, honey. More or less." The way a person appeared, against the way she actually felt. Calm and confident to the world, panicking on a high-wire in her head.

He got that low, soft tone to his voice, and it went right through her the way it always did. "Like you said about my ma earlier. Wearing a mask."

She thought again of McKee, how heavy a cross he lugged beneath that jocular, flippant exterior. If she hadn't stroked and seduced and whispered her way in, if she hadn't jimmied the doorway to his fractured past, even she wouldn't have a clue.

She considered herself in light of McKee. She had a reputation for a hard shell and a sharp stinger, it was true. But as Yak himself would no doubt attest, and maybe Houston, too, she also had a hell of a lot of love.

She reached over and took his whole hand this time. "We all put on masks, I guess. And sometimes they fall off. There's a lot of that going around, these days."

They went quiet in the glittering chill, holding hands and hoping for a meteor. None other appeared. "Think you'll head back?"

She didn't have a clear answer. Flashes of uncertainty or not, she hadn't been to McKee's place in weeks, and she was as conscious of it in the moment as though the low drone of a fan had suddenly vanished. Awareness by absence. She had an ache for the flow of Highlander at her lips, across her hungry tongue.

Other things, too, of course. She knew her mind had ricocheted into the dire ether, and now the warmth of her cousin's hand felt like a reach back for earth. A couple of her fingers had threaded through his, almost of their own volition.

She said, "I know I need to. I'm . . . worried about your mother, though. Sort of pulled in two directions. Give me another day or two to work this out. Get my mask tied on again."

"I'm glad you live here, Annie," he told her, a little later. "I know it ain't a big fast place like Los Angeles, but still. I'm not going to like it when you leave."

"Hush," she whispered. "Just hold my hand for one more meteor. I'm almost too cold to stay out here now."

They lay there until their meteor appeared and kept where they were a while longer. With the moon like a dim bulb over the black rim of the plains and not a single electric light anywhere, the wide band of the Milky Way tapered like some great cosmic roadway, traveling who knew where.

The world was cold around her here, but unimaginably so out there. As she stared into all that vastness, with its twinkling pinpricks and wide, solid band, she felt the actual physical terror of spiraling out of control the way she had in her dream, only upward, into that great unknown, a free fall into some mystery eternity, and the thing holding her down now wasn't gravity but the tight comfort of his grip. Maybe, she thought, it really was better never to leave what you already knew to begin with. Easier, anyway.

"What do you think's out there? Past all those crazy lights?"

"More of the same," he said. "For a long, long way. Beyond that? Who knows?"

Venturi

*Now I'm a practical man. I don't know mathematics much——enough
to figure out the major loadings, wing areas, and so on, but as far as
saying "hocus pocus" to a Reynolds number and having a wing coef-
ficient pop out at me, I'll have to excuse myself.*
———B. H. Pietenpol, 1932 *Flying and Glider Manual*

They were in the fabrication bay, the discarded Hoover vacuum torn
down and a two-year-old edition of *Automobile Trade Journal* splayed
open to a long article on the supercharged Auburn Speedster.

"A hundred and sixty horses," said Huck. "Stock. One hundo an
hour, right from the factory. Guaranteed."

"It's an amazing age, Colonel. I mean, think of it." McKee made
a wide sweep at what was strewn across the bench. "You're about to
possess the world's first flying vacuum cleaner."

"You think this'll work, though?"

"I don't see why not." He tapped the open journal. One full page
bore the heading EXPLAINING THE AUBURN SUPER-CHARGER. A help-
ful diagram illustrated the car's whiz-bang induction system. "Just a
lucky thing they were so generous with the company secrets."

If the goons had phoned again, Huck wasn't aware of it. McKee
remained tight-lipped, other than to say he'd done what he could
and for Huck to keep his fingers crossed they'd seen the last of
them. He did seem more of his old self again, or at least what
Annelise might describe as cautiously optimistic, if she'd ever com-
mit to coming back home. Two more nights had passed and she was
still out there, which was maybe another reason McKee seemed
open to distraction.

They went up Coal Camp Road, pulled the front cowling from around the motor. With a couple of worked-up brackets, the blower housing could install beneath the engine and still fit inside the existing compartment.

"What do you figure you'll need for impeller speed?"

He had to admit he hadn't gotten that far.

McKee was on his haunches with a zigzag rule, measuring from the water pump pulley. "Okay, but it's critical. Not only to get the thing up to pressure, but we also need to know how to size the pulleys. You usually cruise this thing at what, sixteen hundred?"

Huck was already thinking. "Yeah, that's what Mr. Pietenpol arrived at. Shoot. I don't even know how fast the impeller turns when it's just running a vacuum cleaner. Maybe it ain't even strong enough to adapt."

When he'd encountered that offhand line about a supercharger in William Faulkner's whacky barnstorming book, a dim bulb in his brain pulsed instantly brighter. He already knew about the Venturi effect, had witnessed the phenomenon firsthand. He'd followed deer tracks up the funnel of a steep draw one day last hunting season and was amazed at the way the lowland breeze siphoned into an all-out scream when he reached the top. Wasn't something along that line what they were trying to mimic now?

Maybe progress simply boiled down to harnessing what God or nature or both had put into play, as the permanent dictates of the way the world worked. The keystone in the radius of a Roman bridge, say—wasn't that gravity, manipulated to defeat gravity? Watermills, windmills. Seizing the power of running water or the force of funneling air. But dreaming up the idea was the easy part.

He hated to say it, but he knew it was the truth. "Guess I should've figured there'd be some trial and error here."

"Patience is a blah blah blah, and if at first you don't succeed, blah blah again." McKee clamped one eye shut and looked at him with the other. "Get used to it, Huckleberry."

McKee had a friend in Butte with an actual college engineering degree. An hour on the telephone that evening got him some of what they needed, including the number for an honest-to-God professor of mechanical science at the state school in Bozeman. He put a call through first thing in the morning, left the shop number with a secretary and got a ring back that afternoon while Huck was out on a service call with Pop.

McKee thrust a page of tidy but clearly furious notes at him when they came in, all numbers and figures and formulas.

"Voilà." He had his welding goggles shoved up on his forehead. "The good professor came through. He's put a couple of manuals in the mail, but I think we can pretty well figure it from what I've got here."

Huck tried to make sense of McKee's notes. "Whoa. Where's my Tom Swift secret decoder. Can you actually understand that?"

Pop fished out his eyeglasses and took a look. "Nope. I did graduate from the third grade, though."

"I have a general idea, but it hardly matters. The good doc basically worked up the specs while I had him on the phone." He went sidelong to Huck. "I think he's hoping to recruit you to the college engineering department. He was pretty impressed that a high school freshman could build an airplane in the first place, let alone think to hop it up with a vacuum cleaner."

Huck felt himself redden. "He really say that?"

"More or less. He also said your idea stands a pretty good chance of doing what you want it to. But you've got to get the impeller turning at about thirteen grand."

Huck felt his eyes widen.

"Yes, you heard that correctly. So we will be mounting it on ball bearings. In the meantime, what do you know about sand casting?"

Huck shrugged. "I've read some articles, know what it is."

"I've done it. Been a few years," said Pop. He took his specs back off, fished his white hanky from his shirt pocket and wiped a lens. "There's a pretty good clay bank out at the ranch."

* * *

They band-sawed the patterns out of plyboard and built up a series of wooden flask boxes to hold the molds. Huck was amazed yet again at how quickly and cleanly McKee could work, which he guessed was the reason Pop had hired him in the first place. The three of them worked through the long northern light of evening. By full dark they had the wooden models for three pulleys cut out and glued up and ready for sand.

In the morning Pop rousted him early. Huck had reclaimed the bedroom only a couple of nights earlier, with Annelise lingering on at the ranch. He found himself sleeping so deeply in an actual bed, he could hardly get his eyes open at full daylight.

"Hey there, fifteen," said Pop. "Always thought that was a good number. Has a ring to it."

Huck mumbled through the fog. "Guess it does. I was wondering if anybody'd remember."

Pop handed him a cup of coffee. "You think I'd forget? Or Mama, either? We need to get out to the place, she's got breakfast planned for you."

Later with the hash and eggs cleared they drove down and shoveled a load of bentonite from a deposit by the county road, not far from the ambush site a mere six weeks back. Time flew and crawled at the same time. Same old water under the same old bridge. He'd tried to cajole Annelise into coming along, but once again she'd pleaded out, although this time for a reason he could hardly contest. It seemed she and Mother had a birthday cake planned as well.

Pop had sold a good bit of the clay off as tank lining the past few years and they cut deeper now with their shovels, into the straight, clean scars from the last front-end loader to come through.

"That Yak is sure a dern wiz, ain't he?"

"Oh, he's all that." Pop leaned his shovel, pushed his hat back on his head. "He ain't the only one, though. Know why I hired him?"

"Why's that?"

"So you could learn from him."

Huck's foot slipped right off the spade, and the shovel handle caught him in the chest. "Shit," he said. "*Shoot*, I mean." He felt the heat come out of his chest into his face, straightened the shovel and sunk it hard this time.

"You all right?"

"Yessir."

"You can say *shit*, kid. It's what guys say when they're working."

They both shoveled again, dumping the sunbaked bentonite into a galvanized washtub. "I have learned a lot from him."

"You and me both. Like I said, though." Pop leaned his shovel again, swiped at his forehead beneath the hat. "He ain't the only dern wiz."

Now Huck leaned his, too. "I guess you mean I'm no slouch myself?"

"True enough."

"Well. Shit, then."

Pop's gold tooth grinned. "Not every shaver gets it in his head to put his own airplane together. And actually pull it off, which you would have eventually, even without McKee. Look, you have a gift. I had it too, somewhat, but you're coming up in a whole different time."

"You really hired him just so I could learn?"

"More or less. I did need the help, but it was big in my mind to get the right guy for your purposes. 'Course at the time, I didn't quite figure your cousin into the mix."

They looked at each other and started laughing. "How long have you known about that?" Huck asked.

"Oh, probably about since it started up. Old Mr. Neuman ain't as deaf as he lets on." He shook his head. "That girl is a handful. God love her."

They finished shoveling, hoisted the tub into the back of the REO, and went around to the cab. Way up the draw they could see the edge of the wheat table, beyond the tapering shelf of the buffalo jump. Any day now Pop would take the tractor up and plow the pigweed under, ahead of the next planting. Then he'd cross his fingers and hope for the best.

"How much we owe on this place, exactly?"

"Oh, you know." Pop reached across and opened the glove box, fished out his Luckies. "More'n some, nowhere near as much as others. Couple good solid crops like the old days, we'll get ahead of it. Imagine we'll get some rain again, one of these years."

He hesitated, seemed to turn unusually serious. "Something else I been needing to talk to you about."

Huck had a flare of panic, and also guilt. If McKee really had turned everything over to the police, Cy had almost certainly gone straight to Pop, and Pop would no doubt be feeling pretty duped. Hell, even now, he had no idea why they were supercharging the motor, because Huck hadn't dared tell him about that incident with Katie, either. He braced himself to take his deserts.

"I want you to quit cutting school."

Huck blinked.

"I've been thinking about it, and it's the only thing makes a lick of sense. Your days as a truant are officially over, at least on my account."

"Oh. Shit."

"You're hearing me, though."

He could only nod.

"And you heard what Yak said, about that professor in Bozeman. You can have opportunities. But we've both got to start taking it seriously. You've got a gift, Houston."

He had to admit, he never much thought of his own life as especially spectacular. He knew he was maybe pushing ahead a bit, first with the glider and now with the airplane, but in all truth he barely ever stepped outside the nuts-and-bolts effort of whatever task he'd set himself to long enough to consider the way things might appear otherwise. The way he saw it, Pop's long ride from Texas clear to the Yellowstone to avoid an orphanage seemed a whole lot more eye-popping than merely following somebody else's manual to piece an airplane together.

"So no more hooky. Not even to help out at the shop?"

Pop ground on the REO's starter. The truck shuddered wearily back to life. "I wouldn't, if I was you. Fifteen, already. Turn over a new leaf."

Huck felt the tug of a grin. "Sort of like a New Year's resolution. Guess we ain't gonna hear any argument out of Cy, anyway."

Pop leaned out the window and backed the truck around, nosed it for the county road. "Hey, Houston? Don't say *shit* around your mother." He caught Huck's eye. "And I wouldn't let on about this professor, either."

Gloria

II

On the other hand, there are girls who have really cast off conventions—who feel no spiritual or moral connection with their sex conduct. How do they come out? Usually they are deserted.
—Margaret Culkin Banning,
"The Case for Chastity," 1937

That girl was a panther the way her own mother had once been, and Victoria was a fool to think Annelise could ever be totally controlled. But that was my sister, always having to be in command of something while never ceding to an inch of such herself. Two sides of a coin. I cannot lay blame exactly, for I always envied so much about Victoria. But envy—a different sort of coin, with its own opposing side.

I took one look at my niece that first night, and even bedraggled from days on the train and whatever flogging or browbeating Victoria had already inflicted, she had a composure I had to acknowledge. A cunning, really, like a creature too smart even to be seen, unless she'd chanced into a trap.

She was a woman already, and in every sense of the word. I could have guessed that, too, even if I hadn't already known why she'd been banished from the castle in the first place. I myself was barely any older when I married Gilroy, and many girls her age even now are betrothed and tending children, at least in backwater Montana. But Annelise had experience of a more worldly variety, the sort of thing that had taken hold in the big fast cities. Neither shame nor contrition seemed likely.

The times had indeed changed, faster than anyone could sort. I knew full well Victoria had let her don breeches and take up horseback riding, and that was years ago. To tell the secret truth, I envied Annelise a bit, too.

Once the traveling revivalists moved on to their next destination, a few of us who'd felt the strong fire of the Lord that week continued to meet, for the better part of two years. We subscribed to periodicals put out by missions in Chicago and Portland and modeled our gatherings on the Apostolic conviction that any member could be equally inspired by the power of the Spirit. Before long, even Mama could not ignore the call.

The three of us and a few other members traveled by rail to larger gatherings, too—once south to an enormous revival in Indianapolis and again the same summer to a meeting in Chicago. That's where Victoria met her match.

Robert Clutterbuck. An earnest young lawyer from Los Angeles, who himself had witnessed the famous Azusa Street Revival a few years previously. He was far more reserved than Victoria, as I suppose befitted his profession—his cup did not runneth over with the more obvious gifts but he did have a scholar's grasp of the Word, and the ability to share that knowledge with others in a way that seemed almost like an elixir. I think that quiet conviction, so contrasting to her own youthful fervor, may be exactly what drew Victoria to him. Two sides of a coin.

We traveled back home and Robert to his own out West when the revival adjourned, but their very spirits seemed to have meshed during those days of rejoicing. It seemed a letter came for her every day from California. And yet again, Victoria had my envy.

*   *   *

Twenty-odd years in the interim, and how can it be? At one moment it seems only a breath ago, and in another as though an entire biblical age has passed.

By then we had heard plenty of Sister's tours through the East and the South, of the power of her preaching and nearly unheard-of crowds she'd begun to draw. Her ability to inspire healing, though— crutches cast aside, blindness cured, hearing restored—the amazing frequency of such was even making the regular newspapers, as though to document for the wider world that there was more to this age than politics and fashion, or the pretty distractions of modern times. Eternity was upon us. Take heed.

The most recent reports had her burning up the Sawdust Trail in her Gospel Car across Georgia and Florida. Her power nevertheless reached us, in one of those mysterious ways the Lord uses from time to time, to startle even the faithful with His abiding presence.

Now ordinarily we might go weeks without any sort of mail, but ever since Chicago I'd come to expect the daily sputter of the rural delivery driver and his gasoline runabout coming up the drive. I couldn't imagine what my sister and her faraway beau could find that was new to say on a daily basis, and I guess maybe Robert ran out of ideas himself, for one particular day his missive arrived not in an envelope but inside a box.

Curiously enough, the only other item in the post came from Georgia—a copy of the very first edition of Sister Aimee McPherson's brand-new periodical.

Victoria was of course totally distracted, tearing into her package. I leafed through the magazine, tried to feign more interest in the pages than I had in Victoria's mail. I had never received so much as a card before, let alone a mysterious box. Then again, in the absence of anything from Robert, Victoria would have claimed first dibs on the magazine, undoubtedly. I looked at the cover, tried to tamp down that awful green feeling that seemed to rise up from the pit of my stomach, like a frog trying to eject through my throat. But I could not restrain my human tongue.

Oh look, Victoria. Sister Aimee has titled it Bridal Call.

Victoria in that moment defeated the binding on her package. *What did you just say?*

I said, Bridal Call.

When I looked up, Victoria held a diamond ring. Signs and wonders.

I'd begun to wonder if I really was damaged beyond hope. Did boys notice me at all? Had word gotten out? Victoria had been the one to tell me—maybe the secret was not for my ears alone? Whatever the case, I did not draw the suitors my sister always had, did not seem to catch the attention of a single one.

I knew I was sanctified in the eyes of the Lord, and in fact actually innocent of anything that should have truly damaged a girl's reputation. The troubles with my hips and back and of course those infernal headaches had returned—the other members of our little congregation laid hands on me and prayed over me once again, and we knew that not every healing could be considered permanent anyway. The Lord wanted us to supplicate to Him not one time, but always and forever.

I remained unsure of my maidenhood and certainly did not know how to check for myself. Neither Mother nor Victoria brought it up. I truly wished I could believe, but each new tightening in my spine, each painful throb in my temple, inched me further into doubt.

By the time of my birthday, I'd become quite concerned I might end up an old maid. That was not the cross I wished to bear.

Within six months Victoria was married to Robert and living out in that exotic place herself. I loved my sister, truly I did. And I missed her, too. But should all the signs and wonders have been hers? All the gifts?

I myself should not have cared to live in the city, anyway. Chicago had been alarming enough, with its teeming streets and taverns and dance halls unabashedly in view. Surely Los Angeles must be all of that and more, churning out its glamorous movies with which to deceive the world. Victoria's first letter home described the great crashing Pacific Ocean, however, and I must admit, I wish I had even once gotten a look at that.

But, oh, those mysterious ways. Sometimes He withholds what you anguish over in prayer in one season, only to grant what you need in His own perfect time.

Early the following summer, Mama and I took a train west, to meet up with the newlyweds and to have a time together. An adventure, really, at Yellowstone National Park, which I had read a little about but never imagined I might one day visit in person. Robert paid our fare and also secured lodging for us. We were to spend several weeks in the mountains of Montana, at a place called a dude ranch.

Never had I witnessed such spectacular scenery. I remember it as though it were yesterday—Mama and I practically pasted to the glass in the passenger car, two creatures who'd never known much beyond cornfields and flatlands suddenly faced with the grandeur of what people understandably call God's Country.

Three mornings into our stay, Victoria announced that she and Robert would be going on a trail ride, and would I care to join them. I looked at her, fairly certain I understood, but a little incredulous, too.

A trail ride?

Yes! Robert and I have gone a few times, out in California . . . It's more and more common. For ladies, I mean. I have my own riding habit, in fact.

You are talking about horses?

Of course! Trust me, Gloria. It's the spirit of the West.

Mama to my surprise did not seem particularly shocked. These days, she pointed out, hardly anyone even batted an eye at the lady cyclists.

And we are to ride like the English ladies? Sideways?

Not in this day and age. And you can thank those lady bicyclers, I guess. Nowadays we use split skirts and a regular saddle.

I looked at my plate, at the steam still rising off the eggs. Victoria read my mind.

Don't worry. They have them on loan here at the ranch. Along with proper riding boots. It is not at all uncommon, Gloria.

I looked again at Mama.

She and Victoria exchanged a glance, and I realized they had already conversed. She shrugged. *Goodness, even the Virgin Mary rode to Bethlehem on a donkey. What is the expression? "When in Rome"?*

Later it occurred to me that she and my sister were both relieved—the age had gotten beyond the trappings of propriety, in a way that might provide me with some second chance. He does work in mysterious ways.

When we showed up at the stables that day, Victoria in her jaunty riding attire from California and I in my awkward borrowed skirts, we learned that the usual trail guide had taken ill. We were not to worry as paying guests, however, for the ranch blacksmith had been called away from his bellows to assist.

And that is how I met my husband.

I understand why Gilroy finally did what he did, when he took Houston off the ranch and into town all those years later. The world marches along and, so long as He tarries, we must march in time with it. Much as I worry over some of the blasphemy taught in the schools these days, I could never deny that Houston has a clever enough mind to deserve an education, beyond what he could ever acquire on the ranch. I guess a part of me truly hoped Jesus would come first and save me the strife of having to give my own only begotten over to that fallen old world, out beyond the fence line . . .

But the truth of it is, the day they headed down that long lane without me, the truck diminishing into the distance until finally the land simply swallowed it altogether—that day remains the most forlorn of my life, the night that followed my longest and most despairing. It was as though the Rapture of the believers did in fact occur, only it was I who'd been left behind.

I suppose my sister saw the error of her own ways when she sent Annelise here to be with me.

Victoria did not of course say so directly, caught up as she was with the original indignity of the thing, but surely she had her reckoning. I know she thought of Montana in the long golden hue of memory, cast by that first trip she and Robert made all those years ago. I know she imagined Big Coulee to be more the sedate farming village of our own young lives than it actually is, with liquor sales restored and the obligatory den of ill repute out across the tracks. And I have always led her to believe things were less hardscrabble here than they truly are. My pride, again. My secret rivalry, against my own luck-charmed sister.

So I am not without faults. Not without cunning, not without lies. What is the expression, lies of omission?

When Victoria appealed to me to keep Annelise here, to get her away from the fast city and from whatever boy she'd dallied with, my sister was of the belief that I had already moved into town from the ranch as well. Because that is what I led her to believe. She believed that I would be right there on hand to manage the tiller of her wayward daughter. My wayward niece. And so that is what I let her believe.

She was a panther indeed, and what felled her spirit, I could not have predicted.

But I recognized the symptoms. I'd sunk to my own depths, in a not-unfamiliar circumstance. Sister Aimee had also vanished into an ocean. I prayed hard, and that prayer was answered when she walked like Lazarus out of the hot Mexican desert. And I pray for Miss Earhart, as a matter of course.

But the Lord giveth, and the Lord taketh away, and He will indeed use a tragedy for a greater good. If the U.S. Navy had found her safe and sound, washed up on an island or maybe floating about on the sea, Annelise would almost certainly never have returned to me. Which has become, I must admit, its own answered prayer.

And it's true that my spine's murderous tightening has begun to relax, my longest relief from those crippling headaches in many a year. For all my faults, all my omissions, I have nonetheless been an instrument of His will. Even my deceit has led to some roundabout version of truth, for here was my sister's wayward daughter after all, in my care, and perhaps even my friend.

Does He not work in mysterious ways?

Rapture

Pop had a couple of bags of sand left over from some concrete project or other, and Huck sifted out the bigger aggregate and got a supply of straight silica. They mixed it three to one with the bentonite, plus an almost imperceptible amount of water. Packed into the square halves of the flasks, the green sand had just enough stick to hold a perfect impression of the wooden patterns.

They formed sprues and risers out of chunks of three-quarter pipe and, with the patterns eased back out of the mold, carved a run into each blank cavity. Huck fired the forge out back and dumped an assortment of scrap aluminum pieces and a couple of virgin ingots into the crucible, and in the waves of swelter off the furnace, they watched a mound of cold solid metal melt into fuming silver soup.

"Don't breathe this crap," McKee told him, "it's pure poison," and he grabbed the crucible with a pair of tongs and moved to the first flask, tilting hot burping aluminum down through the sprue. The excess ran up out of the riser and pooled like giddy mercury. He moved to the next flask.

Ten minutes later they snapped the hasps and pulled the still-warm blanks for three pulleys out of cooked crumbling sand. They headed for the lathe.

By noon the next day they had three gleaming pulley-wheels milled out and turned down and ready to install. Two mornings after that, with the charger bolted on and the gas line rerouted through what had previously served as nothing more than a dust-sucking carpet cleaner, Huck flung the prop and fired the engine out on the runway.

They watched everything work for a while with the cowling removed. Watched and listened.

Huck let out a holler. "You hear it?"

The motor roared with a whole new hum, this hopped-up howl from gasoline and oxygen whipping rather than trickling into firing cylinders. They let her run up to temp and idle a bit, watching while everything appeared otherwise normal.

Finally Huck went to the cockpit and killed the switch. Blank summer silence, shocking as ever.

McKee leaned in. "You like it?"

Huck was already heading for the cowling. "You know, I think I may be in love."

Ten in the morning and already shimmering out toward the Bulls in the high summer air. Huck throttled up on the strip, and the ship lunged like a racehorse out of the gate, the sudden flex of the wings like a leap of streaming mane. He throttled higher and felt the rush at his face, felt the drag of the gravel drop away in forty feet of travel.

She climbed like gravity in reverse. A plummet for the sky. He let her rise a bit from velocity alone, and before he knew it, she was way out over the sage flat and already at five hundred feet, and he pulled back on the stick and pressed into the seatback. He watched the altimeter gain five hundred more in seconds.

He'd gained the Bulls already, too, or nearly so. The acceleration was beyond belief. He banked her in a wide sweep to the north, came around again, and straightened her out with the airfield back in view.

He was higher now than he ever had been on an actual approach, although farther out, too, and the long, straight hash of unpaved strip looked from this vantage like some eerie linear feature scribed upon the earth in the far-off past. Just dun-colored line against dun-colored terrain. He had a flash of the first time Pop showed him the figures in the face of the buffalo jump on the ranch, how even as a mumblety-peg tyke he'd done a double-take to see those scrapes in the stone become a picture in his mind.

Hard to believe any of it could possibly be real, when he thought about it. Not the symbols left behind by whoever had left them all those eons ago, and not this outrageous exercise in the here and now, all these eons later. He was already at an altitude to make McKee's Studebaker and the little tin shed appear no more discernible than the receding past itself, yet indisputably fragments of endeavors beyond the unassuming turn of the earth.

The white panel truck gleamed like a polished pearl. The shed even at this height formed a perfectly minuscule gunmetal square. He thought maybe—*maybe*—he could pick out Yak himself down there. *Maybe*. Leaning against the front fender of the Stude. Couldn't say for sure, though. He was at a distance in the air to reduce a man on the ground to little more than a speck in the dust.

He banked around again and watched the Bulls reel back into view. Even the mountains appeared to have shrunk during the brief time he'd had his back to them. From the corner of his eye he saw the clouds.

They were building a good way to the east, maybe as far off as Rosebud County, but stacking in billows with all the brilliant glare of an explosion inside heaven itself. He had a moment of doubt.

On the one hand, he wanted to test the ship on its own new merits, without the aid of anything other than straight mechanical advantage. On the other, flying, *true flying*, meant identifying whatever advantage presented itself and using it. He could test mechanical basis any old time, under whatever conditions prevailed. For now, he tilted the stick and flew toward the clouds.

He could perceive the lack of resistance to forward travel but didn't know for sure whether this was a matter of tailwind or the additional jump in the engine's performance. Some of both, probably. He pushed the throttle up yet again and watched his speed climb beyond seventy, then on past seventy-five.

She cruised at nearly eighty an hour with no real strain, his throttle knob still shy of the three-quarter mark and the engine's revs barely up beyond the operating specs for the original conversion. With the tach steady at 1,600 there still remained, in Mr. Pietenpol's words, plenty of soup in the old gal yet.

He edged the throttle up again and took his speed past ninety in a heartbeat, leaned back on the stick and let her climb. He was already at nearly seven thousand feet, singing along smooth as glass. The verdant corridor of the river bottom wound like loose green yarn. He could practically feel himself chortle, a-flood with the rush of success. He had thunder in his heart, lightning in the tips of his nimble fingers. He felt like some mythical hero, galloping across the ether on his silver winged steed.

He could see the rail bridge across the Musselshell up ahead at the county line, also the black belch of a chugging, toylike train. A bump jarred him back.

He'd hit the updraft, farther out from the cloud mass than he would have expected but undeniable in its giddy lift. He watched the needle climb in response, as though the clouds were drawing him into some magnetic field. He pushed the throttle forward and leaned the stick back and gave the eternal rhythms of nature all the help he could.

He shot simultaneously up and ahead, could feel the accelerating climb right in the seat of his pants. So far he'd deliberately avoided any sort of extreme pitch to an ascent, for fear of hitting the wing's stall-off point—that crucial angle in which the cant of the wing lost its airfoil and gravity again took over—and not knowing how to deal with it.

He didn't intend to find out firsthand, at least not on this jaunt. Just crossed his fingers he'd recognize the warning shimmy and bogging power in time to correct, and otherwise held as steep a rake as he dared. He throttled up as far as he could, felt his speed surge again in spite of the incline.

By the time he centered beneath the billows, he'd gained elevation so rapidly he could feel the air temperature coming down around him. His altimeter showed 9,200 feet, with the needle still rising. Back on the ground the thermometer on the airfield shed read just shy of eighty degrees, right before he'd taxied to the strip and lit off. The air was noticeably cooler at this altitude, as though it were still summertime down there but the first of October up here. Sixty degrees, maybe? And while Mr. Pietenpol may never have intended the ship as anything more than a low-and-slow hedgehopper, between the boost from the clouds and the mod to the engine, she showed no sign yet of hitting any kind of a plateau.

At 9,600 he bumped around a bit on the far edge of the cloud column, felt himself exit the hard pull of the updraft. His needle showed him still at a moderate climb, but nothing like the ascent he'd just experienced.

With the bulk of the column running now to the north, he dropped the nose a bit and put the ship into a left bank, came back around and bumped into the thermal again. He leveled out and nosed up and watched his gauges. The altimeter passed ten grand and kept right on going.

He followed the draft in a shallow bank, corkscrewing into thinner and thinner air, the temperature dropping and dropping, until the down on his forearms rose against his skin like hoarfrost.

He called it at twelve thousand feet. He felt like he'd flown past October and well into November. Thirty degrees, maybe? Twenty-five? No matter—his rate of climb was indeed finally tapering, and anyway, if he stayed with it much longer in this flapping summer shirt, he'd start to turn blue. He nosed down and leveled and flew out beyond the reach of the clouds.

The reefs and big buttes jutted no larger than anthills, fainter and fainter in the distance, and finally ghostlike at the lavender haze of the horizon. The one tiny hamlet he could see had barely the scale of a postage stamp. No people, no cars, not even a single identifiable structure, more just a mottled, telltale grid of green foliage and vague rectilinears, surrounded on all sides by that rolling brown ocean. Even Dunn Mountain off to port looked like some schoolkid's papier-mâché geography project.

He backed off the throttle, pointed the half globe of the compass in the gauge-cluster west and a little south. He dropped through the warming air.

Five thousand feet down, the air patterns were evidently all a-swirl. He felt the wall of a headwind push like a palm against his chest, while a couple of miles away the cloud column seemed to move in the same direction he was moving. He bucked around a bit in a patch of chop, feathered the stick in response and came out level with the wind again at his back, the ship leaping with the shift. He throttled back up.

He was still fairly far out from the airfield, intent on reaching the foothills of the Bulls and angling along the ridge back toward home. He bumped around through another rough patch, worked the stick somehow intuitively to ride it out, and a tremendous sidewise slap out of the west rocked the ship as though the fuselage might barrel-roll around an invisible spindle. His heart leapt straight for his throat even while the force of the thing subsided and his attitude stabilized again.

He wondered if such a gust qualified as wind shear. He'd read about the phenomenon mainly as a landing hazard, in which a blast of air colliding at a right angle with the prevailing wind created the atmospheric equivalent of a sucker punch.

He was still wondering when another one hit. He rode this out as well, leveled again a little off course for the mountains. He banked back toward them and ran the throttle fully forward. Evidently the wind was really howling now down at ground level, for the river bottom was not far off, and he could see the flash of leaves in the crowns even from here. That fluid green flicker.

The rough air at his own elevation continued in punctuated bursts, for some reason from the opposite direction than the course taken by the cloud column, and he had to correct and correct again to stay on course. Finally he wound up with the Bulls not far at all to the west, which would at least put him in the direction of the airfield. He went ahead and gambled and put the ship into a fairly hard bank. With the ground tilted toward him, the corner of his eye picked out a flash of motion down below.

He looked over the cowling and saw the square box of a structure, tucked up tight to a juniper-studded bench. A homesteader's twelve-by-twelve shanty, or maybe a cattle company's line cabin, with some commotion going on around back of the thing, what looked at a fast glance like a couple of guys wrestling a sail in the wind.

That didn't make any sense. He checked the position of the mountains again, held the bank and looked back to the ground. Of course it wasn't a sail but a canvas tarp, and evidently the wind was really screaming down along that bench because they were having a heck of a time managing the billowing thing, so much so that the one guy lost his grip on it altogether.

The ship was around a thousand feet AGL, too far by a long shot to recognize a person with any certainty. But once the loose-blowing canvas flapped up and ripped as well out of the other guy's hands, Huck saw plain as day what rested underneath: a gray Plymouth coupe, with a smudge of damage visible even at this height to the roof.

He pointed for the airfield and poured on the coals.

Release

1

She'd felt herself approaching dry land, even before that night of the meteors with Houston. By the time Roy roared up in the middle of the afternoon a few days later, the slightest of currents could have washed her into shore. Without even gathering her things, she roared right back down the lane with him.

"Complete stroke of luck on the kid's part," he told her. "Went out to test this gizmo he made for the airplane and wound up spotting that dern Plymouth coupe, way out by Rattlesnake Buttes."

"Appropriate."

He laughed. "Reckon he found himself the easiest possible way to keep old Cy off his case, too. When I left for the ranch, the two of them and about twenty reporters out of Billings were all heading up to the runway for a demo."

He let her off at the bungalow and went on to the airfield.

She took a hot bath, ran a razor over herself for the first time in a while. Lined and shadowed her eyes.

She wriggled into that same summer dress she'd worn to Billings that day, same black-and-white heels, an outfit she knew made him a little crazy. No lipstick to smear, though, and no way she could plead heat-of-the-moment or any other sort of momentary lapse. She held her chin high in the mirror, narrowed her painted eyes. Mea culpa, all the way.

They'd gone at each other like beautiful animals, no sooner, it seemed, than she'd crossed the threshold into his little room. Half danced and half crashed their way to the bed, clawing at clothes and biting and breathing. Then he was falling atop her and how quickly he'd plunged inside her and how quickly she seemed to launch, her wrists pinned along her head, and in no time he roared in her ears because he was launching, too, which made her rack even harder. She heard herself cry out, just about the time some lever dropped her through her own foundation and into a whole other plunge, and she began to rack not so much with spasms as great heaving sobs.

Release, in more ways than one.

She fought away from him and he let off her wrists. She curled tight and let him hold her, let him shush in her ear. She shook so hard, she couldn't even nod.

Finally it passed. She lay there a bit and patted his wet wrist. Got her breathing under control. One of the droplets had rolled, started to tickle her chin. She twisted away and sat up.

She wiped her eyes. "Wow. I'm sorry."

"You shouldn't be. Probably just what you need."

"It's just such a relief, you know? Even with everything else going on—Amelia and all. I've been in knots ever since you shot their cars up. Longer than that, even. Worried sick."

"I want to tell you I'm sorry, for putting you through any of it. Hell, for even attempting that stupid bushwhack in the first place." He stalled, shook his head at his own hindsight. "I guess I must have been so festered after what they did to you that night, I just . . . wasn't thinking straight."

"Hush," she told him. "It wound up working out. Crazy as it seems."

"Roy tell you they had bullion when they got pinched?"

"No . . . what? Out of the cemetery?"

"No doubt."

She could feel her wheels turning, those old gears getting back in the habit of working ten miles down the road. "Houston thought you turned everything over to the police. In exchange for staying in the clear yourself. But I guess that's not what happened."

He shook his head. "Nope. The kid was right, I started to get pretty worried myself, especially once we knew about that gold stash. So when they came back around, I just turned it all over to them. Watch, ledger, map—all of it. Figured if they got what they were after, they'd hightail it for Argentina or something."

"What did they say about us beating them to it?"

"I never told them we did. Not even with the map and the lock-box. I just put the whole caboodle in a burlap sack and left it in the boondocks, as instructed. Three o'clock in the morning. Figured that was the end of it, until a couple of days later when Houston happened to spot them from the airplane."

"By which time they'd gone for the stash."

"Looks like it."

"Well. Guess I missed the whole show." She kneaded at her eyes again, saw the makeup on her fingers. "On top of that, I must look like a real fright."

He appeared to give this some serious mulling. "That is, ah, one way to put it."

She slapped his face, not very hard. God, she'd missed laughing with him.

He kissed the hand that hit him. "You're gorgeous. Like a raccoon."

She laughed again, had to catch herself again. A sound like a hiccup. "Careful," she warned. "I might start back up."

"Want a beer?"

"God, yes . . ."

"I was starting to wonder if you were going to come around at all," he told her.

Her eyes felt like withering gashes in the skin of an apple, curdling with some sickly color. She took a small sip of Highlander, let her tongue absorb it. "It wasn't you, I promise. Just all the other *stuff.*"

"Thought for sure I'd lure you right to my lair, that first time you seemed to shake it. My wheels were a-turning, believe me."

She gave him a little look.

"After you figured out the ledger? That trek down to Billings?"

She couldn't read his face now, and with the light lowering outside the window she realized he almost certainly couldn't read hers, either. "I know. You were close. Believe *me.*" She pulled another swig, this time a healthier one. "Guess it wasn't over, though."

She was quiet a moment. Down on the main floor of the house something banged and thumped, then the circular clatter of a dropped lid. An agitated French harangue came through the floor.

"Half in his cups," said McKee. "Probably tripped over his cat."

"It was that little girl's body. In the crypt." Somehow she was only just realizing it. Should have been obvious. "That's what set me back. I probably never should've seen it."

"One of those things, though. You don't know until it's too late. And no way to unsee it afterward."

"True enough." That tiny sleeping face, with those tiny teeth. Now and always and maybe forever, peering away through some hazy glass in her own mind. She didn't know how many times she'd startled awake already to that very image.

"Tell you the truth, I had my doubts about letting you down in there that day. Not that I think you couldn't handle such a thing, under regular circumstances."

"Well, I appreciate the sentiment, looking back. But I doubt you could have stopped me, short of not inviting me along to begin with. Which would've made me even angrier."

"It's a fine line, wanting to protect someone."

She thought about Gloria, out there alone once again. Roy had been in such a wild rush, she'd barely even said goodbye. She said, "Ignorance might be bliss, but only if it's honest. Otherwise, you just wind up feeling mollycoddled. It's insulting. Can you close the window? I'm freezing."

He swung his feet to the floor and stood and slid the window down. In an instant that simple gesture sealed the two of them from the air and the noise of the rest of the world, and in another instant he was right back beside her as though he'd never been gone. "You feel pretty warm to me," he told her.

"Like a raccoon?"

"Not sure. Never been to bed with one."

She yawned, still thinking about her aunt.

"That was supposed to be funny."

"It is funny. I'm just"—another yawn and she talked right through it—"really worn out. Been a rough month."

She lay there for a bit while he drank his beer in the gathering dark, feeling herself settle into this amazing drowsiness, knowing something had sure drained out of her. She'd sleep like she'd been drugged and she knew it, knew as well she should rouse herself and head to the bungalow right now, before she slipped past the point of return.

"Might be a touchy subject, but are you gonna get back in that bird again? The kid sure wants you to."

She heard the blow of her breath, that old dying balloon. *Touchy*, that was one way to put it. "I will if you will."

"Great. Let's do it."

She lifted her head off his shoulder, put it right back again. "Yeah, right."

He laughed. "I mean it. Probably. Have to put me in a diaper first, but for you? Sure. I'd do it."

"I don't believe you."

"Well, you're smart. Anyhow, none of that's the point. You're the one's got to do it, for you alone. My horse ain't in the race."

Only a moment ago she'd been borderline chilled and now a flush went through her like ninety-proof whiskey, right down her throat and somehow straight to her blood. "It makes me look pretty weak, I know." Her face practically burned against the pillow.

"Not what I'm saying. Hell, look at me—I won't even climb up on a roof. But you can fly a plane, and that's your *life*. Maybe you can't get Miss Earhart back, but you can get *you* back."

She realized she was holding her breath, realized as well that her old stinger was starting to rise. Evidently she *was* getting herself back, little by little, misguided as it might be. She'd also shocked awake more than once to Amelia's face, that famous gap in *her* teeth, also behind glass. Glass, and water.

She forced herself to let the bottling air back out. Forced the sting back down.

"You know he took that thing to twelve thousand feet the other day?"

The words sank in and her head came back off his shoulder. "You're kidding."

"What he said. But he was a speck in the air in no time, that much I can for sure tell you. He told you he supercharged the engine, right?"

"With a vacuum cleaner?"

"Yeah. A busted vacuum cleaner."

God love that kid. "He told me he thought he might be able to. I guess I'm not surprised he actually did it."

He nudged away from her and went across the room to the ice-box. "Yeah?"

"I'd better not. I need to get back to the house." She heard him pop a single cap. A moment later he climbed back in beside her.

"So how was it out there, with Miz Gloria? Huck said the two of you were getting along like thieves."

"I saw another side of her, definitely." She'd put herself in her aunt's position and couldn't help feeling some of her pain. "It's hard not to feel bad for her, because she's just muddling through like the rest of us. Unfortunately, she sort of forced her own rejection by the people she loves. I don't think she knows how to atone for it without appearing to deny the same sense of belief that carried her through her other troubles for so long."

"Rock and a hard place."

Now she did want another beer. She reached over and took his. "She's incredibly lonely out there. I actually feel sort of guilty, like I abandoned her myself, all over again. It happened pretty quickly, but I could tell she was . . . crestfallen, or something."

"How did she take the news about the airplane?"

She drained the rest of the bottle. One easy gulp. "She doesn't know yet. Roy was in a rush, I don't think he really expected me to come back with him." She realized something else. "He probably thought I should be the one to explain it all to her. Given the way it's been going."

"Want me to run you back out there?"

"Looking like a raccoon? No, I don't. There's plenty I haven't told her, either."

McKee laughed.

"Anyway, it's something the three of them really need to pow-wow about. I don't mind going, but they've gotten way too used to not being themselves around her. It's made a real mess for all of them." Plus there was something else, something she could hardly resist now that she'd plunged back in. "Besides that, you feel good."

"You're welcome." He had her tight. "I hate to say it, but we should get you back over to the house."

"Yuck."

"I know it." He yawned again. "But the rumor mill."

"Dodging that's"—this yawning was a real contagion—"mainly for my aunt, in this case. Save the poor woman from the scandal." She felt almost bad again, even as she said it. Who was mollycoddling whom, exactly? "I can hardly move, though. What on earth did you do to me?"

"Just my sworn Christian duty."

"Oh, Yak," she said, and she couldn't keep her eyes open, her own voice ten thousand miles away, floating at her from the inky deep. "I do love you."

"Careful, now." He was tight against the back of her neck. "That way lies madness."

Maybe an hour passed or maybe only seconds, but whatever the case, she knew she'd already been asleep. Maybe still was, although she'd remember it clear as a bell later.

"Where on earth did you come up with Yakima?"

"Huh? Oh. Stole it, actually. Met this . . . rodeo rider. Bronc buster. A real hot dog. Years ago, over in Kalispell.

"He was from Oregon, somewhere. Washington, maybe. Told me his name was also Enos and I should"—yawn—"change mine like he did. On account of the ladies. Something with more of a . . . snap to it." He sounded practically etherized, slurring his words through the half-light of his own lazy slumber. "Just went ahead and used his. I ain't even been to the Palouse."

Years later, she would remember smiling against his arm . . .

2

She heard the yell of her name and a bang at the door, and she jarred into the wince of full daylight. The room was already hot, Yak already pulling on his pants, half hopping across the room. The door took another pounding.

"Hang on," he yelled. "I'm coming." He buttoned his fly and looked back at her. "So much for the rumor mill. Sorry."

She half blinked against the light, half cringed against the blunt force of reality. Mouth like cotton. "Not your fault."

"Sure it is," he told her.

He turned the lock and Houston burst through like a G-man. Or maybe the wild man from Borneo—eyes the size of flight goggles, electrocuted hair. Waving around and babbling like he was speaking in tongues, something about it had finally happened, finally happened, that the end was here, and he wished he could go back and do it all differently.

She realized he'd been crying. She forgot she was naked, sat bolt up and immediately grabbed for the sheet when it slid down her chest. He didn't even seem to notice, just went babbling on.

McKee had him by the shoulders. "*Houston.*"

He clammed up but looked wild-eyed around the room, breathing like a cornered animal. Finally he managed to fix on her.

"What is going on?" she said.

He spoke around his own ragged air. "It's Ma. We got to get back to the ranch. She's sick, I mean really, really sick this time."

"Like headache sick?" said McKee. "Does she need to come in to the doc?"

"Doc's already been out there, and it's no headache. Thinks it's her appendix. She might"—he sucked in another massive, halting draught—"she might *die*."

Annelise shucked the covers entirely and spun her legs to the floor. She reached for her dress and underthings, all in a heap near the foot of the bed. "Where's your father?"

"He's out there. I came back with Doc Lipton."

She got into her brassiere and got the dress over her head and reached behind herself and zipped as far as she could. Her shoes were in the kitchen and she moved toward them, then on second thought pushed McKee out of the way and took Houston's hands. "What do we need to do?"

"Get back to the ranch . . . no." He was nearly frantic with fear, goggle eyes ricocheting around the room again. "I just ran from the hospital to the shop and then over here. Trying to find you." He found her eyes again and a whole other look of disarray came across him. "We need to get back to the hospital."

McKee was pulling on a shirt. "Go start the truck. I'm right behind you."

"Acute appendicitis, that much I'd bank on." Doc Lipton ran his fingers through his crazy mop, tested the bristles on his cheek with his palm. He'd been summoned out of bed and straight to the ranch, and now here they were in his office, in what passed as the Big Coulee Hospital.

Annelise had seen him around but never met him. Younger than her father and definitely more rakish than doddering old Doctor Weems back home, but she wouldn't trust either of them with emergency surgery.

Evidently he didn't trust himself. "Look, these ain't the old days of field experiment, learn as you go, whatever. We aren't equipped to help her, is the upshot.

"Generally we'd try to farm this out to Deaconess down in Bill-ings, but we're up against a wall there, too—I just called down and the chief surgeon, Art Movius, is over at the Bozeman Deaconess. Training nurses." Fingers in his hair again. He looked back and forth between her and McKee. "Rotten luck."

"What are the options?" said McKee. Annelise turned to look at Houston and caught a startling glimpse of herself in a mirror on the wall beyond. She looked almost masked, with that streaked black makeup. A girl Lone Ranger. God, her hair had grown out, though.

"I'm working on it." Lipton hammered his forehead with an index finger and looked at McKee. "You smoke? I need a cigarette."

"Uh-uh. But the clock's ticking, I take it."

"Yeah." He glanced at Houston. "Kid, you sure you're okay hear-ing all this?"

"He's living it," Annelise said. "Better he hears it, too."

The doc gave her a deferential nod and started again. "She was out there by herself all night and now this thing's pretty far along. I can tell that by her fever and level of, ah, let's say, discomfort." He meant *pain* and she knew it and it was like he wanted to tear his own hair out.

"Thing is, even if Movius were in Billings, I'm not sure how easy it would be to get her there, at this stage of it. I was just down there a week ago and parts of that road are rough as a cob. Probably what we'd do is have him drive up here and use the delivery room as a sur-gery. Or maybe meet him partway in Roundup. Anyway, it's beside the point. Movius ain't in Billings."

"Bozeman's what, six hours?" Houston, the first time he'd spoken since McKee's kitchen. But he seemed to have steeled himself.

"At least, and I know there's grading crews between here and there, so you'd have to figure even longer." He shook his head. "Even if we can get Movius on the road in the next five minutes, he's a long way out." He blew a long deep breath, as though he actually were exhaling a drag. "Look, push is coming to shove here. I may have to give it a try myself. Get her pretty morphined up. Strap her down and have a go."

Houston stood. "How far's Bozeman?"

Annelise looked at him. Maybe he wasn't hearing any of this after all.

"Mile-wise, I mean."

"Two hundred or better. It's a clip."

"Yeah, but that's driving. West and then south a good ways, and then west again. How far as the crow flies?"

McKee got to his feet as well. "That would cut it in half, or nearly so. Like one-twenty, one-thirty? I've got a map in the truck."

They were moving toward the door and Annelise hit her feet, too. "Hey. *Hey.*"

Both of them paused.

"You're doing what I think you're doing?"

"I've got that bird cruising at eighty-five an hour, no problem," said Houston. "If we can get my ma in the front bay, we can fly her there in no time. He turned to the doc. "Clock's ticking, ain't that what you said?"

Lipton gestured at Yak. "Actually he did, but it's a point. How rough a ride is it?"

"Depends. Cooled off good last night, though." He shrugged. "Shouldn't be any trick to get a couple-thousand up and sail right on over. Be a lot smoother than that bounce to Billings, and probably quicker."

"You do have Bozeman Pass to get over. That's pushing six thousand feet."

"I just flew her past twelve. Not worried about six."

The doc scraped at his hair again. He looked at Annelise. "This is probably our best bet. I can call Deaconess in Bozeman, get Movius on the horn."

Why on earth he felt the need to sell it to her, she had no idea. "Can we drive her to the airfield, at least?"

"Waste of time," said Houston. He started for the door again. "Yak'll run me to the plane, you two get back to the ranch. Tie a white rag on a stick and go on up to the wheat table."

3

She thought she could hear the buzz of the ship coming in and she shielded her eyes and scanned, and before she'd picked it out of the blue yonder a different glimmer caught her eye down below. She looked toward the county road and saw Yak's white Studebaker, turning up the lane. He bumped over the cattle guard. Sunlight flashed on the glass.

The drone of the plane came on louder. She scanned again and found it, lower than she would have thought, coming in across the tables from the direction of town. Another moment and he cleared the house, just about the time Yak lurched to a stop beside the ambulance she and Doc Lipton had brought from the hospital, and also Pastor White's black sedan. She saw the plane's shadow appear across the front wall of the barn and then vanish again, like a silhouette passing a shade.

He descended light as a bubble, traveling so slowly she could hardly believe he stayed in the air, the sight so mesmerizing she nearly forgot to hold up the cloth. Just as he cleared the lip of the jump and passed, looking at her over the cowling through those goggles, she put the thing straight up over her head.

It hardly mattered. The hanky lay slack as a noodle. He accelerated and banked out beyond the far edge of the field, came around over the farm lot again and set down on the two-track at the south edge. He taxied out, bobbing across the shallow furrows, the stunted weeds blasting flat in the rush of the prop, then turned and smoothed out and cut the motor. He ripped the harness loose.

She went out toward him, her feet greasy with sweat inside the rubber muck boots she'd grabbed off the porch. Still in her dress, though, and still with the mask of streaked makeup around her eyes, which she could see in the ambulance's side mirror the whole ride out.

Down in the house the atmosphere had been tense indeed. Aunt Gloria was fairly wringing herself and curled into a hard little knot, clutching Roy's hand like a clamp but trying not to so much as whimper because even that triggered jolts of lightning through her middle.

Pastor White and a couple of men from the church were laying hands on her and praying. Doc Lipton had his bag open at the foot of the bed when Annelise left the house, prepping a morphine shot.

Houston hauled a gas can and funnel from the front cockpit, undid the cap in the wing, and started pouring. He had the tank topped before she even got there.

"Barely burned a drop, but still." He handed her the can and jumped down, and they started back across the furrows. "What's happening inside?"

"Sort of a two-pronged approach. Pastor White's trying for a miracle, but the doc's loading her up with dope."

"We're still on with this, though?"

"Hence the painkiller."

"How's Pop with it?"

Her heart was breaking for him. Roy was nearly as sweated-through as Aunt Gloria was, sitting there with her and trying to hold himself together, but white as that handkerchief she'd hoisted and no doubt riven with agonies all his own.

Fear, guilt, regret—she saw all of it, wished him none of it. When she'd only just arrived, he'd taken one look at her coming through the door and tried to speak to her and couldn't at first, he was so choked up.

"He's managing," she said. "Scared out of his wits, poor thing."

"But how is he with the Bozeman plan?"

"Oh." They were hoofing it down the grade to the base of the jump, where she'd parked the REO. "He just asked if that's her best chance, and the doctor told him it's more like her only chance."

He paused and looked back up the two-track to the wheat table, and Annelise looked too, but the airplane wasn't visible from this low vantage. He kept looking, though. "It's not even a question. Sure, if it were ninety degrees already I'd think twice, really damned hard."

Finally he looked across the hood at her. "But it's not ninety degrees, not even close. And what's that old saying? God helps those who help themselves?" He shook his head. "I reckon there's some kind of truth to it. If I don't use what I can to help my own ma, there's nobody to blame but me."

"I understand. But I still wish this Doctor Movius were in Billings, where he belongs."

Houston climbed in and fired the REO. "Got to eat what's actually on your plate. At least we have an airplane."

He put the spurs to her and barreled for the house, hitting ruts and dips a few times at such a speed the bench seat seemed to drop beneath them like the hinged floor of a gallows, only to slam right back up with a nearly tooth-cracking wallop. He had a death grip on the wheel and could tell Annie was hanging on for dear life beside him, one hand fairly welded to the edge of the dashboard and the other splat against the roof above her head.

He'd left the bungalow with Pop before six that morning, the both of them figuring it was sure enough time to come clean with Mother, just begin at the beginning, before the news reports started squawking through the radio and beat them to it.

He'd known something was amiss before he'd so much as passed the doorway. No coffee on, no radio on, not even the start of a fire, and a morning dawdler Mother was not. Headache, probably, although those usually came later in the day. The stillness, though— that struck him next, in the flash of time it took to find his own voice.

Silence, like a strange scent in the air.

The kitchen windows were closed and the place had an eerie bottled stasis that reminded him of something he didn't at all want reminding of, and he fought the automatic workings of his own brain because he knew the unruly thing was even now trying to conjure exactly what he wished to avoid, the way he found himself wishing at times that he'd never seen that dead little—

Bingo. That was it. The stillness took him to the blank air in the crypt. He was afraid to move, afraid that actually entering the house and exiting this uncertain state would lead only to a place he couldn't return from, and though he knew he couldn't stand in the doorway forever, he realized that for right now, he'd rather stay terrified and hopeful than fully aware and doomed.

If by some miracle she wasn't dead in her bed, he'd get right onto the straight and narrow. Be a better son, take better care of her. No more secrets, no more falsehoods. *Please, God, please.* He promised, he promised, he promised he would . . .

Behind him in the yard something banged like a shot and he jumped, practically out of his skin but definitely into the room. Pop, knocking mud from a shovel against the bumper of the REO.

He'd landed nearly in the middle of the kitchen. *Ma?*

He heard his name, faint as a wraith, so faint he thought it might be a figment of his own desperation. He held his breath. Then a sob from her bedroom, like the merest creak of a floorboard.

She was doubled up on the bed, barely able to lift her head. The covers trailed and her night shift was drenched with sweat and probably tears and for all he knew the release of her bladder, and quick as a flash he was back at the kitchen door roaring for Pop.

Mother was already on the stretcher when he slid to a stop and cranked on the brake. They had her wheeled to the back of the ambulance. He looked at Pop and Pop looked at him, and for the first time Huck could remember, his father simply looked old. Huck gave him a little nod, and the hard set of Pop's mouth started to quiver, and neither of them could look away quickly enough. He didn't know which way his father's eyes went, but his own went straight to the gurney.

The drug had set in. She seemed half lost in a dream, with her breathing deeply steady and her eyelids fluttering. The doc was talking to her, telling her she was doing good, telling her she should feel some relief until they got her into good hands, and evidently she could hear what he said because she gave her own nod there on the pillow. Little more than the flutter at her eyes or that quiver to Pop's mouth, but he had no doubt he saw it.

He'd never considered that Pop might know the clutch of actual fear. Pop always just seemed like Pop, maybe caught between a push and a pull at times, but steady as a clock and amiable, too, even when everything otherwise went into a tailspin.

Huck stole another sideways peek. Now Pop was petting Mother's shoulder, Annelise petting Pop's, and the one on the stretcher seemed at the moment frankly in better straits than the one still on his feet. McKee stood a few feet away, oddly enough in some confab with Pastor White and the deacons.

Whatever the case, he needed to keep his own face on, just a bit longer.

"You all set?" Doc Lipton, looking at him. "We ought to get this show on the road."

"One minute." Huck strode for the house, leaned in and grabbed a pair of overalls from the line of hooks beside the door. He rolled them in a wad and came back into the still-rising slant of light, out of the cold shade of the porch. Somehow the day was hardly along at all. Doc Lipton and McKee and one of the deacons were lifting the stretcher, passing Mother into the back of the ambulance.

"Annie."

She looked over from where she stood beside Pop.

He threw her the overalls. Not his oversize patched and frayed pair, but a new set actually sized to fit. Deep indigo, deep as some lightless depth of the sea. Pop had brought them to her days ago, when she moved out from town.

She caught them by one of the legs that had loosened from the wad.

"Put those on."

"What?"

"I ain't doing the flying. You are."

She practically erupted. "NO, no no no," she began, and he'd seen this coming and was already slashing a finger across his throat to shut her up. He hooked a sly thumb at Pop. They walked off to the side.

"I'd do it myself in a second if that was absolutely our best option. But it's not." He lifted the hem of his shirt. "What's different?"

Her striped eyes shifted to his waist. "Your pants fit."

He'd filled out somehow, practically overnight it seemed. Eating lately like a starveling at a king's banquet, and no longer requiring that cinch of a belt with its auxiliary hole. Even his shoulders strained his shirts. "I've got fifty pounds on you at least, and for all I know, that's the difference between blowing over that pass like a leaf and bogging out like a pig in a mudhole."

She clutched the wadded-up overalls like a thing she wished she could hide.

"You already flew her to twelve thousand feet. You and your vacuum cleaner. Yak told me, and you said it yourself. In the doctor's office."

"Yeah, I did. With some help from clouds, I admit. But I don't totally know how much gas the Hoover contraption sucks down, especially on some cross-country haul, two passengers, maybe in a headwind, maybe no thermals. God only knows.

"You are a better flier than I am, Annelise. I've had two lessons and what, ten, twelve hours?" He shook his head. "Nothing."

"Baloney. You studied it, you built it, you *know* it, inside and out. And besides, I'm not"—she tripped on her own voice, looked away as though she couldn't face his eyes—"I'm not who you want me to be."

If anybody else saw the streaks around her eyes, nobody said so. This sight exactly had stopped him cold, when he'd burst through the door into Yak's apartment. She'd shot bolt up in the bed without a stitch of clothing, but all he could remember was the wreath of gold around her head, and that black stripe across her eyes.

She was wrong now, though, clutching her overalls there in the yard. He was himself, and Annelise was herself. Yes, she had her own life to muddle through. But she was *exactly* who he wanted her to be.

He said, "You've got two hundred hours, Annelise. What, two *years* of lessons? Fact of it is, I did build the airplane, I do know it inside out. But you will always fly farther and climb faster than I can. That's the plain truth."

She threw her head back and looked straight up at the sky. "Why me?"

He and Yak pulled the bolts connecting the front stick from the controls and fished the linkage out from beneath the gauge panel. More room for Mother and more to the point, no chance she could accidentally interfere with the actual piloting.

Doc Lipton had the ambulance backed to the edge of the harrowed field. Huck gave the sign and they popped the doors, began to ease the stretcher out. He watched McKee walk over to Annelise, a few feet away in her overalls and a pair of sneakers she'd chanced to leave at the house. Flannel work shirt up top with the sleeves rolled. She was studying the map out of McKee's Studebaker.

Pop and Doc Lipton and the men from the church came toward them with the gurney, across the corrugated ground. Huck looked the other way, out across the tables and rims. He could just see the faint blue spine of the Absarokas in the haze above the western horizon. Something moved at the corner of his eye and he shifted over there.

A whirl of loose soil came up at the far side of the table, spin-ning and whipping into a gyrating yellow devil. It hovered in place a moment, its mad swirl stretching higher and higher, then darted and danced toward the edge of the jump. It hit the plunge and simply stopped, dispersed into drifting particles again. Over here the air remained still as a church.

"What's that mean?" Annelise asked.

"Means the wind is at your back," Huck said. "Don't know if it's a sign from God or not, but it could be worse."

The gurney was nearly to them. "So I keep the compass south and west until I see the big river, then follow it due west."

"You can't miss it," Yak told her. "Once you hit the corridor, if you do have to land for some reason, you've got the roadway and plenty of good flat hay meadow to boot."

"Then the river turns south at Livingstone—"

"Livingston—"

"—Livingston, right, but I stay west, follow the road and the rail tracks up over the pass. And there's Bozeman."

"You got it," said McKee. "Can't miss that, either."

They came up with the stretcher, set it by the ship with Mother's feet pointing toward the prop. She seemed to be asleep now, her eyes fully closed and the rise and fall of her chest fairly regular. Doc Lip-ton pulled the sheet back and she looked hardly bigger than a doll, there in her night shift.

They passed her into the front bay as gently as they could, with Pop and the pastor reaching through the warren of cables and struts on the port side, McKee leaning in at starboard to guide her feet. The doc and the deacons lifted her off the gurney and passed her to the others beneath the wing. She murmured a bit and seemed to struggle against the hands and arms that supported her, and actually cried out and shuddered once as they tried to contort her through the maze, but even this seemed more like a reaction from the depths of a dream than anything she was aware of. Yak steered her legs into the bay.

They got the harness fastened and padded her with blankets. Pop stood on the tire and leaned in and said some things, and Huck saw him kiss her forehead. Yak was already at the prop.

Huck laced his fingers into a step. Annelise put one hand on his shoulder, the other on the cowling. Put her sneaker into the web he made for her. She stepped up into the cockpit.

"I wish it was me," he told her.

She fastened her helmet. "I wish it were, too."

"If they have to cut the plane apart to get her out, tell them to cut the plane apart."

"I will."

Pop came out from beneath the wing and gave the two of them a curt little wince. He paused as though he wanted to say something, then walked off at his own angle, not toward anybody else at all and maybe not in any direction at all, but simply away. Annelise pulled her goggles down.

"Hey," he said. He could see her smudged eyes through the glass. "Thank you."

"Don't thank me yet," she said, and McKee swung the prop out front. A blast of dust went up.

One minute later he heard the motor wind, and the ship moved forward down the furrows. Stalks and fronds rippled like water. She was up to speed even on the tilled ground faster than he would've predicted, trailing a roil of dust out behind. The tail came up out of its dragging skid and her speed advanced yet again, and the wheels left the earth, too.

She passed through the air across the lip of the jump. She started to rise.

Signs and Wonders

I

Churned field or not, the ship raced up to speed beyond what she could have imagined, dust fairly billowing off the tires. Even so, the dread in her chest and the terror in her mind taunted like demons, whispering and snickering, ready to chant and laugh the second she reached that ancient edge and plunged straight to the hard ground below.

Except the whipping dust fell away long before she'd even approached the end of the furrows. It took a moment to register that she was airborne and climbing, smooth and steady as a department store escalator. The demons weren't totally cast off, but when she hazarded a look over the cowling, the only thing in free fall was the face of the buffalo jump itself.

She flew on straight ahead, hardly able to take her eyes from the altimeter and yet hardly able to comprehend it. Climbing and climbing, right on through whatever angst-driven stupor she knew she was going to have to get herself beyond. She cautiously edged the throttle forward, eased the stick back with her other hand to tilt the elevator. The seat seemed to lift right up against her bottom, while her belly dropped to meet it.

The rail trestle across the river caught her attention off to starboard. Cottonwood crowns like vibrant green clouds, that same stretch of river Houston had once showed her from this vantage exactly, where he and Raleigh had dredged the body from the floodwater.

Nearly six months ago, could that be right? In one sense it seemed like minutes and in another like eons, but here she was, hurtling through time and space even now, the river a mere trickle of what it must have been then and the Crazy Mountains revealing themselves steadily above the horizon, and it finally began to filter through her muddled, addled brain that she really needed to start piloting already.

She could see the top of her aunt's head through the little wind-screen above the panel. White tendrils, lifting and dancing. She checked her gauges.

She was a shade under a thousand in the air and holding steady, had apparently marshalled the wit somewhere in her torn and frayed mind to level out and cruise. She couldn't quite remember. She was only moving at sixty-five an hour, taching below 1,600.

She glimpsed a flash of something off to port, like silver foil or a signal mirror, angled against the light. Another ship, probably, but when she scanned out to the south she saw nothing but endless sky above endless broken-brown ground.

She fixed on a big crumbling mesa, or maybe butte, directly to the south. She didn't really know the terminology, but this one had the look of a gigantic upside-down ice-cream cone, melting with time and slowly spreading at the base. She glimpsed that silver-foil flash and again looked up.

Nothing. What on earth. If she were merely on a lark and not this particular cruel mission, she'd bank immediately south, maybe close some distance and get to the bottom of whatever it was she couldn't quite see.

Another flash, this one in her mind. The proverbial lightbulb. Tacking due west but she wasn't supposed to be, the tip of the blue mountain to the south and west not a tip at all any longer but an entire saw-toothed ridge, pyramids beside pyramids, rising off the horizon by the second. South and west. The direction she was sup-posed to be tacking now.

She tilted the stick and banked left, watched the compass rotate. She leveled again with the needle at SW, the peaks of the mountains swung around now to starboard.

One decisive move led to another and she leaned on the throttle, heard the hop in the engine out front and for the first time in this whole hair-raising exercise felt a corresponding hop in her own pumping blood. Something along the lines of exhilaration. She throttled up again.

She could hear the difference in the motor, hear the whir and whine of Houston's miracle centrifuge. The force of speed pushed her into the seatback.

The tach had jumped to 1,800 and already she was pushing ninety an hour. The acceleration was pretty remarkable—most of her lessons had been in a Curtiss-Wright training plane, which had little if anything on this reborn bullet that shot her along now.

The tables and buttes began to soften and melt into muted rolling hills, with towering mountains off to the west and another saw-toothed range looming well to the south. Then the land below unfurled again into hay meadow and pastureland, flat green atolls of sheared-over grass and bunched-up masses of black or red cows, and also a series of ranch yards with crimson outbuildings and houses nestled within islands of shade trees. Big spreads, too, obviously not hardscrabble family places. Then Annelise saw the river.

She'd been somewhat aware of it on the train to Billings all those months ago, but had paid only scant attention. Now she spotted it, probably at least five miles off and broad as a thoroughfare, lined on each side with the usual vibrant green rind.

She hurtled along with the speed indicator pegged at ninety-five. Otherwise nothing looked out of the ordinary, with even the gas gauge barely down from a full tank.

Ninety-five miles an hour, though. Hadn't Houston said eighty-five? Did she have a tailwind behind her or something? Or were the air and the atmosphere just somehow exceedingly perfect? In her experience the best-laid plans typically went awry rather than the other way around, although she knew uncanny good luck was a thing as well. Lindbergh certainly had it in spades, hence the nickname— Lucky Lindy. Amelia had owned an outsize share herself, once upon a time.

It crossed her mind that she didn't actually have to reach the river but merely bank around to the west and keep it in sight off to port. She began to tilt the stick, then had a second thought and leveled. She flew straight on for the water, passed over the railbed and the roadbed up along the higher ground, and finally crossed over the river channel and banked out across the breaks on the south side. She watched the half globe of the compass rotate around and settle, just about due west. She could see not only the river off to starboard but the rail tracks and the highway too, a couple of minuscule vehicles crawling even now.

Something caught her eye and she looked back up. That silver flash again, she could've sworn, but no sooner did her eyes come back from ground to sky than they locked on the most obvious feature in view. The Crazies, of course, fully revealed and utterly enormous to the west and north. But something else, too—an even more enormous range not of mountains but of seething black clouds, roiling from the back side of the peaks like an ogre clearing a fortress wall. If there was in fact another plane flying, she still couldn't spot it.

The Yellowstone ran out of the west. She could see a little town not far ahead but clearly it wasn't Livingston, where the river angled in from the south. She looked back at the clouds in time to see an actual flash, not the silver skin of an airplane but a bolt of lightning, dancing out of that black-fog abyss.

What had Houston called a storm cloud? An anvil? Was that ever appropriate now—the top of the mass had flattened like an iron table, with a long, tapering wedge jutting like a devil's horn off the near end. She'd thought at the time that this was his own original description, a natural metaphor for a kid who'd practically cut his teeth in a blacksmith shop. Maybe she was wrong.

The entire ominous black system was apparently not content to stay put beyond the barrier of the mountain range but seemed to want to bear down in this direction, and quickly. Already the leading edge had swirled out beyond the facing slope, and the skies behind it to the north were growing broader and darker and seemingly nearer by the second. She saw another purple skitter of lightning.

At this rate, a wall of weather might cut her off in a matter of minutes. So much for a new lease on luck. Her aunt's hair fluttered in front of her. She'd asked herself a million times, at one crossroads or crisis or another, what would Amelia do? Now it seemed entirely the wrong question, but the words muttered in her head anyway, muttered like a sad taunt.

Maybe just those demon voices, whispering all over again. She looked at her gauges, tried to keep her head on straight. She'd pulled her speed down to eighty-five back across the river and she ran the throttle knob up again now, shooting for the erstwhile ninety-five if possible, in the hopes she might outrun that towering juggernaut before the thing could get in front of her.

The plane did indeed respond. She felt it, saw it. She made speed again in not much time at all but now the throttle was advanced entirely, and ninety-five was evidently the top end. Still the black mass came on like a ghost of the mountain itself, leaving its own solid corpus behind. The river stretched ahead.

She felt the air temperature drop. Ten degrees at least, like flying into the reverse of a furnace blast, a wall of cold not heat. Weirdly she could still feel the beat of the sun on her left arm where her sleeve was shoved past her elbow, but she felt as well the breath of a chill on her opposite cheek, against the incoming weather.

The light around her had gotten weird too, as though she were flying right at the edge of a collision of dark and bright, and somehow the presence of each made the other all the more extreme. The outer billows of the approaching front loomed pewter and silver and gray, but the heart of the thing may as well have been cloaked in a drape of black velvet.

The first blast hit the plane and she screamed, so violently did the little ship roll sideways. She corrected by sheer impulse in the buck and shake of turbulent air. No way she could outrun this thing, and how on earth could it move so fast, the sky overhead already a piling canopy of seething vapor and the sun divided and stabbing through in shafts here and there, even those blinking out one by one as the heart of the mass rolled like a cold black wave over the river and the land and indeed her own airplane.

So what *would* Amelia do, exactly? The only thing she could, she supposed—hold her direction and keep on flying. She had roiling gray mist all around her now although evidently she was right within the bottom strata of the storm, because she could still glimpse the river from time to time through shifting apertures in the clouds.

Just about the time it struck her that she should probably drop her elevation, an outright explosion of electricity streaked like a serpent's tongue out of the black maw of the storm and shot right by the starboard edge of the wing. The plane went to bucking all over the place again, and she was screaming her bloody head off.

Gloria

III

*And I will shew wonders in heaven above, and signs in the earth be-
neath; blood, and fire, and vapour of smoke:*

*The sun shall be turned into darkness, and the moon into blood, be-
fore the great and notable day of the Lord come:*

*And it shall come to pass, that whosoever shall call on the name of
the Lord shall be saved.*

—Acts of the Apostles

I felt always I would Rapture, never die.

Knew it, even, if that's not too strong a word, as surely as any of
the great prophets and seers knew the truth of their own revelations.
Isaiah, predicting the coming of the baby Jesus, or Daniel, foretell-
ing of the restoration of Jerusalem. Some of this they witnessed in
dreams, the way I have seen my own fate in dreams. Escaping mortal
death like Enoch, or Elijah in his fiery chariot, up and up and into
eternal life, in blessed heaven.

I have been through my own tribulations, that much is also true,
and some of them not inferior to the testing of Job at times. Some of
them should have killed me the way they should have killed him, but
that was not the plan then and I have been shown by their defeat that
mere death is not the plan now, and so here I am, the victor of my
own prophecy, traveling up and up. Traveling home.

I had long imagined my actual body rising, victorious over the manacles of the earth and over the prince of the power of the air, with the other faithful right around me as far as the eye might see, all of us rising and rising, and the angels coming down. I imagined our earthly attire simply falling away, shedding like the old and brittle skin of a snake. It had crossed my mind that we might sail heavenward in a state of innocent nakedness, the way Adam and Eve wandered without shame in that pure original state.

What I did not see in those other visions was the roar of the passage now upon me, the rough and hazy terror of the transport itself. Mysterious ways indeed. Where is Gilroy? Where is Houston? Where is anybody? What is that howl in my ears, and why am I bound within this cocoon? Where are the magnificent trumpets?

The chariot itself feels as though it might blow apart into bits and pieces around me, its strange canopy humming and vibrating above my head like the wing of a giant moth. Somehow we've passed from light unto dark—did we leave the sun behind while I slept? Are we far, far into the firmament, beyond a place where the sky appears blue? Where is everyone, and why is a journey toward Paradise, of all places, so fraught with this violent, abusive battering?

A streak of light shoots out of the roaring air and surely it must be Him, for the blinding flash of the thing cannot even be looked upon, as though a star has been fired into existence out of the finger of the Father Himself. I feel a leap in my heart and at once an awesome terror—what must be a true manifestation of the fear of the Lord, and I wait for that moment in which the flare itself subsides and the holy figure I have counted upon finally, *finally* appears.

The next shock strikes not my vision but my *hearing*, in the form of a tremendous boom, as though a stick of dynamite has exploded in each ear to leave me ringing with deafness, the puzzling roar of the air now fully drowned by the persisting gong.

I am not hearing and I'm not seeing the streak of light, either—not the way I thought I would. What I am is simply blinded by that first searing glimpse, the way the apostle Paul was stricken on the road to Damascus. Eyes open, eyes shuttered, no matter. The white strobe remains. I am only hurtling along, seeing and hearing nothing, as senseless and as helpless as an embryo.

Except for that pain in my middle, recurring in faint waves at the tremors and turbulence, not constant and not even necessarily there but perhaps a memory? A lingering sense of a pain that once was . . .

I could not sort the real from the ethereal in 1918 either, when the greenish man led me through the hot jungle of the Spanish fever. I remember seeing Gilroy and then losing him in the green dappled light, and feeling so sad for him because we had only just started and now here I was already departing, but when I opened my eyes a long time later, or maybe only a few seconds along, I saw him again, no clearer than an apparition, but his voice soughing through the wet heavy air, saying my name, saying *Gloria*, and though the greenish man beckoned whenever I closed my eyes I tried with all my might to keep them open, and sometimes when I thought I had been with Gilroy all along, I would come up out of the addled depths once again and find him anew and have to start all over again, try to stay with him all over again and make the greenish man go on without me, which finally he did.

When I came back to myself, out from that hot green jungle, my hair had turned white as the garb of an angel. I was eighteen years old. No older than Annelise, and already married.

When Roy came out to the ranch that day, I knew he'd come to take her away again. I saw them talking in the yard, and I knew. She did not talk to me about it, and she did not have to. I should have known anyway, for she had already told me she did not wish to travel home to my sister but to continue on here awhile, even with her schooling behind her. She said maybe she could handle the office at the smithy for Gilroy, take calls and keep the books. Which meant eventually she would return to town, and in my imagination and, yes, in my pride, I saw myself there as well. But in the end, she never did ask.

So again I was left behind. Alone in my separation to puzzle over the times of grace and the times of trial, alone under that roof, which felt in that hour like it might well come down on top of me. Barely were they down the lane before the tightening began in my back, the racing in my heart.

By nightfall another sensation entirely. The region behind my left eye throbbing away and a sear in my navel as well, making me think at first that my moon had arrived earlier than it ought.

By midnight however the sear had become more like a twisting skewer, or a devil's pitchfork rending my insides. I considered in flashes and waves all of these things, began to experience in flashes and waves both the boiling of my blood beneath my skin and trembling icy chills to make the down on my arms stand aloft. I saw again the greenish man, recognized him as though my time in that fevered Spanish jungle happened only yesterday.

But was it just last night? Or the night before? Or am I now in a place where the passage of time means nothing at all?

My eyes have been closed, or perhaps my mind's been asleep, but the turbulent passage shoots another stab through my center like a Roman's piercing lance, and I return to some stunted form of awareness to observe again the fiery beam above my head, my chariot now a cross, and in this now I am not, I believe, the one left behind.

But this lightning storm of Rapture is not what I expected. There is pain and there is fear, and that old haunting abandonment. Why, O Lord, hast Thou forsaken me this way?

Wherever is Mama? Where is Gilroy and where is Houston? Where is Annelise *now*, and why did she leave me when all I'd wanted was to save her, and so save myself?

Signs and Wonders

II

Who is the third who walks always beside you?
When I count, there are only you and I together
But when I look ahead up the white road
There is always another one walking beside you
Gliding wrapt in a brown mantle, hooded
I do not know whether a man or a woman
—But who is that on the other side of you?

—T. S. Eliot, *The Waste Land*

The blast from the lightning hit the depths of one ear and also the starboard side of the fuselage with the same concussive force, and she shrieked in reaction and felt the ship roll sideways.

The concussion traveled past. She got the ship level again. Even with the roar of the engine and competing roil of the air she could hear the ringing inside her helmet, her right ear feeling like somebody had jammed down with an ice pick.

Lightning flared and flared again, but farther off this time, cloud to cloud, like a pulsing filament inside a flickering bulb. The noise when it came rolled in a delayed series of receding booms, nowhere near as deafening as the last explosion that seemed to detonate right off the wing.

What *would* A.E. do? She had asked herself so many times for so many reasons, and always she could conjure some useful way forward.

A crisis with her mother, a row with a classmate, ogre behavior from a boy—in every case, the question had proved useful. Only now, when it truly mattered, airborne in an open plane at the heart of an actual maelstrom, nothing came to her at all.

Then that other irony. Six months in drought-parched Montana with barely so much as a drizzle and now here she was, flying a life-and-death mission through what amounted to a hurricane. As Yak might say, you couldn't make it up.

The first real drops were coming at her, huge beads of water splattering on the windscreen and sailing by like bees. Another flash lit up to port, and she saw the glint of a million diamonds hurtling down.

The land and the river below were completely lost to view. Even in the lowered light she could see the gauges well enough to know she was still tacking west, but the wind out of the north had to be pushing her sideways, too, and at what rate she had no idea. Her chest was tight as a drum, her heart hammering like a timpani, but even so she saw in another flash that the one thing Amelia Earhart would *not* do was freeze under pressure.

She remembered Houston that night of the meteor shower, his story about taking Katie up and getting into a jam. He'd thought his way through it, and with less than a week's piloting experience, flew his way out of it. Big Coulee Lindbergh.

She couldn't save her aunt if she herself died in the process. That much was obvious. And if she was going to die, she was going to die trying. That's *exactly* what A.E. would do.

Her altimeter showed nearly 1,500 feet AGL, which meant she'd climbed a bit on the air currents. Still, she'd have to climb yet again to clear the pass into Bozeman, assuming she made it that far. But here she was, barely back in the game and already getting ahead of herself.

She needed her bearings. That was the first thing. She needed to drop below the clouds and orient herself to the river. Bumps or not, she was still somehow clipping along at nearly eighty-five miles an hour—no wonder the raindrops appeared to be flying past sideways.

She dropped the throttle back and moved the stick forward. The altimeter crept back down.

She couldn't see a single land feature through the rain and fog. No way to judge where any of the mountain ranges were, and though her rational mind tried to tell her she couldn't possibly have blown or traveled far enough in any direction to cause one of them suddenly to loom up out of the mist, the inability to confirm this had dread at her nape like a coiling snake. She told herself that if she did manage to get below the clouds and spot a reasonable place to land, she might well have to try for it. She tried not to think about what this would mean for her aunt.

The ship hit another patch of tooth-jarring air and she worked the stick around to keep more or less level, and somewhere in all the thudding and battering she caught a glimpse of the ground below. She came back again with the throttle knob and dropped through the floor of the clouds.

The turbulence did not diminish. Rain fell in curtains but she could see the river again, maybe a half mile to port now, which meant she had indeed blown off course. She thought she could see the base of the Gallatins well ahead, beneath the wet bank of clouds, though not the turn of the river toward the south.

She banked back toward the river bottom, brought her speed down to seventy. She still had half a mind to ditch the whole effort if she could find a place to land, and the highway made more sense than anything else. The rain came down like the deluge in Genesis, blasting in a weird aureole off the prop. Despite the circumstances she found this a little mesmerizing. Interestingly most of the downpour went well around the cockpit, so even her goggles remained fairly clear.

Another jagged bolt streaked down just ahead and to the side, connected with something on the ground in a burst of sparks and white-blue light. The ship jolted again in the concussive boom. Another streak reached behind the first, and she glimpsed the cottonwoods along the river bending and writhing. She knew she was stuck.

The wind in the corridor whipped even harder than it did up here. She was over the highway now, the river already behind her, lightning flashing like cannon fire in the clouds. The ship bounced like a rodeo bronc and she knew she had to bank west, had to keep herself on course at the least. She didn't know what to do otherwise, only that she couldn't go down into that wall of wind below. Couldn't sit here in this wretched turbulence, either.

She went back up. Ran the throttle forward, leaned back on the stick. The plane settled immediately, speed indicator and altimeter both steadily rising. She climbed up out of the chop and let the mist of the clouds again blot her view of the land. She took the ship back to eighty and climbed above 4,500 feet, her brain scrambling at the math of it all.

The land below couldn't deviate much from the field elevation at Big Coulee—three thousand above sea level, give or take a few hundred feet. The pass into Bozeman in the great wall of the Gallatin Mountains was higher yet, and in short order she was going to have to start climbing to clear it, assuming she could find it to begin with. But she still couldn't rule out the possibility of an emergency landing, somewhere between where she was now and the very same mountains she would otherwise have to top.

The devil, and the deep blue sea. The longer she waited to climb, the less likely she was to get the necessary altitude, but once she committed, an emergency landing became out of the question. Whatever the case, she was still tacking north from the effort to get back across river to the roadway. She put the ship into a shallow bank, watched the compass rotate inside its bubble.

She came around due west. By the time she leveled, she just about had herself convinced to descend one more time, make one last assessment of the landing conditions, when another blinding arc shrieked out of the clouds overhead and blazed on by to starboard. She felt the scorching blast of it like steam out of a boiler and she veered to port, and this time the instantaneous boom of thunder seemed to detonate beneath the ship rather than right in her ear. She felt the shock wave like a swell on the ocean, watched the altimeter needle jump with the sudden lift.

She could smell static in the air, smell the ozone scorch of agitated particles. Scared as she was, she could only watch in disbelief as a purple ball pulsed to life out on the wing tip and traveled in a line along the trailing edge, like the ports of an oblong burner in a gas range, flaring and flaring one at a time, until the entire perimeter rose up in flames.

She watched the luminous shimmer move toward her along the wing and then right over her head and away from her down the starboard edge. Out ahead the whirl of the prop and the top of the radiator were also aglow. The panel had a lavender shimmer, right before her eyes. Even her hands and arms danced with it, though she could feel nothing.

Saint Elmo's fire. Blix had described it and she'd read other pilots' accounts too, and Roy told her he'd once observed it dancing on the horns of a herd of cattle, hopping from cow to cow. Supposedly it couldn't hurt a plane, and that was all well and good, but at the moment it was as though the very cockpit had come alive with phantoms, just one more thing she wished weren't happening.

She looked through the purple specter at her gauges and tried to make a decision. She was clipping along again at nearly ninety, rain slinging and the ship bouncing through another patch of chop. She considered with still more certainty that she should just point the ship down and try again to land. If she pulled it off, she would probably doom her aunt entirely and lay a lifetime's second-guessed guilt upon herself. But how on earth was she supposed to fly across a mountain range when she couldn't see where it was? And even that assumed the ship didn't get knocked out of the air by lightning in the first place.

Guilt or death. Those were the options. Of all the times to have that cursed biblical drought break—you just couldn't help but see the irony as some form of cosmic punishment, some mockery of human folly. Only this morning she'd been jolted out of bed, seized by that same old fear of getting caught, getting punished.

Maybe that's exactly what was happening now, in some cruelly reverse way nobody but God could have contrived. She'd spent weeks with her aunt and nothing, not even a headache, then gone to town to get her ashes hauled one time, and now all this. As though she'd been judged and sentenced, simply for returning to earth. She understood why God might want to forsake her, but Aunt Gloria? Why on earth would He put *her* in this terrifying position?

She realized that somewhere within the twisting maze of her consciousness, she'd been praying. Pleading, actually, begging God to give her one more try at this thing called life, to save her aunt, and so save herself. Had Amelia prayed too, out there in her own dire straits?

She'd behave herself, as best she could. She'd deny temptation, as best she could. *Please, God, please.* Just show her some sign, an opening in the clouds or a shaft of light to follow, or best of all, wake her just one more time from this petrifying, hopeless dream.

But those things weren't going to happen, and she knew it as surely as she knew the chrome taste of fear behind the edge of her teeth. Was it all a parable, visited in real time upon her? Like Abraham, raising the knife above his own son, at God's behest?

She was being tested. That must be the answer. God had put her aunt's life in her uncertain hands, to force her own salvation. Maybe that's what this was. She couldn't save Gloria and maybe wasn't expected to, because Gloria was *certain* of where she was going when she departed this sad old painful world. So where could that possibly leave Annelise, except with a duty at least to save herself?

The entire ship was engulfed in lavender shimmer, even the wisps of her aunt's fluttering hair dancing with eerie blue light. Annelise saw her aunt's head shift slightly and wondered how long the effects of the morphine would last. She thought, *I am so, so sorry*, and with that, she reached over and came back with the throttle knob.

She feathered the stick forward to begin a descent and as though on cue an entire barrage of lightning came down across the span of sky, bolt after bolt snaking and dancing, forking and forking across and within the interior of the clouds, and she squinted against this frenetic voltage even while she found herself unable to take her eyes from a sight that, despite its sheer menace, she could regard only as beautiful.

She felt the waves of thunder before she actually heard them, felt the plane jump and thud in the epileptic air, and finally a branching charge of berserk energy went off so close and with such overwhelming flash and heat that her eyes clamped fully closed by sheer reflex.

The sonic blast punched again to the depths of her ear, the other one this time. She was stricken both deaf and blind, rocketing along in a sort of sensory stasis while the rolling shock tossed the plane like a windblown leaf. For all she knew the sky itself was splitting around her, and it crossed her mind that maybe she'd actually *been* lightning-struck, that maybe when she again opened her eyes she would find she'd passed through some cosmic portal, shuffled off this coil into another plane altogether.

Was she afraid for her life, or afraid for her afterlife? She didn't have a clue anymore. All she knew was that she was scared out of her mind, and that eventually she was going to have to open her eyes and simply take whatever awaited there.

She peeked with one eye, fully expecting anything other than what she glimpsed, and what she glimpsed caused her eye to clamp itself closed all over again.

Another airplane, flying out ahead, angled off to port through the struts and cabanes.

Couldn't be. Her own ship shuddered through another patch of rough air, and she saw even through her eyelids the vivid kinetic blare of more lightning. She thought again of that silver-foil glimmer earlier at the corner of her eye, before she'd encountered the storm.

She forced both eyes open and there it was, moving through clouds and rain and swirl, radiant with the same purple glow. She watched it disappear into a bank of mist and immediately doubted again.

She ran the throttle forward. Her speed had dropped to not much above seventy, and though she couldn't hear the whine of the engine out front she could see full well the instant launch of the tach, also an exuberant jump of the speed indicator. She flew into the mist herself, saw the wet haze around the ship catch the electrical shimmer and glow like a neon corona.

Visibility was nonexistent, the fog like frost across a windowpane. She did see the bright surge of another lightning bolt, but not the branch of voltage itself. Her speed had climbed nearly to eighty and she tried to ignore the fact that she was more handicapped in this very instant than she'd been at any prior point, flying totally on some kind of delirious faith. The blazing image of that phantom ship burned yet in her mind, right along with the taunting whisper of doubt, assuring her she'd only been seeing things in her feeble mind, that she was crazy and amateurish and irresponsible for not immediately descending for ground.

One more glimpse, was all she asked. *Please, God, please.* If she got it, and if she could stay with it, she'd make the leap, and she would follow. On the faith that whoever else was also out here in this mess, in a real airplane, must surely know more than she did. Must surely know how to get over the mountain. One more glimpse.

Her air speed passed eighty. The watery mist surrounded her yet. She remembered in a flash that she could travel in two directions— straight ahead and also upward. Would have to, in fact, if she were to clear the elevation of the pass. She cranked back on the stick and started to climb.

She watched her altimeter and gained another hundred feet in a matter of seconds. She came up out of the fog and into the gray wet vestibule of the storm.

Nothing at first, or nothing that she could see. She banked slightly to starboard to clear the view out front. Still nothing, and what the hell—those voices starting up again at the nape of her neck, laughing and whispering, tides of foolishness and failure, and all she could think was, *Get behind me, Satan*, and lo and behold.

A long lavender-blue smear appeared in the mist at the top of the fog bank out ahead, coming up through the wet haze like a luminous cross, and she hardly had time to hope before the glowing wings and long, broad back of an Electra breached the mantle and climbed fully into view.

She practically choked on ten things at once, terror and elation and the sheer ghostly weirdness of seeing a glowing airplane suddenly materialize from the storm clouds as though the thing were more apparition than actual. But there it was, floating maybe a hundred yards out.

It was not, she realized, necessarily a Lockheed Electra. She'd automatically jumped to that because of the mystery ship's general size and architecture, also probably the name coupled with the fact that this particular specimen actually *was* bathed in a writhing energy field, as though it had just risen out of the sea and swarmed yet with plankton. But it could have been any number of other airplanes. A big Douglas DC or a Boeing passenger carrier.

Or the Tri-Motor from that day she'd first flown this very ship up at Coal Camp Road. One could certainly hope—she'd rather follow that high-country hotshot through a tempest and over a mountain than anyone else she could name. She couldn't tell whether the plane she now followed had retractable landing gear or not, but that would be a clue.

Another jolt of lightning streaked the sky out ahead. She lost sight of the other ship in the gray-bright burst of lumens, then perceived it again as soon as the lightning ran out. She realized it was still climbing, at a faster rate than she was, and she put more angle into the elevator and did her best to keep up.

She watched it bank to starboard, held her breath when she lost sight of it behind the pillar of the radiator out front and breathed again when the big luminous bird edged back into view through the opposing struts. Though she hardly dared take her eyes from it, she forced herself to peek at the compass, saw she was technically still flying due west, which meant the blue phantom out ahead had angled slightly north. She zeroed on it again and banked as well.

She managed to keep it in sight until it leveled out and tacked dead west. She positioned herself slightly to port to keep it in view, and just about the time she'd settled enough to make a somewhat objective assessment of the whole surreal situation, another raw chain of lightning throbbed and forked against the clouds out ahead. The Electra or Tri-Motor or whatever it was vanished again in the flash.

The lightning flickered and held for an inordinate amount of time. She tried to ignore the livid flare of it, to keep her eyes fixed on where she'd last seen the other ship. When the voltage finally did blink out, the big glimmering ghost was rising in another climb and she lost sight of it yet again, only this time behind the barrier of her own glowing wing. She cranked back on the stick and checked her altimeter.

Coming up on 5,500. She had her speed upward of ninety and holding, the throttle wide open. She edged the stick farther back and tilted the nose up as far as she dared, and evidently the other plane was still really climbing, because she sure couldn't manage to tilt her own wing at enough of an angle to get another reassuring glimpse.

She had an absolute dread of stalling off in this particular crate, the mere thought of which brought those awful spiraling dreams rushing back, that spiraling ground rushing at her own spiraling mind. The dreams felt real enough in the moment the way this other nightmare felt real enough now, and in any case she couldn't afford to give up even an inch of gain, never mind risk plummeting into an actual tailspin.

She had to find it again, though. Had to convince herself, once again, that what she'd seen was really there. She climbed another couple of hundred feet, and when the missing phantom failed to appear beneath the edge of her wing, she went ahead and banked to port.

The big soaring bird immediately tilted into view, still awash in that hypnotic energy and thank God, thank God. She banked back toward it, lost it again behind the angle of the wing. She checked her altitude.

Evidently she'd hit an updraft in the swirl of the storm, because even now she'd topped six angels and still climbed like a kite. She gave it another two hundred feet, hoping the mystery ship would again drop into the aperture beneath her wing. When it didn't, she banked again to port and to her surprise saw the big plane *right there*, much closer than it had appeared before, maybe two hundred feet above her and about the same distance out ahead.

God, it looked just like an Electra. Or did, until another blinding flash in the ether caused it to vanish again into thin air, and the instantaneous blast of turbulence behind the flash had her fighting her own bucking ship back to a sort of wobbling level.

She rode out the worst of it and checked her gauges: 6,200 and flying steady, speed down to around eighty with the chop. She came back on the stick again to resume her climb and in a matter seconds watched the other airplane come back into view beneath the wing. She held her attack a little longer, then moved the stick ahead and came out of the climb with the Electra again positioned just off her starboard struts. She had it in her head that they were high enough now to clear the pass.

Twice again a jagged tongue of lightning strobed the dark cavern of the storm, and twice that gigantic apparition vanished before her eyes. And both times it reappeared, though seemingly much farther out ahead than when she'd lost sight of it. What a weird phenomenon.

Finally she saw what must have been a break in the wall of the gale, dead ahead and circular and bright, like looking up to see the filtered disk of the sun through the last atoms of a fog. The Electra seemed to tack right for it, still alight with that charged wreath around it, and now she understood the difference in sheer power because the other plane accelerated like a racehorse, pulling down the stretch and diminishing by the second, heading straight for that platinum hole in the swirl.

She couldn't keep up. Her throttle had been jammed all the way forward for a while now, with her speed in the headwind topped at eighty, about half what a twin-engined Lockheed ordinarily cruised at. She kept her eyes on the ship as long as she could, squinting against the bright glare at the break in the clouds, watching as the electrified glow contracted into a mere blue dot, smaller and smaller, and finally dissipated entirely within that silver-white window at the edge of the storm. Annelise flew toward it herself.

The rain had tapered off somewhere behind her, she hadn't really noticed when, and she seemed to have outpaced the lightning and thunder as well. Even the charged shroud around the skin of her plane had diminished, though she thought she could see a remnant glimmer dancing and forking at the tip of the wing. Up in the front bay, Aunt Gloria's white hair fluttered above the seat.

She drew nearer and nearer to the nucleus of the light, the billows and clouds limned with silver, forming a tunnel, swirling like a slow vortex that sucked her along, and she wasn't certain she'd be able to keep her eyes open against the increasing brilliance much longer, as though she were flying into the very sun itself, just beyond that last screen of fog.

Finally, with her eyelids narrowed to the merest slits, the plane cleared the grip of the storm entirely and burst into the crystal blue jewel of open sky.

She could see the road far below, like a ribbon winding down from the mountain. What had to be Bozeman lay out ahead, buildings and trees and streets, nestled at the foot of another soaring range. The land unfurled all around.

The bright clear air was almost painful to look at, but she held her squint and scanned everywhere, looking for another airplane.

None appeared in any direction. She passed over the city and began her descent.

She spied the airstrip out where they told her it would be, just west of town. She buzzed the runway and checked the wind sock and took a quick scan around for anything resembling a Lockheed Electra, then did a double-take at what appeared to be McKee's white Studebaker, parked just off the tarmac.

Not McKee's rig but an ambulance—she could see the red cross now. She flew on out past the end of the runway and made a broad bank around, came back with the wind behind her to face the east again. The black tower of the storm hung out there still, rising up over the notch in the mountain. She flew toward it, saw one last flare of lightning stretch down toward the ridge south of the pass. She banked again and put the storm at her back, once and for all.

She slowed her speed and came down light as air to the runway, ran out past the hangars and a handful of berthed ships here and there, but nothing resembling either a Lockheed Electra or a Tri-Motor. She steered around and maneuvered toward the ambulance, could already see three or four men with a stretcher.

She steered within fifty feet and killed the motor, was already fumbling at the safety belt before the plane had reached a stop. The men with the stretcher were running toward her, and she wriggled up out of the seat and ripped helmet and goggles loose. She half leaned, half crawled across the windscreen and deck. She peered down at her aunt.

"Gloria."

Gloria's eyes were closed, her mouth slightly parted so that Annelise could see her teeth against her bottom lip. Tiny little teeth. *Please, God, please.* The stretcher was nearly to them, and she could hear their feet on the tarmac.

"Gloria."

Her aunt's eyes opened, met her own. And she smiled.

Epilogue

75 Point Lookout
Milford, Connecticut
February 11, 1985

Dear Annelise,

Many thanks for your kind condolences. I think Mother was more surprised at her longevity than most anyone, but she did indeed see eighty-five, still on her feet and still more or less as she ever was, right to the end. She talked about you often, and I know she always prayed for you, which of course was entirely her way. She always thought that God, in His mysterious ways, sent you to Montana solely for her rescue.

Of course she never knew the half of it. We had us some times, didn't we? Some of the best of my own life, in fact. Reading your letter again, I have to believe it is the same for you—after so many years it is like hearing a voice from the long past, even while bringing the events of that hot summer roaring back as though they happened only yesterday. Nearly half a century, though—how on earth can it be?

To answer your question, yes, the Piet is still in storage in Big Coulee, with the wing detached. I saw it again only a few weeks ago when I took Mother's ashes to be placed there beside Pop. Gosh, he's been gone so long already now . . . more than thirty years, somehow, and now here we are, senior citizens ourselves, and how on earth did THAT happen?

Anyway, the ship looks its own age, at this point. A dilapidated relic, like an old horse-drawn buggy covered in dust and white pigeon chalk, tucked away and forgotten.

So I have been dickering with the county historical museum to make room for an airplane. Progress is slow. But I would hate for it to wind up eventually in the city dump, after all those wild and woolly times we had. My own kids were limited to Lincoln Logs and Erector sets, and nowadays my grandkids have to make do with plastic Legos. I'd like for future generations to see how we were able to amuse ourselves, back in the "wild old days."

By the way, I finally visited Mr. Pietenpol. The man himself, at his home in Cherry Grove, Minnesota, in 1983. He has since died as well, but he told me he built twenty-one airplanes with numbers, and a number of others that never were registered. Some of his later ships were powered with Chevrolet Corvair engines from the 1960s. I chuckle to think that if old Yak could've let fly with Pop's big buffalo gun at a chintzy little Corvair, the whole car would have probably disintegrated on the spot! Mr. Pietenpol certainly got quite a kick to learn that we supercharged our own little ship with a Hoover vacuum cleaner.

I know we've sort of skirted this subject over the years, but I often think of that day you flew to Bozeman and saved Mother's life. Now that she has in fact departed for some other place in the sky, or maybe nowhere at all, I can't help finally circling back. I've run it through my head so many times now, as I imagine you must surely have, too.

Mother certainly did. She had no real memory of the storm itself, exactly, only the darkness and roar and the roughness of the passage. She told me that she did not even understand she was in an airplane but believed she must be in some sort of flaming chariot, like in the Bible when one of the prophets—Elijah, I think—rides up to heaven without dying. You described it as Saint Elmo's fire, which I'm sure is correct. I myself experienced several episodes of the same in 1944, when I served on a B-17.

How that storm should have coincided with the events of that particular emergency seems a whole other question. As you no doubt recall, we were deep in drought to that point, and I believe that Independence Day 1937 still qualifies as Montana's record high. No rain had been predicted at all and certainly not a storm of that magnitude, or I would never have suggested such an endeavor, and Mother very likely would not have reached the age of forty, let alone eighty-five.

The rest of us could see the sobering dark tower of it as we drove south toward the Yellowstone River, although even with McKee hauling like a maniac whenever the road would permit, the trek was in general slow-going, and the weather had continued on toward Billings and beyond by the time we reached the junction heading west. The land was still soaked, though, the river a little off-color and potholes full to the brim in the roadway, water vapor steaming all around.

If the situation had been different, we would've been grateful for every drop. But if the dread over Mother's condition were not enough, we had to spend a couple of hours further dreading the sight of a wrecked airplane over every hill and rise. I remember very well our immense relief when we got to Big Timber and were finally able to call ahead to the hospital. Not only had you made it through, but Mother was already well along in the surgery that certainly saved her life.

I remember being caught off guard in the days after that, when you chose to return home to California. Or maybe it was simply disappointment to see you go, although even then I knew not to take it personally. We had the blood-oath bond of conspirators that summer, it's true, but in retrospect I think we were all pretty frayed.

I've often puzzled over what you told me you saw, battling your way through that storm. You swore me to secrecy at the time, and I have made good on that, never have mentioned it to a soul, including you, until now.

However, I have also come to understand that it's not an isolated situation. I very much recall reading Lindbergh's book from 1953, in which he finally after twenty-odd years confessed that he'd been visited and assisted by what he called "phantoms" there in the cockpit with him while he fought to keep himself awake. I nearly fell out of my chair.

You looked like you'd seen a ghost, too, when we finally got to you that day in the hospital. At first I figured it must have been just plain circumstances, the pressure on you with Mother's ordeal, multiplied into something else entirely by that killer storm. Until you pulled me aside and tried to tell me what you witnessed up there. A glowing airplane, leading you through darkness. A Lockheed Electra. Possibly.

You said you weren't even sure it was real, and yet it was the most real thing you'd ever experienced. You said you thought you'd had a religious experience. Or maybe you said "mystical," but it was something along those lines. At first I thought you were afraid people might think you were simply crazy.

Eventually I understood it as something else. I know Mother always regarded the event as a confirmed miracle, and she never said a thing about another airplane, glowing or not. But isn't that the trouble, being brought up simply to believe? You never can tell what it is you're seeing, even with your own two eyes. That right there is plenty enough to haunt a person for life.

In a way, though, it was a miracle for other reasons. Mother of course moved with us into the house in town after that, of her own choosing, which was plainly a relief to both her and Pop by then. Not so long after that I flew the ship to Bozeman myself, to enroll in the engineering college, but you already know that part of the story. Just for the record, the sky was clear and the conditions perfect. I thought of you the whole dern way.

To answer your other question, your memory is sound. We did indeed find a crate of gold, right where you remember. I know myself how the long-ago past can braid in and out of dreams, until you can't really tell what actually happened from an imaginary figment, way back behind you, down the long hall of memory.

Truth be told, I've thought about retracing our steps to that old forgotten time capsule and walking down those stairs to that cool, steady dark once again, just to see. Every time I've traveled home and laid my eyes on our tattered, dust-collecting *Cloudmaker*, in fact. Just to see.

But I never have. Never did tell a soul about that secret, either. Of course neither Yak nor Raleigh survived the war, and with Pop long gone, too, and now Mother as well, I guess it makes sense that we would caution a look back after all this time. You and me.

Times do change, fast as the blink of an eye. I fly a Piper Seminole these days, a far cry from our little low-and-slow homemade Piet. I would like nothing more than for you to come back here to the East and take a hop with me. Or I could fly it out to you anytime. Steal you away from those horses you've done so well with, get you out of your stable and back to the cockpit again, all these years later. You and me. Let me know, while we still have a little time left ourselves.

I love you, very much. I will write more soon.

Your cousin,
Houston Finn

Acknowledgments

Many people had a hand in bringing this book off the ground.

Clay Scott, Danielle Lattuga, Nick Davis, Bryce Andrews, Ken Egan, Jameson Parker, Allison Tierney, Sally Weaver, and Alex White provided insight and encouragement, as did Rick and Marli Davis and my sister-in-law, Lindsay Davis.

Dan Bronson has been not only a tireless champion but a true mentor, and I am eternally grateful. His brother, Ralph Bronson, is a lifelong aviator, and the importance of Ralph's technical critique of my efforts to capture the art of flying cannot be overstated. Michael D. Fox, Curator of History at The Museum of the Rockies in Bozeman, Montana, assembled a remarkable archive documenting the Pietenpol airplane in the museum's collection, and guided me through it.

Shirley and Doug Parrott opened up the Musselshell Valley Historical Museum in the dead of winter, so I could examine David Comstock's Piet from 1932. This was the first Air-Camper constructed from plans in the *1932 Flying and Glider Manual*, taken on its maiden flight by its remarkable builder when he was just seventeen years old. Patrick Kenney of Billings, Montana, spearheaded the plane's restoration in 2006 with a team of junior high students, and provided crucial insight into both airplane construction, and the capabilities of dedicated young people.

Betty Wetzel not only went to high school with David Comstock, but actually flew with him in his airplane. When I met her in 2016, Betty was almost certainly the last surviving witness to those days and times. It was an honor and a pleasure to hear her vivid memories, which very much informed this book.

Bette Lowrey, native of Roundup, spent much time with me road-tripping and reminiscing about the region in which she grew up. I'm forever indebted, both to Bette, and to her hometown.

Julia Whelan, actor and audio performer, novelist and screenwriter, has been incredibly supportive of me and my work despite her own overwhelming array of commitments. I can't thank her enough.

The lives and legends of Amelia Earhart, Beryl Markham, and Bessie Coleman continue to inspire.

Many thanks to the Ucross Foundation, for time and space and support.

Thanks as well to Chris Dombrowski, Robin Troy, and Beargrass Writer's Workshop. My agent, Kirby Kim, has been a tireless advocate and a fine friend. Couldn't do this without you, Pard.

Likewise, my lovely editor and de facto sister, Amy Hundley—once again, this is as much yours as mine. To Liz Van Hoose as well, who stepped in to pinch-hit and smacked a homer.

Everyone at Grove Atlantic—Morgan, Judy, Elisabeth, Deb, John Mark, Savannah, Kait—thanks to you all.

My old friend Dennis Dusek, as capable a soul as ever existed, gave me a model for Huck.

Bernard Pietenpol. Master innovator, grand wit, and champion of the do-it-yourself ethic. Without him, there would be no this.

Finally, to my wife, Miss Manda Davis, who I'm lucky enough to spend this charmed life with. Scorpio perfectionist, Scorpio perfection.